# SURVIVING THE FALL

## A HIDDEN TRUTHS NOVEL

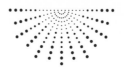

### BRITTNEY SAHIN

EMKO MEDIA

*SURVIVING THE FALL*

By: Brittney Sahin

Published by: EmKo Media, LLC

Copyright © 2017 EmKo Media, LLC

Previously titled: *Deadly Consequences*

This book is an original publication of Brittney Sahin.

Editor: Sarah Norton, Chief Editor, WordsRU.com

Cover Designer: Mayhem Cover Designs /Istock/Deposit photos- licenses

eBook ISBN-13: 9780997842159

Paperback ISBN: 9781719963107

❀ Created with Vellum

# CHAPTER ONE

THE MEN WERE EITHER HORRIBLE SHOTS, OR THEY HAD NO intention of killing him.

The loud punch of gunfire echoed around Jake as he ran. His feet pounded the uneven concrete, the cold hard surface assaulting his heels as he tore through the empty building. Shots sprayed against the floor, nipping at his ankles.

The massive space was nearly empty—a ghost of a building that once housed dozens of men and women who'd churned out products at the assembly line. Scraps of paper littered the floor, sticking to his bloody feet as he tore through the large space. A rancid odor crept into his nostrils as he looked at the staircase that led to the second floor, open to the factory down below.

He tried not to limp as a shooting pain spiraled up through his left leg. Still, he staggered to the set of steel stairs, clenching tight the trigger in his hands. One slip of his thumb and it'd all be over. No overtime. No do-overs.

Upstairs now, Jake started down the hall. He focused on the corridor of rooms that spanned before him as his sight blurred. He blinked rapidly to clear the sweat and blood from his gaze.

The bullets had stopped, but any glimmer of hope that he'd

escape fizzled fast when the thumping of two sets of boots barreled behind him down the hall. So far, every window had been boarded up.

*Shit.* He turned left and halted, taking two steps back to the entrance of an open doorway. He released a pent-up breath as he spotted a large, expansive open window—a piece of plywood lying in front of it. He'd almost missed it.

*Thank God.* The open window, with its glimpse of dusky blue sky, was the most beautiful sight he'd ever seen.

He hurried into the room and braced one hand against the wall. The cool, biting air slapped him in the face, and he narrowed his eyes, trying to get a better look outside. His heart pumped hard in his chest as his insides shook.

He swiped away the blood and sweat from his eyes, ignoring the burning pain, and focused on the rooftop of a neighboring building maybe fifteen or twenty feet below. The jump wouldn't be too bad. Not deadly, at least.

He lowered his hands, the trigger still grasped tight, and spun around as he heard the two men draw near. They stood before him, staring at him with the same brownish-black eyes that had become so familiar. Green bandannas were tied around their faces beneath their eyes and draped down in a pointed V to their chins.

One of the men moved in front of the other and entered the room with slow and cautious steps. He stopped a few feet shy of Jake and pushed a breath through his lips; the bandanna puffed lightly out in front of him. The man's eyes, void of emotion, darted down Jake's chest as he lowered the gun to his side.

Jake glanced down at the timer on his black vest. The red numbers glowed on the stopwatch strapped over his heart, which was wedged between small packaged blocks of what Jake assumed was C4. Wires sprang out of the red blocks and wrapped around to the back of the vest.

Jake cocked his head and slanted his eyes. "You guys have less than sixty seconds to get the hell out of here. You might want to run unless you've got a death wish." He panted a little and swallowed.

When they didn't move, Jake raised the trigger out in front of him. He could set it off now if he wanted to, but the men weren't afraid. They could see it in Jake's eyes—his desire to live, to see another day. To tell his mother he loved her because he worried he didn't tell her enough. To remind his sister Emily how proud he was of her. And to tell his dad—well, his dad was a man of few words and wouldn't need to hear how he felt. But he'd been the rock of the family. Someone he could always count on.

"You Americans think you're so smart." The guy closest to him took a step back. "You think you're so much better than the rest of the world." His accented voice pushed through the dusty air, and Jake tried not to look at the stopwatch. He had to stay strong.

"We don't think we're better or smarter than everyone, but we're for damn sure stronger and smarter than you assholes."

The man's gaze flickered back to the vest for a moment, then he and the other guy turned and disappeared.

Jake now had twenty seconds to get out of the mess he was in.

He worked fast at the vest, attempting to remove it while also keeping his hand on the trigger. If his thumb lifted from the button, he'd be painting the walls with his blood.

He'd trained for moments like this. Although he knew how to deactivate a bomb, there was no use trying with only seconds left. This wasn't some blockbuster movie, and as much as he and his pals always joked he wasn't an action hero. The death attempting to claim his soul was all too real. And he wasn't ready to learn whether it would suck him down to the netherworld of hell or the soft grace of heaven.

The vest finally slipped off, and he cleared the room in two galloping strides to chuck it down into the factory. His veins pulsed in his neck, squeezing tight until he could hardly gather oxygen into his lungs as he sprinted back. Still holding the trigger, he climbed into the window and squatted.

He didn't know how large the blast would be—perhaps not too bad, based on the amount of explosive material on the vest.

*This is shit,* Jake thought as he sucked in a breath and leaped out the window. A hot blast of flames fanned out behind him, propelling him forward.

# CHAPTER TWO

THE SKY WAS LIKE BLACK INK LEAKING FROM AN OLD-FASHIONED pen, covering everything. It was dark. Ominous. There were no stars—just a pool of inky nothingness.

"We need to do this tonight. You think you can get him to his hotel room?"

Alexa pulled her gaze from the sky outside the window and observed her partner, whose dark hair was gelled to the side. His gray eyes were the color of steel, and yet they were warm. Was he worried about her on this mission? Oh, who was she kidding? Xander always worried about her when she went into the field. He'd rather she sit behind a computer nestled in a shroud of safety. But none of them were ever really safe, were they?

How much time did she have left in life?

Being thirty-three and single for, well, it felt like forever, was starting to bother her more and more lately, especially when she spoke with her sister. Lori would get on her case about needing to meet a man, and then she'd remind Alexa of the American—the one her sister insisted was "the one who got away." How cliché . . .

Besides, that guy had been in her life for all of a week before he returned to the States. She had met him at a party in London on New Year's Eve. It wasn't exactly a story for the ages.

But for some reason, Alexa couldn't seem to get "Mr. New Year's Eve" out of her head. Even now, apparently, at a time like this.

"Alexa?" Xander was snapping his fingers in front of her face, and she blinked, her dark lashes fluttering.

"Sorry. What were you saying?" Alexa stared down at her ring finger, sliding the forefinger of her right hand along its length. Would there ever be a ring there?

She rolled her eyes at her thoughts, hating herself at that moment for wallowing in such ridiculous self-pity when she was on an operation. Of course, it's not like there would ever be a good time or place to think of such things, given her current lifestyle.

"You think you can get Gregov to his room?" Xander asked her again, and she finally flashed her hazel eyes to meet his.

"Can't I stay in the van and you go and seduce the Russian?" A smile skated across her lips, and he playfully nudged her in the shoulder with a fist.

"If I was his type, I'd take the bullet for you and do it, mate. But, based on our research, he prefers gorgeous women. Especially those with long, black hair."

"Then we should have had Matt wear the wig," Alexa was quick to respond.

"Funny," Matt blurted through her earpiece.

"You've got this—no worries," Xander added.

"Yeah, well, I forgot to take Seduction 101," she joked. "But I'll do my best." She reached for the door handle, but Xander's hand on her shoulder had her pausing and looking over at him.

"Be careful." Xander's hard jaw strained with worry.

"Always." She winked and got out of the van, careful not to slip on any of the ice that lingered after the storm that had passed through earlier. As she walked, she shivered from the cold, which settled through her jacket to chill her bones. An inch of soft snow coated the sidewalk, but it wasn't the fun, powdery snow that children dream about. No, it was the evil kind—lined with a shield of ice.

A few hundred meters away, Alexa turned sharply and entered the beer hall, which was busy as ever. The live band was playing Bavarian music, and massive wooden tables were filled with people.

Whenever she entered the beer hall, Alexa had felt like she was stepping back in time. It was over a hundred years old, and part of her liked the aged feel of it, but it also creeped her out. The arched, dark wood ceilings were gorgeous, but the paintings on the walls . . . well, many of them were mounted to cover up the Nazi swastika signs from WWII. So, she had been told, at least, by some tourist with a pamphlet of fun facts in his hand.

But tonight, the icy breath lashing at her skin wasn't from the cold outside or the reminder of where she was. No. Tonight, her nerves were raw because she needed to make contact with her target.

It didn't matter how often she went out on an OP—she always got nervous.

She spotted Gregov at the bar as she made her way through the crowd of people. He was sitting there like he had every other night this week, with a stein in hand filled to the brim with dark, wheat beer. She was grateful that he was a man of routine.

Alexa swallowed a lump of emotion and focused on her target as she approached the bar. The man had thick, black hair that was long in the back. He was in his fifties, but his toned physique and the muscles framed beneath his clothes could have been those of a much younger man. He wasn't the typical computer geek, but no one she'd been tracking on her current case had met the stereotypical character profiles the agency had previously used to locate high-value targets. The world was changing.

Alexa sat in the empty seat beside him and motioned for the bartender. "Ein Weissbier, bitte," she ordered.

She could feel Gregov's eyes on her, and she straightened in her seat a little. She realized she hadn't remembered to take off her jacket. Now how was she going to utilize her "assets" (as Xander had joked earlier this morning) to help seduce him?

She untied the straps of her wool coat and shrugged it off, draping it over the top of the seat behind her. As she shifted back to face the bar, she realized Gregov was now focused on the swell of flesh at the V of her red sweater dress. Well, that was easy enough.

He cleared his throat as his eyes drifted up to meet her hazel ones. "American or British?"

*Was my German accent that bad?* she wondered. "English," she responded, and then nodded her thanks to the bartender when he returned with her beer. "And you must be from . . .?"

He took a sip of his beer, and then smiled at her, his dark eyes remaining on hers as he drank. "What do you think?" he asked after setting his stein down on the counter.

"Hm." She tapped a red fingernail at her lips and narrowed her eyes. "I'd guess you're from Texas." She wondered if she could warm him up with a joke. If his personality was anything like his steely composure, she was in for a long night.

He tipped his head back and laughed as a large hand slapped the bar in front of him. "Cowboy, eh? Maybe I could be your Russian cowboy?" His accent, thick and deep, rumbled through her as his dark brown eyes steadied on her mouth.

*So, he's not so stiff.* She breathed a sigh of relief. "Why? You think you might be able to lasso me in?" she joked.

He took another drink before reaching into his pocket for some bills. He tossed the euros on the counter—enough to cover both their beers. "You know I've seen you in this bar several nights for the last week. Always looking over at me. I have to say I'm impressed you had the nerve to finally approach me."

Alexa wet her lips and forced a smile to her face. "Who said I was trying to approach you? Can't a girl sit at a bar and have a beer?"

"Ha." He placed a hand to his chest. "Now you joke, right?"

She leaned in closer to him. "I guess it's up to you to find out," she said in a low, sultry voice.

He pressed his palms to the counter and Alexa caught sight of a gold wedding band on his ring finger.

"My place, then." The Russian dragged his attention down to her breasts again.

"Oh, come on. Make him beg." Alexa straightened in her seat and tried not to roll her eyes at the voice of Matt in her ear.

Alexa stood up and reached for her coat. "If you promise not to keep me up too late. I have an early flight."

She wished she'd known before joining the agency that having a minor in theater would have been more helpful to her in situations like this than her bachelor's in computer science. Of course, she wasn't doing all that bad tonight, given her target was about to leave the bar with her in under ten minutes. That had to be her new record.

"Maybe you don't go to bed at all." He raised a brow and rose to his feet as she slipped her arms into the sleeves of her coat. The man reached for her, gathering the mass of her long black hair, freeing it from where her wool coat had captured it against the skin of her neck. The intimate gesture made her skin crawl, and she hid a wince by lowering her chin to her chest.

"What's your name, by the way?" he asked as they started for the exit. His hand touched her back before slipping lower.

*Oh, please don't.*

His palm rested on the curve of her ass, and she bit her lip to hide her disgust.

"Sylvia Reynolds. Yours?" She feigned interest and looked up at him as he pushed open the doors of the beer hall.

"Boris Gregov," he answered before she walked past him through the exit.

She was surprised by his honesty. Then again, he had no clue who she was. He didn't know that he needed to lie.

Alexa peered back up at the dark sky before her eyes flitted to her surroundings. She scanned each and every person they passed, and her shoulders relaxed a little at the sight of Matt leaning against a building fifty meters away, his eyes casually looking up from the mobile he held in his hand to greet hers.

Alexa dragged out a lungful of air, and her breath floated out in front of her in a small cloud of steam. "I bet Munich was lovely at Christmas." She could still barely believe it was January. Where had the year gone? Another year alone. And she assumed it'd probably be the same this year, as well. Of course, if they finally closed their current case—maybe she could take a week or two of vacation. The last time she'd been on holiday was—well, when she met Mr. New Year's Eve, but she hadn't even left London. No, this time she'd go somewhere warm. Maybe Bali. Get lost in a good book on the beach with some delicious cocktail in hand. A romance book, maybe—since that'd be the closest she'd come to romance for a while.

"Do you live in Munich? Or are you here on business?" She stared at the thin veil of icy snow beneath her boots as she walked, doubting the man would answer honestly.

"Business, and I also leave soon. My employer moves me around a lot."

"What do you do?"

"Nothing all that fascinating. I work with computers."

"Yeah?" She raised her voice an octave to sound surprised. "So do I." Well, that was her cover story, anyway. "I'm with Henderson Intel. Heard of them? We're not that big, but we're working on building our brand." They were one of the agency's shell corporations.

"Ah. Then you are my competition. I must not reveal our secrets."

"Well, maybe if I tell you a secret, then you'll consider telling me a thing or two." She flashed him a smile.

Gregov stopped walking and banded her waist with his long arm, pulling her close to him until her chest pressed to his.

Alexa looked up at him, confident in how her smoky black liner played up her hazel eyes. Her brightly painted lips opened for him. As he angled his head and lowered his lips, she stepped back and chuckled. "Mm. You need to warm me up with a drink, first." She raised her shoulder and winked at him, but he pulled her back, tugging at her arm, jerking her sharp against him.

"You're naughty, and I like it," he growled.

"Feckin' wanker," Matt said into her ear, and Alexa pressed her lips together instead of physically responding to Matt's insults.

Gregov tipped his head to the left, and Alexa glanced over at the double glass doors. She hadn't realized that they'd stopped in front of his hotel. That wasn't like her—she was accustomed to noticing every little detail.

"This is me," he said in a low voice.

*Great . . .*

Once Alexa and Gregov reached his massive suite, he started straight for the small bar alongside the wall opposite of the living area, which had a sofa, TV, and desk. A desk with no computer. *Damn.*

"I'd like something strong," Alexa said from behind as she continued to observe the room. If she couldn't get her hands on the computer, the mission would be a bust. His laptop would probably be in the safe, she decided, trying to calm the worry that had started to pull at her. The safes at the hotel required a palm scan, but Matt and Xander were in position, and they'd be able to help her lug the Russian into the bedroom when it was time.

"So, Boris . . ."

He was standing next to her now, and he smoothed a hand through her hair before gently pulling at the tips.

*Oh, shit. Not the wig.* "You like it rough, huh?" She tried to ignore the impulse to swallow. Without giving her a chance to react, Gregov's mouth moved in. His lips slammed against hers, sloppy and wet. He smeared her lipstick as she fumbled around deep into her coat pocket for the needle. She allowed his tongue to intrude inside her mouth. God, the things she did for this job.

A moment later, he pulled his lips from hers and took a step back as she attempted to gain her footing . . . her fingers finally wrapped around the needle.

"You gonna lasso me in or what?" Her voice was like a soft hiss, and he lunged for her again, grabbing her hips, pressing his body flush against hers—right where she wanted him.

She snaked one hand up to his head as he kissed her. "Mm," she murmured against his lips as she brought her other hand up and around to his neck.

She pricked him with the needle, and he pulled away, a big hand shooting to the side of his neck. "What the . . .?" His brows pinched together as he dropped to his knees in one fast movement, looking up at her in a daze.

She stepped back when his eyes shut and he fell face forward to land at her feet.

"He's out," she informed her partners as she stared at Gregov's motionless body.

"Be there in a minute," Matt responded in her ear.

She started to search the room, rifling through his luggage and finding nothing but a string of unused condoms. "Ugh. Well, at least he was prepared. Lots of rubbers."

"You could still have your way with the cowboy, if you'd like," Matt teased in her ear. "Another snog."

Alexa shook her head at his comment and tried to flush away the memory of the kiss with Gregov, a man she'd been tracking for over a year now. A man she hoped to hell her lips never had to touch again.

"Oh come on, Alexa, I thought that was a pretty good comeback of mine, especially after your comment in the van. Long black hair would look bloody awful on me." Despite being the agent runner, and the man in charge, Matt had a sense of humor, and it helped keep Alexa a bit grounded, at times. Going on missions, always focused on the mark, it could make things dark. Morbid.

Alexa laughed. "I don't know. I think you'd look utterly smashing."

"Huh. We can't all look like models like you and pretty boy Xander, here," Matt said.

"Shut up, you git," Xander answered, and Alexa could visualize the grin spreading across Xander's face. Of course, Matt was far from bad looking. If he wasn't her boss, and maybe in another life—she would have hooked up with him in a heartbeat.

"Would you two stop playing around and get your arses up here? We've only got two hours before he wakes." Alexa kneeled in front of the safe and eyed the palm scan. "Maybe even less. He's a big bugger."

"Outside the door, love," Xander said a moment later.

She pressed off her knees. "Coming." Alexa made her way back to the suite's door and swung it open.

Xander nodded at her with approval of a job well done as he and Matt entered the room.

"Now help me drag his heavy arse to the safe," Alexa said as she squatted by the body, reaching for Gregov's ankles.

"You know, you could have at least waited to knock him out until you got into the bedroom," Xander said as he grabbed hold of Gregov's forearms.

"Sure, and have to snog him even longer?" She shook her head. "No, thank you." Her eyes steadied on Matt's coffee brown ones. "You gonna watch us or help?" Then she stood and stepped back, folding her arms. "Better yet, you two go ahead without me. I did the hard part. You can handle the poor bloke." Alexa watched as Xander and Matt dragged Gregov's dead weight down the hall, and then she followed after.

"Let's hope his computer is in this thing," she said as Xander held Gregov's hand to the palm screen of the safe.

There was a beep followed by a click, and the door of the large safe opened. "Jackpot." Matt rubbed his hands together and grabbed the razor thin laptop before handing it off to Alexa.

"Thanks. Why don't you guys set him up in the bed with the booze and undress him while I work?"

"I don't want to undress him." Xander lifted a brow and stood.

"Well, I have a lot on my plate hacking this thing," she said sweetly, "and if we want him to think he passed out drunk after shagging me . . ." Alexa couldn't fight the smile that spread fast across her face.

"Jesus Christ," Xander grumbled and bent back down.

Alexa went back out into the living area and sat at the desk. She flipped open the computer and powered it on.

She bypassed the username and passcode using the command prompt function, then began creating a login so she'd be able to access the hard drive. "Net user," she mumbled while typing. Soon, she was deep in her own world, oblivious to the sounds of Matt and Xander in the other room. Her fingers moved deftly across the keys, jabbing with grace as she hacked into his computer. "I have administrative access now. I'm in. Now the hard part," she called out to her team.

"You think we'll find anything useful on there?" Xander entered the room a few minutes later and stood over her shoulder, watching as she typed code.

"I don't have time to know what's useful, but I'll create a code that will allow us to copy his hard drive. Hopefully he'll never know we were in here."

"How long will it take?" Xander checked his watch.

Her fingers were moving fast, entering appropriate responses to every black box that popped up on screen. "An hour. Maybe longer. His firewalls are impressive—it'll take me a little more time than usual to get them down."

"The other team will be arriving here in an hour. They'll monitor his activity from here on out," Xander said.

"Okay. Good." Alexa didn't want to waste time in Munich. If she successfully downloaded Boris Gregov's files, she'd want to get back to London ASAP to analyze them and decrypt as needed. There was a terrorist attack to thwart, after all.

Xander reached into his pocket for a USB and set it next to the computer as Matt's mobile began ringing from the bedroom. "For when you're ready."

"Thanks," she said, already back in the zone.

Matt's voice rang in her ear as he moved back into the living room. "That was HQ."

"Everything good?" Xander asked.

"No."

Alexa lifted her fingers from the keys and looked over her shoulder at Matt. "What's wrong?"

Matt swiped a hand down his jaw, and Alexa noticed the slight tremble in his fingers.

"What is it, Matt?" Alexa asked again, her brows snapping together.

Matt glanced at Xander before focusing back on her. "There's been an explosion in London."

# CHAPTER THREE

A DULL NOISE TRANSFORMED INTO A LOW-PITCHED RINGING THAT cut through Jake's ears, making the veins at his temples throb.

"Someone tried to come into the room a few minutes ago who wasn't approved. We have Jake isolated for a reason."

"The nurse is new. She came to the wrong floor. She doesn't know anything."

Jake needed to open his eyes, to see what in the hell was going on.

"That had better be the case."

"He's my patient—I have his best interest in mind. Don't worry."

Jake tried to open his eyes yet again, but it was like trying to solve a crossword puzzle first thing in the morning before having a cup of coffee. Not going to happen.

Not for him, at least.

"How long until he's awake?" The voice was familiar—low and deep, with a hint of Brooklyn.

"Should be anytime. Everyone responds differently to the drugs."

Jake finally forced his eyes open, his fingers twitching at his sides.

His vision was a little blurry at first. It took him a few attempts to adjust his gaze.

"Shit. He's moving. He's waking up."

Slowly, he began to see more clearly. The last voice he heard came from a guy in a suit. "Jake. Jesus Christ. You okay?" His cold fingers touched Jake's forearm, and Jake couldn't help but retract himself from the stranger's touch. The movement created a sharp stab in his side.

"What's wrong with me?" Jake winced as he adjusted to the bright fluorescent lights. "My back. My leg." His hand lingered at his side and then shot up to his forehead, where a fresh pain radiated.

The doctor was at his side, jabbing at a few buttons on the monitor by the bed. "I'm Doctor Richards, Mr. Summers. You were in an accident," he answered, his voice accented—British.

"Can you get me something for this pain?" Jake asked.

"There's been a steady drip of morphine pumping through your IV, but now that you're awake, it looks like you'll need something stronger." The doctor tapped at a few keys on the computer that was mounted on a rolling cart near the bed.

"A lot stronger," Jake grumbled.

"But first, I need you to look at me for a second." The doctor focused a bright light in his eyes that made him blink.

"How's your vision? Can you see okay?" The doctor held up a few thick fingers. "How many?"

"Three. And I can see fine," he rasped.

"After the accident, we put you into a medically induced coma. We worried about swelling of the brain, hemorrhaging . . ."

*Shit.* "Am I okay?"

"Yes. All of the scans were clean. You didn't even break anything from the fall."

"The fall?" *What kind of accident was I in?*

"There was an explosion," the doctor answered.

"What? How . . . where the hell am I?" Jake eyed the guy in the suit, who had stepped back to stand next to the doctor. "Who . . . who are you?"

"What do you mean, who am I?" The man's hand went to his chest, and the strip of lighter flesh circling his ring finger caught Jake's eye. The man was recently divorced, maybe. "It's me."

*Wow, that's helpful.* Jolts of pain blanketed Jake's body and tore through him, traveling up both his shoulders and down his arms. "I feel fucking horrible," he growled out as the pain in his back was like knives pricking his skin. And his head—*Jesus*—it was as if dozens of bells were ringing while someone clapped cymbals on both sides of his skull. "I don't know you," Jake said to the man and studied the bandages on his biceps.

"It appears that you were also hurt before the explosion. Tortured," the doctor said slowly, ignoring the man in the suit. The doctor's voice was like the slow drip of the IV—providing a slight relief, but not enough.

*Tortured?* Jake looked over as a blonde woman in pale green scrubs entered the room.

"That's Lisa. She's on the list." The doctor directed his comment to the man in the suit.

Lisa, the nurse, touched a few buttons on the machine by his bed, and then held the needle in her hand. She flicked her index finger, and a bit of water squirted from the tip. "This will make you feel much better." Her smooth British voice was soft and comforting, but Jake figured the drugs looping through the tubes and into his IV were the true source of the butterflies that fluttered through him.

He leaned his head back and relaxed as the last bit of pain drifted free from his body.

"Why doesn't he remember me? Is there something wrong with him?" the guy asked the doctor. "I thought you said his scans were clean."

*Was* there something wrong with his memory?

Jake's mind started to compete with the medicine, trying to stir up information, but he was searching in a dark room for the light and having no luck. "What's going on? I remember who I am, but shit . . ." Jake's words were slower and more drawn out as the medicine kicked in.

"He might have some temporary memory loss. Amnesia. Maybe PTSD. Between the blast, the fall, and whatever happened to him before . . ." the doctor answered.

That wasn't too comforting.

"Besides, after looking over his prior medical records, he's had his fair share of injuries. A series of blows to the head over time can do a lot more damage than just to his memory. I've already called for a neural consult. But, in my opinion, he's come out lucky after what he's been through."

*Lucky?* He was in a hospital after surviving an explosion. That hardly sounded like luck.

"You sure his memory issues aren't a result of the damn coma you put him into for the last few days?" The stranger by his bed cocked his head and glared at the doctor.

The doctor stared at Jake for a moment, his eyes scanning him, calculating.

"No. That wouldn't have any impact in his case."

The man shook his head at the doctor as if he weren't so certain. "What's the last thing you remember?"

Jake squeezed his eyes shut, trying to rummage through the facts and images in his mind, but it was hard to focus with drugs flowing through his veins.

His hands fisted at his sides as he dragged up the first image that popped into his head—him throwing a football down a field. Jerseys scurrying, colliding. Bright night lights shining down as he was tackled to the ground.

"Football is all I remember. Nothing after college." Jake forced his eyes open. "But hell, I feel a lot older than a college kid." Although maybe that was because his whole body hurt.

The man scratched his square jaw and turned his back to Jake for a moment. "Can we have a moment alone? It's classified."

*Classified? Really?* Jake caught sight of a bulge at the center of the man's back beneath his blazer. Was the guy packing heat?

"Of course." The doctor nodded at the man and Jake. "I'll be outside if you need me. But don't be long—I need to run a lot more tests."

Knowing that classified information was serious, Jake tried to sit up. But his legs and arms were too heavy to lift.

The man pulled up a seat as the doctor left and the chair legs screeched against the floor, grating on his ears. The man pinched the bridge of his nose and focused on Jake. Dark bags were beneath his eyes, adding emphasis to the wrinkles that spread outward from their corners. He was probably in his fifties, and Jake gathered him to be a smoker, judging by the tinge of yellow on his teeth and the thick rasp to his voice. "Jake, I'm Special Agent Trent Shaw from the FBI field office in D.C." A knot formed in the man's tanned throat as he swallowed a lump. He touched his jaw, caressing a fresh nick on his chin, and then said, "You're FBI, too."

Jake didn't know what to say. He needed a minute to process the news. Hell, he needed a lot more than a minute.

"Jake?" Trent snapped his thick fingers.

*I guess that explains my weird desire to note little details about everyone.*

"Where am I? Somewhere in England, I assume."

"You're in London."

"The last thing I remember is scoring a touchdown in college—and now I'm in London?"

Trent's big Adam's apple moved in his throat again. "You haven't been to college in a dozen years, Jake. I don't know why you're suppressing the last decade or so, but it's a matter of national security that you remember, and fast."

*Just fucking great.*

Trent Shaw's close-set, green eyes shifted to the monitors before looking back at Jake.

"How the hell did you guys find me?" Jake blinked a few times. Maybe that information wasn't relevant right now, but despite his current state, he was curious.

Trent coughed a little. "When the British found you at the scene of the explosion, you were slightly coherent, and they managed to get your name. They called the U.S. and . . . well, we were both shocked and relieved to hear it was you." He paused for a moment. "Before the explosion, you were on an OP and had gone missing. You were MIA for over a week." Trent stood. "Jesus, Jake, I never thought I'd see you again. And, damn, when I got to London they'd already put you in a coma."

The drugs were trying to pull Jake back to sleep. His eyelids grew heavy, and it was getting harder to keep them open.

"I need to talk with the doctor to learn more about your condition. Why don't you get some rest, and we'll talk again after you wake?"

Jake looked past Trent and at the open door. "Looks like that won't be happening."

Trent turned to follow Jake's gaze.

"He's awake?" the man standing in the doorframe asked.

That was all Jake needed—another man in a suit.

"Why are you here? We made a deal. No police or agents while he's at the hospital." Trent gripped his temples with his thumb and middle finger and irritation settled between the two men, thicker than the London fog.

Jake shifted his attention to the British guy standing before them. He was tall, lean, and had butter blonde hair that was slicked back. Behind his red-framed glasses were a pair of shale gray eyes.

"You're on her Majesty's soil. We invited you to London, even though we could have waited until we learned more about Agent Summers. This is our jurisdiction, not yours."

Trent's jaw tightened. "You better have called us as soon as you knew you had an American casualty."

"If we're going to find out who was behind the explosion, we need to work together. Not dodging London PD's phone calls, and mine as well. I'm running out of patience, Shaw. We followed your requests about Agent Summers—we have him isolated in a very busy hospital, which is not an easy feat . . . but you have to give us something."

Trent unbuttoned his suit jacket and crossed his arms. He stood firm in front of Jake's bedside, almost blocking Jake from view. "And I told you we'd talk once—"

"—he's awake." The man waved his hand at Jake.

"He *just* woke up," Trent said through gritted teeth.

Jake looked back and forth between the two, his mind drifting in and out of a hazy drug-induced stupor.

"And if it were your city that this happened in, how would you feel?" The British guy took a few steps closer to Trent, to Jake's bed. "A bomb detonated in London, and your guy here is the only witness. We need answers. Now." The man was practically in Trent's face, and the two were squaring off. "Are you hiding something?"

"Until my government grants us the authority to hand over classified intel to Her Majesty's Secret Service, my hands are tied." Trent tipped his shoulders up, and Jake could tell the Brit was near ready to blow a fuse. His cheeks reddened, and his mouth was tight.

The man walked around to the other side of the bed when Trent didn't back down. "I'm Justin King. I'm SS. And I need you to tell me what happened."

"SS?" Jake mumbled, unfamiliar.

"Secret Service, or you might know us as MI5. We go by both over here."

"But James Bond was MI6," Jake said in a low voice.

The man blinked twice and released an exaggerated sigh. "MI5 is domestic. SIS," the Brit began, and then cleared his throat, "or MI6 . . . deals with international threats."

"Well, whoever you are, I'm sorry, but I won't be able to help." Jake showed him his palms. "I can quote a few lines from some action movies, though. That shit comes to mind easily enough. But I still have no clue how I landed in this hospital."

"What is he talking about?" The agent looked over at Trent.

"He has memory loss," Trent answered.

The British agent peeked over at the window behind the bed, where snowflakes began to drift in the air as a breeze swirled the powder. "And you're sure that's the truth?" His voice was colder now. Bitter—matching the chill of the January air.

"And I'd lie because . . .?" Jake touched his forehead and shuddered as the pain in his head went from zero to sixty. Wasn't he on pain medicine? Why was this happening?

"We have no record of his entry to the country. Why was he here?"

"Like I said, I'm unable to share any information with you until I'm given clearance to do so."

The Brit removed his glasses, cleaned them with his silk tie, and placed them back on his nose. "We're fortunate no one died. I'm just trying to figure out what an FBI agent was doing in an abandoned factory wearing a bloody suicide vest. And considering he magically appeared in our damn country right before the explosion—"

Jake's ears perked at the new information. "Suicide vest?"

The Brit sighed with frustration as if he hadn't meant to let that information slip. "We recovered what looks like materials from a vest. There wasn't too much C4, so you're lucky—"

What was it with everyone thinking he was so damn lucky? "So I wasn't just at the site of an explosion—someone was trying to kill me?"

Then chills shot up his spine. *Or was I trying to kill myself?*

"Can you both get the hell out of my room? I need time to think."

"Maybe you'll remember something," the British agent said under his breath before turning away. "We'll be in touch soon."

Jake shut his eyes and gripped the sides of the bed, holding onto the sheets as a memory cranked through his mind at hyper speed. It was a blur of images and sounds that he could hardly tell apart . . .

*A whip smacked against his skin. He released a moan, and his shoulders shrank from the pain as the leather ripped at his flesh.*

*His hands were bound above his head.*

*He was on his knees. Barefoot and in jeans only.*

*The whip ate at his back as it lashed him.*

*Blood.*

*His blood.*

*Dripping from his face down onto the concrete floor as he hung his head low.*

Jake's eyes flashed open, willing the memory away. It was unbearable. His body shook, and he started to sweat as a rumbling in his stomach, a feeling of nausea, swept over him. "What in the hell happened to me?"

# CHAPTER FOUR

ALEXA'S GAZE SLID UP FROM HER COMPUTER AND TO THE MASSIVE screen on the wall. Matt was updating the team on their mission in Munich, even though she still hadn't been able to crack Boris Gregov's encrypted files.

"Gregov is in Cyprus." Matt placed a pin on a wall map next to the screen, marking Gregov's location. "We're not yet sure what he's doing there, but our agents are following him. That does put him pretty damn close to Istanbul, to Kemal Bekas, which means something could be up."

Xander stepped up next to Matt and began swiping his fingers across the screen, moving icons around and opening files. "We were able to copy Gregov's computer, but Alexa," he tipped his head at her, "is still working on decrypting the few files on there that we hope will be relevant."

Alexa scowled at Xander, knowing he was poking at her. But what choice did he have but to push her? He was second in command on the case—the lead intelligence officer. Then again, all the members of the team were itching to close the case. "It's barely been two days, guys—I'm doing my best. Besides, we've been distracted by the incident in London." She hated making excuses, but the files were nothing like she'd seen.

Xander tapped at his wristwatch and winked at Alexa.

"We haven't intercepted any new transmissions since the email about the attack," Matt said, pulling her attention back to him. "Since we have no idea when or where it will take place, we're shooting in the dark. And this time, we absolutely have to connect whatever attack the group is planning on Kemal Bekas—as well as prevent it. We chop off the head of their organization and—"

"You don't think another leader will rise if we take Bekas down?" Agent John Daniels interrupted, looking up at Xander and Matt.

Xander swiped at the smart screen again, pulling up an image of Kemal Bekas. Surrounding his face was a web of other men and women—people MI6 believed were all connected to the group, known as @Anarchy. Although when talking—MI6 referred to them simply as Anarchy.

And as much as the agency wanted to take down Bekas, they still hadn't garnered enough evidence to swoop into Turkey and make the arrest. Or the kill.

Alexa cleared her throat and rose to her feet, leaving the oval table to join Xander and Matt. "Bekas is the brains behind Anarchy. Without him, it'll fall apart." She hoped, at least. "And I don't believe there is anyone," she pointed to other faces on the screen, "who has the money and resources to pull off what Bekas has done. No Bekas, no Anarchy."

Alexa's fingers skimmed her blouse, then rested on her collarbone as she thought about it all. "Of course, the hackers that have joined the group won't up and quit hacking—but if they aren't working collectively for one main purpose than they pose a lower risk, for sure. None of these hackers that work for Anarchy have the same conviction as Bekas. He's motivated by hate and loss. The hackers working with him are motivated by money.

Okay, so some enjoy creating chaos, but Bekas—he's looking for retribution. And revenge is always a much more dangerous game."

There were two other main players aside from the leader, Bekas. The Russian, Boris Gregov, and a wealthy Frenchman, Pierre Reza.

MI6 figured Bekas had named the terrorist group, @Anarchy, to attract other hackers to the organization—the younger generation of hackers ate it up.

Anarchy. Chaos. Money.

Why not?

But after tracking @Anarchy for fifteen months, Alexa and her team realized @Anarchy was no longer just a group of cyber terrorists. The organization's actions had become progressively more dangerous—murderous, even.

Alexa stuffed her hands in the pockets of her tan silk pants and examined the names and faces of the men and women on the screen. The people were of many different nationalities and ethnicities, but they all had one thing in common. They had also been known for their hate of Britain and the United States.

"And since we can't ask the Turkish government to help us nail Bekas, we're on our own," Matt added glibly.

"But Bekas is part Kurdish. You know the current government isn't exactly favorable of the Kurds. We could use that to our advantage and at least smoke Bekas out of Istanbul. Maybe we'd have better luck getting at him in different territory," John recommended.

"It won't work. Bekas won't up and relocate the headquarters of his legitimate business, Bekas Tech, from Istanbul. And we can't convince the Turks to force him out," Matt said, folding his arms.

John's dark green eyes met Alexa's, and he pinched his brows together, the lines in his aging face deepening. "Why don't we just send an agent in and kill the bastard—we can be done with this."

John had been saying the same thing almost every day for the last six months, so he already knew the answer.

"I wish," Xander said.

Alexa grumbled. She'd love to put a bullet in Bekas herself.

But there were rules. These weren't the olden days or the movies. They couldn't go around killing businessmen without approval from Parliament. "So, right now, our focus is to find out what Bekas is planning. The email Gregov sent to Bekas two weeks ago hints that it will be their biggest attack to date," Alexa said. Both worry and excitement pierced her. On the one hand this was the closest the team had come to taking the group down. But on the flip side—what if they failed?

"And we're certain that the message was decrypted correctly? I mean, it's so soon. They don't normally have hits that close to each other, and just last month they took credit for the attack at the British bank in India," Jill Stanley said. She was the newest agent assigned to the team and was still getting her footing.

"They've been speeding up the attacks. They're more aggressive lately," Alexa responded. That was why she didn't have time to focus on the bombing in London, which had been at an empty and deserted factory. She had a real threat to stop.

"Ahem." Matt redirected the group's attention back his way. "It's critical we nail these bastards now and stop this upcoming attack. I don't want to see any more deaths. You got it?" He raised his brows and rubbed his hands together. "So, give me what you have. I need updates on our leads—then you can get back to work."

"Any movement on Bekas?" Xander asked.

"No. Our informant inside Bekas Tech said Bekas hasn't left Istanbul in two weeks," Tenley, another intelligence officer on the team, responded as she looked up from her notes.

"And how is Berat?" Xander had been the one who'd managed to turn the Bekas Tech employee into an important ally.

"Nothing new right now," Tenley answered as she scribbled

something down. Tenley was the youngest agent on their team. She'd only been recruited from Oxford two years ago, but her IQ was off the charts, and her uncanny ability to learn languages had garnered her a position on their team.

"When do you normally hear from Berat?" Matt inquired.

"Every Tuesday morning."

"Okay. Well, I want you in Istanbul. I want you to meet with him in person and try and get eyes on Bekas. Watch him like a hawk these next few days." Matt's hand swooped up to the back of his neck, annoyance spreading across his face. "John—go with her."

When neither Tenley or John moved, Matt's eyes narrowed, and he held his hand up and flicked his wrist twice, waving his hand. "I meant now!" Ever since they heard of the explosion, Matt-the-joker from their OP in Munich had been on holiday. He was all business. As he should be, she guessed.

Tenley popped to her heels and started for the door, and John followed after her.

"We'll get you assigned to a target soon, Jill. That leaves you, Sam. Please tell me you have better news about Reza." Matt's eyes darted toward the computer genius they had recruited from Kenya eight years ago. He had previously been hired by companies to hack their servers and find the faults in their systems, so the companies could better defend themselves from malicious hackers. When Sam had hacked MI6 to show the agency its flaws—on his own initiative—he had been arrested for the breach. Ultimately, however, the bold act had landed him his job.

Sam scratched at the black stubble on his jaw, his dark brown eyes finding Alexa before sliding over to Matt. "Reza has been on the move a lot. He was in Greece, then Italy, and it looks like now he's back home in Paris."

"You manage to intercept any emails or calls he's made in the last few weeks?" Matt took a step closer to the oval table.

"We've intercepted two emails, both encrypted. I'm working

on decoding them. One was a little over a week ago, and the other more recent."

"Maybe it's related to whatever Gregov's working on." Matt nodded at Alexa. "You want to add anything?"

"Honestly, I should really get back to Gregov's files," Alexa answered.

"Sounds good." Matt looked over at Jill. "Let me get you more up to date," he said to her. "We'll all touch base tomorrow."

Alexa sat back down as Matt and Jill left the room, leaving her and Xander alone. She began drumming her fingers on the table by her laptop. "So—has Laney tried to rope you away from our case and on to the bombing?" Sarah Laney was the chief of MI6, also known as C.

Xander rested a hip against the desk and folded his arms. "Not sure if this bombing will fall in our laps or not. Should be Secret Service territory, anyway."

"True."

Alexa focused back on her computer screen and stared at it as the algorithm she'd set up to crunch through Gregov's files continued to work—code scrolled across, becoming a blur. "Have we heard anything new from Secret Service?"

"London PD started sweeping the site of the explosion and is working their way outward—they established a five-kilometer perimeter to check if the American involved in the bombing came from one of the surrounding points," Xander explained. "I mean, I doubt the guy was wandering around the neighborhood with a suicide vest strapped to his chest and no one noticed."

She blinked a few times and dragged her gaze back over to him. "Which means he was in a secluded area before he arrived at the mill."

"Or he was dropped off, and the police need to extend their search perimeter if they don't find anything soon."

"Any change on the American?"

"Yeah. The doctor woke him up, but apparently, he has amnesia."

Alexa narrowed her eyes. "Really? I find that a little hard to believe."

Xander shrugged. "Yeah, me too." He patted her on the shoulder and a breath of air rushed from his lips. "I'll give you some time to work. Be back later."

"Thanks."

Once Xander had left, she pressed her hands to her face, and then rubbed her eyes. She was tired and sore from sitting in front of a computer for such long hours. "Come on, dammit." She shoved her laptop back and stood up.

Alexa moved over to the window and folded her arms. Her eyes fell upon the Thames, admiring the dusky sky's reflection on the grayish water. Pillow-soft snow coated its banks.

*When was the last time I went for a walk?* Of course, it was ridiculous to think of doing anything leisurely. Her only stress relief was the mandatory fitness training.

She touched her stomach, her hand skating to her side as she closed her eyes, a memory moving fast through her like the pull of a ripcord. Then her shoulders shuddered and she stepped away from the window and went back to her laptop.

She sat down, wrapping herself in the laptop's familiar glow, and kept working as the algorithm ran in the background.

Xander was back a few hours later with a mug of tea in his hand. He set it in front of her and sat down. "Still nothing?"

Alexa pressed her palms to the desk and pushed her rolling chair back. "The files we downloaded are basically a bunch of pixel fragments. It's complex."

"And you're the best at complex, which is why we dragged your arse to Munich with us." A smile met his lips. God, didn't he just love giving her a hard time.

"You try and figure out a million-piece jigsaw puzzle when the pieces are all practically the same color, shape, and size . . ." Her analogy seemed lost on him as he shot her a blank stare. "Using our binary systems to decode these files is proving damn near impossible. It's like nothing I've ever seen before. I knew these guys were on another level, but I didn't expect this," she said while waving her hand at her computer as if she were brushing it away.

"So we send it to GCHQ." The Government Communications Headquarters were Britain's, and really the world's, premier cyber agency.

She scrubbed a palm up and down her cheek and glowered at her screen. "Something doesn't make sense—it doesn't feel right."

"At least you were able to bypass Gregov's firewalls and copy his files back in Munich. But if we want to stop whatever cyberattack Anarchy is planning we really need to—"

She held up her hand. "I know. I know. And I already copied the files and sent them off to GCHQ. Maybe they'll have better luck."

Xander touched her shoulder and gently squeezed. "Good to hear you already passed the files on, because we need you to play dress-up again."

Alexa looked over her shoulder at him, her lips parting. This was always her least favorite part of the job. The only time she wanted to impersonate someone else was via computer.

"It's Laney's orders."

"Why?" She pushed to her feet. "This isn't about the bombing, is it? You said Secret Service is on that."

"They're asking for our help now."

"Isn't there anyone else?" She pleaded with her eyes, narrowing them at Xander. But she knew she was wasting her time. If Laney wanted something, there was no arguing. "We're knee deep in our own shit right now."

He shrugged. "Not my decision, babe. Sorry."

"Well, who am I supposed to be this time?"

Xander smirked.

"What?" She folded her arms, growing tense.

"Oh, well, um." He paused and touched his chest, and then his smile spread until she wondered if it would reach his ears. "Laney needs you to play nurse."

"Oh, bloody hell."

# CHAPTER FIVE

ALEXA DUCKED INTO THE HOSPITAL ROOM AND SHUT THE DOOR behind her.

Justin King, the Secret Service agent in charge of the investigation, had informed her that the U.S. government didn't want anyone going near the injured American's hospital room. She couldn't believe the Americans were managing to boss them around, especially given that they were on British soil.

Of course, she understood their reasoning. The Americans wanted everyone to think their FBI agent had died in the explosion. They were trying to protect him. And if you wanted to cover the truth, you couldn't have police running around.

Fortunately, they had made her job enormously easy. Since the hospital wing was practically vacant, there weren't many people to notice her. In fact, so far there hadn't been any at all. The Americans only had one guard dog—another agent. She had waited for him to disappear down a hall before she made her move.

*I shouldn't be here*, she thought bitterly. She'd much prefer to sit behind her screen, breaking through Gregov's snarl of code. It was damn infuriating she couldn't crack it. After so much time tracking @Anarchy, she was anxious as hell to stop them finally.

Alexa moved with slow and cautious steps toward the man lying in bed.

Jake Summers was asleep. White gauze wrapped his forehead, covering part of his scalp.

There were black rings around his closed eyes, and he had a little bit of a swollen cheek.

He wasn't all that banged up for someone who had survived an explosion. But there was something painfully familiar about the man. She couldn't quite place her finger on it.

She turned away from him, even though she was compelled to stare. Reaching for his chart, she skimmed over the details, attempting to verify the information Secret Service had received about the man's condition.

The trauma to his head could have caused temporary amnesia. But what if he was faking it? Then again, why would he lie?

The lashings on his back indicated he'd been tortured. But why terrorists sent Jake to an old mill was beyond her—unless he had escaped?

She returned his chart to where she'd found it and moved to the side of his bed, where she stared down at his hands, which were linked on his chest. Her fingers touched his bruised knuckles, and she held her hand over his for a moment.

*What am I doing?* She pulled her hand free from his.

His chest inflated and he released a ragged breath.

When Jake blinked a few times, and opened his eyes, Alexa stumbled back, turning toward the heart rate monitor.

"How are you feeling?" she softly asked, examining the monitor like she had a clue. Did he know she wasn't supposed to be in there? She'd have to improvise—and fast—if that were the case.

"I feel like hell . . . but I don't want any more meds." His deep, country voice flitted to her ears and goosebumps chased across her skin.

"Are you sure? You must be in a lot of pain." She stole a

glimpse of the hall through the window in the room, checking to see if the coast was still clear.

"I can't think with that stuff in me. And, apparently, I have a lot I should be thinking about."

She listened closer to the rich baritone of his voice, which was like a slow whisper of seduction nipping at her skin. She spun toward him.

It couldn't . . . could it?

Her body stilled, and the hairs on her arm stood.

"Your voice . . ."

Was he a mind reader? Oh, God. It *was* him. Mr. New Year's Eve—the guy she'd spent a week with a year ago and . . . *What the hell?*

He'd said his name was Jake, but he'd never given his last name. She hadn't wanted to do last names—that would imply something more serious.

And she couldn't ever do serious. Not while she was racing around the world trying to stop terrorists.

Alexa's mind scrambled for answers as she turned away again, offering only her profile. Of course, if he truly had amnesia, he wouldn't recognize her.

Would he?

How could this be happening? How could he be lying in a bed twenty minutes from her flat? It was almost unbelievable. Scratch that. It was unbelievable.

She touched a hand to her red wig, making sure it was still in place. As she started to lower her arm, he reached out and captured her wrist. The gesture sent strange, tingling sensations up her arm. Her nipples became stiff against the inside of her bra.

"Do I know you?" he asked gruffly.

"No, of course not."

He released Alexa's hand, but the loss of his touch left a cool imprint in its place.

"Sorry," he mumbled. "I barely know who I am." He forced an

awkward laugh. "Any updates on my charts? I haven't seen the doctor in a little while. You think you could ask him to come in here?" Jake pressed a hand to his face and then gripped the bridge of his nose. Maybe his nurse or the doctor could talk some sense into him and get him to take pain meds. He seemed an awful lot like her, though—stubborn.

"I'll get him." Well, not that she really could. But he'd probably be along at some point.

She inhaled one long breath and took a step back from the bed. "I hope you get better, Mr. Summers."

"Thank you, ma'am."

Ma'am? She tried not to laugh. He had called her that the night they'd first met.

"Take care." She touched a hand to her stomach, trying to fight the sudden emotions that pulled her apart like frayed fabric coming unraveled.

"Miss?"

"Yeah?" she nearly whispered as she looked up at him, finding his eyes. They were the color of chocolate—no. His eyes were more like the color of oak. Strong and dependable.

Those eyes had haunted her for the last year.

Jake's forehead creased, which must have hurt, given the bandage on his head. "Are you sure I don't know you?"

Some small part of her wanted to tell him the truth, but she swallowed back the words. "I don't think you'd be the kind of man I'd forget."

Not so much a lie since she'd never forgotten him.

"Goodbye."

Alexa rushed from the room without waiting for a response, her heart pumping loud in her chest. She lowered her head as she maneuvered down the hall, thankful that no one was around.

She noticed a tremble in her hand as she raised it to press the button to open the automatic doors. When they parted, she rushed through, anxious to get out of there. But once she rounded the next corner, she quickly stepped back and hid inside an empty room. She'd nearly collided with the agent that had been outside Jake's room. She assumed he was Special Agent Trent Shaw, the man whom Justin King of Secret Service wanted to throttle.

"What are you doing here? When you called, I said not to come," she heard the agent rasp to the man that had been standing next to him. Alexa pressed her back to the wall and angled her head to bring her ear closer to the doorway.

The other man had been tall and built, with thick black hair and sharp blue eyes. And he had looked pissed. "And I told you that I was coming, like it or not," the man responded to the agent.

"You're not family," Shaw answered. "And hell, not even his family is invited."

"I want to ID the body. I need to see for myself that it's Jake. That he's gone." A hot warmth of sadness trickled through his voice—an obvious pain.

Alexa tugged her lower lip between her teeth. She felt bad for whoever this guy was—he thought Jake was dead. All of London did, too. But even though he didn't know Jake's true status, he had been knowledgeable enough to find his way to Shaw. That was impressive.

"How'd you even locate us? Hell, you still haven't told me how you found out what happened to Jake," Shaw bit out, his accusation following the line of Alexa's thoughts.

"Don't worry about that. Tell me what happened on his OP in Sicily—how did this happen to Jake?" His voice was raw, near breaking.

"Did Jake tell you about Sicily? How'd you know he was there?"

"He didn't tell me. Jake's a rule follower, you know that." He cleared his throat, quiet for a moment. "Jake *was* . . ."

"Then how'd you—"

"You know who I am. You know my contacts."

"And yet your contacts forgot to mention one important thing to you."

Alexa's stomach muscles tightened with anticipation. Was the agent going to tell him the truth? Alexa's fingertips bit into her palms as she waited, her nerves growing anxious for Shaw to speak again.

"I'm going to tell you something. Well, show you . . . but it's only because of who you are and what you've done for our country. Hear me, though—you're under direct orders not to tell what you learn to anyone," Shaw finally said in a low voice. "And I mean *anyone*."

"Agreed. Now, what the hell is going on?"

"Come with me," Shaw grumbled.

The two men started past her door, and Alexa stepped back, allowing the darkness of the room to shroud her body. She waited a few minutes to make sure they were gone and then hurried to the stairs.

The second Alexa set foot on the first level, her work mobile began to vibrate in her pocket.

"It's me. Code: zero nine five three two eleven."

"How'd it go?" It was Laney.

*Not how I expected.*

Before she could answer, Laney said, "I'm worried. I think the Americans are going to try and swoop him out of London without giving us any intel."

Alexa paused outside the hospital cafeteria, her gaze fixated on a young and probably very normal couple. They were sitting at a small, round table munching on burgers and chips. Mustard dripped down and splattered on the man's shirt. Alexa couldn't help but wonder why they were at the hospital. Was someone sick? Or maybe it was a happy occasion—maybe someone had delivered a baby.

She was craving "normal" more and more these days—well, in

between the moments she wasn't knee deep in code, trying to hack the hackers.

"Well, this Shaw guy seems pretty secretive, but I did learn something that might be helpful," Alexa finally said.

"And?"

"Jake Summers was on an assignment in Sicily before the explosion. I'll tell you more when I get there. Heading to you now." She ended the call and quickly made another.

The phone only rang once. "About bloody time you called me. It's been weeks."

"Lori?" Alexa's eyes averted to the floor as she moved off to the side of the lobby. "Remember that guy I met last year?" She leaned against the wall and bowed her head. "He's back in London." She shouldn't have been telling her sister this—it could compromise the investigation. But her family was all she had, and they were the only ones outside her work who knew the truth about her.

"How could I forget him?" Lori's voice rose an octave, and Alexa could visualize the smile on her sister's face. "You guys shagging again?" She said it so casually, like Alexa had time for such things.

"No. But—"

"You want my permission or something?" She chuckled. "Because you've got it."

"I shouldn't have called," Alexa grumbled. She straightened her shoulders and started moving toward the exit.

"What's wrong?" The humor was gone from Lori's voice. "Alexa?"

"Nothing, Lori. I'm—well, I just miss you. I have to run. Love you."

She didn't wait to hear her sister's goodbye. Instead, she shoved her phone back in her pocket, kicking herself for being weak, for giving in to her desire to share her life.

# CHAPTER SIX

JAKE MINDLESSLY FLIPPED THROUGH CHANNELS ON THE TV. HE tapped at the volume, lowering it to barely audible. Almost any noise was like a banshee howling in his ears.

He stopped scrolling when he came across a news station, then set the remote next to him, happy to simply read the headlines at the bottom of the screen, opposed to hearing them.

But Jake's attention diverted to the tall, broad-shouldered man who was now filling the doorframe to his room. The man's sharp blue eyes steadied on Jake with disbelief as his brows pulled together.

He looked government, that was for sure. Well, at least as far as Jake could tell—he drew his comparisons from TV and movies, and his father's military pals. From what Jake knew, this guy screamed military badass. He was all hard planes—his facial expressions seemed carved from granite, his jaw was probably so tough he had to use a switchblade to shave. There was a grit to him, a roughness. Yet, he was cloaked in a perfectly tailored black suit that matched the sense of danger his presence radiated. The man cleared his throat and brought a hand to the nape of his neck, where his black hair brushed against the collar of his dark dress shirt.

"Who are you?" Jake finally asked, and the man took a step into the room. He shut the door behind him, but not before Jake caught sight of Trent standing with arms crossed, observing through the window from outside the room.

The man fidgeted with the knot on his tie—it was black atop a black shirt. Was he going to a funeral? He cleared his throat, yet again. Either he was sick or nervous, although that didn't really fit. This guy didn't look like he ever got nervous.

The man came to the bed, his eyes assessing Jake. He folded one arm across his chest and rested the elbow of the other against it, tapping his fingers against his lips. There was a thick titanium wedding band there.

Jake's eyes snapped shut as a sharp pain tore through his skull, followed by the image of this man holding a ring box. *"You think you could hang on to this for me until the vows?"*

"Shit." Jake shook his head and swallowed as his stomach became unsettled. "I'm gonna be sick." He grabbed the plastic bowl at his side as his stomach tucked in, convulsing. Tremors raked over his spine as his skin pebbled with perspiration. His jaw opened wide, but only spit dribbled down as his body shook. *Jesus Christ.*

"You okay?" The man's eyes grew dark, and his arms dropped like weighted anchors at his sides.

Jake's throat burned, and his chest grew tight. He pushed the plastic bowl aside and jabbed at the nurse call button. Maybe the red-head was still there.

But it was Lisa's voice that resounded through the speaker above Jake's bed. "Can I help you?"

"I need you."

"Here." The man reached for the tray table by the bed and offered him the cup of water that sat there.

"Thanks."

"I'm Michael Maddox," he said at last.

Lisa opened the door and arrived at his bedside before Jake could decide how to respond. She glanced at Michael and tossed him a nervous smile. "What can I do for you?" She looked over at Jake and angled her head, compassion shining in her eyes.

"Got any anti-nausea meds you can pump in me?"

She frowned in apology at his pain. "Yes, sir. The doctor has meds on standby if you ever asked for them. I'll be back."

Jake rubbed his stomach and tried to sit up a little so he could concentrate on whatever news this Michael character had arrived to deliver.

"It's so good to see you alive."

*So, you know I was in an explosion.* "Are you FBI, too?" Jake released an exaggerated sigh. He must be, right? That tightwad, Trent, wouldn't let just anyone in his room. Maybe he was a general. Although this guy looked like a soldier in a suit, too young for general status.

"Hell, no. That's your department." Michael scratched the side of his head as if he wasn't sure what else to say. "I, uh, just found out that you have amnesia right before I came in here. Seeing you alive was a shocker—an amazing one—but then . . . shit, I'm so sorry. This must all be awful for you. But I'm going to find out who did this to you, I promise. The SOBs will pay."

Jake barely heard what Michael said. Instead, he sputtered, "We must be close if I was in your wedding."

Michael's mouth went round as his eyes widened. "You remember? I thought—"

"Not quite. I had a flash of memory—you were asking me to hold on to some rings." Jake shrugged, which was a bad idea. It brought about a pain like being needled in the ribs with a hot poker. "That's all I got."

"Oh. That's something, anyway. Maybe the rest of your memories will come back soon." The man's voice was low and strained, and Jake wondered what emotions he was tucking away

43

beneath his steely surface. Had the man ever shown an emotion in his life? Did he know how to laugh? Jake couldn't fathom how he might have become friends with someone who was so aloof.

"Every time a memory tries to resurface, it makes me dizzy and nauseous. I think I need a damn break from memory lane." He blew out a breath.

"Sorry . . . I had to come as soon as I found out about the explosion and—"

"What is it that you do?" Jake couldn't help but interrupt. His mind was spinning as he tried to make sense of the stranger—who wasn't really a stranger—standing before him.

It was all so damn odd.

Michael smiled and shook his head. Well, at least the man was capable of a smile. "I do a little bit of everything."

Well, that wasn't entirely helpful. "You have any clue what I'm doing in London, at least?"

"Honestly, no. You're one of the leading specialists on counterterrorism in the U.S., though. You head up the unit in Dallas."

Jake was beginning to miss football. A concussion sounded much easier to deal with. "How the hell did I end up in counterterrorism?" *Oh, God.* He started to shake, and his core squeezed.

He grabbed the bowl and shoved it up to his face, but he knew his empty stomach would produce nothing. "Fuck," he yelled, just as the nurse entered. He blinked away whatever memories tried to resurface. He couldn't deal with them right now.

"Oh no. Again?" Lisa was at his side, prepping a vial. "This will help." She inserted a substance into the IV. "This should also calm you a little."

"Calm me?" Jake looked up from the pink plastic bowl. "What'd you give me?" His eyelids flickered shut a few times as his head grew light and everything became a little fuzzy. "I didn't want that shit."

"You said no pain meds, but this is for anxiety."

"You think I'd want that?" he mumbled before resting his head on the pillow. The medication felt good, as much as he didn't want to admit it. It helped ease the tension in his body.

"Sorry." As she disappeared from the room, he regretted yelling at her. It wasn't her fault.

Michael faced Jake again with a darkness in his eyes, a shield of armor protecting him from whatever emotions he didn't want to reveal. But Jake didn't have that luxury—everything was new to him. His memories cascaded to mind without his permission, absorbing him as though they were happening for the first time.

"I don't want to bombard you with too much right now. I'm just so damn thankful you're alive. And I promise that I'll get to the bottom of this."

"Maybe I want to disappear back in time and forget the last twelve years." Jake shut his eyes, hating how pathetic he sounded.

"Get some rest—you need time to process all of this." Michael placed a hand over his heart. "Hell, so do I." His voice wavered a little as he spoke.

Jake forced his eyes open, and Michael averted his attention to the floor. "Listen, Jake. You may not remember, but you're like a brother to me. You saved me more times than I can count."

*What did I save you from, if you're not an agent?*

"The guys always joke that I'm the glue that keeps us together, but that's just not true."

*What guys?*

"You're the heart of us all, and without you . . . well, shit, we need you. And I'm not gonna give up on you. None of us will."

Maybe the man wasn't cold hearted, after all.

Michael moved to the door and glanced over his shoulder at Jake before nodding goodbye.

Jake pressed his hands to his face. But there was no time to process his emotions. The sound of shoes smacking against tile came nearer.

"He shouldn't have come here. The fact that he figured out your location means we need to scramble out of here faster than I'd like." Trent was standing by the bed, arms folded.

"That's fine with me. I'm itching to get back home."

"You think you're going home? Hell, do you even know where home is?" Trent shook his head.

*Thank you for rubbing that in my damn face.* "And where am I supposed to go?"

"Somewhere safe," Trent grumbled. "We should probably get out of here tonight or by tomorrow, at the latest. You think you're up for a flight?"

*No.* But he wasn't going to admit it. "I'll be fine," he said as the news station grabbed his attention.

He scrambled for the remote at his side and increased the volume.

"Still no updates on the explosion at the old abandoned textile mill just outside of London. Most certainly, American authorities will be investigating the matter in conjunction with the London PD, given the tragic death of the American at the mill. The American, whose name has yet to be relinquished, died during surgery at the hospital following the explosion. Our thoughts and prayers are with his family back in the United States."

*Died during surgery?*

The female reporter's words had the hairs on Jake's arms standing. "We're going live to footage now from our chopper—it looks as though the London PD is investigating a small cabin about two kilometers from the location of the blast."

There was an aerial view of a home surrounded by police cars and flashing lights, as well as vans and other news reporter vehicles. "It appears they brought in SOCO—scenes of crime officers—so we have to assume the London PD have found something in conjunction with the explosion."

"Fuck me." Trent reached into his pocket and grabbed a cell phone.

"You can say that again. Do people think I'm dead?" Jake tried to sit up in his bed, and his mind reeled once again. No wonder that Michael guy had looked like he'd seen a ghost.

Trent lowered the phone in front of him for a moment while directing his attention to Jake. "As soon as we positively identified it was you, we requested the cover story about your death, and we asked for you to be moved into isolation."

"Does my family think I'm dead?"

"Your name hasn't been released, and we haven't told anyone you're even here. So, no. No one other than the bastards who did this to you think you're dead. Michael's got government contacts —that's how he found out you were here."

"Oh." He wasn't sure how he felt about this. Why did people need to think he had died?

"But this is why we can't have you going back home to Dallas. We need whoever held you captive thinking you're six feet under. I don't want them coming after you again."

# CHAPTER SEVEN

ALEXA SAT ON THE WHITE LEATHER SOFA IN THE SITTING AREA OFF to the side of Laney's desk. Her fingernails curled against her thighs as she tried to slow her pulse, staring out the window. Clouds were like steam puffs of fog hovering outside, hanging in the sky above the Thames.

She still couldn't believe Mr. New Year's Eve was an FBI agent and the American involved in the explosion. *How the hell can this be happening?*

Laney was on her phone, standing behind her desk. "I agree with Special Agent Shaw on this—it's a complete circus. Get the media out of there. And let's have London PD removed, as well. We're now working with Secret Service on the investigation, and we don't need all of this news. The media is giving the terrorists step-by-step guidance on our every move." Laney was quiet for a moment, and Alexa could hear a deep male voice snapping out words through the phone.

"Of course it was terrorists who tried to blow up the American agent. What do you mean, we don't know for sure . . . Give me a bloody break." Laney crossed one arm over her chest, supporting her elbow as she held the mobile tight to her ear.

If MI6 was now dealing with the explosion, Alexa hoped Laney would divert other resources and agents to the investigation. She needed to stay focused on @Anarchy to stop their next attack. Besides, Alexa couldn't be involved in this—it was a conflict of interest. Well, Jake Summers didn't remember her, but at some point, he might.

Laney's liquid brown eyes focused on Alexa as she removed her glasses. She shook her head, demonstrating her irritation for whatever government official in Parliament was pissing her off on the other end of the line.

"Yes, I've thought about that. But the Secret Service and I have decided it is in our best interest to let everyone think the American died in the explosion. Besides, the request came from the White House." Another pause followed by more male chatter on the line.

Laney blew out a long-winded breath. "It's not so simple. Whoever held the FBI agent hostage may have been planning a terrorist attack. I hardly doubt the attack was to hit an abandoned mill and only kill one person. I guarantee they were planning something else and this agent escaped. He may have knowledge that can help prevent the next attack."

Alexa tried to wrap her head around what she was hearing. She couldn't imagine Jake Summers being tortured by terrorists—and how the hell did he escape? Or . . . had he? The whole situation was borderline insane.

"If the terrorists think the agent died, they may still go ahead with their plans. But if they know he's alive but don't know he lost his memory, they'd cancel, right?" Alexa interrupted. She had a feeling that this was what the man on the other end of the line was arguing. And he had a point. Okay, so maybe Jake's captors would come after him if they knew he was alive. But he could be protected, and at least they would have thwarted an attack.

"Let me call you back." Laney ended the call and tucked her mobile back into her pocket. She approached Alexa, who was now on her feet in front of the sofa. "Think about this, Alexa. This man might be our only lead to finding out what his captors have planned, but if they think he's alive and they change their plans, his intel will be absolutely useless."

"Isn't this risky? I mean, we're relying on this agent to get his memories back fast enough to corrupt the plans of a terrorist group . . . and, hell, we don't even know who had him or what their true intentions are." Alexa folded her arms and narrowed her eyes. "I think we should let everyone think he's alive and then use him as bait. Then they will be coming to us." *Oh, God, am I really suggesting to use Mr. Wonderful as bait? What is wrong with me?* But the job had to come first. It always came first.

"And you don't think they'll be expecting that?" Lines scattered across Laney's forehead, making her look older than her forty-five years. Her normally smooth, mocha skin was tainted with streaks of worry. Still, her black hair remained perfect in a tight bun, as always, every hair pressed down in place. Alexa would have clawed at it with frustration on a daily basis if she had Laney's job.

"They who?" Alexa shrugged.

"ISIS. Al Qaeda. One of the other many groups we have on our list," she countered.

"It's obviously your call," Alexa grumbled.

"It is," Laney sharply responded. "But I won't drag you onto the case. Clearly, you don't want to be involved. Besides, I need you working on the Anarchy case."

"Thank you." And yet, some strange pang in her stomach had her placing her hands there. "Who will you put on it?" she asked. She couldn't do it herself, but she wanted the best working the case. Her "perfect" man from last year—who apparently wasn't perfect because he was a federal agent—well, his life was on the line.

"I don't know. Maybe I'll have Seth run lead and work with Secret Service."

"He's good, but—"

Laney's hands went to her hips. "Now you have an opinion?" She raised a perfectly arched brow. "And you still need to tell me what you learned from your hospital visit. I had Xander look into Sicily, but he came up empty so far."

"Can't we just ask the Americans? Whatever happened in Italy must be connected to the bombing, right?" Alexa shrugged.

"Well, you don't need to worry about it, remember? You don't want on the case."

Just what she needed—sarcasm from her boss.

A knock at the door curbed Alexa's response, which was probably for the best. Just because Laney had taken Alexa under her wing like a sister didn't mean Alexa could snap at her. The woman was still her boss and the chief of the agency.

"Come in," Laney said.

It was Sam, Xander, and Matt.

"Hey," Xander said, nodding Alexa's direction.

"Got anything?" Laney asked.

"I think you'd both better sit down," Matt said, his brown eyes, which had a touch of honey gold to them, met Alexa's.

*Well, shit, that's not good.*

Laney folded her arms across her chest, and Alexa mirrored her move. "Tell us," Laney instructed.

Matt nodded to Sam, who clutched his tablet tight between his hands and swallowed. "Well, remember I mentioned Reza was in Italy recently?"

"I read your report earlier, but I've been busy." Laney tipped her head for him to continue.

"It took some time, but I finally decrypted the two messages Reza received. I haven't been able to narrow down the source of the emails to a specific IP address, but the messages pinged off a router within two kilometers of the mill explosion site."

Sam's brown eyes focused on Matt for a moment; Xander's jaw remained locked as his eyes steadied on Alexa. She took in a long, deep breath.

"I didn't think much of the messages after I decrypted them—not until Xander mentioned Sicily." Sam looked back at Alexa, and then to Laney. "The first message was sent on January fourth at ten p.m., and it said, 'The Eagle has been received.'"

"Eagle's the code name Anarchy uses for American agents," Alexa blurted.

Sam nodded. "And the other message was sent January eleventh—five minutes before the explosion in London. It read, 'The Eagle is loose.'"

"Loose?" Laney shook her head in disbelief. "So, you're saying you think Anarchy is responsible for kidnapping the American agent? And the agent escaped, that message was then sent, and the explosion occurred directly after?"

Alexa's fingers slipped up to her lips. She had thought the situation was messy before, but if the explosion at the mill was tied to the @Anarchy case . . .

"Yes, we think that whatever attack Kemal Bekas is—or was—planning is somehow connected to the American," Xander said.

"And we're basing this all off a few vague messages?" Alexa asked. She knew they were right to draw those conclusions, but she didn't want them to be true.

"We should confirm with the Americans that Jake Summers was in Italy when he was taken, but given that we know Reza was also there, and he received those encrypted messages . . ." Matt showed his palms. "I'd say it's a safe bet."

Laney walked around behind her desk and pressed her fingertips to the metal surface. "Good catch, Sam. Now, what I need you to do is grab as many agents as you can to help you out—scour every transmission you can find going to and from Reza before and after those emails. I know you already checked, but look again. There has to be something we missed. Come back with something."

"Will do, ma'am." Sam gripped his tablet and hurried from the room.

Xander nudged Alexa in the shoulder and her eyes widened, surprise flickering through her at the sudden turn of events.

"Our main priorities are finding out why Anarchy kidnapped the Fed, and what they have planned next. And we need to be able to link this all back to Kemal Bekas so we have enough evidence for Parliament to give us the green light to take him down." Laney's eyes shifted to Alexa. "Looks like you're on this case, whether you like it or not."

Alexa went over to the sitting area and sat back down on the sofa. "Okay. But," her voice stuck in her throat, "there's something I need to tell you all."

Matt and Xander exchanged looks and crossed the room to join Alexa. "What is it, Alexa?" Xander asked as he sat down next to her, his hand slipping to her back.

"The thing is, I know Jake Summers," she said softly, looking over at Laney.

"You do?" Laney placed a hand over her mouth, and the light from her diamond ring caught Alexa's eye.

"I met him at a New Year's Eve party a year ago in London. He never mentioned he was FBI." Alexa bit her lip, not entirely comfortable discussing her sex life with her coworkers or boss. "We hung out for about a week and then he went back to the States. We never spoke again after that."

"And you're only now telling me this?" Laney sank into her chair and rested her elbows on her desk.

"Sorry. When I realized it was him in the hospital I was in shock, I guess."

"Alexa." Xander's voice pulled her attention. She peered at him over her shoulder; his eyes were focused on hers. "You think it was merely a coincidence that you met a year ago or—"

"Why was he in London?" Matt interrupted.

"He said his sister invited him for the holiday to meet her new boyfriend who lives here." She looked down at her pants as her fingertips buried themselves in the soft material.

"Xander, I want you to check on the story. Find out who his sister is and whom she was or still is dating," Laney instructed, and Matt nodded.

"What? You think Jake lied?" Alexa stood and moved quickly toward Laney's desk.

"I don't know what to think, but I find it strange that a year ago you met this agent in London, and now here he is again. Coincidence, maybe. But let's be certain," Laney said.

"What do you want me to do now, ma'am?" Matt shoved his hands in his trouser pockets, his dark eyes intense and focused on Laney.

"I want you to go talk to the Americans and try and find out what happened in Italy."

"I'm not going, right? He'll know we were spying on him at the hospital." Alexa fidgeted with the ID clipped to her belt as she nervously waited for an answer.

Laney's eyes became thin slits as she turned them on Alexa. "You're off the hook, Alexa. For now."

# CHAPTER EIGHT

"I STILL DON'T REMEMBER ANYTHING—WELL, OTHER THAN BEING tortured that one time, but I already told you about that." Jake shut his eyes for a moment, wishing he could rest. Ever since Trent had transferred him to the Royal Air Force Station in Lakenheath, Suffolk, he'd been hounded by more American government-types than he could count.

He was in a medical bed in the Liberty Wing, which hosted the United States Air Force. His forearms flexed as he clenched his hands into fists, attempting to squeeze out his frustration from the recent rapid firing round of questions he'd endured from another federal agent.

"They got a match," someone called from outside the room.

Trent glanced over his shoulder at the sound of the voice. He'd been sitting at Jake's bedside next to the other FBI agent—or maybe he was CIA. Jake couldn't be sure.

"It's Jake's blood—he was there," the voice added a beat later.

"So, I was definitely being held in that cabin in the woods?" Jake asked. "How'd I get away?" He tried to sit up, but he couldn't quite manage it, so he relaxed back down, his head sinking into the feathery soft pillow.

A man in military fatigues and a hunter green tee entered the room. His dark brown eyes focused on Trent as he approached the bed. "Other than those few drops of blood they found, the British didn't find anything useful at that cabin."

"And I didn't notice anything when I was there yesterday," Trent added. "I didn't expect we'd find much. Whoever had you, well, they were professionals."

"Probably ISIS," the military guy added.

"ISIS? What or who is that?" Jake's brows pinched together, and the guy in fatigues glared at Jake before his brows lifted.

"Shit. Sorry, I forgot. It's a terrorist group. They're our worst nightmare. Attacking us from all over," Trent said as Mr. Military and the other Fed who'd been at his bedside, left the room.

"So. Now what?" Jake asked after a minute.

"Well, I'd like to get you back to our field office in D.C. We have agents here working, and they'll hopefully get something out of the tight-lipped British." Trent rose to his feet and stuffed his hands in his pockets. "In the meantime, we need you to get your damn memories back."

Jake dragged his hands down his face, a tinge of annoyance seeping into his bones. "I'm doing my best to remember, but I don't think going to D.C. is going to help."

"What will help?" Trent barked out, but a moment later he bowed his head in apology. When he looked up again, he raised both hands, palms up. "Sorry, I know this can't be easy. But you might be the only one who can help us."

"Help you do what?"

"Stop a terrorist attack."

"You've got to be kidding me." Jake placed his hands at his sides and forced himself upright in the bed, ignoring the pain that zipped down his spine and the tenderness of his back where he'd been whipped. "Do you know for sure there'll even be an attack? You said earlier the British barely said anything to you, and—"

"And they didn't have to. Whoever had you was planning something."

"What? Killing an FBI agent isn't big enough?" Jake shrugged and rolled his eyes. "You have to stop thinking of me as some Fed. I'm not that man. Hell, I don't know who I am anymore, but I do know that this is way too much. I need space. I need—*home*. I need my family."

Trent pinched the bridge of his nose, a low whistle escaping his lips. "You think being around your family will help you remember . . .?"

Jake thought for a minute. "Yes," he finally said. "Can you make it happen?"

"Shit, Jake. I'll see what I can do."

"Sir." Jake looked over at the door, where another man in military attire stood, his hands behind his back in respect for Trent.

Trent looked over at him. "Yes?"

"There are two agents here from MI6 demanding to see Agent Summers. They have the proper clearance, and they have been approved to enter."

"Jesus. I was hoping to hold them off a little longer, but now that MI6 is involved . . . shit."

"What's to hide from them? I don't know anything. And even if I did, why wouldn't we want to help them?" Jake leaned back against his pillow once again, feeling a little hopeful for the first time as he thought of going back to the U.S. and seeing his family.

"It's not so simple. The operation you were on before your abduction is highly classified, and I still don't have the authority to share the OP with the British," Trent explained. He pushed his blazer back, placing his hands near his dark belt on each side of his hips.

"And whose authority do you need?" Jake asked, curiosity beginning to swell inside of him.

"The President of the United States."

*Oh.*

"Sir?" The soldier at the door took a step closer, his hands falling to his sides.

Trent flicked his wrist in the air and shook his head. "Let them in."

The soldier left the doorway and returned a minute later with two men. They were both dressed in sharp gray suits with black ties.

"I'm Matt. And this is Xander." They were keeping it informal, apparently. No agent titles or last names. It actually made Jake feel better.

The two men nodded thanks to the American soldier, who then left the room. They moved with slow steps toward Trent, and Matt reached for his hand. "Nice to meet you."

"We don't have any updates. I'm not sure why you're here," Trent said after shaking Xander's hand.

Jake wanted to shut his eyes and make everyone in the room disappear. He wasn't interested in hearing any more about the case —well, so he told himself—but there was a twitch of excitement in his core about being in the presence of two MI6 agents. He wondered if the two agents had any spy gadgets on them from the famous Q branch—or if they'd come to the base in a BMW equipped for battle.

He was still Jake, the dreamer, the guy who was in love with action movies. Not a real-life hero. He couldn't quite wrap his head around the idea of belonging to this world.

"We need to talk to you about Italy." There was a slight tick in Matt's jaw as he looked over at Trent. Well, it was more like he was staring him down. Even though the Brit looked about the same age as Jake and years younger than Trent—he faced Trent with a confidence that displayed no sense of inferiority.

"What about Italy?" Trent's lips tightened as he crossed his arms, echoing Matt's posture.

The three men were standing a few feet away from Jake's bed, but Jake could feel the blast of testosterone and heat smoking within them. Who'd break first?

"We believe a case we've been working on is connected to the explosion," Xander said.

Matt began talking next, but his voice was nothing but scratchy white noise as a blinding pain shot through Jake's skull.

*Black boots kicking at sand.*

*Scorching heat.*

*Something heavy on his back.*

*Loud popping sounds all around him.*

Jake leaned forward, holding his stomach, ignoring the pain that roared in his back. "Shit."

"What's wrong?" Trent was immediately at his side, his hand resting on his shoulder.

"Was I in the military?" Jake took in a few calming breaths, trying to suppress the nausea.

"This is good. You're remembering something?" Trent asked.

"Answer the question." Jake opened his eyes.

"Yes. You were a Marine. Special Forces."

"Special Forces? Are you kidding me?" He grabbed the cup of water on the table next to his bed and swallowed the cool liquid. "Why didn't you tell me? Jesus, Trent. FBI was a far stretch . . . but a Marine?" *It's a long way off from what I went to school for.*

"I didn't want to overwhelm you with too much information."

"Oh, sure. But you're pushing me to remember what happened before the explosion." Jake crumpled the plastic cup in his hand, irritation billowing through him like smoke.

"You okay, mate?" Xander stepped closer to the bed.

Jake didn't respond as he stared at the crunched cup in his hand.

"He's not up for questions right now." Trent's voice had Jake flickering his attention back up. Right now, he could hug the big man.

"And since, at the moment, you're on American territory, I'll kindly ask you to leave. And if not, I'm sure I can have someone show you the way out." Trent cocked his head to the right, not backing down.

"The longer you hold out on us, the greater chance that someone will die," Matt said in a low, haunting voice.

"Then give me five damn seconds to think, so I can remember what the hell happened." Jake was on the verge of snapping. He'd had too many people coming at him, needing him to be the savior —and all he wanted was to shut his eyes and go back to the days when losing a football game was the worst of his problems.

"You may not be able to help us right now, but you know something, don't you?" Matt faced Trent.

"And I told Secret Service that I don't have the authority to share anything yet. But, of course, you can tell me about your case . . ." When neither of the MI6 agents spoke, Trent's words floated from his lips, hugged by puffs of air, "Didn't think so."

"Just get the authority so we can talk. Or we'll find out whatever it is that you're hiding. And believe me—that won't be the best of the two options for you," Matt said, his brown eyes holding Trent's. Then both agents turned and walked away.

"Fucking spooks," Trent said once they were gone.

Jake shut his eyes and bowed his head forward. "I can't be responsible for people dying. To know I can save people, and I—" *I'm not twenty-two. I'm thirty-four. I was a Marine. I'm a Goddamn FBI agent! Get it together!* And yet, his body protested with pain that seared his insides, the lashings on his back a reminder that he was weak right now.

As much as he didn't want to be the man he'd become, Jake was beginning to realize that he didn't have much of a choice. People could die, and his memories could save them.

"What if I can't help?"

Trent looked him square in the eyes. "You will."

"But how do you know?"

"Because you always come through."

# CHAPTER NINE

JAKE STARED AT THE RANCH, A GLOVED FIST PRESSED TO HIS MOUTH as he absorbed what lay before him.

Stacked stones supported dark wooden posts, and the one-story home was made of solid burnt orange wood, with expansive windows, and a porch wrapping around the structure. Behind the house, Jake remembered fishing in the trout filled pond. Of course, now, the land and pond were covered by a layer of ice and snow. But the serene rolling hills and mountain peaks had always served as the perfect backdrop for a kid in his cowboy boots. He remembered catching his first trout when he was seven. The thing had been so big that the fishing pole almost snapped as the line became weighted down by the sucker.

But damned if Jake didn't reel it in—only to let it go. He hated killing anything.

Jake tugged off his right glove and brushed away a tear that was nearly hardening like glass to his skin.

A cold chill from the Montana winter air moved through him, and his chest hurt. But this time it wasn't from the pain of the blast.

*He's gone. And I don't remember him dying.* Jake's body trembled as he gripped the glove in his hand, holding it to his heart. It was as if he were experiencing the loss of his grandfather for the first time.

Jake forced himself to remain standing when all he wanted was to drop to the icy cold ground and cry. But that wasn't what a man did—right? He thought of his hard, steely father.

No, Jake had to suck it up. Be the man his father was.

He dragged his gaze back to the ranch, his eyes falling upon a swirl of smoke that filtered out of the chimney and up into the sky. "Do you know when he died?" he choked out the words.

"I checked your records. Your grandfather passed away three years ago, and he left the ranch to your family. You mentioned to me in passing that you liked coming here when you needed to think. It's secluded, so you should be safe out here. We'll have agents posted outside at all times."

"Yeah, this was a good idea. Although you could have mentioned where we were going—and that my grandfather wouldn't be here." Jake forced his feet to move toward the front porch. He was able to walk, thankfully, but his body still felt like one massive, achy bruise.

Trent had booked a military flight back to the States shortly after the MI6 agents had left the base, knowing that they would continue to hound Jake as long as he was on British soil.

"Sorry," Trent said, looking over his shoulder at the other federal agent accompanying them.

"Is my family inside?" Jake stopped in front of the steps. Smoke hovered above the house like small gray clouds.

"Yeah. We booked their tickets using aliases. No one should know they're here."

"What do they know?"

"The basics. You were taken from a case and your abductors think you died. But anything beyond that is classified, so don't share—"

"Not like I know much, anyway." Jake shook his head as he began to tug off his other black glove.

"And the second you remember . . ."

"You'll be the first to know," Jake finished as he climbed the steps. He glanced over his shoulder at the rocking chairs to his right. They'd been hand carved by his grandfather. His eyes became glossy again as a swell of pain in his stomach grew. He remembered sitting on those chairs on his grandfather's lap, studying the constellations in the sky.

"You okay?" Trent placed a hand on his shoulder, and the gesture felt so odd since he didn't know the man—even though Trent apparently knew him pretty damn well.

"Yeah. I'm great . . ." Jake reached for the knob, but he couldn't bring himself to open it.

Of course, he didn't get the chance.

The door swung open, and his mom rushed toward him, flinging her arms around his neck.

* * *

JAKE SAT AT THE FORMAL DINING ROOM TABLE WITH HIS FAMILY, his stomach in knots. The partially eaten pork chops on his plate blurred as he stared down at them. His appetite was returning, although slowly, and he was grateful for that. He didn't think skinny would look good on him.

He sat forward, hating when his back came in contact with anything. The red strips of flesh were starting to scar, to become pinkish white. The crisscross lashes had torn deep, however, and he'd wear the marks of defeat for the rest of his life.

It had only been a few days since Jake had arrived at the ranch, but being around his family was a hell of a lot better than being in a hospital bed overseas. A few flashes of memories had even come to him in the last few days, like catching a trout with his father on the ranch just three weeks before his grandfather had died. Too bad that most of what he had remembered was useless to the FBI.

"Jake, dear, are you okay?"

Jake looked up at his mother, her deep brown eyes finding his. He studied his mom, hating that she aged over a decade since he remembered her last. Her hair was graying where it had once been blonde. But at least he remembered her. And his father and sister. He couldn't imagine not knowing his own flesh and blood.

"I will be, Mom." He hoped, at least.

Jake scooted away from the table and tossed his red linen napkin on the plate, covering the rest of the food he couldn't quite finish. His mom had given him far too much, expecting him to be the quarterback he once was, not the injured man sitting before her now. "You know, you don't have to stay here for long. You have lives to get back to."

"Are you kidding?" His mom's brows pinched together.

"Well, Emily shouldn't be here," he said while nodding his head in his sister's direction. "D.C. is probably crumbling without you there." He couldn't believe his little sister had become a big shot lawyer at the Attorney General's office. Well, technically he could believe it because she'd always been smart, but he still thought of her as an awkward teen with braces.

Emily pressed her napkin to her pink lips and blotted. "You're my big brother, and you're far more important than a few cases."

Jake's father touched his dark beard and toyed with the strands for a moment as his silvery gray eyes fixated on Jake. He didn't say anything, which was typical of his father. That, at least, hadn't changed in the last twelve years.

"Can't you tell us anything about what happened to you? I mean, what if whoever had you comes after you again? What if someone finds out you're here?" His mom stood and began collecting dishes.

"Whatever Trent already told you is about as much as I know." Pretty close, at least. "And no one should be coming after me. I'm dead—remember?"

"I don't like this," his mom said, shaking her head. "And I'm not leaving anytime soon."

What if someone did come after him? He didn't want his family getting caught in the crossfire, that was for sure.

Jake walked into the living area adjacent to the dining room and stared at the unlit, floor-to-ceiling stone fireplace, the half-eaten burnt log drawing his eye.

That's how he felt.

Like part of him was gone. Burned. And all that was left were ashes.

But then there was another part of him, some strange part on the inside that wanted to scream. To tear down the damn walls of shame that he was building and fight back. To find whoever the hell did this to him. He had to assume those feelings came from the man he had become.

A cold chill wrapped his spine, and he flinched a little when his sister's hand came down on his shoulder a few minutes later.

"Jake, I made you something."

He faced Emily and forced a smile to his face. He'd always been there for her in the past, and he hated the idea that now she, along with everyone else, had to take care of him like a wounded animal.

"What is it? A homemade get well card?" he half-joked.

She handed him a folded piece of paper, fighting a smile. "It's a list of your friends, smartass. People you can rely on."

Jake gripped the bridge of his nose as he studied the list, squinting a little.

Emily rested a hand on his forearm for a moment. "Hang on." She moved over to his mother's purse and dug around inside. "Here we go. Mom brought the spare pair you keep at her house."

Emily handed him a small black case.

"I wear glasses?" he blurted, popping it open. They were framed in thick, black plastic.

"Only for reading." She smiled.

"Great . . . I really am old."

"That's for sure," she teased.

He slowly placed them on and looked at the list again—it was a hell of a lot more in focus.

The first name his sister scribbled with her chicken scratch (she should have been a doctor, with that handwriting) was Michael Maddox. He'd been the resourceful one, the one who'd managed to find him in London. He read the next two aloud: "Connor Matthews. Mason Matthews—"

"Brothers. Both former Marines, too," Emily interrupted.

Jake still couldn't believe he'd been a Marine. Going into the military had been about the last thing he had ever considered doing when he was younger. "What do they do now?"

She sighed. "Well, the Matthews brothers inherited their father's business recently, but last I heard they were thinking of starting their own PI firm—or private rescue group. I don't know. They help people—that's what I know."

"Oh." He looked at the next name. "Aiden O'Connor."

Emily smiled. "Irish guy. Great accent."

Jake raised a brow, ready to go big brother on her if his sister had a crush on his friend. Even if it was a friend he couldn't even remember.

"Hey!" Emily shoved her brother in the side. When he grimaced, she covered her hands over her mouth. "Oh, shit. Sorry."

"I was just getting back at you," he lied. "I'm okay."

"Thank God." She pursed her lips together. "And to clarify, Aiden is taken. Engaged to a hot biochemist." Another smile teased her lips, and Jake had to wonder if his sister was hiding something. "Besides, I have a boyfriend."

"Oh yeah? Who?" He probably would hate the guy.

"He's English, actually. Lives in London. I met him at an event two years ago, and we hit it off. The long-distance stuff is hard, but we manage. You came to London last year to meet him . . . well, more like drill him."

Jake touched his chest. "You're telling me that you're dating a guy in the city where I just survived an explosion?" What the hell were the chances?

Emily shrugged. "Sorry."

"Well, did I like him at least?" he grumbled.

"Ha. You barely even saw him. You became enchanted by some sexy Brit you met at the New Year's Eve party."

"Now *that* I wish I remembered." He smiled, almost forgetting everything for a moment.

Emily returned his smile and nudged him in the side. "Anyways, there's one more name on the list. You have a lot more friends than these, but I narrowed the list down to the guys you tend to call—or they call you—when things get hairy."

"Hairy?" This elicited a chuckle from him.

"I don't know. You boys tend to find yourselves in trouble. A lot."

*Great.*

"His name is Ben Logan." Emily flicked at the paper with her index finger. "He has a private security firm out in Vegas. Although he was a pro-baseball player for two years before that."

"Let me guess, before that he was also a Marine. Do I have something against the other branches of military?" The thought made him smile. "What does Dad think about his son becoming a Marine? Did I do it just to piss him off?" His dad had attempted to raise him to become a soldier, which was exactly why Jake had never wanted to be one—he wanted to be as different as he could be from his father.

"Probably. You know how badly he wanted you to be Army like him. And you just couldn't help yourself . . . he got over it, though." She shrugged. "Since you, for the most part, followed in his footsteps."

Jake thought about asking her why he joined, but he held off. "Thanks for the list, Emily. I probably won't see any of them until my memory comes back, though. *If* it comes back." He stuffed the paper in his jeans pocket and walked over to the leather couch in front of the fireplace.

"It *will* come back. And when it does, whoever did this to you will regret it." Emily crossed her arms and smirked.

"You believe in me that much, huh?"

She squinted a little while waving her hand between them. "Well, between you and your friends, someone will go for the jugular."

"And you're okay with that?" he accused.

"After what I've seen you go through—and, hell, what I've witnessed in Washington—very little bothers me anymore." Her espresso brown eyes met his, and he cringed at the thought of his sweet little sister dealing with Washington cronies and criminals.

"Well, I don't know if I want to be that guy anymore."

Emily shook her head. "Jake, I don't think it's possible for you to escape your past so easily. And as much as I'd wish my big brother would quit being in the line of fire, that's just not who you are." She touched her collarbone and exhaled. "You are strong. Dependable. And although I don't want you getting a big head, you're kind of amazing."

"Gee, thanks."

"Jake?" His father's voice stole his attention from his sister.

He was standing in the doorway with a laptop tucked under his arm. His dad hadn't said all that much since he'd been there, and Jake wondered if they'd grown even more distant in the past twelve years.

"I'll be in the kitchen." Emily looked at her brother out of the corner of her eye, and then brushed past her father and left the room.

"What's up?" Jake's shoulders rolled back a little as if he felt the need to be taller in his father's presence.

"Hm. Well, I have something that I thought might help you remember things."

His words caused a slight twitchy reaction in his stomach.

Some part of him didn't want any more memories. Maybe it was the part of him that got sick every time he remembered some part of his past. The nausea was like a greeting card from hell.

"Okay," he dragged out the word like it was stuck in molasses. "On the computer?"

His dad nodded and motioned for him to have a seat on the couch.

Jake sat down, pulling an extra pillow behind his back for support. Still, the pain crept through his skin—like he was still stripped naked, his back bleeding.

His dad opened the laptop and went into his email account. "Here." He slid the laptop over to Jake. "There are at least a hundred emails from you on there. Most of them are to your mother, but a few are to me." His dad stood. "And most of these emails are during your time in the service." He lifted his shoulders. "Maybe they'll help trigger something for you."

Jake stared at the computer screen in a daze and when he looked back up, his dad was gone.

He sat alone in the room; the only sound was the slight clank of dishes as his mother cleaned up the kitchen, that and the low hum of her voice as she spoke to his sister.

He stared at the list of subject lines, not sure if he wanted to read his own words. He clicked on one at random and stared at the few lines that came onto the screen. The message was dated November 2005.

*Mom, the training is harder than I expected. But don't worry about me. I'm doing good. Better to be over prepared, right? Well, give Emily my love. Tell Dad hi. Miss you. –Jake*

*Did I become a man of few words? When did I turn into my father?*

Jake closed the message and scrolled through the list. He opened one from two years later.

*Mom, you need to stop worrying about me. Afghanistan's not that bad. Promise. And I'm working with a good group of people.*

*They have my back. I won't be in touch for a while because I'm going out on an OP. Love you, Mom. –Jake*

Jake read a few more emails, but he couldn't bring himself to read his mother's responses. He remembered how stressed she had been when he was a kid, and his father was deployed in the Army. He could only imagine what his own time in the Marines had done to her. And he wasn't ready to relive whatever agony he had put her through.

He shut the laptop and shifted it off to the side on the couch, unwilling to torture himself anymore. He'd had enough torture to last a damn lifetime. He bent his head forward, pressing his face into his palms. The sound of shoes walking on the old, beaten up floors had him straightening.

Jake couldn't take his eyes off his father as he slowly moved the computer out of his way to sit next to him. "Jake." There was a crack in his voice—a sound Jake had never heard from his composed, controlled father.

"Yeah, Dad?" Jake touched his quads, grounding himself.

A hand on his shoulder had Jake flinching. Then he sagged as his dad tugged Jake against his shoulder, unable to believe the gesture, desperate not to do anything that might make it end. His father pressed his face against the side of Jake's temple. "We could have lost you."

Jake couldn't remember his father ever crying, at least not when he was younger. Hearing him do it now . . .

So, Jake did the only thing he knew that made sense. He let go with a sob, suddenly feeling like a child again in the safety of his father's arms.

\* \* \*

WARM BEADS OF PERSPIRATION TRAILED FROM HIS SCALP DOWN HIS face. His spine dripped with sweat as he kicked at the covers and turned over in bed.

Jake fisted the sheets as images poked into his mind—a nightmare or memories, he wasn't sure which.

In his mind, he was back in the desert.

*Helmet. Black boots—heavy and practically glued to his feet.*

*The air was layered in yellow and gold, fumes baking the land. So thick. So hot. It was hard to breathe.*

*The city before him was quiet. Eerily quiet.*

*The buildings were in ruins. Freshly burned.*

*Then he heard it—gunfire spraying in the distance.*

*The screams.*

Jake rolled out of bed and thudded loud against the floor. He winced as he pressed his palms to the hardwood and stood up.

"What the hell?" He wiped the sweat from his face and pulled back the curtains that covered the window near his bed. The sun had yet to rise.

As he dressed, Jake pushed back the choking sensation in his throat.

The heavy jacket and cowboy boots he'd found in the closet looked as though they'd seen better days.

The ranch felt empty now that his family had left. Trent had decided it wasn't a good idea for them to stay for long, that it wouldn't be safe for them. Jake was happy to go along with any plan that meant keeping his family out of danger.

But the three days he'd spent with them had been good. Snippets of his past had slowly edged back into his mind, and some of them had been almost . . . nice.

Jake stepped out onto the porch, automatically searching for the federal agents who were supposed to be on guard outside.

What he didn't expect was to see a woman standing behind the agents' car.

Not just any woman.

He took a step closer and squinted as the first bright rays of sunlight pierced the horizon.

He could only see her profile, and her hair wasn't red, but a deep brown. His eyes must have been playing tricks on him, he decided. There was no reason why the nurse from London would have followed him there.

But when the woman looked his way, there was no mistaking her eyes. They could shred a man like a bullet, even in the hazy morning light.

She slowly walked the stone path, which had been shoveled by the agents yesterday. He stared in shock as she stopped at the bottom of the steps.

"Hi, Agent Summers," she said in a soft voice, looking up at him.

# CHAPTER TEN

A LEXA RUBBED HER GLOVED HANDS OVER THE ARMS OF HER jacket. It was freezing.

Jake was staring at her, his lips parted and his arms relaxed at his sides. He looked healthier than when she had seen him last. His cheeks had more color, and the bandage on his head was gone—in its place was his dirty blonde hair. Shorter on the sides, and longer, slightly messy on the top.

"Do you recognize me?" she asked.

"You're not a nurse, huh?" Jake perked a brow and slowly turned back toward the house and started for the door. He moved without a limp. He didn't look like he was suffering—that was a good sign.

Alexa looked over her shoulder at Xander. He sat in their rental car, a hand draped casually over the steering wheel. He was parked behind two American agents, who were sitting inside a black SUV. They served as Jake's security.

Alexa had asked Xander to stay in the car for now. She figured Jake would want answers, and she couldn't believe she was about to reveal her identity to him.

The whole situation was surreal.

Alexa tilted her head toward the house, letting him know she was going inside, and he nodded back.

She climbed the few steps, but as she rested her gloved fingers over the doorknob, her nerves got the best of her. *You can do this.* She forced herself to go inside after a deep breath. "Hello?" she called out. The place smelled of pine, and the dark, exposed wood and stone fireplace screamed comfort. The fireplace was the kind you burn wood in, the kind that could actually heat a home.

"In here," Jake answered.

She tugged at her black leather gloves, removing them and set them on top of the brown sofa as she chased the sound of his voice.

Jake's back was to the kitchen counter, his arms crossed. As she moved through the room, stopping a few feet shy of him, he pinned her with his brown eyes. Her lips closed tight, and she watched the movement of his throat as he swallowed, her mind racing with what to say.

Jake's eyes flashed shut, and he squeezed his brows together as if in pain, his dark lashes splaying against his golden skin.

"Are you okay?" she asked and took a cautious step forward.

His head lowered as his hands moved to each side of him, bracing the tiled counter. His knuckles whitened as his fingers gripped harder. "I'm fine," he said with a strained voice.

She could tell he was anything but.

Her gaze flickered over to the fridge, and she went over to it, skirting him, careful not to touch. She grabbed a bottle of water from the fridge and returned in front of him.

"Here." Her eyes dragged from his tanned throat to his hard chest, all the way down his denim jeans to the worn out brown leather boots he wore.

A cowboy FBI agent, huh?

Jake opened his eyes and reached for the bottle and held it tight in one hand. "Do you always make a habit of going into men's homes uninvited?"

She took a small step back and pressed her hands to her outer thighs, drumming her fingers there as she tried to remember the lines she'd planned to say. Lately, she was beginning to feel more like a stage actor than one of the top cyber intelligence officers at the agency.

But what she hadn't planned or anticipated was how her heart would move in her chest like a tap dance, or how her stomach would lurch at the mere sight of him. She'd been too surprised to feel anything but shock when she saw him in the hospital in London, but now that Mr. New Year's Eve was in front of her, all she could think about was how he'd given her the best orgasms of her life.

*Get it together.* She needed to delete those memories. Like Jake had.

He set the unopened bottle of water down on the counter and, in one quick move, closed the small space between them. "You're a spook, aren't you?"

"A spook?" She almost laughed. "I'm with—"

*Am I really going to admit the truth to him?* "I'm an agent at MI6," she said slowly. Some strange weight, which felt like a hundred or so kilos, lifted from her shoulders.

Jake blinked a few times before brushing past her. He grabbed a navy-blue kettle and brought it to the sink. "Coffee?" he grumbled.

Well, that wasn't the reaction she'd been expecting.

"Oh. Um, yes, please." She preferred tea, but she wasn't about to argue.

"You gonna stay standing all morning, or would you care to sit?" He turned on the burner and placed the kettle down before facing her.

She tried to fight the smile that pulled at the edges of her lips. "I didn't know if you'd want me to get comfortable."

His broad shoulders relaxed. "I don't, but you came a hell of a long way. And since the agents let you waltz up here, I'm guessing they don't think you're a threat."

He was taking this better than she'd thought. She hadn't been sure what to expect of a man who'd lost part of his life. Well, his memories.

"So, you'll hear me out?" Of course, he didn't have much of a choice. The orders had come from high-ups in both their governments. Although the Americans still hadn't come clean about Italy—about anything, actually—but they wanted her and Jake to work together.

Jake lowered his head and placed his thumb and middle finger at his temples. Did he have a headache or was *she* the headache? "Now, I didn't say that." His Southern voice wasn't twangy like in some of the films she'd seen. No, it was smooth. Just as sexy as she remembered.

She took off her coat and hung it on the chair next to her, and then pulled out a seat from the small table that was in the middle of the large, country-style kitchen. The place needed updating. The cabinets were an outdated light brown wood, the hardwoods scratched and dented, and the counters were made of a light cream tile. Of course, it was still an upgrade over a London kitchen, which you were lucky to find in half this size.

Unless you were her sister, who had married a football player in Manchester.

Alexa smoothed a hand over the maple table and looked up at Jake from the corners of her eyes.

"You could tell me why you played nurse back in London." Jake leaned his hip against the counter by the stove as he waited for the water to boil.

"Well, I was just checking to, um . . ."

"See if I was telling the truth about my memory issues?" Jake glanced over and caught her staring at him.

Her skin pebbled from the eye contact, a bristle of inappropriate need coursing through her—*what the bleeding hell is wrong with me?*

"And are you?" She straightened, forcing herself to focus on

Jake as a part of the mission, not as a man she'd once spent every waking hour with for a week straight. A man who had kissed her in the London Eye above the Thames—giving new meaning to the feeling of 'weak knees.'

"What do you think?" he asked. Steam shot out of the pot and a high-pitched whistle spread into the air, disrupting her thoughts.

"I believe you," she whispered as her cheeks flamed. And a minute later, Jake slid a coffee mug of dark black liquid along the table.

"Not going to sweeten it?" She looked back up at him.

"I didn't think you'd want me sticking my finger in it." Dimples appeared as he smiled. He still had his humor, even now . . .

"Thanks," she forced herself to say, warming her hands against the steaming mug.

Jake scratched at the stubble on his jaw and took a seat opposite of her. He looked more rugged than she remembered. It probably had to do with the flannel and boots.

"So, what do you need from me? I take it you didn't come all this way just to stare."

She choked a little on her coffee and wiped at her lips with the back of her hand. "Your memories would be a nice start," she said dryly.

He set his mug down and leaned back in his chair. "I honestly don't know if I even want them—are you sure you do?" He bowed his head and stared at his hand, which was pressed to the table. His fingers trembled.

"I can't believe you're able to function like this after what happened to you last week." Her thoughts had slipped from her tongue. She had meant them, although she'd never meant to say them. What kind of man could survive being tortured and blown up —and then make coffee a week later?

He lifted his hand from the table and swept it to his lap, his

77

eyes landing back on hers. "Apparently, what happened is like a Monday for me."

"A Monday?" A genuine smile flirted with her lips. "Wow. And I thought my Mondays were rough. What've you been up to for the last decade or so that this is the norm for you?"

"If I knew the answer to that, I'd probably be able to offer you a lot more help."

"True."

"So, since you know I can't help you, why are you here? Why not bother the FBI agents who actually might know something?"

"Believe me, we're bugging the bloody hell out of them. But I got assigned to you." Alexa scooted back, wincing as her chair scratched against the heavily abused floors.

"Lucky you."

She stood and moved over to the counter, keeping her back to him.

"And do you spies have some sort of pill that can help me get my memories back?"

"I wish." She spun around, needing to face him, but she didn't expect to find him right there. She hadn't even heard him stand, but there he was . . . and her hands had landed against his hard chest.

Alexa stared, her fingers resting on the hard planes of his body, unable to move them, but then he gently seized her wrists, holding onto them until their eyes met. His face hovered near hers, and he leaned closer, a puff of his breath warm on her skin. "I know you from somewhere, don't I?"

*Oh, God.* "Of course not." She was frozen in her position, unsure of what to say next.

"There's something familiar about you." His words came across low and smooth, gliding across her skin, making her nipples harden. *Dammit.*

"We don't know each other," she said with dramatic emphasis on every word. She tugged her wrists free of his grasp.

Jake took a sudden step back, relieving her of the cage his body had made. She exhaled when he turned and shoved both hands through his hair, which was starting to grow out. He probably had missed his usual haircut.

Jake bent forward and touched the kitchen table before his hand curled into a fist. His knuckles pressed down against the tile.

"What's wrong?" She came up behind him and rested her hand on his back, but he flinched and moved away. When he faced her, his pupils were dilated, and his breathing was heavy.

He was in pain. He had to be.

"I need you to go," he said in a tense voice, and then left the room.

"Jake!" She followed after him into the living room.

"Please go." His hand cut the air between them as he stopped by the front door.

"I can't do that."

He lowered his head for a moment, looking down at the floor, and when his attention swept back up to her face, she could see the pain there. "I'm not sure if I'm an agent anymore. Or if I even want to be. I don't know how I ended up in this life—but it's not me." He placed a fist over his heart. "Maybe I'm done, memory issues or not." His voice was a cool whisper that moved across her skin, chilling her spine.

"Don't say that. You help people." She had to assume he had done a lot of good as an agent. "Without you—"

He shook his head. "Without me?" He faked a laugh and crossed the room, grabbing a remote control from the end table by the sofa.

The TV powered on, and he scrolled through the channels until he found a twenty-four-hour news station. "Have you seen this?" He pointed to the flat screen TV on the tall, oak stand on the other side of the fireplace. "What in the hell has happened in the twelve years I can't remember? People are dying all over the place. The world has gone fucking mad. You can't even go to the mall, anymore. Clearly, I've done nothing—and maybe no one can."

She struggled to find the right words. How could she make him understand that even in such a crazy, messed up world, people like him still made a difference? Alexa took a step closer to him, her hand out in front of her as she moved with cautious steps. "There'd be even more violence if people like you didn't exist." Her voice broke a little as she spoke. It tore her up at night, as well. She hated the idea of her nephew being raised in a world like this. She wasn't sure if she ever wanted kids, herself, because of the insanity she lived and breathed every day.

But his face remained unchanged.

"If everyone thought like you, the world would be in chaos." *Bekas wins*, she thought. "We'd be living in hell on earth. But Jake, you do make a difference, and I need you." She hadn't meant to say "I," but it was too late to go back. "Without you, we may not be able to stop him."

"Stop who?"

She didn't want to get into the details about @Anarchy right now, and she didn't have approval to do so. "Whoever tortured you. Whoever is planning the next attack," she said instead, trying to buy time before he threw her out.

"That's not enough for me." He blew out a whistling breath and turned off the obnoxious chatter of news reporters debating the recent election.

"It has to be enough."

But Jake's back was already to her as he moved out of the living room and down a hall.

*Now, what do I do?* She considered going out to get Xander for reinforcement, but she worried he might further aggravate Jake. And Laney was demanding results. So, she stalked down the hall in search of him.

The door at the end was open a crack.

Alexa pushed the door all the way open to find hardwood

floors that were a faded burnt orange, rife with scratches—from an animal, maybe. The room had a whisper of a scent still floating in the air . . . vanilla cigars. It reminded her of her father's study. A warm flash of pain settled in her stomach as she lifted her eyes to find Jake. He sat behind the massive oak desk, a rifle mounted on the wall above his head. He looked sexier than any man had a right to be, sitting there with black framed glasses on. She'd always been a sucker for a guy who could pull off glasses in a devastatingly handsome way.

Jake gripped something between his hands. Pictures, maybe.

Seeing him sitting there gave her the sensation of tiny little jolts within her, flapping wings beating fast in her core as her skin tingled. She remembered that feeling from the first night they met.

Jake squared his shoulders and looked up at her.

She approached the desk, walking across what looked like the Turkish rugs she'd seen sold in the bazaars in Istanbul—red, gold, and blue thread weaved together in intricate details. The rug helped serve as a reminder to her as to why she was there.

Kemal Bekas was in Turkey. And the man needed to be stopped. Soon.

"Whose place is this?" It must have been a place that was familiar to Jake, but she was surprised the FBI would risk taking Jake to any place he could be recognized.

"This was my grandfather's ranch. He died and left it to my family," he finally said.

"I'm so sorry."

He set the pictures he'd been holding down in front of him and removed his glasses, pinching the bridge of his nose as he shut his eyes. "He was a good man. He was Army. My dad was Army, too." Jake opened his brown eyes, and she braced her hands on the edge of the desk.

She could barely look into his eyes; it was almost too much, seeing the pain laced in the light lines around his eyes and thick in his irises.

"I have absolutely no clue how I became a Marine."

"Instead of Army?" She angled her head, studying him, trying to get a read.

"Military in general." He pressed his hands to the edge of the desk and pushed back a little in the rolling chair. "I never wanted to be in the military. I didn't want to be like my father," he said somberly.

"And what did you want to be?" She lifted her hands and folded them across her chest as a chill rushed up her spine.

A small smile tugged at his lips. "A teacher and football coach."

Her eyes widened at his words, surprised by both his candor and his comment. She could definitely imagine him standing in front of a classroom with those glasses on . . . although no teenage girl would be able to concentrate in his class. "I guess you changed your mind."

"Looks that way." As he lifted his shoulders in a shrug, he winced with pain. "I don't mean to be rude. Hell, I don't even know your name, but—"

"Alexa. It's Alexa." She took a step back as he rose to his feet, feeling small in his presence.

He came around in front of her and hooked his thumbs in the pockets of his jeans. "Well, Alexa, if I could help you, I'd tell you everything so you could be on your way. But I don't think—"

Alexa did the only thing she could think of. She pressed up on her toes and touched her lips to his. She snapped her eyes shut, waiting and hoping he'd respond, and when he did, her knees almost buckled as her palms lifted to his chest.

His hand swooped up to her back, pulling her closer to him. His tongue dove into her mouth while his other hand weaved through her thick, silky hair. Regardless of what else he'd lost the man hadn't forgotten how to kiss.

Alexa stumbled backward, feeling breathless and light as she broke their kiss.

His brows pulled together as he cocked his head. "And that was because . . .?"

She swallowed, searching for words that made sense. "Call me crazy, but I thought maybe it'd work like in the movies—you know, I kiss you, and you remember everything."

He covered his hand over his mouth for a moment as he studied her. When he lowered his hand, he said, "Isn't that for waking someone up from a spell?"

She released a small laugh.

"I think it's only supposed to work for true love," he added.

"And how do you know so much about fairy tales?"

He folded his arms. "I have a younger sister, and I'm kind of a movie buff. Although I prefer—"

"Eastwood," she finished and then bit her lip. How could she forget so easily that she was supposed to be a stranger?

Jake took a step back. "And how do you know that?"

*Shit.* "Uh, you kind of have a Clint Eastwood look about you. Or more like his son." She wasn't lying. "So the kiss didn't work, huh?" She wet her lips and started to turn, but he reached for her arm and gently pulled her back around.

She bumped up against him as his hand came to her chin, tilting her head up so their eyes could meet. "Alexa?"

"Yeah?"

"What is it that you aren't telling me?" he asked gruffly.

That was her cue to leave. "I should go. My partner and I are going to check into a hotel a few kilometers down the road." Well, more than a few kilometers, actually. They were in the middle of nowhere.

He kept his hand tucked beneath her chin, his brown eyes gleaming as they held hers. "I'll come back tonight. Get some rest." She took a step back and started for the door. She glanced over her shoulder at him, stealing one last look—his eyes were still on her—and then she grabbed her coat and rushed from his home, needing time so that she could breathe again.

When Alexa slid inside the rental car, Xander scratched at his chin and shot her a huge smile.

"What?" she asked, buckling herself.

"Your lipstick is smeared."

She immediately opened the visor and checked her reflection. "I'm not even wearing lipstick." She shut the visor and smacked her partner in the chest as he began to reverse out of the long driveway. "Asshat."

"So you did kiss him, yeah?" How could he chuckle at a time like this? "Laney called while you and lover boy were inside."

"Oh my God, Xan. Call him that one more time and . . ."

"And what?" When she didn't say anything, he smiled. "That's what I thought."

"Damn you, Xan. The man lost his memories—he doesn't even know about our past or what happened."

But he kind of remembered her, didn't he? He had asked if they knew each other, after all.

"Just tell me what Laney said." She looked out the window at the snow-covered hills as they drove. Fir trees and mountains served as a beautiful backdrop in the distance.

"We have a secure webcam call with her tomorrow. The FBI agent in charge, Trent Shaw, will be setting up the call at Jake's home."

"And what do we hope to accomplish with the call?"

"We'll hopefully learn something of value."

"And if I don't get Jake on board, we should probably head back to London."

"You think you can get to him?" He pressed his lips together as his gaze met hers for a brief moment, amusement softening his eyes.

"I do," she murmured. "Just let me handle Jake Summers."

# CHAPTER ELEVEN

"WE HAVE DIRECT ORDERS. I'M SORRY, JAKE. I TRIED TO HOLD them off for as long as I could, but you're the only witness. Just talk to them. Then you can be done."

Jake held the burner phone Trent had given him close to his ear as he peeked out the blinds and into the darkness, locating the car with two agents in it parked in the driveway.

"Didn't you guys tell MI6 anything? You clearly have more information than I do. A lot more." Jake still couldn't believe the woman he'd thought was a nurse was a spy. How had he gotten caught up in all of this? He wished he knew.

He went back over to the desk in his grandfather's office, his eyes settling on the rifle on the wall. His grandfather had attempted to teach him to hunt when he was younger, but when it came down to it, he couldn't take the shot. He couldn't kill an animal.

But had he killed a person?

As a former Marine and FBI agent, he had to assume the answer was yes.

"We haven't shared any intel yet," Trent answered.

"And why is that?" Jake was curious. What was so bad the FBI couldn't tell the British?

"Why don't you try and get some rest? I'll be over tomorrow." Trent hung up before Jake could respond.

He tossed the burner phone on the desk. It slid up next to the photos he'd been looking at earlier before Alexa followed him into the office.

The photo sitting on the top of the pile was from a wedding. Jake was standing in a penguin suit next to Michael, alongside a few other guys, one of which was a guy he'd remembered from his dream the other night. The man had an Irish accent. He must have been Aiden, the man his sister told him about.

He started to reach for the photos again, but a stab of pain to his gut had him keeling over and gripping his stomach. A fresh wave of memories prickled his skin, and his spine jerked back upright as if he'd been whipped.

*Muffled and indistinct voices.*

*Like a hot iron on the flesh, the whip ate through his skin.*

*His eyes burned as he opened them, focusing on what lay before him.*

*Then a fist cracked against his jaw.*

Jake opened his eyes as the memory drifted from his mind . . . but the pain remained.

"What the hell?" He reached around, and his fingers splayed over his back. It felt like the fabric of his shirt was sticking to him. He quickly fumbled with the buttons and peeled off the shirt. He lowered his head, trying to catch his breath.

He heard a faint noise in the distance, but he couldn't move or call out.

The sounds of screams echoed through his mind. He had no idea who was screaming—and he couldn't make it stop.

He sank to his knees and held his hands over his ears, rocking—shaking.

When warm hands moved over his shoulder blades a moment later, he lowered his hands from his ears and swiveled around on his knees in one hot movement, pinning someone beneath him.

"Jake, it's me."

He could hear a female voice, but his vision blurred as he tried to know what was real.

There was the taste of gravel and dirt on his tongue.

Heat.

Fire.

Yelling.

"Jake!" someone cried. "I don't want to hurt you."

"They're all dead," Jake mumbled. He lifted his hands and slid backward and into a seated position on the floor, his legs stretched out in front of him as his vision came back into focus.

"Who's dead?"

It was Alexa. Shit, had he hurt her? She was on her knees before him, her hand raised between them. "Are you okay? What happened? I knocked and called out for you, but then I heard you screaming."

"*I* was screaming?" He blinked. "No." It couldn't be.

"What's wrong, Jake? Talk to me. Who is dead?"

"I—I don't know." He dragged his palms down his face. "I don't remember now."

"Let's get you up." Alexa scooted closer to him and held her hand out between them. "You should be in bed."

"I don't want to be." His warm palm met hers, and they rose together.

When he turned around, he heard her gasp. She must have seen the markings on his back. He'd been stunned the first time he saw his welted flesh in the mirror, as well.

"When was the last time you applied medicine to your back?" Her voice nearly broke as she spoke, which wasn't what he'd expect of a stranger. Especially of a seasoned agent. Why'd she give a damn about him?

He reached down for his shirt and faced her, clutching the material between his hands. "I don't know. It's not exactly easy to apply myself."

"Oh." She rolled her tongue over her teeth as she stared at his chest. "I could do it for you."

Jake angled his head, holding his shirt even tighter. What the hell was it about this woman that was so comforting, so easy? Her gorgeous hazel eyes held him captive for a moment, and then he lowered his head and blinked. "You don't mind?"

"I'd like to help. Get the medicine, and I'll meet you back in the living room."

When Jake looked back up, she was already gone. His hand slid down his outer thigh, massaging for a moment where pain spliced through him. The fibrous bands of tissue were hard to his touch, his muscles feeling as though they were on fire. "Jesus," he muttered under his breath, wondering if he should give in and take the pain meds the doctor had prescribed.

He slowly moved out of the office and to the bedroom to grab the ointment. He glanced over at the oxycodone next to the cream and curled a hand around the bottle and tossed it into the trash bin by his leg. He wasn't sure why he had such a distaste for the meds, but his gut told him to fight through the pain on his own.

When Jake came into the living room, he found Alexa bent over in front of the fireplace.

She was wearing black tights and a long, cream sweater. The sweater had shifted up to her waist as she placed a few pieces of kindling inside the fireplace. The tights hugged her ass, and Jake took a slight step back, trying not to go stiff at the sight of the perfect body before him.

"What're you doing?" He almost laughed when she looked over her shoulder at him, a smudge of soot on her cheek.

"I'm trying to figure this thing out. I thought it'd help you relax to have a fire, but I've only had fires that require the flicking of a switch."

He tossed his shirt on the couch as he crossed the living room, forgetting the pain in his leg, his back—hell, his everywhere.

Alexa rose to her feet, and Jake stopped in front of her, his heartbeat ticking up a notch as her eyes steadied on his mouth. He swept his thumb to her cheek, wiping at the smudge there. Somehow, he couldn't bring himself to step away, and she didn't seem too interested in him moving, either. His palm remained on her cheekbone. His brows drew together as she slowly wet her lips, her eyes drifting up to meet his. The woman had killer looks—pouty lips he wanted to sink his teeth into, and a bone crushing beauty that would get any enemy of hers to spill all the secrets of his life . . .

And that was exactly the point, wasn't it?

He stepped back, dropping his free hand from her face, his other still clutching the ointment. "We probably don't need the fire." He scrubbed a hand through his thick, dirty blonde hair, which had become darker than he remembered. "Shit . . ."

"What's wrong?" Alexa folded her arms, bringing them tight beneath the curves of her breasts.

"Just pissed. I've already forgotten something I sort of remembered earlier. It's like a vacuum went into my brain and sucked everything back out again. It's weird, right?" He was standing in front of one of the couches now, the back of his jeaned knees brushing against the cushion.

Alexa unlocked her arms and stepped closer to him. "Sounds like you're suffering from post-traumatic stress. I'm sure it must be difficult." She placed a palm on his forearm, and her hand on his bare skin had his stomach muscles tightening.

He kept his eyes on her long, graceful fingers. "You sure you don't mind rubbing a stranger's back? Won't be too weird for you?" Alexa didn't know him, but maybe she was used to strangers since she was a female James Bond, he decided, trying to shrug off the suspicions that ricocheted through his brain.

"I wouldn't have offered if it bothered me." Her hand glided down his arm, and her warm skin covered his fingers, which were tightly wrapped around the white tube of cream.

BRITTNEY SAHIN

He swallowed at the contact and unclenched his fist, allowing her access to the tube. "Where do you want me?"

"Um." She scanned the room and motioned to the couch. "Not sure where you'd be the most comfortable. Would you like to sit or lie down?"

If he were to lie down with a woman who looked like she did, his injuries would be the last thing on his mind. Then again, maybe that wouldn't be so bad. But he said, "Sit."

She tapped the tube against her chest as she studied him. "I don't think that'd be comfortable."

He almost laughed. "Then why'd you ask?"

She smiled.

Damned if he didn't love her smile.

"Since we're not lighting the fire, why don't you go back to your room and lie down on the bed? I'll make you some tea, and then come in and put the medicine on."

Now he was the one smiling. "Do I look like a guy who drinks tea at night?" He shrugged. "Hell, do I look like a guy who drinks tea at any time of day?"

Her beautiful mouth opened as she squinted at him. "You have any beer, then?"

Beer, his bedroom, and her hands on his body? Was the woman out of her mind? Injury or not, he was still a man. And it felt like he hadn't been with a woman in years. Meanwhile, Alexa was a hot MI6 agent—a fantasy come true. Well, at least for the twenty-two–year-old guy he remembered himself to be.

Alexa's eyes dipped down to his naked chest for a moment and then found his brown eyes once again.

"You're just trying to loosen me up so you can get information out of me," he said, joking but not joking. He gently tapped at the side of his skull where the swelling from the accident had finally disappeared, leaving in its place only a sensitive spot near his temples. "But you can't squeeze blood from a stone."

"I don't want to see you in pain."

90

He stepped closer to her, his eyes pinning hers. "And why is that?" She was supposed to be a stranger, but it sure as hell didn't feel that way. She'd felt familiar to him since the moment she stepped into his hospital room.

"I'm sure I don't know." She raised a brow and tipped up her chin. "Now get in bed."

He flashed her a grin.

"Oh, bloody hell. You know what I mean." Her sexy English accent heated his skin.

Jake left the living room, trying not to walk with a limp, forcing himself to ignore the pain in his body that he remembered as soon as she wasn't right in front of him. Jesus, he'd take her over the oxy any day.

He flicked on the lights and stared at his bed. The gray cotton sheets were still crumpled at the bottom. He hadn't exactly been interested in taking the time to make the bed since he'd been at the ranch. He released a breath as he sank onto the plush mattress, pressing his hands on either side of him as he waited for the sexy spy to join him.

"How are you feeling?"

He looked up from the floor. He'd been staring in a daze at the scratches there, remembering his grandfather's hunting dogs.

"I'm great." A smirk lit his cheek, but he stiffened at the sight of her leaning against the inside of the doorframe to the room.

Beautiful wasn't quite a powerful enough word to describe her.

He brought a fist to his mouth for a moment as he tried to suppress his desire, and yet strove to capture the image of her in his mind before he lost, that, too.

"You think you can lie on your stomach? Will that hurt?" She stepped into the room and approached the bed, her eyes never leaving his.

"Yeah, I think I can manage that." So long as he could turn over without her noticing his hard-on. He was losing his damn mind thinking about her hands on him, even if it was to apply medicine.

Jake scooted further back on the bed, his biceps flexing as he used his upper body strength to shift in the bed. His legs were throbbing, but he didn't want to look weak in front of her, so he bit back the lick of pain that cut through him when he twisted to his stomach.

"Jake?" Her voice was soft, a whisper of seduction racing across his skin and to his groin.

"Yeah?" He raised his arms up and rested them on each side of the pillow as he peeked up over his shoulder. The weight of the bed slightly shifted as she sat down next to him.

"This might hurt."

He lowered his head back down. "I can handle it. Besides, it's supposed to help in the long run." He shut his eyes.

He could hear a slight hitch in her breathing as her fingers touched his back, the cream cooling and soothing his skin. He flinched a little as her hands smoothed over his shoulder blades, and then down his spine, working the medicine in small circles over the markings on his back.

He sucked in a breath and shifted his face into the pillow, biting it a little. As much as he'd been turned on at the prospect of her fingers trailing down his back, the pain was fierce.

Her fingers lifted for a moment. "You okay?"

"Mm hm," he murmured into the pillow.

"Jake?"

He held his head up long enough just so that she could hear him. "I'm good."

"Okay." Then, she rubbed the medicine into his back more before her hands went to his outer arms where there were no scars. She began softly massaging there.

"What are you doing?" he asked before burying his face back into the pillow to smother a groan. Damned if it didn't feel good.

"I thought I'd help you relieve some tension after you suffered through me touching your wounds," she said a moment later, her voice slightly strained.

"Does it bother you? Seeing my back like this?" he asked a few minutes later, as her skilled hands worked at the base of his neck.

"It's not easy seeing someone hurt. You risk your life to help others, and this is the consequence."

Jake pressed his palms to the bed and did his best to push up without showing the pain.

"I'm probably not good at giving a massage."

He swung his legs down to the floor so he could sit next to her. He rested his hands in his lap as he thought about what to say. "You're amazing, actually. I almost forget that I survived an explosion," he said with a smile.

Her cheeks flushed beneath the soft lighting of the sole lamp that lit the room.

"I'm just curious about something." She was clutching the tube of cream between her palms. She didn't look like an MI6 agent— just a woman in pain. He wondered what her story was, but knew it wasn't his place to ask. "You said to me earlier that the world needs me. But now you're talking as if—"

"The world does need you. But that doesn't mean you don't need something, too."

He reached for her chin, tipping it up. "Who are you?" His brows slanted, his lips going tight as he stared at her in amazement.

"What do you mean?" Her voice was like silk to him, soft and beautiful.

Jake kept his hand beneath her chin. "I want to kiss you again."

"You—what?" She had inhaled a sharp breath and started to pull away, but he brushed his hand up to her cheek, holding it to her warm skin . . . and she leaned into his touch.

"Because nothing in my damn life makes sense right now. And then you come here, and I know you're just trying to pump me for information, but for some reason, the insanity in my head stops when you're around. I just feel so . . . calm. I don't know how you're doing it, but—" He lowered his head as his hand fell on his lap.

"What?" she whispered as his gaze met hers again. "Why'd you pull away?" She slid her hand over to his, reaching for his wrist. She brought his hand up to her face again.

A lump of emotion moved through his throat as his body heated at her words, at her touch. She kept her hand on his, and he wasn't sure what the hell he was supposed to do. "Tell me why I'm so comfortable around you, Alexa."

Her eyes flashed shut. "Maybe it's because we're both in the same line of work."

"That's bullshit," he was quick to respond, and her eyes opened back up. "I don't even remember my line of work." He started to pull his hand away, but she tugged at it, keeping it in place as she scooted closer to him, her mouth hovering near his.

He couldn't stop himself—his lips slanted over hers, and she moaned against his crushing kiss. His tongue slid into her mouth as his hand snaked around to the back of her head. His fingers threaded through her long, dark locks.

His heartbeat started to pound as her short fingernails grazed across his chest.

His mind skipped like a broken record, flashes of a memory slipping inside.

He'd been in a large room—colorful confetti landing on his head and shoulders. People cheering. Horns sounding.

And Alexa was there, too.

But it didn't make sense. What he was remembering couldn't be possible.

Jake pulled back from her and pushed up to his feet, ignoring the pain that spread through his limbs.

"What's wrong?" she asked breathlessly and rose.

He raked his hands through his hair and dragged them down his face, leaving them over his mouth for a minute. This memory —it didn't hurt. It didn't make him sick like the others.

So, was his mind playing tricks on him?

"What is it, Jake?" Alexa took a step closer, reaching out for him, but he backed up and held his palms out between them.

"What's going on, Alexa?"

"What do you mean?" She wet her lips and tucked her arms against her chest like a shield.

He cocked his head and studied her. "This isn't our first kiss."

Her lips parted. "Yeah, this morning—"

"No. We've done this somewhere else. Somewhere before. I know you, don't I?"

His words had Alexa moving back until she bumped into the bed. "I—"

Jake stepped forward, his body tense and rigid. His hands snapped to his sides as he shut his eyes, trying to drag what he had remembered to the forefront of his mind. "There was a countdown. New Year's Eve, maybe? I was standing, and you were near me—I remember looking over at you, and when everyone screamed 'Happy New Year's,' I grabbed your arm and pulled you against me . . . and we kissed."

"Jesus, Jake." Alexa covered a hand over her mouth.

"So," he stepped even closer to her, but she remained locked in place, simply staring at him, "tell me, Alexa, how do we know each other? And why the hell didn't you tell me before?" His voice was sharp as a razor.

"I can't believe you remember. They thought I could help, but I didn't actually believe . . ."

"They who? What are you talking about?" he accused.

"MI6. When I saw you at the hospital and realized I knew you, my agency thought I might be able to help trigger your memories."

"So you're using me? They sent you here to Goddamn use me?" He turned away from her and lowered his head. But why was he surprised? He already knew they wanted his memories. Why wouldn't they do whatever they could to extract them?

95

Her fingers on the back of his shoulder blade had him shutting his eyes.

"It's not that simple."

Jake spun around, almost knocking into her as he moved quickly, not caring about his injuries.

She stumbled, and then slowly brought her gaze back up to his. "I'm trying to stop a possible terrorist attack. Maybe even multiple attacks. I don't know. I've been after a group of people for fifteen months now, and I think you might be able to help bring down some pretty bad people."

"So being used for information is just another occupational consequence, huh?" A flash of anger shot through him. "And how do we know each other? Where does that fit into this plan of yours?"

Her hazel eyes darkened, the soft green overtaken by the chestnut brown. "We met at a party a year ago in London. You were visiting your sister, and that's it—we kissed and . . ."

"So it's some happy fucking coincidence that you and I know each other? An FBI agent and a spy?" An angry smile met his lips as he stepped away from her. "It's like a bad joke. Kind of hard to believe, don't you think? A spy and FBI agent walk into a bar—"

"What are you suggesting?" she asked, raising a brow.

He lowered his head, fighting the urge to be sucked into the vortex of her beauty.

"You think I met you on purpose?" She laughed. "Funny. My boss thought maybe you had tried to do that to me."

"Yeah, well," he said, looking back at her from the corner of his eye, "it is kind of unbelievable. But then again, nothing about the last week of my life screams normal." He gripped the bridge of his nose, trying to work through the intense emotions that were becoming more prominent than the blistering aftereffects of the explosion.

"Leave, Alexa. If you're not going to be straight with me, then leave."

"I—"

"When you're ready to tell me the truth I'll be all ears, but until then, do me a favor and stop pretending to give a damn about me. Get what you need from me and cross back over the ocean and go home." He left his bedroom, in desperate need of that beer. Hell, maybe he'd even go back to the bathroom and grab the oxy from the trash bin.

"Jake."

He opened the fridge and grabbed a bottle. "Go." He remained facing the open fridge, the bottle in hand, the refrigerator door blocking her from his sight. He couldn't face her. The last thing he needed were these awful mind games. He had enough shit to sort through in his head without someone muddying it up.

"I'm sorry. I should have told you this morning, but I—"

"Because you care about saving the world? Which is great." A bite of sarcasm flavored his voice as he faced her. "But to hell with the consequences, right?"

He heard her sigh but made no attempt to look her way. His shoulders relaxed a little at the sound of her moving behind him.

Once she was gone, Jake slammed the refrigerator door shut and smacked the freezer door with a balled fist.

He needed out of this black hole. Sooner rather than later.

# CHAPTER TWELVE

"WHY ARE YOU AT THIS SHITTY GYM?"

Alexa slowed the speed on the treadmill and switched from running to walking. She swiped at the sweat on her brow and grabbed her water bottle out of the holder to swallow several mouthfuls of the cool liquid.

"I take it your meeting with Jake didn't go so well?" Xander crossed his arms and stood off to the side of the treadmill, studying her.

"Oh, yeah. It went great." The sarcasm was baked into her voice as hot as black cement on a summer day. "He actually remembered something." She screwed on the cap of the water bottle and slipped it into the holder before staring down at the rotating fabric beneath her feet.

"Well? Is it something important?"

She faked a laugh as she looked back over at Xander. "Depends. You think I'm important?" She jabbed at the stop button.

"He remembered you? You serious?"

"Well, he remembered that he knows me, at least." She stepped off the treadmill and grabbed one of the complimentary hand towels by the cooler. As she draped the towel around her neck, she studied her image in the full-length wall mirror. They were alone in the small hotel gym.

"So how'd you handle it?"

She swiped the towel over her face, and then their eyes met in the mirror. "Like an arse."

"I should have gone with you." He came up next to her and placed a hand on her shoulder, his gray eyes still holding hers. His brows quirked up as his lips twitched. "You still have feelings for this bloke?"

"Ugh." She tipped her head forward, pressing a hand to her face. "No," she grumbled, not sure if she was lying to him or herself—maybe both. Because there had been something between them tonight—something that went beyond words. She wasn't quite sure if she *could* describe the moment when she saw Jake bent over in pain in his office when she had first seen the scars on his back.

And when they had kissed, for one tiny fraction of a minute she felt like Alexa Ryan, the woman. Not the agent. Not the person who had to lie to every man she met.

No, she felt like someone who could have more, even if it was for only a moment.

Her fingertips bit into her palms as she tried to reel in her emotions, not ready to share them with her best mate and partner. "Xander?"

"Yeah?"

She wet her lips and sucked in a breath. "You ever get lonely?" She swallowed as her eyes found his again. There was a warmth there, despite their steely color.

He dropped his hand from her shoulder and swiped it over his hard, square jaw before bringing it up to the nape of his neck. There was a flicker of seriousness there, but it passed as quickly as it had come. "Of course not, love. I have you. I have the agency.

And I have a woman in every city I travel to." He lifted his shoulders in an innocent manner.

"Even here? In Montana?" She almost laughed.

"Maybe not here." He winked at her and patted her on the back. "Come on. Get yourself some rest. We have a long day tomorrow."

"Yeah. Okay."

She said goodbye to him outside her hotel room and then went into the bathroom for a shower.

Once undressed, she stared at herself in the mirror as her finger traced the scar by her hipbone.

She shut her eyes and skirted her hand up her breastbone and to her lips, resting them there as she remembered Jake's kiss.

*I'm in so much bloody trouble.*

\* \* \*

"Just got off the phone with Matt. Sam hasn't found anything new from Reza. And GCHQ says they haven't found anything of use on the drive yet—"

"Wow. You're full of good news." Alexa focused on the snowflakes drifting outside the window as she and Xander sat parked in Jake's driveway. They were waiting for Special Agent Trent Shaw to show up for their web conference. Xander unbuckled his seat belt and turned on the radio. Soft country tunes drifted into the air for just a moment before Xander jabbed at the buttons, trying to switch the music.

"They'll find something eventually," Xander said. "We need to be optimistic."

"Any news from Tenley and John? They were supposed to meet with Berat today in Istanbul, right?" It was Tuesday, their normal day of contact.

"Not yet."

Just then, she noticed taillights reflecting off the dark wood of the cabin. Alexa peeked at the side mirror and spotted a SUV pulling in behind them. "They're here."

"You ready for this?"

"As ready as I'll ever be." She fought back the urge to check her appearance in the dashboard mirror, knowing that Xander would give her hell for it. "Let's do this."

Xander came around next to her once they were out of the car, holding on to her forearm as if to protect her from slipping on the snowy driveway. "Don't want you busting your arse," he said as a smile met his lips. But the smile soon faded once the two men in suits stepped out of the SUV.

The men posted to guard Jake, who were sitting in the car parked in front of Xander and Alexa's rental, remained in their vehicle. They must not have had the clearance to be a part of the web call.

"You must be Agent Ryan," Agent Shaw mumbled as if the words were an inconvenience to his mouth. "And good to see you again," he added when looking Xander's way.

Alexa recognized Shaw from the hospital. "Thank you for meeting with us," she said when she realized Xander wasn't going to speak.

"Not like we had much of a choice," Shaw said dryly, and then tipped his head at the tall man to his right. "This is Special Agent Harris. He's from the D.C. field office."

"Ma'am," Agent Harris said and nodded.

"We can drop the formalities, right? Call me, Alexa, please." She smiled, hoping to bridge some sort of alliance with the closed mouth Feds—she needed them to open up to her agency finally.

"Works for me, Alexa. I'm Randall." He smiled at her and gave her a slight wink, and she was relieved he seemed to have a little more of a personality than Shaw.

"Call me Trent, then," he grumbled.

After a moment, she flicked Xander's hand from her forearm, embarrassed by her partner's protectiveness over her. They were the same age, so why he treated her like a kid sister was beyond her.

"Let's get this over with so we can get back to London," Xander said, mimicking Trent's grumpiness.

They followed after the agents and Alexa swallowed and shut her eyes for a brief moment when Trent's fist tapped at the door. She wasn't ready to see Jake again. To face the anger in his eyes.

Her eyes flashed open when she heard the click of the door latch. Alexa's eyes landed on Jake as he stood there in the doorframe, his broad shoulders hidden beneath a dark brown, button-down shirt that made the color of his eyes appear even darker.

He looked straight at her. Practically through her.

Xander rested his hand on her back, offering her support, sensing her nerves.

Jake's eyes shifted down in one quick movement, taking note of Xander's arm behind Alexa's back, and then his jaw clenched. *Shit. Did he think . . . ?* Not that it mattered what he thought. She and Jake weren't together, after all. Hell, they'd never technically been a couple. And besides, she was here to work a case, not get her head and heart twisted up in some insane mess.

"How are you?" Trent asked Jake.

"Just great." His voice was icy, and she missed the sweetness and humor she'd heard from him before. He stepped back and waved his hand, motioning them in and out of the cold.

Alexa shrugged off her winter coat and unwrapped the scarf from her neck. She took her cue from the others, resting her things over the top of the couch in the living room. Her gaze flickered to the hall to where his bedroom was. Where they had kissed.

When she looked up, Jake was watching her from across the room, his arms crossed as he stood in front of the lit fireplace. The flames roared, and the heat from the fire radiated throughout the room, warming her. Or maybe it was Jake who was making her hot.

"Where should we set up the computer?" Trent asked, clutching a laptop bag.

"Kitchen is fine," Jake answered.

Trent and Randall went into the kitchen, but Xander remained at Alexa's side. Jake also hadn't moved.

"Jake, you remember my partner, Xander, right? He met you at the base before you came back stateside."

Xander approached Jake and held out his hand. "Good to see you again, mate."

Alexa took a few steps closer as the two alpha males stared each other down. Both were tall and muscular, strength rippling through every inch of their bodies. But Xander was like family to her, and Jake—well, he was something entirely different.

Jake didn't say anything, but he finally shook Xander's hand.

"Shall we?" Xander tipped his head to the kitchen.

"Could you give us a minute?" Alexa asked Xander.

"Sure." Xander nodded at Jake and moved into the kitchen to join the agents.

"How are you?" she softly asked while stepping up in front of him.

Jake placed a hand on the mantel above the fireplace and looked down at the dancing orange and red flames. "You mean after what happened last night?"

"Um. Yeah."

When he looked back at her, she could see irritation burning in his irises. "How do you think I am?" Jake lowered his hand and moved past her, his shoulder brushing against her as he left her alone in front of the fire.

She released a deep breath and went into the kitchen. Randall and Trent had set up a laptop on the kitchen table, and they were pulling up a secure network.

"Looks like they're online. They're ready," Randall said. A few seconds later, Laney appeared on screen alongside two men Alexa didn't recognize. She had to assume they were members of Parliament.

Laney didn't introduce herself or the men she was sitting next to at the table. And Randall and Trent didn't say their names, either. Alexa assumed they already knew each other. They'd probably been going back and forth for days.

"We're waiting for the information, Special Agent Shaw," Laney said, clasping her hands on the desk in front of her, appearing confident as always. "We've already been working with NSA on a case, and that case appears to have crossed into FBI territory. So, now we'll be needing to work with your officers as well."

Maybe they hadn't chatted as much as Alexa had thought— wouldn't they have known this already? What in the hell were the Americans hiding?

"What does NSA have to do with this? I wasn't informed that they were involved." Trent looked over at Randall, his brows pinching together.

"Maybe if you had bothered to take at least half of our dozen calls—you'd know this." Laney shook her head, clearly irritated with the Feds. "Speak first, and we'll explain next." She leaned back in her leather chair.

Jake folded his arms and stood off to the side, out of the view of the webcam. He stared out the window over the kitchen sink as if he had nothing to do with the current conversation.

"I'm not prepared to talk about classified information just yet," Trent answered.

*Of course, not. This is a waste of time.*

Laney chuckled, and it wasn't her polite laugh. No, it was her "I'm going to kill you" laugh. "Then what the bloody hell are we doing having this conversation right now—and why did you leave London in the first place? Are you planning on taking a plane back here then? The agents you left in London for investigative purposes aren't ranked high enough to give us a damn thing."

Clearly the Americans had done that on purpose.

"What *do* you want to tell us, Special Agent Shaw? Because I'm losing patience and running out of time. We have sources that have verified an impending attack on British soil, and this attack is from the group that we believe was holding your agent."

"And you were working with the NSA about this before Agent Summers' abduction?" Randall asked.

"Yes. We're tracking a cyber terrorist group known as Anarchy. Well, they use the computer 'at' symbol before their name. 'At Anarchy.' Are you familiar with them?" Laney asked.

"Heard of them, but cyber is not our territory," Randall answered.

Alexa's lips parted. "That doesn't make sense." Alexa looked up at Trent, confused. "I assumed you were after Anarchy, which is why they took your agent."

"We have nothing to do with hackers or cyber terrorists." Trent rubbed a hand down his jaw and glanced over at Jake. "Why do you think our mission prior to the explosion is connected to yours? What is it that you're not telling us?"

Alexa was about to speak, to yell at him again for being such a roadblock to their investigation in the last week, but Laney held up her hand. "We decrypted intel after the explosion from a hacker connected to Anarchy that led us to believe your American was taken by their group." Laney looked over at the men at the table and then stood up, pressing her hands to the desk and leaning forward a little until she seemed to fill the computer screen. "So, Special Agents Shaw and Harris, are you ready to share your information? Could you please enlighten us on what your agent was doing in the U.K. prior to the explosion, so we can figure out how our cases are connected?"

Jake's attention was now glued to the back of the computer, the muscles in his jaw tight, his chest lifting in deeper breaths. It had to be hard for him to listen to all of this, to know he might be able to help if only his memories hadn't betrayed him.

"We're not at liberty to go into depth, but what I can say is that we were a part of a joint task force in Sicily. It included CIA and the military, as well as Jake and one other FBI agent. Jake was chosen for the assignment because of his unique knowledge of the HVT." HVT—high-value target. "We've been tracking Qasim Ansari, one of the military commanders of ISIS, for two years now, and Jake's been the lead agent in charge of counterterrorist activity related to Ansari on American soil. We received credible intel that Ansari would be in Libya, and so we set up at our base in Sicily to take them out. Unfortunately, our mission was compromised, and our men were attacked off base."

Jake's brows furrowed, his eyes darting to Trent. Alexa wondered if this was the first time Jake had learned of the nature of his mission. Although Qasim Ansari wasn't a man that Alexa had personally been after, she'd heard of him. He was one of the most wanted men in the world by all agencies.

"And what happened to the other agents with him? Did they see anything? Did they see who took Agent Summers?" Laney asked.

Trent and Randall exchanged looks once again, and Alexa got a bad feeling in her stomach. She could see it in Jake's eyes, too. He knew that something was wrong.

"Jake was the only survivor. Both SUVs transporting the agents were ambushed. The first was taken out by a long-range missile. And the second vehicle flipped as a result of the explosion. The men in the second vehicle were shot and killed. Except for Jake, of course." Trent's voice took on a softer tone this time. There was pain in his voice as he had spoken. He'd lost men.

Alexa looked over at Jake. His head bowed, his eyes closed. For an agent, it was almost a fate worse than death to be the sole survivor on a mission.

"I'm sorry, Jake. We wanted to tell you, but—" Trent stepped out of view of the camera and approached Jake, placing a hand on his shoulder.

"Why me? Why'd they take me?" Jake asked.

"I don't know. Could've just been the way things went down," Trent answered.

"I'm sorry for your loss, but if we want to prevent more deaths, we need to get a handle on this and fast. I don't know how much time we have until the group makes their move. My assumption is that they were using your agent for information. Or for more dramatic purposes," Laney said.

Jake stepped away from Trent and turned to the counter, bracing the edges of it. Alexa wanted to go over and console him, but she remained in place.

"Perhaps they wanted to use him to transmit a message. We've seen that plenty of times with ISIS," Randall said.

"But this isn't making sense," Alexa spoke up, pulling her gaze away from Jake's back and shifting, so her face was fully in front of the screen. "There has never been any connection between ISIS and Anarchy. Anarchy has funneled money to anti-Western militant groups, but never once to ISIS. In fact, they have denounced ISIS's actions in the past. Anarchy only supports attacks against Americans and the British. And they're not motivated by religious fundamentalist ideas."

"They've given money to Al Qaeda before," Xander noted.

"But that's only to support efforts to rid Americans and British from Afghanistan and Pakistan. They have never shown any interest in anything related to Syria or Iraq," Alexa said.

"Well, it looks like they've started. We have intel suggesting that Anarchy took Agent Summers. If he was taken from Sicily while on an OP to kill an ISIS leader, we have to assume there is a connection between ISIS and Anarchy now," Laney said.

Alexa had been studying the group for the last fifteen months, and there was nothing to indicate that Bekas would support ISIS. It was completely outside his MO. "With all due respect, I have to disagree." Alexa straightened her spine and faced Trent, hoping

Laney wouldn't cut her off. "How'd you know Ansari would be in Libya? Where'd you get your intel?"

"What are you saying, Alexa?" Laney's voice echoed through the laptop speakers.

Alexa waited to see if Trent would answer the question before she directed her attention back to Laney.

"NSA intercepted several emails relating to Ansari and his whereabouts. We followed up and verified that Ansari was really there, and then we pushed for the go-ahead to send in a team," Trent said.

"Do you think we could have a look at the messages?" Alexa's eyes met Xander's, and she could see the acknowledgment in them —he saw where this was going.

"I'll see what I can do, but why?"

"Alexa, are you suggesting Anarchy was behind this?" Laney asked.

Alexa released a breath. "I think that is more likely than Anarchy being affiliated with ISIS." Her hands landed on her hips as she confronted her boss. "I know Bekas, ma'am. And I know this wasn't a coincidence. If Anarchy took Jake from Italy, then they were the ones who made sure he was there in the first place. Maybe not him, specifically, but they wanted an American agent."

"So, you're saying the messages we intercepted were planted by this cyber terrorist group?" Randall scrubbed a hand down his jaw, his voice echoing an edge of disbelief.

"She might be right," Xander said. "They dangled some forbidden fruit in front of you all—Ansari—knowing you'd take the bait."

"I'll talk to the Director of the NSA," Laney said. "I know him. I'll get those messages."

"And what will that prove? If this group lured our men there, we already know why, right?" Randall asked.

"I'm betting not," Alexa was quick to respond, "because anytime Anarchy does something, it's never as it seems."

"Fine." Trent exhaled. "I'll look into Anarchy, as well. But I'm not as familiar with the group—would you give me a quick rundown?"

Alexa's stomach lurched. She looked over at Jake, and a harsh pain crawled up her spine. She felt so sorry for him. And for all the people he'd lost that he couldn't even remember.

"Three years ago, there was an American and British joint OP to take out a leader of Al Qaeda," Laney began after a moment. "He was a couple of kilometers outside Kabul in an area deemed relatively safe from civilians, but the building was close to another home."

Laney switched the screen to show her computer instead of the conference room. A picture of Kemal Bekas displayed in the lower right-hand corner of the screen. Although she'd never met him, she knew his olive skin, jet black hair, and piercing blackish-brown eyes by heart. "Government officials gave the go-ahead for a drone strike, ruling that the neighboring home was empty."

Images of the aftermath of the drone strike were displayed on the screen—a decimated home where the Al Qaeda leader and his men had been. A hundred meters behind the house was debris—a child's doll and suitcases scattered about.

"I remember this," Trent murmured.

"Kemal Bekas's wife and twin eight-year-old daughters had just arrived at the home near the targets a moment before the drone took out the Al Qaeda leader. Bekas has Kurdish and Turkish backgrounds, as well as English. But his wife was Afghan and English. She was visiting family in Afghanistan on holiday." Laney switched over to a screen showing the Bekas Tech Tower in Istanbul. "Bekas is a wealthy businessman. His headquarters were in London, as he held British citizenship. But after the loss of his family, he demanded answers for what had happened to his family. Answers we couldn't give him." Laney's face was back on screen now.

"So what happened?" Trent asked.

Jake's back was still to everyone, his shoulders hunched forward, one hand now covering his face.

"He moved his company to Istanbul two years ago since he had Turkish citizenship from his father. Then, a few months after that, we began noticing unusual activity surrounding Bekas. We had decided to keep an eye on him after he threatened our government. We're pretty sure he created the group as a means of retribution. He wants vengeance against us and you guys for what happened to his family."

Laney removed her glasses and clasped them in her hands in front of her stomach as she stood in front of the long, oval table. The men beside her had yet to speak, and Alexa wondered what their purpose was in this. Were they just watch dogs there to ensure that no one said too much?

"Drone strike, huh?" Trent looked down at the floor for a moment, and everyone remained quiet for a minute.

"They say for every drone strike we use to take someone out, we get fifty new enemies as a result," Randall said.

Alexa couldn't agree more. She'd never been an advocate for the use of drone attacks unless absolutely necessary.

"Just curious, but why the name? Why 'at-Anarchy'? I'd expect something a bit more focused on hating Western civilization." Randall looked at the computer screen, and then over at Alexa and Xander.

"He only has two people in his inner circle. A Russian businessman and a wealthy Frenchman. Most of his followers are in their twenties. They're from all over the world, and they're looking to create trouble and make money. I doubt they even know Bekas's true motives. We think he used this hacker group and the name to recruit young hackers to do his bidding and uses the organization as a front for what he really wants," Alexa explained.

"And what do you think the ultimate goal is?" Trent asked.

Alexa raised her shoulders. "If you became mentally unstable and sickened by grief after you lost your wife and daughters, what would you do?"

"So tell me something. If you know this Bekas guy is the head of a terrorist organization, why aren't you arresting him? Hell, why aren't you murdering him?" Jake suddenly asked, facing them.

Xander looked over at Jake. "This is the real world. We can't simply go and murder people, especially a millionaire businessman. Bekas is unlike any terrorist we've faced recently. He hides in plain sight behind this network of hackers, and we still haven't directly connected him to any of the crimes committed by Anarchy. It's not that easy to arrest someone, or even kill them, in friendly territory. We need to catch him with his hand on the trigger, so to speak."

Jake glanced up at the ceiling, and Alexa didn't envy the man. How was he expected to exist—to thrive—in a world that he had no clue about?

"I suggest we work together," Xander said when Jake remained silent. Of course, they didn't have a choice, did they?

Alexa glanced at Laney as she pulled her chair out and sat down.

"I'll have to talk to my people in D.C." Trent thrust a hand into his pocket and pulled out his mobile.

"Fine," Laney noted. "For now, Alexa, Xander, you can come back here. Unless you think—"

"No." Jake spun around, his hands curling into tight fists at his sides. His eyes went straight to Alexa, and she couldn't break his hold. "Alexa stays."

"And you think you get to make the orders because . . .?" Xander approached him, angling his head to the side as he peered at Jake with narrowed eyes.

Jake released a lungful of air and looked over Xander's shoulder at the others. "I'm beginning to remember things, and I think Alexa is why." Jake maneuvered around Xander and stood in front of Trent and Randall.

"Shit, Jake. What do you remember? Why the hell didn't you say something sooner?" Trent lowered the phone.

"You should have bloody led with that," Laney said.

"I was planning to say something, and then you guys began talking about all this intense shit." Jake gripped the back of the kitchen chair as if he needed it for support. Maybe he did.

"And what do you remember, Agent Summers?" Laney asked.

"I've been remembering moments from my time in the military, so yesterday when something came to my mind I thought it was related to that. But then again this morning it was clearer. And after this meeting, I realized my memory is from the ambush in Sicily."

Nervous anticipation spiraled through Alexa.

Jake shut his eyes as if he were trying to drag the memory to his mind. "I remember the SUV in front of me exploding. Right before my vehicle flipped, the driver was shot straight through the neck. Me and another guy tried to get out once the SUV was on its side, but we were trapped. I scrambled to get my sidearm, but—" He opened his eyes. "Shit, that's all I can remember."

"Not what anyone looks like or . . ." Xander pressed.

"No, but there's something else." Jake sucked in a breath, and then released the air through his nose. "I don't know what the men looked like who tortured me, but I remember being beaten, and I remember seeing something. There were maybe a half a dozen vests lying on a bed in the room, all weighted down with explosives and wires."

"Suicide vests? In my Goddamn city?" Laney was back on her feet and reaching for her mobile.

Jake came around in front of the camera to look at Laney. "Ma'am, I'm sorry I don't remember more. Believe me, I want to stop these assholes who killed my teammates—even if I can't remember the names of the fallen men. But I can feel it . . . the memories. They're there." He tapped at the side of his head. "I just can't seem to access them, yet." Jake looked over his shoulder at Alexa. "But I think Alexa can help me get them back."

"And why the hell would she be able to do that?" Trent asked.

"Because we know each other," Alexa answered for him.

"Come again?" Trent angled his head and moved around Jake to confront Alexa.

She remained firm in her wide stance, refusing his attempt to intimidate her. "We met at a party a year ago," she told Trent.

"And I think being around her is helping trigger my memories. So, you see, I need her." Jake held his hands in front of him, palms up as if he were pleading for a handout. "I think being around anything familiar from the last ten years of my life will help." He squeezed his eyes shut for a moment. "I want to be a part of the team. I want to be on the OP that brings down the sons of bitches who killed my partners," he gruffly said.

"Hell, no. You're still in pain. You were in a damn explosion and tortured. You can't be running around Europe." Trent folded his arms, shaking his head.

"It might be a good idea." Xander looked at Laney. "Whoever had him thinks he's dead. No one will be looking for him. And maybe if he's part of the OP, it will help him remember something important. It might help us bring these motherfuckers down."

Alexa was surprised by Jake's sudden willingness to help. He'd been resistant to the idea yesterday. Maybe learning he was the sole survivor of his OP had changed his mind. Or maybe he was becoming the man he had once been as he slowly regained his memories.

Maybe he had even remembered more of their time together. She didn't think he'd ever want to see her again after last night, but now he was asking for her to stay with him. Something had changed, at least.

"I need time to think about this," Trent said.

"Me too," Laney echoed. "Alexa. Xander. Call me when you

leave the house and hold off on booking your flights for now. I'll be in touch."

The transmission ended.

"I, um . . ." Alexa tugged her lip between her teeth as she studied the room full of men. "I need some air." She darted out of the kitchen and went straight out the front door, not taking time to grab her jacket.

She glanced at the agents in the parked car and wrapped her arms around her, hugging herself as she walked to the left side of the front porch. It was still snowing. Fat flakes fell from the sky, splattering the white-coated terrain. She was freezing, but the numbness exhilarated her.

"Alexa."

She looked over as Jake came out of the house with her jacket in hand. He shut the door behind him and slowly approached her, offering her jacket even though he hadn't bothered to grab his own.

"Thanks." She took it from him and pulled it on.

"I thought you hated me," she said. He came up next to her and rested his wrists on the railing, leaning forward as he looked off in the distance.

"How could I hate someone I barely know?"

"Do you really think I can help you get your memories back?"

"I don't know. Maybe." He pushed off the railing and cupped the back of his neck as she faced him. "I don't know if I still want to be an agent when this is all over, but I do know I can't live with myself if I don't try and help. I may not remember the man I became, but I'll damned sure try. There's no way I can stand back and let people die when there's a chance that I can help. And I want justice for the other men on my team who didn't survive . . ."

She knew how he felt. She wasn't prepared to tell him why or how she knew, but she hurt for him. And she needed him to know that. "Jake, you don't need to be alone in this." She rested a hand on his forearm and realized that the material of his shirt was already chilled from the icy cold.

"I don't?" He raised his brows as his eyes found hers.

"I came here so you could help me." She lifted her shoulders in embarrassment as she heard the echo of her words. "I mean, help the case. But if I can help you—"

"You know," he interrupted, taking a step back. "I don't have a wife or daughters, but like you said in there—if someone hurt my family, I don't know if I'd snap, too, like this Bekas guy."

"You would never hurt innocent people."

"No, maybe not, but I'd sure as hell kill whoever was responsible." He gritted his teeth and looked down. "And you know what scares me?"

"What?"

"That wasn't who I was twelve years ago. I wasn't a killer. Hell, I'd catch a spider in my house and let it free outside instead of squashing it." He turned from her. "And now I'm a man who wouldn't think twice about murder. I'm not sure if I like being this guy, but I feel him inside me . . . and he's clawing his way out."

She reached for his arm, trying to turn him. "There is a big difference between you and Bekas. If you've killed in your past, it was to save others. And I'm sure the military and FBI changed you." He faced her now, his eyes growing darker, his breathing heavier. "How could it not?" Her fingers still rested on his arm, trembling slightly as emotions coursed through her. "I don't know the man you were twelve years ago, but I know the kind of guy you were last year."

"Oh yeah?" He took a step closer to her, and she lowered her hand. He angled his head, his eyes dipping to her mouth for a moment.

Was he remembering their kiss? Their kisses?

"You were incredibly funny and charming. There was nothing hard about you—well, other than . . . um, your body." Her cheeks warmed as Jake's gaze slid back up to her eyes. "Shit, I didn't mean to say that."

"I take it we did a lot more than kiss last year."

Before Alexa could respond, she looked over Jake's shoulder to see Xander and the FBI agents coming out onto the porch.

"You ready to go?" Xander asked as he put on his coat.

"We'll be at the hotel, Jake. I'll call you later tonight or in the morning," Trent said as Randall went ahead to their SUV.

"Sure." Jake shoved his hands in his jeans pockets, pulling his shoulders forward a little from the cold.

"I don't think you're physically or mentally ready to go out into the field," Trent said in a low voice. "But if I get approval, then I won't stop you if that's really what you want."

Jake only nodded at Trent before he left.

Xander was still standing a few feet away. He was waiting for her, but she couldn't seem to make herself leave.

"You going to be okay?" Alexa asked Jake.

"I'll be fine," he finally answered before turning away from her and walking with slow steps into the house.

# CHAPTER THIRTEEN

"You came back. Why?" Jake stood on the other side of the door, staring at her with parted lips as she held a white bag with red Chinese symbols on it, and clutched a DVD with the other hand.

The sky was a dark blue. The snow had finally let up, and now there were only stars in the sky, the twinkling lights moving about as if they were on the ends of puppet strings.

"Things are about to get real tomorrow. If MI6 and the FBI agree to let you on the case, we'll be diving head-first into a shit storm. I thought maybe you and I could use a bit of normalcy before all of that." She smiled.

He stepped back, allowing her entry from the cold. "Normalcy? I think my life will never be normal."

She handed him the food and movie so she could remove her jacket.

"You went and bought *Dirty Harry*?"

"It was that or *Bridges of Madison County*. I know you're a Clint Eastwood fan, but I didn't take you for a sappy romantic." She spun around after tossing her jacket, almost bumping into him.

"So you brought Chinese food, my favorite, and one of my all-time favorite movies?" He eyed her cautiously. "I guess this answers my question from earlier."

"Which question?" She clasped her hands together, and she looked far too innocent for who he knew she was. Was she playing another role?

He thought back to her red hair at the hospital. How could he trust her when she had lied about their intimate knowledge of each other?

"Oh . . . you mean about did we do more than kiss?" Her lips split into a grin. God, what was this woman doing to him?

He trailed after her as she marched the food into the kitchen.

"We spent a day eating Chinese food and watching old movies while you were in London." She looked over her shoulder at him before beginning the business of opening cupboards—probably in search of plates. "Does that answer your question?"

"Hardly. I'd like to know more." He set the food and movie down on the kitchen table and tried not to focus on her backside, but her slender waist, perfect hips and ass—*Jesus, what is wrong with me?* And yet, he couldn't find it in himself to feel bad. He didn't notice the pain in his body right now. He didn't even remember any of the horrid information he had learned earlier today. Every time he was near her, Alexa was like . . . medicine.

How could he have possibly forgotten this woman?

Alexa found two plates, and set them on the table. She opened the bag of food and the mix of sweet and sour aromas floated to his nose as she retrieved chopsticks from the bottom of the bag and began pulling out boxes of food. Yup, she knew his favorites: spicy orange chicken and rice with vegetables.

"I don't have much of an appetite."

"Sit and eat. You want the truth, right? Eat with me, and you'll get it." She sat down and popped a piece of chicken in her mouth with the chopsticks. She licked the sauce from her lips as he sank into the seat opposite her.

"Fine." The tender meat of the chicken and the sweet flavor met his tongue, the spice warming his mouth.

She looked up from her plate a few minutes later and smiled at him. When she still didn't speak, he waved a chopstick her way and narrowed one eye. "I'm eating. So, talk," he said after swallowing.

Her hazel eyes greeted his, and his pulse quickened at the simple look. She rested her chopsticks on the table and touched the napkin to her lips before pressing back against the seat. "My sister is married to a big-shot football player in England. He has a lot of friends. And I guess your sister is dating one of those friends, which is how we ended up at the same party."

"And?" He stopped eating for a moment, his heart racing as he waited for answers.

"And you kissed me at midnight, and that kiss led to us chatting. You called me ma'am until I finally gave you my name."

"Your real name?" He raised his brows.

"First name." She rolled her eyes at him. "You weren't exactly forthcoming with information, either. You didn't tell me you were FBI."

"Keep going," he urged.

She pushed her plate to the side and locked her hands together on the table in front of her as if the conversation was making her nervous. The woman could hunt terrorists, but talking about how they met was difficult for her . . .?

"We had way too much champagne, and we slept together," she quickly said.

He filled his lungs with air, intoxicated by this confirmation of his desire. Her saffron and vanilla perfume met his nostrils, and the muscles in his biceps tightened.

"I tried to sneak out of your hotel room in the morning, but you caught me—and you wouldn't let me go."

"You tried to ditch me?"

"You were bloody persistent on me staying." Her cheeks

heated to a rosy color that gave her cheekbones a soft glow. "And then you kind of coerced me into spending the day with you." She looked down at her hands. "And one day turned into seven. We were both on holiday, after all. Then you had to go back to the States, and that was that."

"We spent seven days together and then I left?" He pulled his lips together and nodded as he processed what she'd said. "Did we ever talk again? Did I call?"

"No." She cleared her voice. "We decided it'd be best to chalk it up to what it was—an amazing seven days." Alexa pushed away from the table and stood, shifting away from him.

"And why don't I believe you?" He was on his feet, but as he started for her, a sharp stabbing pain greeted his side and jolted down his thigh. "Dammit."

"What?" She whipped around and went to him as he grabbed hold of his outer thigh.

"It fucking hurts sometimes," he bluntly responded. Even though he didn't break a leg, he must have landed on his side after the explosion—his hip and leg taking the brunt of the fall.

"I'm sorry," she whispered.

"It must have been a hell of a week we had together." Jake's eyes locked with hers.

Her lower lip had trembled a little before she caught it between her teeth. "It was one incredible week," she said in a soft voice. Her eyes slid down to his mouth, and her chest slowly rose with deep breaths. "Really, really incredible."

Jake gulped as her words baited him like sin. He leaned closer. "Just doesn't seem like something I'd do," he said in a low voice and stepped back.

"What do you mean?"

"To meet a woman like you and never look back."

"Maybe the you-at-twenty-two wouldn't do that, but maybe last year you would."

He tipped his shoulders up. "Maybe. Or maybe not." He left the kitchen, not waiting for her to speak or to follow.

"You're angry at me again?"

He turned at the sound of her voice as he stilled in front of the fireplace, which was still blazing. He'd been chucking wood in there all afternoon. The fire had helped calm his nerves.

He crouched down in front of the fireplace and grabbed the poker, shoving at the logs as sparks met the air. "I'm sick of you holding the truth back from me."

"And what makes you think I'm lying? Hell, if you can't remember everything, then why are you the expert on what happened?"

Her voice was as cool as the Montana air, and it straightened his spine. He pushed back up to his feet, ignoring the throbbing in his thigh. "I'm the one with the memory issues, but it looks like you're having some trouble yourself." He kept his back to her.

"How can you be so certain that I'm not telling the truth?"

"I think you don't know when you're acting and when you're being real." Maybe he had no right to question her—he couldn't even remember anything but their first kiss. But something inside him screamed that he was right, that she was afraid, that he would never have turned his back on her.

"You might be right," she said as her voice grew farther away, and he realized she was probably leaving. He turned and faced her as she was putting her jacket back on. "But I definitely never pretended when I was with you."

Jake sucked in a breath as she twisted the doorknob.

"I'll see you tomorrow, Jake. If you still want to work together, that is."

# CHAPTER FOURTEEN

ALEXA PRESSED HER EAR TO THE DOOR OF THE MASTER BATHROOM but heard nothing.

"Jake? Are you okay?" He'd disappeared into his bedroom within minutes of their arrival and hadn't come out for over half an hour.

When he didn't answer, she touched the doorknob and turned it, hoping it wasn't locked.

It wasn't.

She slowly pushed open the door and her breath caught in her throat. He was sitting against the bathroom cabinets. One knee was bent, and the other stretched out in front of him on the peach, travertine floors. His eyes were closed, his neck bared to her. Small white tablets scattered over the floor from the open bottle near his right hand.

"You didn't take a bunch of these pills, did you?"

He rolled his head to the side as his eyes opened, landing on hers. "I didn't take a damn one of them."

"Then what happened?" Alexa knelt next to him, not sure what to do. She wanted to touch him—to do something—but she kept her hands pressed to her thighs.

"Don't worry about it," he grumbled with a dark edge to his voice.

He was clearly still pissed at her, and how could she blame him? Things hadn't ended so well last night. "Please, Jake. I'm sorry for last—"

"I remembered why I joined the Marines," he suddenly said, cutting her off.

*Oh.*

He reached for the pill bottle and clutched it in his right hand. It wasn't what she'd been expecting him to say, nor did it explain why there was oxy all over the floor. But he was talking to her, so that was a start. "And?"

He cocked his head and looked over at her. There was so much pain in his eyes that it was nearly impossible to look at him without absorbing some of it.

"My best friend joined the Marines when he was eighteen," he said slowly with a steady voice. "He got hurt four years in, but it wasn't bad enough to force him out. He was on leave for a bit . . ." He lowered his head until his chin almost touched his chest, and he heaved out a deep, ragged breath. "I had recently graduated college and was applying to teaching positions. I was wrapped up in all of that and didn't notice what was happening to him."

*Oh, God.* Her eyes drifted to Jake's beat up cowboy boots, and then over to the pills again as she lifted a hand to her mouth.

"He got addicted to the pain meds, and they discharged him from the Marines. I didn't know any of this, of course, until I found him with a suicide note clutched in his hand." His voice fell until it was hardly a whisper. "He overdosed."

Alexa's hand swept to Jake's arm in one fast movement. "You found him?"

He nodded.

"And his death made you want to join the Marines?" She might have done the opposite, to be honest—she would despise the people who stole a friend's life.

"I hated seeing him go out like that when all he'd ever wanted was to be a Marine. I felt that I'd be honoring him if I joined. I told myself that for every man I could save in the field, that'd be one less soldier lying in a hospital bed. One less potential victim of addiction."

*Wow.* "That was bloody brave of you." She chewed on her bottom lip, and then reached for his hand and wrapped her fingers around it.

"Or maybe stupid. I probably should have taken my rage out on the military instead of on strangers in the Middle East." He faked a laugh as his gaze swept to their hands. "Now I'm a killer . . . they were nameless people to me, but to others, they were husbands, brothers, fathers . . ." He lifted his free palm to cover his face.

"They weren't innocent people."

Jake dropped his hand and gaped at her. "Really? You so sure about that?" He pulled his other hand free from hers and stood, but then clutched his leg, fighting back a grimace as he put weight on the injured leg. "What about this Bekas guy? Were his twin daughters and wife dangerous? And, hell, all the people he's killed as a consequence of that drone strike are on the military's hands, too." He turned and braced the bathroom counter, staring at his reflection until Alexa was on her feet next to him. His eyes flickered to meet hers, and he lifted his hands, staring down at his palms. "How much innocent blood do you think is on these hands?"

She touched the middle of his back. "Jake, you can't do this to yourself. It will tear you apart. Please."

"Have you ever killed someone?" His dark brown eyes lifted to hold her gaze once again.

"Yes, but maybe we can save that story for another day," she said softly and took a step back, kneeling down to the floor to pluck up the pills, one by one. "We should—" She stopped herself when she stood, finding herself alone in the bathroom.

She sighed and went to the toilet and flushed the tablets, staring as the swoosh of water circled the drain. She cupped a hand to her mouth, her shoulders trembling slightly as she focused on the toilet basin. She recalled the memories of her past—of her ex—in a daze. Memories of the one time she had pulled the trigger.

And then the very real sound of gunfire close by turned Alexa toward the door in a panic. She reached behind her back for her weapon as she started for the noise, but realized she wasn't carrying. She cursed under her breath as she skidded to a halt at the entryway between the hall and living room.

"Get down!" Xander screamed, crawling with his head tucked down. Another bullet tore through the fractured windowpane with a tiny sonic boom.

Trent was crouched on one knee with his pistol extended alongside the sofa. He shifted up for a moment to take a shot out the window, but as he did, there was another loud crack . . . and the dull wet thud of a bullet against flesh.

Trent's arm lurched back, his Glock smacking the ground as he fell onto the sofa behind him. Blood started to seep from the wound. "Fucking bastard!" Trent shouted.

"Get him out of the line of fire," Randall shouted to Xander. *Where the hell is Jake?*

"Stay here," Xander commanded to Alexa, and she squatted down and watched with shallow breaths as Randall and Xander grabbed Trent by the shoulders and stooped low as they tugged him over to her.

A whizzing sound—ffsh!—hissed toward the kitchen entryway, and Jake was standing there. He barely flinched as the bullet went right over his shoulder.

"Get down, Jake!" Alexa hollered.

"We need to get this son of a bitch," Randall said, turning to Xander. "You carrying?"

Xander nodded before reaching for the piece he had strapped to his ankle. "See if you can patch up Trent," Randall told Alexa, but she couldn't take her eyes off Jake.

What was he doing, just standing there? Xander's eyes followed her own.

"Get cover!" Xander shouted, but Jake did the opposite. He rushed to the center of the room and lunged to the ground, snatching Trent's Glock in stride. As he came back upright, a bullet tore into the hardwood floor where he had been.

"Bloody hell!" Alexa screamed. Xander's arm was extended in front of her, blocking her as she pushed against her friend, wanting to run to Jake.

"I've got him," Xander said when Jake barreled out the front door.

Did Jake have a death wish? Did he even remember how to fire a gun?

Xander and Randall raced through the kitchen, heading for the back door.

Alexa sank to her knees and pressed both her hands to the wound at Trent's shoulder, now wishing she had the oxy back. "You'll be okay." She kept her hands over the bloody hole as she stared at the open door through which Jake had fled.

A gust of wind suddenly slammed it shut, and she found herself alone with Trent.

# CHAPTER FIFTEEN

JAKE HELD THE COMPACT FIREARM IN HIS HANDS AS HE PURSUED the gunman. The grainy, pebbly feel of the metal handle felt like he had slipped a well-worn leather glove over his fingers.

It was familiar. It fit.

The shooter dodged shots, his white ski jacket and matching pants blending and blurring into the snowy terrain, and then appearing in stark contrast against the dark Douglas firs.

And then he was gone.

Jake blinked as he searched for the shooter. Had he fallen through the ice on the pond?

No, not this time of year.

And the guy wouldn't flee the scene until the job was done. So, where the hell was he?

Jake hunkered down and scanned the yard, ignoring the bruising pain in his body and the lashing cold chill as winter burned his face.

"Come and get me, you asshole," Jake shouted when he saw Randall and Xander sprinting around the side of the house. He shut his eyes and listened. If only he could be the man he had once been

—just for a second. Of course, maybe he was already becoming him again.

Then again, a trained FBI agent probably wouldn't have gone right out the front door in plain sight.

Jake opened his eyes and peeked over his shoulder. Randall and Xander had disappeared.

A wave of dizziness washed over him. Was this just another one of his sick dreams?

"Did you kill my team?" Jake slowly stood, hoping that the shooter would show himself if Jake drew his fire. Wherever Randall and Xander happened to be, Jake hoped they would be faster on the draw than the man who had begun this attack.

Of course, there could be more than one guy, right?

He extended the gun forward, holding it tight between his palms, his finger resting gently on the trigger. Then his stomach began to roil, and his head sagged as memories clawed to the surface. *Shit, not now.* He groaned as he faltered, his arms lowering as he took a step back. The snow was thick and heavy here. It clung to his calves.

And then, somehow, everything changed.

His eyes widened, and his body trembled. Surrounding him were crumbling, war-torn buildings that had been obliterated by recent bombings and the raining of gunfire. Before Jake was his friend who had visited him at the hospital, Michael Maddox. Michael was sprawled out on the ground, trying to rise despite the blood that dripped into the dirt beneath him. Michael was gasping for air, but he wasn't giving up. Before him was another Marine with a knife to his throat.

"No!" Jake screamed, and he wasn't sure if he was saying it now or if he'd shouted it back then. He squeezed his eyes tight, trying to comprehend what was real and what was the past as he heard the sound of a bullet splicing fast through the cold air.

His eyes flashed open as he saw the shooter lying face down in the snow some fifty feet away. The gunshots he'd heard—he had thought they were in his head, but apparently not because the snow seeped red, soaking with blood like a disgusting slushy.

Randall took giant steps, trudging through the snow in his direction, while Xander approached the shooter's body, gun still drawn. The faint sound of sirens pierced the air as Jake lowered his weapon.

"Shit!" Randall tapped Jake on the shoulder as he passed by, lifting his feet high up over the snow with every step. It only took him a moment to realize where Randall was going. The two agents who had been posted outside the house for security were still in the car in the driveway and seemed very still.

"He's dead!" Xander straightened up from crouching over the shooter's body. "Jesus Christ. We needed him alive!"

Xander's lips continued to move, but Jake turned his head, focusing solely on the agents in the car. Was he responsible for their deaths, too?

Flashing blue and red was all the movement Jake could see at the end of the driveway. Randall waved his arms over his head, running toward the ambulance. "I need a medic over here!"

# CHAPTER SIXTEEN

Alexa's pulse spiked as a slow ribbon of heat tore through her body. Jake's hands were on her.

*"I'm going to touch you everywhere, Alexa,"* Jake whispered in her ear, and her heart raced.

Her shoulders shook as she clutched at her chest and blinked her eyes open.

"Shit, where am I?" she mumbled, trying to slow her heartbeat although her body still clenched with need.

"At the police station in Helena."

It was Jake's voice—low, husky, and sexy as hell.

She sat upright, realizing she'd been leaning against Jake as she slept, dreaming about their time together last year. "Oh."

Dear God, what if she had said something? What if she had moaned?

"I don't even remember coming here," she admitted.

He stood, bracing his leg. He shouldn't have gone running after the shooter—for multiple reasons.

"Any updates on the agents?" It was coming back to her now— the agents parked outside had been flown via helicopter to the hospital in Helena, which was better equipped for emergency surgery than the clinic in the small town where the ranch was located.

"One of the agents didn't make it, but the other—well, he's in surgery. The doctors are optimistic." His face was grim, and she could tell he was blaming himself. "Trent's fine," he added. "He'll have a sling on his arm for a bit."

"Oh." She rubbed her hands down her face, hating that they lost someone. She wished they still had the shooter alive to interrogate him. Randall hadn't aimed to kill, but he'd been off by a few centimeters, and the bullet had nicked the man's heart. Now they wouldn't be able to pump the gunman for information.

"There was just the one shooter, right?"

"Looks like it."

"How long have I been asleep?" she asked after a few moments stretched across the room.

"Just an hour or two."

"And have you been sitting with me this whole time?" Her voice was soft as she stood, and he turned to face her, nodding.

"And how are you holding up?"

The stubble on his jaw was thicker than yesterday, and his lips were raw. Some crazy part of her wanted to kiss those lips—to try and make him feel better in any way that she could. To make her feel better, too. To pretend they hadn't lost any lives—and they were just two normal people who didn't stand between life and death.

"I'm fine, but—"

She angled her head and focused on his eyes as she waited for him to continue.

"He was there."

"He?"

"The shooter." He swallowed. "He was in London. He wasn't responsible for thrashing my back, I don't think. But he was there before the explosion. I'd never forget those eyes. I'd been looking right into them before the bomb went off."

"You recall the explosion?" She nearly choked on her words. Did he remember her, too?

"A little. I was at a factory or something, and then I saw that shooter. I worked at the vest, trying to get it off. Then I jumped out a window." He tapped at his skull with a closed fist. "I must know something if he came all the way over here to shut me down." He clenched his hands at his sides and took a step closer to Alexa, which had her taking a deep breath.

"The damn memories are hanging there, so close, but I can't seem to grab them. But soon, Alexa . . . and then we'll bring these sons of bitches down."

His sudden confidence was a message to her—Jake was coming back.

The Marine. The agent. The man who had swept her off her feet . . .

Before she could say anything, the creaking sound of the door pushing open had her mouth going tight.

"We have orders." It was Xander.

She nodded at him and brushed past Jake, wondering what would happen between the two of them when Jake finally did remember everything . . .

She followed Xander out of the office and into a conference room two doors down. She didn't check to see if Jake trailed behind her. Then again, she didn't need to. She could feel his presence. It was like warmth and comfort moving through her, wrapping her tight.

For some reason, it was like she didn't need to be as composed, firm, and steely when she was around Jake. With him, she could be herself, without worrying about appearing weak. He made her feel delicate, almost. Fragile. And for a small glimmer of a moment, she liked the idea of being like that, of allowing someone to protect her, to make her feel safe.

She hadn't felt like that since her father had died. She had always been Daddy's little princess, a girl who played with dolls . . . and now she played with guns. So much had changed.

As she sat down at the conference table, her hand unconsciously fluttered to the scar at her side, and she closed her eyes.

"You okay?" Jake's mouth was at her ear, his hand on her back as he took the chair next to her.

Wasn't she supposed to be the one asking that?

"I'm fine," she murmured and opened her eyes, turning her attention to Randall and Xander, who were the only other men in the room.

Xander stood with crossed arms on the other side of the long, maple table. "The CIA, FBI, and NSA are teaming up to try and get at Kemal Bekas and the members of Anarchy at every angle possible," Xander began, his voice tightly controlled. "They'll be working full throttle on this. The time for chasing and waiting for Bekas to slip up is over." Alexa could detect his seething anger in the wry smile he shot her way. "We're taking Bekas out, one way or another, within the next week."

*Within a week?* They'd been after Bekas for a year and a half, almost. That they could meet this goal in only a week felt . . . well, surreal. Alexa's face flushed; her body trembled.

"I can't believe the Joint Committee approved it," she said wonderingly. In 2015, the British government had established a panel of six members from the House of Lords and six from the House of Commons, to hold a special constitutional convention to debate the merit of drone strikes when taking out high-value targets.

The drone strike that killed Kemal Bekas's family had occurred a week before the establishment of the Joint Committee, or JOC. Once agents and military personnel had realized that the area wasn't clear as had been reported, the order to withhold the firing of the missiles came one second too late. The two-second delay between the pilot's joystick and the MQ-9 Drone Reaper had meant the deaths of Bekas's innocent daughters and wife.

When Xander didn't answer her question, Alexa knew why.

If MI6 was bypassing the JOC, they must have been turning this over to the Americans. If her government wouldn't authorize the capture or kill of Bekas, certainly the Americans would . . .

"What role will we play, then?" she asked softly. She didn't want to be cut out of this after all the time she'd spent hunting @Anarchy. She couldn't imagine that Laney would surrender easily, either. But Laney would always put her country ahead of her pride, which was one reason that Alexa knew she could trust her.

Jake pinched his brows together as Randall rounded the desk and came to stand next to Xander. "You'll be assisting us with intel —we'll keep you in the game. This is still your baby. But any orders to take down Bekas will not fall on you. MI6 will pull out before then to keep you all good with Parliament." Randall patted Xander on the back.

At least MI6 and the FBI finally appeared to be on the same page.

"Have you talked to Laney?" Alexa rubbed her hands against her jeaned thighs as she tried to adjust to the new situation. "Have we found out yet the origins of the intel that the NSA received that sent Jake and the agents to Sicily? Was it Anarchy?"

"Laney won't be able to take point on this, but she agrees with the change of plans," Xander answered. "And Sam has the intel from the NSA," he tipped his head toward Randall in thanks for supplying the transmissions, "but he hasn't yet traced the origins of the emails. He's still working on it."

"Okay," Alexa said. "So, what's the plan?"

"The CIA director has been in a briefing with the NSA director for the last hour. They're sending a team to Barcelona," Randall said. "And they have agreed to send the both of you, as well as

Xander and me, along. You know more about this case than anyone."

Alexa pushed away from the desk and stood. "Of course I'm in." She looked over at Jake, who was bracing against the table as if worried that he might fall out of his chair. His lips were tight, and his eyes cast down. "Should Jake be going? Anarchy tried to kill him," Alexa wondered aloud. He had a target on his head, after all. "And how the hell did they discover he's alive . . . and his location?"

"We're not sure how Anarchy found out. We're interviewing the few hospital members who were aware of his survival, as well as London PD. We'll find out how the information was leaked, and the responsible party will be held accountable." Xander's attention shifted to Jake as he slowly rose. "Do you want in, Jake? Now that they know you're alive, there's no reason to hide." Xander raised a fist to his mouth and cleared his throat. "Well, other than to stay safe."

*Staying alive. Sure, who wouldn't want that?* But a Marine and FBI agent would do what was right, and part of that scared Alexa. She didn't want anything to happen to Jake, especially when he still didn't remember exactly who he was.

"I'll help under one condition." Jake's eyes flashed up to Randall's face. "I want my family held somewhere safe until this is over. I don't want them becoming collateral damage because of me."

Her stomach squeezed at his words.

"Done," Randall said without hesitation.

"When do we leave?" Jake asked in a low voice, but Alexa raised her hand up in the air.

"I'd like to know why we're going to Barcelona." She stole a glimpse of Jake from the corner of her eye, and she realized he was nodding in agreement. How bizarre that her fling was now her colleague.

"I should have led with that news. Sorry," Xander said. "One good thing that came from the attack yesterday is that we got a new lead. Our facial recognition software identified the shooter. He goes by the name Ray, and he flew from London to Barcelona a few days ago before he came here," Xander said. "He's a British citizen with Egyptian origins. In his forties—a militant for hire. Has no known ideologies."

Jake walked up next to her and folded his arms.

"No connection to ISIS?" she asked.

"No," Xander responded.

*Good.* This confirmed her suspicions that ISIS and @Anarchy had nothing to do with one another. "So, why was Ray in Barcelona?" she asked.

"Because Reza is now in Barcelona, and since we're speeding up the timetable on Anarchy, we've decided to go after them hard and fast," Xander said. "Instead of merely stealing files, we're going to download malware onto Reza's computer so we can track his movements. And hopefully get a hit on what they're planning since we failed with Gregov's files."

Alexa rubbed a hand down her jaw. They'd considered such a move in the past, but the risk of detection had been deemed too high. If they got caught, their operation could be compromised—everything they'd built in their case could become useless if Reza knew they were on to him. "Can we take that chance? These guys are the best we've ever seen." *Well, almost the best.* There was still one hacker better. "Reza will pick up on it."

"We have to try, Alexa," Xander said solemnly.

"And we can't just take this Reza guy into custody and question him, right?" Jake's voice filled the room.

"The problem is that we know we won't be able to get Reza or anyone to talk, and I'm betting the attacks are already in motion—so killing Bekas and the rest will have no effect," Xander answered.

"You guys already have agents in Istanbul on Bekas, but we're sending some guys there, as well. Gregov is in Cyprus, so there are two additional men on the way there, too. We have the major players covered," Randall added.

"Yeah, I think I need some water. Excuse me," Jake said.

Alexa noticed Jake's hand sliding to his outer thigh as he exited the room, and she wondered how much additional pain he was now suffering as a result of his confrontation with the shooter earlier. "You sure bringing him along is what's best?" she asked Xander.

"We need his memories, Alexa." Xander came around and placed a hand on her shoulder. "There will be plenty of people who will have his back." His steely gray eyes steadied on hers, but she didn't find comfort in his words. Not even a little bit.

"Who is going to download the malware to Reza's computer?" she asked, and Xander dropped his hand and glanced at Randall. "I think I can do it," she offered, hardly believing it herself.

"No offense, Alexa, but this will be different from anything you've done before."

"What about Sam? He's good," she said.

"Sam's great, but I don't think he can do it. Besides, we need him working with the NSA to identify the source of the emails, to check out your hunch on that intel. And . . ."

"And what?" Her face blanched.

"Sam said our servers at MI6 are running a little slow. He said it's barely noticeable, but well, you know Sam. He noticed it. He's going through some diagnostic tests," Xander said.

*That's not good.* "So—who are we bringing in, then?" *Oh, God. Don't say it. Don't say his name.*

Xander gripped the flesh at his throat for a moment as his eyes shifted to the floor. "We need the absolute best hacker we can get. We have to bring in Jason Holms. I'm so sorry."

"Jesus Christ, Xander."

Jason Holms—the greatest living arsehole of all time.

Although Kemal Bekas was giving stiff competition for that spot.

*No. No. No!*

"You know that's the last thing I want, too, but we have no choice—" Xander started, but she didn't care to hear any more. She turned away from him, and when he placed a hand on her arm, she yanked herself free, too bloody pissed off to even look at her friend.

How could he go to Jason for help? He knew she couldn't work with the man, and Xander had his own reasons for hating him. It was absurd.

Alexa hurried out of the room, feeling as though her lungs were coated with paint—sticky, heavy, hardly inflating.

She bent forward and clutched her chest.

"You okay?"

Alexa's gaze slid up Jake's strong, jeaned legs, and then found his torso before lifting to his face. "Yeah." She merely mouthed the word, unable to speak.

She straightened, and he placed a hand on her shoulder as his brows furrowed. "You don't look okay."

Of course, she wasn't okay. She could hardly believe this was happening. But she softly responded, "I'll be fine once this is all over." She forced herself to move past him and get outside, desperately longing for the harsh slap of winter on her skin.

# CHAPTER SEVENTEEN

THE CONSTANT HUMMING NOISE AND THE VIBRATION BENEATH Alexa's feet was like a serenade when one was sleepy, making it even easier to drift off into the night. And the soothing, turbulence-free ride was what she needed right now.

She'd been unwilling to sit next to Xander on the plane, and so she had swapped with Randall. But that presented a new problem. She was now shoulder to shoulder with Jake.

She reached for the glass of wine—well, the plastic cup of wine—that the flight attendant had given her a few moments ago and swallowed the chardonnay. It wasn't the best in the world, but it would suffice.

In seven days or less, the @Anarchy case might be over. She only hoped it would end without any further bloodshed unless that blood came from the men of @Anarchy.

Alexa set her cup down and casually glanced over at Jake. He was looking out the small window, his eyes focused on the plane wing as white puffs parted around it. He had dyed his hair dark—an espresso brown color, and he was growing his stubble into a beard. When he exited the bathroom earlier, black framed reading glasses perched on his nose, she almost hadn't recognized him.

His new look was part sexy mountain man and part nerdy teacher. He'd been garnering glances from the flight attendants and even from the mom who'd been walking up and down the aisle, trying to soothe her crying baby. Alexa could understand the stares —Jake was sinfully hot.

He stretched his long legs out in front of him and shifted his broad shoulders against the seat, arching his back against the pillow that created a wedge between the lashings on his back and the not-so pliant airplane seat. She bet that it was going to be a long flight for him.

They had only spoken a few words here and there since the meeting at the police station. She wasn't sure what his mood was about her right now.

She couldn't help but remember the first time they had met. He'd offered her a glass of champagne after his eyes found hers from across the room moments before.

When he had smiled at her, his face lit up. His gorgeous dimples making her speechless.

"Alexa?"

"Hm?" She blinked and tipped up her chin to meet his deep brown eyes.

"You nervous at all?"

Her fingers brushed across her collarbone and slid down the front of her black cashmere sweater. "I always get a little nervous when I go on—" Alexa stopped herself—she had almost forgotten she was on a plane full of civilians. "Yeah, I am." For more reasons than one.

Tomorrow wasn't bloody well guaranteed.

She thought about Jason Holms, the two-faced bastard and ex-boyfriend she would be working with in Barcelona. He wasn't the reason for her lack of a love life—he hadn't stolen her ability to love. No, but he stole her ability to trust. Still, the agency held the strongest claim on her life. As long as she was buried in undercover operations and bouncing around the globe, she would never get the opportunity to know if she were even capable of trusting a man again.

Jake's arm was draped over the armrest, his fingers curved over the end, clenching tightly. His muscular biceps rippled strength beneath his long-sleeved, brown cotton shirt. What she wouldn't give for another week of bliss with Jake, like the one they'd shared last year. She'd damn near sell her soul if it meant spending even one day wrapped up in those arms.

"I'm not nervous," he said with a calm ease, an almost impassive look on his face.

Jake's words pulled her right out of her head, and her gaze snapped back up to his face. "You're not?" she asked with disbelief.

"I'm not sure what to make of that, either." He raised his arm and rested a fist against his lips—lips she suddenly had the fighting need to kiss. "How can I not be nervous about what we're going to do?" he asked in a low voice.

She glanced around at the plane full of passengers, and at that mom who came walking by again, bouncing her baby, wrapped in a soft blue blanket, in her arms.

It wasn't safe to talk too much. "I think you're settling back into your life. The pieces are fitting together more and more as you remember. And this is becoming natural to you, this life."

"But you've got nerves. So, shouldn't I?"

But she always got nervous, even when she was confident about a mission. "We're all different." Her arm went over the armrest, and she touched his leg, trying to reassure him, but it also produced a tingling sensation in her fingers.

"Alexa." The vein in his neck throbbed, and she watched his Adam's apple move as he swallowed. He touched her wrist, shifting it back to her lap. A feeling of rejection sputtered through her, and she looked away.

But out of the corner of her eye, she noticed him raising the armrest.

He reached for her hand and brought it back to his thigh, where he laced his fingers with hers. Then he shut his eyes and tilted his head back. She stared at their intertwined hands as if she were studying a work of art—trying to interpret its meaning.

And then she, too, shut her eyes. Some things were better left alone.

\* \* \*

"THAT IS COMPLETELY CLICHÉ." ALEXA FOLDED HER ARMS AND eyed Xander, noting the mischievous look in his eyes. What the hell was he trying to pull—salvaging her love life while also taking down terrorists? Of course, it wouldn't be the first time Xander had tried to play matchmaker. "I am not rooming with Jake." She looked over as the man in question leaned against a white column in the hotel lobby. Jake's gaze was on her, his eyes questioning.

She shook her head and looked back at Xander. "Why can't you and I be the honeymoon couple?"

"I thought you hated me right now."

"Shit. I do." She bit her lip. "But still—"

Xander tapped the small envelope against his jeaned thigh—inside it were the two keycards for the honeymoon suite. "What are you afraid of? There are two separate rooms in the suite. Two beds."

"I'm not afraid of anything, but—"

"Good. It's settled." He handed her the envelope. "Randall and I are checking into Reza's hotel across the street." The team didn't want Jake in the same hotel with Reza. They had to assume that Reza knew what Jake looked like, and they weren't sure if his disguise would hold up under scrutiny.

"Are you and Randall sharing a room?" She squinted at him as a smile met her lips.

"No, but—"

"Bloody hypocrite." She shook her head. "Fine. What's the plan?"

Xander looked at the large face on his wristwatch. "It's late. Randall and I will meet with the other Americans who are arriving here in a few hours."

"And Jason? When does that arsehole get here? Who is escorting him?"

"Matt was going to come, but he's heading to Istanbul to meet with Tenley and John, instead. Our informant, Berat, is missing."

"That's not good." Alexa wasn't sure how much more bad news she could tolerate.

"Christ, I know."

"Tell me you have some positive news. Like, did Sam find anything out?" Xander had called HQ before they checked in and this was the first update she was getting. "How were the diagnostic tests on our servers?"

"No news, yet." He released a deep, frustrated breath. "I'm getting a bad feeling, Alexa."

She was, too, but the fact that Xander was willing to admit how bad things seemed made her even more worried.

"Anyways, Seth is heading here in the morning with Jason." Alexa remembered that Laney had originally planned to assign Seth to Jake's case before they discovered the explosion was related to @Anarchy.

"Matt really approves working with Jason?" she asked in surprise.

"It wasn't his call—Laney's orders." Xander touched her elbow and urged her farther off to the side of the lobby where no one was standing. "We need Jason's help, Alexa. I hate saying that. You know I do. I despise the bastard, but he's the absolute best hacker we've ever encountered. If we're going to have a chance at this, we need him."

Jason should never have been allowed to consult with MI6. He should have been locked up in a maximum-security prison.

"I need a drink." She glanced back at Jake.

"Get some rest. I'll come to your room in the morning before we meet up with the crew at my place." Xander patted her on the shoulder and started for the sliding doors of the hotel entrance.

She fidgeted with the envelope in her hand before striding across the lobby and over to Jake. There was a small duffel bag by his feet—they'd done some last-minute shopping at the airport in Chicago during their layover. They hadn't had time to go back to Jake's ranch, which meant that he didn't have medication to treat his wounds. They'd have to stop at a pharmacy at some point.

"I need a shower and something strong to drink," she said. Thoughts of Jason hovered above her like a dark, ominous rain cloud.

"We still sharing a room?" He reached for the bag, and she could have sworn he was hiding a smile.

"Yeah. You good with that?"

He lifted his brows. "As long as you are."

She looked past his shoulder and at the boutique that was off to the side of the lobby. "Here's your key." She handed it to him. "I'm going to get us something to wear that's a bit nicer than jeans."

"Why do we need to look nice?" He cocked his head to the side.

"We're close to the boardwalk." She shrugged. "We can grab a bite to eat and have a drink."

"Is it safe to leave the hotel . . . with Reza so close?"

"If there's one thing I've learned, it's how to blend in."

Jake raised a brow. "Blend in. You?"

She slapped at his pecs, and then quickly retracted her arm. "And you're rocking a new look, too. So, we'll be good, yeah?" She could feel a sudden heat emanating from Jake, and she wondered what was going on in his head.

He cleared his throat. "Well, maybe I should at least pick out my own clothes."

She dragged her gaze up and down the length of his body. "I've got it covered." She winked, trying to ignore the small lump of fear that was beginning to unfurl within her.

But she was a good actress, at least. For one night, she could pretend that everything was okay.

"I'll be up in twenty minutes. Why don't you hop in the shower?" She started to turn toward the shop, but he caught her by the wrist.

"Nothing too stuffy," he said as his eyes met hers.

She laughed. "I know."

Alexa could feel his eyes on her as she went into the store. Her fingers danced across the fabric of a red silk dress that hung beautifully on a mannequin. She'd worn a similar dress on the night she'd first met Jake.

But it wasn't exactly New Year's Eve anymore, was it? Still, she wanted to look nice. She might never see Jake again after the case was over. Maybe they could make the most of the little time they had . . . as they had last year.

A stabbing pain of regret wrapped its way around her throat. What if he remembered how things really ended between them? Would he hate her for holding back the truth?

She pushed the worry aside as she stopped in front of another mannequin wearing the perfect outfit. She was determined to enjoy this night because she had to become Agent Ryan again in the morning.

And when the sun kissed the sky, and the folds of darkness fell away—she'd have to face Jason.

But tonight, she could be the woman Jake had kissed on New Year's Eve.

# CHAPTER EIGHTEEN

JAKE FACED THE STEAMING HOT WATER IN THE SHOWER, CAREFUL to keep his back out of the spray. The scalding water would destroy him if it touched his scars.

He shut his eyes and tipped his face up, relishing in the heat. Then he heard a door open and close. Alexa must have been back.

A night walking around Barcelona with Alexa seemed almost too good to be true. Xander had said they wouldn't be diving into anything until tomorrow, so there was no point in ruining the night, right? Besides, it was almost sixty degrees outside, and he was less than a mile from the Mediterranean Sea. It was a nice change from the negative temperatures of Montana. Hell, a nice change from everything.

He only wished Alexa would open up to him more. As frustrated as he had been the other night at the ranch, he didn't have it in him to hang on to the anger. He was dealing with far too much reconciling the past with the present, distinguishing between memories and nightmares. When he had fallen asleep on the plane ride over, he'd woken up with sweat on his brow and chest, his hands firmly locked against his thighs as he remembered standing over his grandfather's casket, saying goodbye one last time, with his sister weeping at his side.

"I'm back!" Alexa called out from behind the closed door. "Gonna jump in the other shower."

"Okay," he answered, turning his shoulder as he did. The hot water splashed against his shoulder blade and skated down his back—burning his wounds. "Fuck," he moaned under his breath, pounding a fist against the wall.

Then he bowed his head as he turned around and decided to allow the water to lash his back. His shoulders jerked, and he winced, but he forced himself to remain, inviting the heat to strike at his scars.

Punishment for living when his teammates in Italy had died.

Punishment for an agent dying in Montana when his job had been to protect Jake—and he did so with his own life.

His biceps tightened as he fought against the pain threading through his body, wrapping itself around every one of his limbs. Strangling him.

His hands curled into fists, pressing against the tiled shower wall as his breathing became labored.

And when he could no longer feel anything, when he was numb, he finally turned off the shower and stepped out.

He yanked a plush white towel from the back of the door and scrubbed his face with it before draping it around his waist, cringing as the material touched his skin like a blade ripping open old wounds.

He released a sobering breath and wiped the steam from the large mirror, bracing against the counter as he studied his image.

He was a long way from the teacher he'd planned to be. While a history teacher taught about the world, he had been making history. In the crossfires of death.

He shifted his body to view as much of his back as he could. The crisscross patterns were a reminder of the impending terrorist attack, and that he might know something to help stop it.

"Focus," Jake whispered to himself as he shut his eyes and pressed his fingers against his eyelids. He took a deep breath and tried to pull forth the memories, but it was like a black veil had dropped over his mind. Pokes of light pierced the darkness, but they didn't reveal what awful truths his mind was hiding from him.

A low whistle sounded from his lips as he exhaled and opened his eyes.

When he returned to the bedroom, there was a bag of clothes on the bed.

His frustrations were momentarily buried beneath a smile as he thought about her picking out clothes for him. The woman had thought things through—black slacks and socks, a white button-down shirt, and even a pair of loafers.

He checked the size of each—how the hell did she know? Was that a talent of MI6 agents?

When he entered the living area, he was dressed in the clothes she had bought him. Her door was still shut, and he could hear a hair dryer beyond the door. He went over to the window and looked out over the city, which appeared as a blanket of glittering lights below. Street lamps and restaurant signs illuminated the walkways, compact cars and motorbikes crawled past palm trees and mini parks. It would be a nice place to vacation. He'd always wanted to try authentic Spanish cuisine.

His hand went to the glass as his body became heavy and head light—the contrast making him dizzy. Maybe he'd overdone it with the shower. Then his jaw clenched tight, and he was overcome with the feeling that hot rocks were burning his chest. Jake realized that his mind was trying to peel back another memory.

"The clothes fit."

At the sound of Alexa's voice, Jake released his breath and lost whatever had attempted to rise from the dead part of his mind.

"No glasses tonight, I see," she said when he faced her.

His eyes roamed over her body. She was wearing fitted black jeans with black heels. A black leather jacket was draped over her black, V-neck top. She looked lethal all in black, like a spy from an action flick. And she looked hot—entirely too damn delicious for him to resist. She raised a hand to her cheek, and then pushed it through her long, wavy locks. "You ready to get out of here? We can slip out the side exit, so we don't run into Reza if he happens to be leaving his hotel at the same time."

He raised his hand to his mouth and tapped a fist at his lips for a moment before pulling it away. "You look nice," he finally said.

"Thank you." She tipped her head to the door. "Let's get out of here."

"And you're sure Xander won't kill us?" Not that he really cared what Xander, or even Randall, thought. But he also knew this wasn't a vacation.

"I'll worry about him. Besides, he might be my boss, but I'm pissed at him right now. I think he'd understand my need to have a drink." She started for the door. "Or five."

Jake came up next to her. "Why are you angry at him?" he asked when they were alone in the elevator.

She chewed on her bottom lip for a moment, and Jake wondered if she and Xander had ever been a couple. He took an uneasy step back. Every moment with her just twisted his emotions tighter.

But when his eyes landed on hers, he saw that they had become glittering gems, coated over with a sheen of liquid. Was she going to cry? He moved forward without thinking, closing the gap between them, but as he did, the elevator doors parted. Just outside the door, someone cleared his voice, signaling the presence of an outsider.

Alexa straightened her shoulders and quickly brushed past Jake as he nodded at the elderly couple waiting to board the elevator.

"Alexa?" He caught up to her and reached for her wrist. "What's wrong?"

She didn't turn to face him, but she halted in her steps. "Can we get a drink and pretend that the world doesn't exist?" She sighed. "That my ex-boyfriend Jason hasn't been invited to work the case with us tomorrow."

*Ex?!* He released his grip and waited a moment before following after her.

When they reached the outside, he paused on the sidewalk, allowing his lungs to fill up with the night air. He couldn't ask for anything more than this beautiful night . . . well, other than not to have the threat of a terrorist attack looming over his head. Or for Alexa to be upset.

"You coming?" Alexa looked back over her shoulder at him, and he nodded and caught up with her.

"Have you been here before?" she asked as they walked down the crowded street toward the boardwalk.

"No, but I've always wanted to come."

"Probably not like this, though, huh?"

He smiled and pushed his hands into his pockets, resisting the strange urge to hold her hand. "No, not so much. How about you?"

"Been to Madrid on a case, but never here. And I was pretty much stuck inside a van the entire time, behind a computer screen." She tucked her hair behind her ear, revealing a small diamond stud.

"So, you're a cyber expert? That's your thing?"

Her lips spread into a beautiful smile. "Yeah, that's my thing."

"How long have you been doing it? I know I'm not making you repeat yourself since we clearly wouldn't have had this conversation last year." He peeked at her and noticed her eyes cast down at the pavement.

"No, we didn't talk about our work."

"Did you give me a cover story?"

"I told you I worked with computers. So, not a total lie. I've been with MI6 for eight years now. I was recruited from my job when I was twenty-five."

"Hm." He looked straight ahead and tried to hide the pain that had begun to dart up his leg. This was the most he'd walked since the explosion—although he'd stupidly run after the shooter. Now, he was paying for it. "What'd I tell you that I did for work?" He was curious about their time together; he wished more than anything that he could remember more than their one kiss. Even though the memories weren't in his mind, he could feel them inside—in his heart. The woman must have made one hell of an impression.

"Well, you said you had some boring government job in Dallas. I guess you weren't too interested in sharing your line of work either, even though—"

"I'm not some kickass spy like you."

She laughed. "My job isn't all that exciting. It's for sure nothing like the movies."

As they approached the boardwalk, where the sidewalks bustled with people, and he could hear the soft sounds of the Mediterranean Sea eating at the sand, he stopped and faced her. "Tell me one thing. Do you really have all those gadgets from the Q branch, like in Bond films?"

"We have a few things. But if I told you," she said, squinting, "I'd have to kill you."

He held his hands up in the air and amusement flashed over her face.

They both remained quiet for a moment, standing still as they looked into each other's eyes. He knew she could feel what he was feeling—the tension, the pull between them . . .

He finally broke contact by rubbing a hand down the nape of his neck and looking out at the sea. "What else did we do when I was in London?"

"We went shopping, which is how I knew your size. You wanted some trendy new digs, so you had said, and we spent a couple hours bouncing around the city as you rejected almost all the clothes I had you try on."

"What on earth did you try and get me to wear?"

"Oh, you know . . ." She paused as her brows pulled

together. "I—oh wow, I have pictures. I don't know why I didn't think about it before. They might help you remember something."

"You kept pictures of us?" His eyes went to her hands, which now clutched her phone.

She looked up at him and nodded. "I kept a couple."

He watched her swallow like she was uneasy. "You going to share them or what?"

"I want you to remember, but—"

"But you're afraid?" He cocked his head, studying her. How could this woman fight terrorists but be fearful of her own feelings?

"A little."

"Why?" His hand curved up to her cheek as he stepped in closer.

"Because then last year becomes real. You become real."

His hand fell from her face, and he reached for her wrist and raised it to his chest, pressing her hand near his heart. "I am real, Alexa. Memories or not, I'm right here in front of you."

She kept her eyes over his shoulder, her lip trembling just enough to notice.

"Look at me, Alexa."

"I—I can't."

"Why not?" he rasped.

"Because I'm afraid of wanting you, Jake." She yanked her arm free and turned away in a hurry, starting back down the sidewalk.

He lowered his head and rubbed his palms down his face, taking a minute to breathe, and then he went after her, but he couldn't move as fast as he wanted with the damn pain spiraling up his side.

He didn't catch up to her again until she stopped outside a restaurant. "Listen, Alexa, I'm—"

"In the mood for some tapas?" she interrupted him, forcing a smile to her face, and he could tell the real Alexa was gone. In her place was the actress who played the part of an MI6 agent.

"Sure," he grumbled, annoyed to be adding her caginess to the long list of issues he had to face.

He swung open the door and motioned her in.

The hostess ushered them through the restaurant, past a glass wall where hundreds of wine bottles were displayed. The wood floors, which looked like board planks from an old ship, stretched along across the entire room. There was a man playing a grand piano and singing in Spanish, just off to the side of a small dance area, where a few couples were slowly turning to the music. The dim lighting and music were entirely too romantic for Jake's mood.

He sat down opposite of Alexa and listened politely as the hostess rattled off the chef's specialties. Once the hostess had left, Alexa pressed her hands to her lap and leaned back against the red leather, looking out at the dance floor.

"This is nice," she said over the music. "Being here makes me almost forget everything." She looked up at him from beneath long lashes, and he stiffened as her eyes found his. Her cheeks blushed, dark beneath the soft lighting. "What a poor choice of words, about the forgetting . . . I'm so sorry."

"It's fine."

The waitress appeared just then. Alexa ordered a sangria and some tapas to share. Jake wasn't all that hungry, however. A Jack and Coke was about all he wanted.

He tried to relax but after subjecting his flesh to the hot water in the shower, he had to stay as upright as possible. His hand slipped beneath the table and he gripped his thigh, willing away the achiness.

"You're hurting." It was a statement, not a question.

He hadn't realized she could tell. He'd been doing his best to hide it, afraid they might pull him off the case if he showed any weakness. Jake shook his head and glanced around the restaurant, unable to look her in the eyes. "I'm good."

"We should stop by a pharmacy soon and get you something for your back. I could help—"

His hand went in the air. "I don't need it."

"Yeah, but—"

The waitress arrived, effectively cutting her off. He was grateful for the distraction and nodded his thanks and whisked the tumbler off the table and raised it to his lips.

"I'm sorry, Jake," she said after a few minutes of awkward silence.

"For what?"

"For being such a bloody coward when it comes to you." She pushed her hand into the pocket of her jacket and grabbed her phone. She tapped at it and then swiped her finger a few times before offering it to him.

He took it as if she were handing him a grenade. Slowly. Cautiously.

On the screen was an image of himself. He was standing in front of a tall mirror wearing a long, wool, tweed coat accompanied by a top hat. He looked like Sherlock Holmes. He had a ridiculous smile on his face. "This is what you recommended for a trendy look?" He couldn't help but grin.

"Oh, that one was your idea." She bent forward to swipe at her phone, and his eyes drifted down to the top of her blouse, where the swell of her flesh was exposed.

She glanced up, catching him in the act. She sat back down and reached for her glass.

He looked at the new photo and shook his head. "Come on? What is this? A yellow blazer and scarf? You have got to be kidding."

She pressed a hand to her lips, stifling a laugh. "You look adorable."

"Ha. Adorable isn't exactly what a guy wants to be!"

She held her palms up. "Okay. Okay. You didn't buy it—no worries."

"I would hope not." He swiped to the next image, and his lips parted as he gaped at it.

"Where is this?"

"In the London Eye. The Ferris wheel."

It was a selfie of them kissing. Their eyes were closed as their lips touched in the photo.

"Those are the only ones I have."

"Interesting ones to save." He handed her back the phone and took a drink. The liquor warmed his chest.

"Sorry to disappoint you. I got rid of the sex tapes."

He almost choked on his drink. As she chuckled, he wiped his mouth with the back of his hand, his eyes narrowing on her as he wondered what might happen later tonight.

"Kidding." She waved a hand in the air. "I'd never get rid of those." Her eyes pierced his, and he could feel his body thrumming with excitement, with desire.

He needed another drink, he realized as he swallowed the smooth liquid, enjoying the way it eased the sorrow inside him.

A soft English song began to wail from the singer, and it had Jake slowly shifting out of the booth to stand. He extended his hand, holding it palm up, waiting for her. "Dance with me."

"What?" She looked over at the dance floor where a couple was moving in a slow and steady rhythm. "This is crazy."

"Nothing about our lives is exactly normal, is it?"

"Good point." She stood, graceful despite her black heels, and tucked her hand inside his, allowing him to guide her to the small dance area.

He pulled Alexa close to him, sharing a smile with the couple to his right. He brought his hand to the base of her back, feeling the soft leather of her jacket. She tipped her chin up, and his eyes captured hers. "You're beautiful."

She smiled up at him, and his chin rested against the top of her head when she stepped closer to him, pressing her cheek to his chest. They moved side to side, barely dancing. More importantly, he was holding her in his arms.

When the song ended, Jake stepped back, and their eyes met. He knew one thing with all certainty—he needed this woman more than he needed their memories together. The here and now would be more than enough.

He placed a fist beneath her chin and guided her face closer to his.

"When I kiss you, Alexa, I want you to do something for me," he said in a husky voice.

Her eyes remained fixed on his. "What?" she asked softly.

"I want you to kiss me back," he said gruffly before he lowered his face to meet hers and kissed her parted lips.

* * *

ALEXA'S BACK HIT THE DOOR, AND JAKE PRESSED A HAND TO THE wall alongside it as his lips worked over her mouth. It felt like he was stealing her breath, reaching into the very depths of her existence with every slow kiss.

"Key," she mumbled, the word vibrating against his mouth as she shoved her hand into her pocket in search for the card.

As she found the small piece of plastic between her fingers, his hand came down on hers, and he pulled it toward the door. He was breathing heavily, and his large, muscular chest moved as his eyes darted down to her breasts, which were aching to be touched by him.

It had been too long. Too damn long since a man touched her. Since a man she had truly desired had been allowed within reach.

"Hurry," she cried as Jake swiped the card and the green light came on.

She stepped to the side as he shoved the door open with one hard push, and then grabbed her wrist and pulled her in after him. Her purse fell to the floor at her feet, and her back was once again to the wall, but this time within the safety of their hotel room. Alexa angled her head, and a soft hiss released from her lips as he kissed her neck and gently tugged fistfuls of her hair. She'd been thinking about this moment since she laid eyes on him at the cabin in Montana. It was almost unreal.

Her fingers moved over the material of his dress shirt, landing on the strip of buttons down the center. She began to work at them without breaking their kiss.

He shifted her jacket back and pushed her shirt off one shoulder, his lips moving up her throat and over the skin there, as well. Her body sizzled with his every touch.

She had vowed never to have sex while on a mission, but somehow she could find nothing in her that cared.

She pressed her hands to his chest and pushed him back a little. He straightened and ran a hand over his head as his smoldering eyes remained on hers. Her fingers skimmed up his open shirt, and she yanked it back off of him, exposing his tan chest and hard, sculpted body. He was so strong—a man with a body that could protect her.

A body that was injured.

"Are you okay for this?" she asked, her stupidity crashing over her like a cold wave. How could she not have remembered his pain?

"Damn, Alexa. I think this is the only thing I'm okay for." He pulled her back to him, his naked chest slamming hard against her breasts as he pressed both palms to her cheeks. He stared at her for a long second, and then his mouth seized hers once again.

Her chest heaved as his hand glided down her neck to the base of her throat, and then traveled beneath her shirt and bra, pinching her nipple. His other hand cupped her ass, his fingertips biting into the material of her pants. She instinctively pressed her groin against his hard-on, needing to feel him.

A few intense moments later, Jake stepped back again and reached for her hand.

"Wait." She bent forward and grabbed her purse, searching inside for the small box she'd purchased at the gift store. "I, uh, bought these . . . just in case," she said as a smile danced up to his eyes.

He took the three-pack of condoms from her and raised a brow. "Only three?"

She chuckled, and he gently pulled her along to his bedroom. Alexa took in a calm breath as she crossed the threshold, grappling with the reality of being in Jake's arms once more.

A tinge of guilt over their past filtered into her lungs, causing her to inhale sharply as he looked at her. They were standing in front of the bed in his room, which was dimly lit by the light that spilled through from the bathroom.

Then a ribbon of heat tore through her, making her forget the guilt, the regret. When the sun came up in the morning, they'd be two agents focused on destroying a terrorist organization. But right now, they were two people who needed to feel something deeper than they could manage alone.

"Are you sure you can do this?" she couldn't help but ask again, even though she'd probably lose her mind if he answered no. She was too primed for the moment.

He tossed the box on the bed behind her, then came at her so fast she stumbled backward and fell onto the bed. He leaned over her in one quick movement, and she tried to ignore when he squeezed his eyes against the pain . . . but when his brown eyes settled back onto hers, his one arm bracing himself above her, she knew he wouldn't let anything get in their way.

Her hand curved around his neck, gently drawing him closer. "I don't know if I've ever wanted anything more," she whispered against his lips, and he shifted back just enough so their eyes could meet again.

"Ditto." His eyes smiled, his dimples deepened, and then he kissed her again. It was a kiss that obliterated all other kisses. It started warm and tender. Then, when his tongue found hers, the kiss intensified, almost bruising her in a sinfully delicious way.

He groaned, or maybe it was a growl. To her, it sounded raw. Carnal.

He moved to his side, probably trying to find a more comfortable position for his back. They remained like that for a few minutes, simply enjoying each other's mouths and the feel of their hands on each other.

Both their shirts were off now, and she sat up to unsnap her bra. Then she stood and unzipped her jeans, watching the way Jake's eyes followed her hands—her every movement—as he sat up, bracing against the bed with a hand on either side of his legs.

Her fingertips had glided over her swollen lips before she kicked off her heels and pushed her pants down. Standing before him only in her flesh colored knickers, Jake reached out and placed his hands on her hips. He gently urged her forward, and his lips brushed warm kisses across her belly button before his fingers caressed her hipbone.

Then he pulled back, his brows pinching together.

"What?" she asked in a daze as she looked down at him.

He tipped his chin up to look at her. "Your scar . . ."

"Hm?" Her hand came down to cover his, which was resting over the thin, six-centimeter mark on her hip.

He'd noticed the scar the first time they had sex, and he hadn't pressed then. Would he now?

He leaned forward and kissed her scar, and she snapped her eyes closed, her chest constricting as emotions wedged deep in her throat. She rested her fingers over his shoulder blades, trying to maintain her composure. But her mind drew up images of her past—the good and the bad—and she felt as if the weight of her feelings would bury her.

His hands were trailing around to her back, and he locked his fingers behind her before once again peering up at her.

In her past, she'd had sex because she needed to let go, to

release stress, to satiate some bare, animal desire. But the way Jake was looking at her now seemed to go so much deeper. She wasn't prepared to face it, though—it didn't make sense. They hardly knew each other.

"I want you," she whispered, giving him the permission if he felt he needed it. He had been a gentleman with her their first time. Of course, to him, this would feel like their first time all over again.

"Give me a minute to look at you." He swallowed. "The past and present keep getting muddled in my head, and I want to enjoy every second."

He rose to his feet, his hands giving her chills as his fingers ran up her spine. Then they shifted to her chest, palming her breasts. She rolled her tongue over her teeth as pleasure moved through her, warming her in all the places she hoped he'd soon touch.

She reached for his belt buckle and worked at his trousers. They fell to his feet, and she stepped back, admiring his toned physique.

She dropped back onto the bed, her hair fanning out behind her, her mouth curving in appreciation as she looked at his body before her. He grabbed hold of his shaft as he moved toward the bed. He knelt on top of her, bringing the hot breath from his mouth to tease her inner thighs.

She bucked as he tugged at her knickers, moving them out of the way, and his lips teased her sensitive flesh. She clawed at the comforter at her sides, resisting the urge to grab hold of his scarred back as he pushed her legs up a little and toward her chest.

"Jesus, Alexa," he murmured, and then stroked her with his tongue again. He'd clearly not forgotten how to make a woman lose her mind.

She cried out a few minutes later when she could no longer handle the mounting pressure that had built inside her. "Jake." His name was like an exhaled breath rushing from her lips. "I need you," she begged, demanding that he fill her. He was like a missing piece she didn't know she'd been without.

His hot mouth had lifted, but her body still tremored and rocked with orgasm as he sheathed himself. She bit back her worry for his injuries as his tip met her center. He held himself above her, and when he plunged deep inside of her, she gasped and her eyes shut. She crested on a wave of sensations that utterly wrecked her, but in the best of ways.

He thrusted slowly at first, building up with a gradual intensity that had them both breathing hard as she moved with him. She reached up for his biceps, her fingers grazing his muscles as she resisted the urge to climax again.

She wanted this to last longer—forever, even . . . but suddenly everything felt too bloody good to fight. She opened her eyes as she recovered from another round of sensations that had felt almost blissfully painful, and she could see that Jake was struggling to hold on.

She watched his throat as he swallowed, and then his head fell forward as he came, his body gently thrusting before he collapsed off to the side of her. He shifted his head on the pillow to look at her, his nose brushing against hers.

"Are you okay? Your back—are you in pain?"

His eyelids fluttered shut briefly. "What pain?" His husky voice was raw.

"Funny." Her fingers skimmed over his knuckles as his hand splayed on her stomach, and she wondered how it was possible to be so comfortable with him, despite everything.

It felt so . . . natural.

And she wasn't used to natural. Not in her line of work.

"You should rest. It's been a crazy last few days, and it might get even more intense tomorrow."

Jake nodded. "You, too." He pulled his hand back and sat up, carefully rolling the condom off. He stood from the bed and started for the bathroom. His bare ass was an unbelievable distraction. Firm and muscled.

But when her gaze lifted, his scars reminded her of the bastards who had ripped his flesh with a whip. His markings—a God awful memento that he'd survived something horrible. Even worse, she knew it was eating at him, that he'd survived when his team hadn't. Once his memories came back, the guilt would be even worse.

A few moments later, Jake returned, his eyes sharp on her, the line of his shoulders relaxed. "You're amazing," he said as he slid into the bed. She was tucked under the covers, luxuriating in the softness on her bare skin. She didn't have the energy to dress, and she relished the idea of pressing her naked body against his as they slept. But then it dawned on her that he might want to sleep alone.

Instead, Jake nudged Alexa to her side, pulling her back tightly against his firm chest. She could feel him hardening against her again, and his thick arousal pressing into her made her legs tighten with a need she didn't recognize.

"Goodnight, Alexa," he said into her ear as an arm draped over her side, resting on her hipbone. Some wild part of her wanted his hand to slide down to her center and make her come for a third time. But she squashed the urge and sucked in a breath, knowing that he needed to rest after the hell he'd been through.

But maybe in the morning, before they had to meet Xander and Randall . . .

Sleep pulled at the corner of her mind, and she fell into fantasy.

# CHAPTER NINETEEN

"THAT WAS XANDER. HE'LL BE HEADING OVER IN AN HOUR."
Alexa rolled back to her side and faced Jake.

He was on his stomach, his hands resting on the pillow above
his head. He must have been so sick of sleeping on his stomach.
She had heard him groaning in his sleep, and she wasn't sure if it
was from the pain of his injuries or his memories.

Jake moved his arm down, offering a better view of his eyes,
which were focused on her breasts. A smile was tucked firmly on
his face. He shifted all the way to his side, and his fingers danced
up her stomach before pinching her nipple.

"If we're about to start working, I don't think it's a good idea
to be lying in bed together naked." Even though she wished they
could stay in bed all day.

His hand wandered back down her body before reaching
between her legs. God, she was already so wet from the thought of
having Jake inside her again. But then she thought of Jason, and
she stiffened, every muscle in her body growing tense.

"What's wrong?" Jake retracted his arm and propped his head
up, studying her with guarded eyes.

"I don't want to see Jason. This case is hard enough, but

working with him is a bloody nightmare." She gulped, pushing the emotion down her throat as she sat upright. She tugged the covers to her chest, feeling her desire subdued by a gritty shield of anger.

"How long ago were you together?"

"Oh, not for ages. We were dating when I got recruited to MI6. I wasn't allowed to tell him who I really was."

"But isn't he MI6, too? I mean, he's working with you guys, right?"

"It's complicated. But when I started with the agency, he was definitely not MI6."

"Oh." Jake sat up next to her and propped a pillow between his back and the headboard. "Do you want to, uh, talk about him?"

She wasn't sure if he was simply being nice. "I think it's best if we don't talk about him."

"But you're upset about seeing him, so—"

"He absolutely gutted me, Jake," she said quickly, wishing she'd thought before she spoke.

Jake looked away from her and down at his hands, which were clasped over his core. His rippling stomach muscles moved up and down ever so slightly as he breathed. "You loved him, then?"

"I thought I did, but he's an ace at deception, and he's one of the most brilliant bleeding hackers in the world, which is why we have to work with his sorry arse." Anger wrapped itself around her spine, her blood chilling as she came to grips with the fact that she was actually going to have to play nice with the bastard. "I think I need a cool shower to calm myself down. I'm seething just thinking about him, and I—"

Jake's lips crushed against hers, distracting her from her thoughts. He cupped the back of her head and pulled her even closer to him until she became almost lightheaded from the kiss.

"What was that for?" she asked, breathlessly, when he released her.

"A distraction."

"Oh really?"

"You kissed me in the office in Montana, trying to help me. So, I thought I'd give it a shot."

A surprising smile found her lips. "It worked." She rolled her tongue over her teeth. She'd forgotten almost everything, in fact. "Do it again," she whispered, her eyes locking on his.

This time, his tongue roamed inside her mouth, deepening the kiss. Her body pulsed with desire. They still had an hour, and they were both already naked . . .

She briefly considered asking him to shower with her, but she worried about his back. Instead, she broke their kiss and climbed on top of him, straddling him. "Does this hurt?" she asked softly, wondering if he'd even tell her if it did.

"Not at all." His hard cock throbbed against her warm center, and she began moving against him, grinding into him as their lips met again. She ran her short fingernails across his hard chest.

"You'd better let me strap something on," he said a minute later.

"Oh." She had been so caught up in the moment she'd almost forgotten, which was so not like her at all.

He softly bit her lip, and then winked at her. "Not that I wouldn't love to feel you without a rubber between us."

She laughed as she reached for the condoms from the side dresser and handed one to him. She started to move off him, realizing that there was no way she could be on top without jarring his back, but he dropped the condom to grab hold of her behind, yanking her back over him. "You're not going anywhere," he said as their eyes connected.

"You promise?" The words tumbled from her mouth before she could catch them. There was so much meaning compressed within those two words, but she hoped Jake wouldn't read into them. Not now, at least.

But as he studied her, his brown eyes intensely focused on her hazel ones, she understood that the Jake who had tried to win her over a year ago was back again.

"This is crazy."

"I was thinking the same thing," she replied. *Honesty. From me?*

"How come even though my brain is shit and we only hung out for a week a year ago, I still feel like I've known you my entire life?" His hand swooped up to her face, and he brushed his knuckles against her cheek. Her lips instinctively parted.

She thought about how to answer, but she had no idea what to say. She was equally dumbfounded by the intense reaction she was having to this man.

Her hands pressed against his chest as she leaned back a little, still nervous that she was hurting him. "Maybe after we take these pricks down, we can try and answer that question." She shrugged and her mouth tightened.

His large hand skimmed to her neck and threaded through her dark hair.

"You're different, aren't you?" *From other men . . .* She'd known it a year ago, but she had been scared to admit it.

"What really happened between us, Alexa?"

She didn't want to ruin the moment.

"I shouldn't have let you go, is all." She was about to kiss him, but her mobile vibrated against the nightstand.

"Don't," he said, touching her arm as she started for it.

"What if it's important?"

He released a breath and nodded.

She scooted off and his fingers spread over her back like the sun's rays on a gorgeous day. The sensation was warm, relaxing, delicious. She wanted nothing more than to toss her phone and get back into bed with him, but she was an agent and never one to put anything before the job. As much as she wanted to put this man first, there were other lives at stake.

"We need to move up the timetable. Coming to you now." Xander's voice had been rushed.

"Everything okay?"

"Reza just left his room."

"Okay," she mumbled.

"Be there in five." Xander ended the call.

Alexa tossed her mobile on the bed. "Xander's on his way."

Jake grumbled a little but got out of bed. "I'd better get dressed." He looked over his shoulder at her for a brief moment as he clutched his clothes from the night before, and then he quietly left the room.

She sank onto the bed for a minute, hanging her head and pressing her hands to her face, trying to come to terms with the fact that she was about to face Jason for the first time in years.

Would she be able to check her impulse to slug him?

She'd have to do her best because right now @Anarchy was the enemy. Well, it was the current threat. Jason would always be her enemy.

* * *

JAKE HATED THIS.

The fact that he'd made love to Alexa before and couldn't remember was driving him completely crazy.

What had he been expecting—in the midst of an incredible orgasm that lightning would strike him and his memories would rain over him?

Although the sex had been beyond great—his past was still trapped beneath a damn steel coating. Only glimpses of horrid moments had leaked through the crevices.

He tossed his hands up, rushing them through his dyed hair and glanced at her bedroom door as he heard a knock.

He checked the peephole before opening it.

Xander came in and quickly shut the door behind him. "We're set up in my room, but I wanted to talk to you guys briefly before you meet up with everyone."

Jake wondered if Xander had wanted to come to their room first to make sure Alexa was okay to face this Jason character.

"Where's Alexa?" Xander narrowed his gray eyes at Jake, a curious look spreading across his face as if he could smell sex in the air.

"She's coming." Jake smoothed a hand down the front of his shirt and eyed Xander. They were the same height, or close enough, and Xander was fit. He had that whole James Bond look, while Jake still preferred a pair of worn jeans and a wide-brimmed hat.

They both turned at the sound of Alexa's door. Jake brought a fist to his mouth and cleared his throat, wishing that all the tension in the room could be cleared so easily.

Alexa strode cautiously toward them in jeans and a soft red sweater that brought out the rich color of her eyes. Her skin was still glowing, and he relished in the fact that he'd at least been responsible for one good thing.

"You all set up?" she asked.

Xander stepped past Jake and stopped in front of her. "Yeah, everyone is in position. Reza is out in the city right now. We have a team following him. He has his laptop case with him, so we'll stick with the plan to strike later. For now, we thought we could get into his room and place a camera and listening device."

"If he's some cyber expert, won't he pick up on those?" Jake had seen it happen in the movies, at least.

Xander looked over at Jake. "Maybe if we planted a device in his suitcase, he'd discover it at some point, but I doubt Reza is checking his room for bugs. He has no reason to worry."

"If you say so," Jake grumbled. He wondered if he'd had a bad experience in the past with something similar because right now his skin crawled with unease.

"You remember anything of use yet?" Xander asked.

"No. Sorry, man."

Xander sighed. "Well, maybe we can pull this off either way, but since Anarchy knows you're alive and tried to kill you, I assume you must know something of value," Xander said.

"And do you think they changed their plans now that they know I'm not dead?" Jake asked.

"It's possible, which is why it's important that we get this malware embedded into Reza's computer. We need to figure out what the hell they are up to." He frowned. "Kemal Bekas has gone off the grid. And our team lost sight of Gregov in Cyprus." Xander's voice was gravely calm, a lot calmer than Jake's would have been.

"What do you mean they're gone?" Alexa's face flushed. "We've had eyes on them since the beginning, and we've never lost them once." Alexa rubbed a hand down her smooth skin, her fingers dipping to the small diamond pendant at the base of her throat.

"I don't have any feckin' idea how Bekas and Gregov slipped the agents, but they did it before the American reinforcements came in. So, it's on us to find them." Xander shook his head with disappointment. "But I have to assume that some shit is going down soon. Getting into Reza's computer is our only hope of figuring out what's going on in time to stop it."

Alexa's face blanched. "This is it," she said softly as Jake moved to her side. "Bekas's end game. The final blow . . ."

"Which means it's going to be—"

"God awful if we don't stop it," Alexa rasped as she tucked her arms across her chest. She went to the window and peered out. "Jesus, Xander. What if we can't stop them?" She spun around and faced the two men, her forehead pinched together with concern.

"We will," Jake answered without hesitation, which induced a look of surprise from Xander.

"And how can you be so certain?" she asked.

"Because I refuse to let you down." Maybe that was a stupid answer, but he had to believe it. If he trusted his instincts and fought for the courage to be whatever kind of man he had become

—a man who'd survived Afghanistan and Iraq—well, he could do this then.

What other choice did he have?

Maybe he'd been scared when he first woke up in that hospital in London and tried to make sense of his life, but now, memories or not, he knew what he had to do. And he'd be damned if he was going to let the terrorists who'd abducted him and murdered his team get away with it.

"We'll get this fucker," Jake bit out with searing confidence, hoping she'd believe him.

She stared at him for a solid minute, and he almost forgot Xander was with them. She finally nodded at him. "Okay . . ."

"Okay," Xander echoed. "Let's do this."

Alexa moved to the door and grabbed her leather jacket, which was still on the floor from the previous night.

Jake noticed Alexa's cheeks turn crimson when Xander faked a cough, a smile pulling at his lips.

"What?" She raised a dark, arched brow.

"Oh. Nothing." Xander opened the door and waited for them to exit first.

A few minutes later, they were standing outside of Xander's hotel room.

"I suppose Jason is in there." Alexa's spine was stiff, her lips drawing into a tight line.

"Yeah." Xander peeked at Alexa as she pressed her hands to her core. His keycard hovered near the sensor. "You good?"

"Sure." She tipped her head forward, giving Xander the go-ahead.

Jake's stomach rolled with worry, and he wanted to reach for her hand, to walk her through whatever pain was eating at her. But he resisted the compulsion. She was at work, after all.

When the door opened, Randall and two strangers were directly across the room. One guy was sitting on the couch with his back to the door and a computer on his lap. His head looked like a large oval egg—it was shaved to the scalp, with not a lick of hair in sight. The other man was sitting at the room's only desk, thrown into shadowed relief by the expansive window beyond. His attention remained fixed on the screen in front of him, and he was wearing huge, full-coverage headphones. The faint echo of rock music drifted over. The guy was going to lose his hearing at that decibel.

Randall looked up from where he was standing once the door closed. His hip was perched against the back of the couch, and he was holding a hand over his ear. "Alpha team is in position, and we have eyes on the target. He's at a coffee shop a mile away from here, and he's on his laptop."

"Okay. Let's not lose him—he's all we have right now," Xander said, his eyes lingering on Alexa.

She was standing absolutely still, staring at the man at the desk. That had to be Jason, then.

Jake squinted, adjusting his eyes. The guy's black hair was cropped. His neck was thick, his shoulders broad—it looked like this computer genius also frequented the gym.

Jake moved around in front of Alexa. Her face was ghostly pale as her hand slanted to her side, curving over her hipbone.

"Are you okay?" Jake asked softly.

Alexa's hazel eyes met his, and her stance softened a little, but only for a moment. She blew out a breath and sidestepped Jake. She crossed the room to stand in front of the desk. "Jason."

The man shifted his gaze up to Alexa, and his frenzied tapping of the keys ceased. A grin spread across his face as he reached for his headphones and slipped them around his neck. He leaned back in his seat and folded his arms across his chest, angling his head.

"Alexa." Xander came up behind her and placed a hand on her shoulder.

"Alexa Ryan," the man's voice was a cool whisper, his graphite gray eyes devoid of emotion. He wasn't just an ex. Jake could see it in his eyes, in the curve of his wry smile—he was a killer.

Jake tried to curb the sudden anger that bubbled beneath his skin. He glanced over at Randall and the bald man, who had come around to the other side of the couch. Was this some sort of showdown?

"We don't have time for this, Alexa," Xander said in a low voice. He lifted his hand from her shoulder, took a step back from her, and peeked at Jake.

Jake tensed. The muscles in Xander's face and throat were tight. He was holding himself back from the blistering hatred that simmered in his eyes. So, it looked like Jason had pissed off more than Alexa.

Xander gave a quick nod to Jake. Beckoning him for help, maybe?

In a few strides, Jake swapped places with Xander and stood firm at Alexa's side, his eyes now focused on Jason as he placed a hand on the small of Alexa's back.

Jason cocked his head, his gaze briefly flickering to Jake's arm. "It's been years, Alexa." Another smile slithered to Jason's mouth. The bastard wet his lips as he assessed Alexa with gleaming eyes. As Jason leaned over the laptop on his desk, Jake caught a glimpse of the black hawk tattoo that spread from Jason's ear down the side of his neck. The man was dark. Dangerous.

Was this the kind of man Alexa liked?

Was that the man Jake himself had become?

"Ahem. Beta team is now in position." Randall's voice broke through the tension that had veiled the room like a dark storm cloud.

Alexa took a step back, her eyes closing for a flash, and then she turned away from Jason and moved toward the bald man by Randall. "Good to see you, Seth. Sorry you had to be the one to bring this lying arsehole here."

"Now, baby girl, wasn't it you who did all the lying?" Jason came around from behind the desk, brushing past Jake, which had

Jake's hands locking into fists at his sides. He'd love for this guy to give him a reason to throttle him.

Alexa looked down at the carpet, crossing her arms over her leather jacket. She was trying to maintain her composure, to resist the pull of anger that was clearly tugging at her heart as Jason poked her.

Xander quickly stepped in front of Jason. "Get back to work," he ordered.

Jason rubbed a hand down his jaw. The outer edge of his hand was covered in black ink. "Just catching up with my girl, here. Haven't seen her since she had me arrested."

Xander pressed a hand to Jason's chest and glared at him. "I think it's best if you don't open your bloody mouth until I say you do."

Alexa kept her back to the scene, picking at a loose thread on the top of the couch at her side.

Jake remained stiff, torn between whether or not he should punch Jason in the face for simply being a prick.

Once Jason retreated to his desk, Xander moved over toward Alexa. "Get some tea in the kitchen and take a breather," he said softly.

Jason scoffed and looked up at Jake. "If you're screwing that fine arse, then you should probably watch your back. She might be a good lay, but she's a bitch," he rasped, his accent thick and heavy.

Jake's heart may have hardened over the years, but he had a feeling that assholes like this had something to do with it. And damned if he didn't want to kill this man, but before Jake could even form a fist, Xander was there—grabbing Jason by the shirt. The smug bastard remained sitting, looking up at Xander.

"Shut up before I put a bullet in your head my-Goddamn-self," Xander growled, his jaw locked tight.

Xander released Jason's shirt as Jake fought against his own anger. The man deserved a lesson. But Jake knew it would be better to trade in his anger to focus on Alexa, instead.

Jason cracked his neck as he tilted his head from side to side and then positioned the headphones back over his ears.

"Come on," Alexa murmured, motioning for Jake to follow her to the kitchenette.

Jake kept his eyes on Jason as they walked past the desk.

"Sorry about that," she whispered once he stood in front of her. She offered Jake a mug of coffee, probably remembering his distaste for tea.

"Thanks." He heaved out another deep breath and brought the hot liquid to his lips.

She folded her arms and leaned her back against the counter of the breakfast bar. Her lips tightened as her eyes darted over his shoulder, and he assumed she was probably peering at Jason again.

"You don't need to apologize, by the way," Jake said in a subdued voice, careful not to attract attention.

"We need to focus on stopping Anarchy and putting an end to Bekas. Dealing with my feelings for that arsehole—well, it's not the time or the place." Her words were weighted down by emotions.

Jake took another sip of his black coffee as he thought about what to say. "We'll take Bekas down, but after that—"

"Alexa, we need your help," Xander called out, interrupting Jake.

Jake had wanted to say no, to give her one more minute to work through her feelings, but he refrained.

She broke eye contact with Jake, and her gaze flickered to her cup as she swallowed. She set the mug on the counter and pressed her hands to her thighs for a moment as if she were mentally preparing herself to re-enter the fray. "Yeah?"

"Eh, Jason hacked into the hotel's system earlier and created a keycard that can access every room in the hotel. He's overriding the surveillance cameras at all the surrounding points to the building, and then I'll need you to hack into the video feeds for Reza's floor and put them on a loop. I don't want any evidence that we were in his room. Not that he has a reason to check the hotel surveillance, but we need to cover our bases."

"That's no problem," she said.

"We need about ten minutes of time looped. Enough to go and install the devices."

"What'd you bring from Q?" Alexa looked over at Seth—he didn't look to Jake like some badass spy. Then again, that was probably the point.

Jake's hand touched his face as he remembered he'd forgotten part of his cover—his glasses—back in the hotel room.

Seth went over to a bag on the table by the couch and dug into it. "This," he said, holding up a red ball-point pen, "can monitor conversations up to twenty meters, and we can hear everything after a ten-second transmission delay." He handed it to Randall, who was now at his side.

"And this beauty," Seth held up a small silver object that looked like a quarter, "is the camera we'll place near the safe, so we can sneak a peek at the combination. Fortunately, we don't need a palm scan for this one."

Jake remained in the kitchen, keeping himself far enough from Jason so that he wouldn't lose his cool.

"Should be easy enough," Xander said. "I'll be going into Reza's room. Randall is monitoring Alpha team. And Seth has Beta team."

"And what is Beta team doing, exactly?" Jake asked.

"Scoping out the casino," Xander replied. "Getting a feel for it, so they can better keep an eye on Reza tonight."

Jake crossed his arms, surprise moving through him. "A casino?"

Alexa nodded. "We've been studying Reza's behaviors for a while. If a city has a casino, he goes practically every night."

"I wouldn't have suspected," Jake said.

"He's a card counter. Has a real addiction to it." Xander approached Jake. "Listen, while everyone is doing their thing, I thought maybe you could take a look at some images from the case files. Maybe they would help trigger something for you."

Alexa came up behind Xander. "Do we have anything new?" she asked while removing her jacket.

Xander glanced at Alexa and responded with a brief nod. "We have traffic camera footage of the Montana shooter in London a few kilometers away from the site of the explosion last week, and he was with someone. We haven't gotten a match on the other guy yet, but we're talking to Interpol and working with other agencies to get a name."

"You have the man's picture?" Jake cleared his throat, wondering if he could help.

"Yeah. I have two laptops set up in the bedroom. I thought you guys might want some space to work." Xander glanced at Jason before pointing to one of the doors off of the living room. "Without distractions, yeah?"

"That works. Thanks." Alexa pressed a hand to Xander's shoulder. "I'll get working on the video cameras."

Jake watched Alexa leave, but when he started to move, Xander's hand fell on his arm. "Listen, mate, when this is all over—"

Was he about to go big brother on him?

Xander leaned in, his voice at his ear. "Don't let her get away." He cleared his throat. "I want her to be happy." Then he moved back to where the team was set up. It took Jake a minute to process Xander's words.

It hadn't been what he was expecting, but it made him like Xander a hell of a lot more now.

# CHAPTER TWENTY

ONE SIDE OF THE SPLIT SCREEN SHOWED ACTUAL FOOTAGE, WHICH Alexa was deleting in real time. On the other side was the looped feed she had created to hide Xander's entry and exit from Reza's room.

Alexa and Jake had only been in the hotel suite's bedroom for fifteen minutes, but that was all the time she had needed to get things going. A simple hack into surveillance was easy for her. But working in the same room with Jake after the crazy tension that had smoked them out of the living room after she'd confronted Jason—well, that wasn't so easy.

She peered over at Jake, whose brows furrowed as he scrolled through the images in the @Anarchy file. He was sitting by the window with the laptop resting on his jeaned thighs.

She inhaled a small breath as her attention swept over his shoulder and to the window. Her hotel was across the street, and her mind wandered to her time with Jake earlier. To the slow, sensual licks of his tongue. To the way their bodies had locked together during sex as if they were tethered together—bound forever. And would that be so bad?

No, eternal bliss sounded pretty bloody good right now.

She glanced above the gleaming building across the way, admiring the soft pink and blue streaks layering the sky like cotton candy. It made her hungry for a time when life was much more straightforward. When she was in primary school, and her greatest problem was when she and her sister liked the same boy.

"We got word from Alpha team. Looks like Reza is heading back to the hotel." Randall's voice quickly diverted her attention back to the mission.

"Shit. Did you hear that?" Alexa pressed a hand to her ear, not wanting to miss Xander's response.

"I'll be done in less than a minute. There's plenty of time—no worries, love," Xander said, his smooth voice filling her ear.

She breathed a sigh of relief. "He's about done," she told Randall.

Of course, the hard part would be tonight, when Jason uploaded the malware into Reza's computer. She still couldn't fathom why they were trusting him with something so critical, but she also didn't know if she had the finesse for the job. And it was too important to depend on a prayer. She'd uploaded malware dozens of times, but @Anarchy was a group like none other they'd faced, and they would have to make sure Reza wouldn't detect any changes in his computer, which wasn't easy for even the most brilliant of minds.

"How are you holding up?" Alexa spoke to Jake for the first time since they'd come into the room together.

But before Jake could answer, she blurted, "Shit!" Alexa pulled the screen closer to get a better look and then zoomed in on the tall, built man who was striding down the hall.

"Xander, you've got a problem," she rasped. "Boris Gregov just stepped out of the bloody lift on Reza's floor."

"Are you kidding?" Xander answered. "Fuck."

How had Gregov gotten right under their noses without anyone noticing?

"Do I have time to go out the door?" Xander asked, and Alexa's heart hammered in her chest, pulsing in her ears.

"I don't know if he has his own room, but I doubt he has a key to Reza's, yeah? Maybe Reza is on his way to meet him, and he's going to wait outside the room."

"Which means I can't leave. Jesus Christ," Xander mumbled. "Where is he now?"

"He's two doors away."

Jake was on his feet and moving to look at the computer.

"Tell me, is Reza walking down my side of the street? If I go out to the terrace . . ."

"Where's Reza?" Alexa raised her voice so Randall could hear her in the other room. "We have a situation."

Randall came into the room. "Where's the target?" Randall was talking to his team through his own earpiece. "He's already in the lobby."

"Okay. He won't see you from the street, but he'll be at his room in a few minutes. You can't get down from the terrace, though," Alexa quickly said.

"Jesus. There's a knock at the door," Xander muttered in a low voice.

Her mind raced as she pulled up the hotel information. "Give me a second." She began tapping at the keys, her fingers working furiously. "Thank God," she cried. "Xander, the room has a connecting door to the neighboring room. Your key is set up to access every room in the building, and the couple staying in that room aren't scheduled to check in for two more hours."

There was no word from Xander—he couldn't talk with Gregov outside the room. Alexa prayed that the deadbolt on the other side of the door remained unfastened.

Jake's hand wrapped around the back of his neck as he stared at the footage on the screen, with Randall at his side.

"It worked. Thanks, mate," Xander said a minute later, and Alexa's head hung with a sudden, relieved exhaustion.

"He's okay. What's Reza's position?" she asked Randall.

"Location?" Randall sputtered to Alpha team.

"Never mind. I have him on camera—he's heading down the hall." Alexa studied the screen, her heart burning in her chest. "They're going into the room, Xander. Give it a few minutes before you leave, and then hurry the hell back here."

"Will do," he answered.

"Well, that was intense." Jake angled his head to look at Randall.

"Hey, now we know where Gregov is. You think Bekas is heading here, too? Is everything going down in Barcelona?" She squinted as her mind scrambled for answers. She highly doubted that Kemal Bekas's master scheme would unfold in Barcelona. But she'd been wrong before.

"I don't know. I'll go give MI6 a call and let them know we have eyes on Gregov." Randall left the room, and Alexa stood up and flung her arms around Jake's waist without thinking, relief pouring through her.

Jake responded by locking his arms around her back, tugging her closer to him. He rested his chin on top of her head, holding her, and she was grateful for the few moments alone. She breathed in his cologne, relishing the warmth of his touch. The world slipped away at that moment, and she was safe.

Terrorists didn't exist.

Her father hadn't died of lung cancer ten years ago.

And she'd never met Jason.

"You okay?" Jake asked shortly after, and she pulled herself free of his embrace, embarrassed at how tightly she'd been holding onto his back.

"Shit. Are *you* okay?"

He didn't flinch or show any signs of pain. Maybe he was getting better. Still, she shouldn't have been so careless.

"I'm good." He whisked a few hairs out of her face and tucked the long, dark strands behind her ear. She inhaled at his touch and shut her eyes.

When she no longer felt his presence nearby, she peeled open her eyes to find him. His back was to her, and he was looking out the window. One hand pressed against the glass as a soft glow from the bright sun shone through the window, wrapping around him like the glow of a crystal. "Did you, uh, see anything helpful?" she asked after a long silence, and then reached for his laptop.

The images he'd been viewing hit her like a train. They were pictures of Jake. One of his body sprawled out amid debris after the explosion at the mill. Another of his injuries, when the lashes on his back had been fresh.

"How can you look at these?" She set the laptop on the bed by hers and crossed the room to meet him by the window.

"It's fine," he said, but the slight tremble in his voice betrayed his words. "I'm alive, although my team's not. That's what I'm struggling to deal with."

She understood, perhaps more than he knew, but before she could say anything Xander's voice sounded in her ear.

"I've activated the listening device. Is it working?" She could tell from the slight breathiness in his voice that he was on the move —probably heading back.

"Let me ask Randall." She touched Jake on the back for a brief moment before grabbing her computer and going out into the main room.

"Are we getting anything on audio?" she asked Randall. He was hunched behind Seth, who sported large, black headphones.

Seth shook his head as Alexa set her laptop down next to his. "It's fuzzy. They must be blocking us."

"But how would they know?" It was Jake. His body was rigid in the doorway as his eyes fell upon Jason.

"They probably always use an audio jammer for protection. It'll impede all eavesdropping devices as well as Wi-Fi connections. These guys aren't amateurs," Alexa glibly responded.

This was another reason that she wasn't overly optimistic about Jason's malware.

"Will the camera still work?" Jake asked.

"I doubt they'll have the jammer on all day—just while they're talking," Randall answered. "But we'll have a back-up plan in case we can't get the combination for the safe."

"They seem to be ahead of us at every step." Alexa's shoulders sagged with disappointment. "Maybe we should grab these guys while we have the chance and hope they'll narc on Bekas."

"You know as well as I do they'll kill themselves before they turn on each other," Xander said, softly closing the door behind him. Alexa had hardly heard it opening.

"We're going to get him," Jake insisted.

"He's right, Alexa. We always get our guys, yeah?" Xander tossed his earpiece on the desk by Seth's laptop.

"And what do we do if Reza doesn't go to the casino tonight? Or if Gregov stays in the room while Reza leaves?"

"We'll keep following these guys until we can make our move. Hopefully tonight." Xander placed a large hand on Jake's shoulder. "How are you holding up, mate?"

Jake was staring at Jason's head like he was willing it to self-combust. She couldn't help but like the feeling of being protected for once. Not that Xander and Matt didn't look out for her, but that was different. Jake had a strength that lit a fire in her belly. She wanted to get lost in his muscular arms, to let someone else take care of her.

What would it feel like not to be this strong, tough woman for five minutes?

*Just five minutes.* She didn't want to give up her own strength altogether, but five minutes would be relaxing.

Okay, so maybe ten would be a little better.

It'd be nice to enjoy a sunset every once in a while. Or have a cocktail at the beach without worrying that the world might explode.

"I'm fine," Jake said. "I didn't recognize the man in the images with the shooter. Sorry."

Alexa blinked a few times, forcing herself to look away from Jake's arms. When she swept her gaze up his chest and to his face, she found his eyes focused on hers, and her breath hitched.

"Okay. Maybe it will come to you." Xander folded his arms. "We'll monitor the cameras to see when Gregov leaves, and we'll have Alpha team in place to follow him. I'll call Beta team back to keep an eye on Reza."

"Who is going with Jason to upload the malware?" She looked over at the man who made her blood ice cold.

"Me," Xander answered.

Alexa went for her jacket and slipped it on. She couldn't stomach being in the same room as Jason. "Do you need me right now?"

"No. You guys go get room service or something and stay put for now. And Alexa, be careful. We don't want Gregov recognizing you from Munich," Xander ordered.

"Let me know when Gregov is on the move," Alexa said. As she went to the door, she could feel Jake at her heels.

Neither of them spoke as they left in a hurry, and then crept inside the side entrance of their hotel, and took a set of stairs to their room. Once there, Alexa dead bolted the door and faced Jake, dying to let the words fly loose. "I really am so sorry you had to meet Jason." Her eyes wandered to Jake's hands, which were clenched at his sides.

"What did he do to you, Alexa?"

Alexa hung her head and pressed her fingertips to her temples. She looked up when Jake's hand swooped next to her, his palm pressing against the wall. His eyes were dark, and a swirl of pain showed in the lines of his face. "Tell me, Alexa. Give me permission to put this guy six feet under after this is all over. I'll kill him with my bare hands."

And he could, too, couldn't he? The prominent veins in his forearm attested to that.

But she didn't want to think about Jason or her past. Right now, she just wanted to lose herself in Jake's arms, to use those hands for passion, instead of anger.

She wanted to will away the evil in the world and bury him deep inside her until she was screaming his name.

Jake had so many sides: humor, strength, conviction. *Love?*

And rules, she couldn't forget. The man outside the hospital room back in London—the dark-haired guy with blue eyes—he'd said Jake was a rule follower.

Maybe Jake wasn't being serious about killing Jason. Or maybe he truly had forgotten who he was. It was crazy to think that he'd gone from a man unable to kill a spider to a man telling her he wanted to murder her ex-boyfriend. Was he changing for her? Or was he trying to adapt to this new world he'd woken up within, where he remembered fragments of his past as he tried to negotiate the present?

"Jake?" His name was like a hiss from her lips as she lifted her chest and rolled her shoulders back.

The back of his hand caressed her cheek, and the desire in his eyes seemed as strong as her own. She glanced down between them and saw his hardened length pressing against his jeans. "Maybe I can tell you about Jason after . . .?"

He arched a brow as his hand slipped down her throat and to the leather collar of her jacket. "After what?"

She roped her hands up to his neck and brought her face close to his. "After this." Her lips found his, and he groaned against her mouth. His hand gently tugged at her hair as he moved a few steps back.

She gasped as Jake swept her into his arms. "Put me down. You're injured." Her palms went to his chest, but he only looked at her with gleaming, brown eyes.

He ignored her protests, nipping at her lip with his teeth as he carried her into the bedroom. She wanted to holler at him for being so completely daft, but she could barely remember words under the heat of his stare.

He gently set her on the bed, and he went for the button on his jeans. He stood there for a moment, the button undone, the zipper still up—just studying her with hooded eyes.

She wanted to cry out for him to come to her—she needed him, and she rolled her tongue over her lips, wetting them as he shoved off his jeans and boxers and stepped out of them.

His hard, beautifully sculpted body was on display for her, and she wanted to run her hands over the curve of his muscles and plant kisses everywhere.

Jake gripped his shaft, and his mouth tightened as he swallowed. "Your turn," he said in a throaty voice.

She sat upright and removed her jacket, then tugged her sweater over her head. She unsnapped her bra, freeing her breasts and started for her jeans.

Jake moved on top of her in one quick movement.

And when his mouth came down over her belly button, she knew she wouldn't be capable of surviving another day without Mr. New Year's Eve.

But a sharp blitz of pain in her chest reminded her of how impossible that could be.

# CHAPTER TWENTY-ONE

JAKE PINCHED ALEXA'S NIPPLE; THEN HIS HAND GLIDED DOWN HER core to her thighs, where it teased her sensitive flesh. "You make me forget all the crazy shit." He could lie next to this woman and be forever happy. He didn't need anything else. But that was nuts —how long had he known her? His strong feelings for this woman were insane, and yet, he couldn't resist them.

She moaned and covered his hand as he slid his finger up and down her wet center. "You ready to go again?"

"Not quite. But it feels like you are."

A lazy smile stretched across her face, and God did he need that smile right now.

"We're out of condoms," he said with a well-intended pout. "I might have to get you off with my mouth, instead." He winked. "Lucky for you, that suits me fine."

"Mm. But we're in the middle of an OP. We can't screw all day." Amusement flickered in her cheek. "Well, maybe we can until Xander calls."

He laughed. "That's my girl."

*Shit, she's not mine. Not yet, at least. And maybe never . . .*

He felt her stiffen at his words, and her thighs squeezed, locking his hand between them. "Jake?"

"Yeah?" He retracted his hand.

"Well, maybe we should take a few minutes to talk about what happened earlier."

*Jason?* Even thinking the man's name heated his blood. Jake hardly recognized the pacifist he'd been when younger. Now, he wondered if he really would grab Xander's 9mm and shoot that motherfucker, Jason, in the chest. *What is wrong with me?*

"I'm kind of worried about what thoughts might be brewing in that head of yours, and I'm thinking I better just be straight with you, yeah?" She was on her side now, head propped up in her hand, mirroring him. Their naked bodies were so close.

Maybe she should cover her incredible tits when she told him about her ex?

"Um . . ." he started.

Would he really ask her to hide her body? No, he didn't think so.

Alexa's hand grazed down the center of her chest to her stomach, and his cock hardened in response. *Fuck me.* But then her fingers settled over her scar, and he noticed her brows pulling together as she looked down at the marking on her skin. His lungs deflated.

*Did Jason do that to you?* Anger burst through him, and his fingertips curled into his right palm.

"I was on an OP over seven years ago. We were in Copenhagen tracking down a terrorist cell. It was only my second mission in the field. I was in the surveillance van while my team went after the target." She sucked in a deep breath, and it was then that she reached for the creamy silk sheet and pulled it up over her breasts. "I was watching when everything went down—they were ambushed. I rushed from the van clutching my gun, prepared to die if I could save my teammates."

Jake reached for her hand when she placed it between them on the bed. He gave it a squeeze, offering her as much support as he could. He understood all too well the pain of reliving the past.

"My teammates were dead by the time I got there, and only one guy was still inside—he came out of nowhere and swiped at me with a steak knife. We were in the kitchen of an empty restaurant—a front for illegal activity. The knife sliced my side, and then the man pinned me to the ground, trying to cut my throat." Her eyes flashed shut, and Jake was so grateful that she was alive right now to tell him the story.

"The guy wasn't big. Thank God. So, I fought back. He couldn't get my gun from me, and we struggled . . . and I killed him." Her big hazel eyes were open and on Jake now. "So, I know what it's like to be the only one to survive a mission. It's horrible. I should have been in there with them. I should have died, too."

Her eyes became glossy, like greenish-brown crystals. "That was the only time I've had to kill. And it was Jason's fault."

He held her gaze, attempting slow and deep breaths to maintain his cool. He was dying to pull her into his arms and tell her she didn't need to say anymore if it would hurt too much, but he knew that she needed him to just listen right now. Still, seeing her hurting was worse than any remnants of pain from his abduction.

"Jason and I were dating before I was recruited to MI6. We met at a tech conference in Dublin. He was passionate about computers, and so was I—we'd been dating maybe six months when I was hired." She pulled her hand from Jake's and sat upright, clutching the sheet tight to her chest as she leaned against the headboard, and Jake followed suit.

"What happened?" he finally asked.

"I'd been an agent for a few months when I was assigned to the case involving that Danish terrorist cell. We'd pegged the terrorist group for an explosion in Liverpool, and we learned the leader was in Copenhagen. We just needed more evidence, so we went after him in Denmark. But the guy knew we were coming. There was a hacker that MI5, GCHQ, Interpol—hell, everyone in the U.K.—had been trying to track down for years. Terrorists and criminals hired the hacker to watch out for them electronically. To keep track of the agencies and monitor our activities. For a hefty price, of course." She stopped talking for a moment. He could see the pull of anger in her face and the tenseness in her shoulders.

"Jason?"

She gave a soft nod. "After we were ambushed in Copenhagen, we realized this hacker—this no-name arsehole—had probably tipped off the terrorist cell." Her arms lifted and her hands darted to her temples. "I was dating Jason while hunting the son of a bitch down. Completely unaware it was him that got my teammates killed." Then Alexa was on her feet, standing naked in front of the bed with a hand over her mouth.

Jake quickly stood, ignoring the flash of pain in his hip. "Shit, Alexa. I don't even know what to say." He knew what he wanted to do, though. Now, more than ever, he wanted to kill the SOB.

"He didn't know I was MI6. It was hard for me to believe at first, but he was as shocked as I was when we went in for the capture. I mean, I thought for sure he'd been using me, but it was just a massive coincidence. Some feckin' coincidence!"

Jake wrapped his arms around her hips and tugged her body against him. She pressed her face to his chest and remained there for a few minutes. Not crying, just breathing.

Thinking, maybe. Blaming herself, probably.

He could understand, for sure.

"Why the hell is he working with you guys?" Jake finally asked.

She reached for her underwear off the floor and slipped them on. "He had an insane amount of intel on terrorists all over the world." Alexa shook her head as if disgusted.

The agency had made a deal with the devil.

"In exchange for the intel, and for cyber assists when needed, they put him in a very comfortable prison—a mansion in London.

It's guarded at all times, and he can't go anywhere in the city without security, but still . . ."

"Fuck me. That's so messed up." Jake rushed his fingers through his hair and looked down at the carpet.

"Tell me about it," she grumbled. "Any time the agency brings him in, I always steer clear and ask to be reassigned from the mission." She grabbed Jake's white T-shirt off the chair by the bed and put it on. "This is the first time I've been in the same room with him since we first interrogated him."

"God, Alexa." He braced his hands on her forearms as their eyes met. "I'm so sorry."

"He let my team members go in to die by helping the terrorists. I should have died, too. There's not a day that goes by that I don't relive that night. So, when I say that I understand what you're going through—"

He pulled her back into his arms, pressing his chin to her forehead. His hands wrapped around her waist.

Alexa stepped back from him a few minutes later, rubbing a hand over her cheek. "You feel like a rest? I'm exhausted, and tonight will be . . . well, you know."

He nodded. "Sure." He put on his boxers and got into bed. She stretched out next to him, and he banded an arm over her hipbone and pulled her back flush against his chest, holding her tight.

"This feels right. Just like last year." Her words floated to his ears, and the hairs on his arms rose.

*"Kiss me one last time, Jake," Alexa had said.*

*"No, but I'll kiss you for now—until next time . . ."*

Jake's eyes screwed tight as he clung to this memory of him and Alexa. When had it happened? It was confusing.

But he was too exhausted to hold onto the memory, and he didn't want to make sense of it right now. So, he focused on Alexa in his arms, rather than what happened last year. He embraced the moment since he never knew how long it would last.

# CHAPTER TWENTY-TWO

"GREGOV HAS A ROOM ON THE FOURTH FLOOR. HE'S DUE TO CHECK out tomorrow," Xander said. Alexa and Jake had just arrived, freshly showered.

"Did he keep his audio jammer on?" she asked.

"We got the code. Saw the bastard punch it in myself when he tucked his computer into the safe twenty minutes ago . . . right after we got Gregov on camera leaving his room, heading to his own suite," Xander said.

"Thank God. And where is Reza now?" It was almost ten p.m., and twilight had given way to utter darkness. Of course, Barcelona was only just starting to wake up for the night.

Xander looked over his shoulder at Randall, whose dark brown eyes shifted to meet Xander's. Randall nodded. "Reza just entered the casino."

"And Gregov?" Alexa asked.

"Still in his room. He actually flew in from Istanbul under a different name," Randall said.

Alexa sat on the sofa, wanting to stay as far away from Jason as possible. He was leaning against the breakfast bar in the kitchen, his arms crossed, his eyes pinned to her. It made her skin crawl.

And she didn't have to look at Jake to know how he was feeling. His anger radiated off him like the heat of a summer day on the Mediterranean. Waves of tension speared the room, its silent vibrations ebbing back and forth between Jake and Jason with increasing intensity.

"You think Gregov met with Bekas?" she asked, pulling her attention back to the mission.

Xander reached for his 9mm, tucked it into the waistband of his pants, and then slipped a black blazer over his shoulders to conceal the weapon. "We have agents scrubbing traffic cameras all around Istanbul to see where Gregov was before he came here, and whom he met with there. Hopefully we'll find a connection to Bekas."

If only Parliament had given them the go-ahead to capture Bekas and his men a year ago . . .

"If we're going to do this, we need to get it done now. You ready?" Xander was eyeing Jason. How the man could work side by side with that monster was beyond her.

"Not going to wear a vest?" Alexa swallowed, pushing thoughts of Copenhagen out of her head, the story entirely too fresh in her mind with Jason there.

Xander's lips curved down as his shoulders arched up as if she were being ridiculous. "It's a quick in and out. We're good." Xander flashed her a smile to comfort her, but it didn't do much to adjust her nerves down to the fine tune of normal. Not even close.

"You in place, Alpha team?" Randall waited for the bug in his ear to respond. Then he nodded at Xander, giving him the go-ahead. "Beta team is outside the hotel," Randall added.

Alexa slipped next to Seth at the table and studied the screen of her laptop, which was already hacked into the hotel's surveillance cameras. "I've got you," she finally said to Xander, hoping she came across confident.

"Jake, why don't you come with us?" Xander asked, now standing near the door.

Alexa immediately looked up, her eyes wide. "Wait. What?"

"He can back me up." Xander looked to Randall as if he were asking permission.

"Up to you, man." Randall unsnapped the Glock from his side and placed it in his palm, offering it up to Jake. "I know you remember how to use one from that stunt you pulled in Montana."

Jake was staring at the gleaming black metal in Randall's hand, and then he looked over at Jason for a brief moment. Alexa knew exactly what had crossed his mind—did he not trust himself with a gun in the same room as Jason? Would he want to take revenge for Alexa into his own hands?

No—she knew his heart. He wouldn't really kill someone in cold blood, would he? Even if the thought had crossed her mind about every other day of the week since Jason had been arrested.

"I don't think you need Jake with you," Alexa rasped. She stood, bracing her palms against the table.

"He needs to get back in the game. Things might get ugly soon, and I need to make sure he can hold his own." While Xander had a point, she didn't like it. And she also didn't see how watching Jason upload malware would get Jake all that comfortable with missions again.

"I understand, but isn't there—"

Xander held up his hand, and Alexa fell silent. There was a glimmer of something in Xander's eyes. It wasn't fear, but . . . he wanted Jake to come. Maybe it was Xander that didn't trust himself alone with Jason. He'd lost a friend the day Jason had sabotaged their mission, seven and half years ago.

"I'm good, Alexa. I can babysit this piece of shit." Jake's voice was laced with a bitter iciness to it.

She didn't know what to say, and she knew none of this was her call anyway. "Be careful, the both of you."

"What—no well wishes for me, love?" Jason had the damn nerve to wink at her.

"Fuck you," she responded without hesitation.

Her gaze flickered to the gun Jake was holding in his hand. He looked over at her, his mouth tight and jaw locked. He gave her a slight nod, his brows drawn together, and her heart sank as he turned his back. This was why she'd never been able to date an agent—the not knowing if he'd come back alive. Her teammates who'd died had families . . . and had left behind widows and fatherless children.

Once they left, she swallowed back the lick of fear that blew across her skin like a cold chill as she studied the image of the men on her computer. They became a blur before her as they walked down the hall to Reza's room.

\* \* \*

*DON'T KILL HIM. DON'T DO IT.* BUT HIS BODY WAS ON FIRE, HIS fingers trembled at his sides, dying to destroy the man who had inflicted so much pain on Alexa. He should have had the death penalty for what he'd done . . . although, now that Jake thought of it, the U.K. may not even have a death penalty.

"You good?" Xander asked as they made their way into the stairwell.

"Could be better." Jake glared at Jason's back.

"Agreed," Xander said as they reached the sixth floor.

When they entered Reza's suite, Xander gestured to one of the doors off the main room. "I'll go get the computer. Keep an eye on him, will ya?"

"Of course." Jake reached for the gun tucked beneath his shirt and held it tight, but kept his arm hanging loose at his side. He didn't think Jason would make a move, but as the guy was a scumbag criminal, there were no guarantees of good behavior.

"How is she?" Jason sank on the couch and pressed his palms to his thighs. "As feisty in bed as I remember?"

Jason was just trying to rattle him, and Jake had to try to stay calm. They needed the son of a bitch, after all. For now.

"Shut your fucking mouth," Jake bit out—that was about as close to calm as he'd get.

"You don't even have the balls to try and come at me, do ya? I read your file earlier today. You've lost your mind, so it seems." Jason tapped at the side of his skull.

Jake wondered what information MI6 was keeping on him and why the hell they would let Jason look at it. Of course, Jason's skill as a hacker gave him access to whatever he desired.

"Do you even remember how to shoot that thing?" Jason tipped his chin up, his eyes on Jake's Glock.

Jake raised the weapon in front of him, extending his arm and cocking his head. His breathing was more controlled than it should be for someone who couldn't actually remember having ever shot a man.

"What's wrong?" Xander asked.

Jake glanced up as Xander entered the room, laptop in his hand. "Nothing," Jake finally said while lowering the weapon.

"We don't have much time." Xander handed the laptop to Jason.

Jake crossed the room and went to the window, which had a view of his hotel across the way. He rubbed the butt of the gun against his forehead.

This situation seemed eerily familiar.

A black curtain of darkness appeared behind his eyes as memories tugged at the corners of his mind. He resisted, gritting down on his teeth and keeping his eyes open as he took in shallow breaths. He narrowed his focus to the street down below.

It wasn't the time or the place for a memory hangover.

Jake must have been standing in a daze for longer than he realized. Before he had fully recovered, Jason's voice sounded behind him: "I'm done."

It was the first time Jason had said anything that gave Jake a sense of relief.

"You're sure Reza won't detect—"

"Trust me, I know what I'm doing," Jason interrupted.

Jake turned to face the two men. Xander's back was stiff as he glared at Jason.

"Sure . . ." Xander drawled and started to reach for the laptop, but his hand went to his ear as his brows pulled tight together. "Say that again."

Jake took a step closer to Xander. Worry crawled across Xander's face.

"Shit." Xander pulled his sidearm from his holster and extended his arm. "Did you help them?" He aimed his gun at Jason, and Jake followed suit, even though he had no idea what the hell was going on.

"What are you talking about?" Jason rose from behind the desk and lifted his hands, palms up.

Xander came around to the side of the desk and jerked his chin up. His arm moved like lightning, bringing the gun closer to Jason's temple. "You know what I'm talking about." Xander's jaw locked tight as his gaze narrowed.

Jake stepped to Xander's side and pointed his gun at Jason as well. If Xander was upset, clearly he had a reason to be. And if his anger was directed toward Jason, Jake was more than willing to get on board.

"Shit, mate. I don't have a bloody clue what you're talking about. You guys brought me here. I did what you asked, now back the hell off." Jason took a step back and pivoted to face Xander full-on. The gun was no longer at his temple, but right in the center of his forehead.

Xander was absolutely still for a moment, but before Xander could make another move, the lights flickered off, and the room was swept by darkness.

"Fuck. You there?" Xander cursed under his breath. "We lost comms."

Jake tried to adjust to the dark room, which was lit only by lights from the streetlamps outside and the soft glow coming from the windows of the hotel across the street.

"Now I know you did this." Xander surged toward Jason, pushing him back until he was against the wall.

Jake focused his eyes on the two figures, and moved to press his forearm against Jason's throat. He cocked his gun and found Jason's cheek—pressing the nozzle there.

"Are you working with Anarchy, dammit? Did they get to you somehow?" Xander asked.

"How the hell would that be possible? Drop your guns," Jason pleaded.

Instead, Jake shifted his gun to Jason's mouth. He'd ram it down the man's throat if he had to.

"Shit!" Xander yelled. "Get down." A pin-sized red light speared the room and landed just over Jake's shoulder on the wall.

Jake dropped to the floor, dragging the son of a bitch, Jason, down with him as a bullet shattered the glass and tore at the wall.

Jason was cowered next to Jake with his hands over his head. The big guy wasn't as tough without a computer in his hands.

"We need to get out of here," Xander said.

But Jake couldn't move.

"Jake!" Xander shouted. "Come on, man."

Jake's eyes shut—he was unable to do a damn thing.

Memories surrounded him. All he knew were the blinding moments of his past.

*"Semper Fi! Ooh Rah, brother."*

*Enemy fire.*

*IEDs.*

*Quantico.*

*Tombstones.*

*. . . Alexa.*

Loud, screeching noises grated against his skull as the gun slipped from his hand. He pressed his hands to his temples, trying to work through the memories that drilled from one side of his skull to the other.

"We've got to move," Xander urged, but Jake could barely hear him. "Fuck. We've got company," Xander whispered as Jake opened his eyes at the sound of a gunshot.

# CHAPTER TWENTY-THREE

A FEW MINUTES BEFORE . . .

"HOW ARE THEY?"

"Jason's almost done," Randall answered.

*Thank God.* Alexa hoped it would work, though. Jason was the best, but what if @Anarchy was better? She pulled her bottom lip between her teeth as she glared at the footage on screen, impatience burning through her as she waited for their escape.

Her burner phone began to vibrate.

It had to be MI6, but she was so high strung she forgot to deliver her code. "Yeah?"

"Alexa, shit."

It was Sam from HQ, and his tone wasn't exactly comforting.

"What is it?" She sat back in the rolling desk chair and tucked an arm against her chest.

"You guys need to clear out of there now. Laney's orders."

"We're almost done. What's going on, Sam?"

"We've been breached, Alexa. Hacked," he said the words slowly as if giving her the chance to process it.

"What?" She was on her feet, signaling to Randall with an

urgent wave of the hand her way. "Get Xander and the guys out of there now!"

Randall nodded and placed a hand over his ear as she listened to what Sam was saying.

"We traced the origin of the emails the Americans received that sent them to Italy to attack the ISIS leader, Ansari. And, Alexa, the digital fingerprint is a match for the intel we intercepted about the Anarchy attack. The intel that sent us to Munich."

She cupped a hand to her mouth. "We were both set up? But why?" She jerked upright and to her feet.

Then everything became clear to her. Like a film had been lifted from her eyes and she could see the truth.

She couldn't decrypt Boris Gregov's files because there was no actual content. @Anarchy had known they were coming to Germany because they'd lured them there. She played right into Gregov's dirty hands.

"Jesus Christ. The USB we used to download Gregov's files . . . Shit, we downloaded the Trojan right into our servers." She looked over at Randall as her eyes widened. "Are they out?" she whispered.

"Xander is confronting Jason—he thinks . . ."

"Tell them to get out now!" Concern darted up her spine.

"Get out of there, too, Alexa. They know everything. You might be walking right into an ambush."

She braced a hand to the desk and looked up at Randall. *Not again. Jesus, no.* "Sam? Hello?" Silence.

She looked down at her phone just as the room went black.

"What the hell!" Randall yelled. "Shit. I've lost comms, too!"

"We need to get to them," she cried, working her way toward Randall, fumbling in the dark.

"We've lost contact with Alpha and Beta teams, too," Seth shouted.

"We've got to get to Xander. To Jake. They're in trouble," Alexa rasped as she tried to power her mobile on with no luck. "I need a gun. Get me a Goddamn gun!" Her hands were trembling, her body locked in position.

*I did this. Me. I'm going to lose them.*

"You're staying here," Randall ordered. "Seth and I will find them."

"To hell with that. I'm coming!" she demanded.

"Alexa," Randall warned as they found their way out of the room.

A few hotel guests were in the hall as Alexa, Randall, and Seth pressed against the wall, seeking the stairwell.

Guests were talking—trying to figure out what had happened.

"Stay close to me," Randall ordered, but damned if she needed that right now. She didn't care about her own life, not with her best friend in danger, along with the man who'd brought her heart back to life.

No, she couldn't lose Jake again. She just got him back.

People scattered down the stairs, fumbling in the dark, two-by-two, helping each other down—a horde of bodies moving like shadows. Why were they trying to get out? Unless they were afraid . . .

Alexa had kept count in her head as they reached each landing until she knew they were on Reza's floor. There, an indistinguishable babble of language sailed over her shoulders as she brushed past people, fighting against the crowd that was suddenly pushing forward faster. People were fleeing like their lives depended on it.

And then she heard the screaming and the pop-pop-pop of gunfire.

Alexa, Randall, and Seth waited as the throng of people pressed past them to exit the floor. There was no way they could fight through the doorway when it was filled with such panic and chaos.

Alexa's fingers itched with anticipation. She needed to get to Jake and Xander. Her heart was ground to ashes, pumping hard in her chest, obliterating her rationality. Were they too late? The second there was a lull in the crowd, they rushed through the door. Alexa forced herself to draw up a map of the hotel in her mind, which she had memorized to make sense of the surveillance cameras.

The gunfire had ceased before they'd entered the hall, which seemed empty as far as she could tell. But that didn't mean they were alone. Someone could be waiting and watching in the dark, using night vision goggles while she was blinded by the darkness. She could be two seconds from losing her life, but she couldn't think like that. She needed to get to her team.

"To the right," she directed as a hard metal object slapped against her palm. She secured the gun in one hand as her fingers glided along the wall. Reza's room was the fifth down from the lift. "Follow me."

When her hands touched the lift, she began to count.

"Should be the next door," she whispered. "Here." She paused in front of the door.

There was a hand on her back, gently nudging her out of the way. She could just recognize Randall's profile—he was taller and broader than Seth.

But then the door began to open.

Even in the dark, Alexa recognized Xander.

Her heart leaped from her chest as she lunged at him, tossing her arms around his shoulders. "Oh, God!"

"We were attacked. We need to find him," Xander mumbled as he stepped back from her.

"Find who?" Alexa asked.

"Jason," came Jake's voice.

"Jake!" Her entire body quivered with relief. A burst of oxygen shot through her, and she could breathe again. Xander and Jake were both alive. Her team had survived.

She wanted to go to Jake, to fit herself tight into his arms and lose herself in his safety, but she checked the impulse. There were more important things to do.

"They took that son of a bitch, Jason," Xander said. "Shot the room up and grabbed him, then got out through that damn connecting door—the one I used earlier."

"Who?" Randall asked. "Jesus, we probably let the son of bitches right past us in the hallway."

"And Jason didn't make a Goddamn peep," Alexa noted.

"I don't know who—I couldn't see a thing. There were two guys from what I could tell," Xander answered. "Does anything work? I lost you on comms soon after you told me to get out."

"No. They killed our mobiles, too," Seth answered.

"We have to get Jason back." Xander started to move down the dark hall as if he knew where he was going, determination propelling him forward.

Alexa hooked her arm around Jake's, and he flinched. She softly let him go. "Are you okay?" she whispered.

"Fuck no," Jake said.

*Stupid question.*

"We need to split up. Where were Reza and Gregov before we lost power?" Xander stopped walking and faced her, a figure in the dark.

"As far as we know, they were where they were supposed to be. Gregov was in his room, and Reza was at the casino," she answered.

"Try and find Beta team—they were just outside the hotel and in the lobby when this all went down. Let's rendezvous at the Columbus monument at Rambla in thirty minutes," Xander instructed.

"That works," Randall answered.

"Jake, you stick with Alexa, okay?" Xander stepped in front of Jake. "You have ammo?"

"I'm good," Jake answered, and Alexa could sense something different about him. She wasn't sure how she knew it, especially given their current shit situation and the fact that she couldn't even make out his facial expressions, but nevertheless, she could feel it. The man was cold.

But he'd just been in a shoot-out—could she blame him?

"You think Jason was working with Anarchy somehow?" Alexa asked Xander.

"I don't know, but we need to get him back."

"Randall, Seth, can you guys update Xander on what we found out?" she asked.

"Will do," Seth said.

"See you in thirty, and be careful." Xander's hand found her shoulder in the dark and gave it a squeeze. If she could see his face, she knew there'd be worry behind his eyes.

She turned around when she realized Jake wasn't on the move. "Jake?" She went to him. "Are you hurt?"

"No."

"Then we should leave, yeah?" She sucked in a breath and tightened a hand around her weapon.

"Just give me a second, okay?" His voice cracked.

*Is this too much for you?* How could it not be? It was almost too much for her, and she wasn't the one who'd been tortured and had amnesia.

She turned from him, feeling shameful and guilty for what had happened. How could she have missed the Trojan? How had she uploaded a virus from @Anarchy into the servers? She'd run tests on the USB to ensure there wasn't any malware, but clearly, she'd missed something.

When she felt Jake's hand settle on the small of her back, she stiffened. He came up close behind her, his face near her hair. "Alexa, there's something I have to tell you."

"What is it?" She couldn't move or face him. Her nerves twisted inside her at the feeling of his breath near her ear.

"I remember . . . *everything*." His words nipped at her skin, lifting the hairs on her arms.

"Wh—what?"

His hand went to her hip. "The showdown in there was like a smack in the face. Suddenly, I was back in Iraq. I was undercover in an Al Qaeda terrorist cell in Texas."

Her body stilled at his words, and she inhaled a sharp breath.

"I remember every battle. Every fight. Every man I've killed." His deep voice penetrated her flesh and shot straight to her core. "I remember every moment we were together, too. I remember you, Alexa."

She lowered her head. So now he knew the truth about what had happened.

"Jake, I'm—"

"Don't, Alexa." His hand was gone. "Right now we need to get to a phone. We need to call your government."

Her voice was a whisper. "Why?"

She pressed a hand to her chest, struggling to breathe.

"I remembered that they're planning to hit Westminster."

"Oh, God. The suicide vests."

"I'm pretty sure they have something much worse for it planned than that."

Alexa's pulse throbbed in her neck. Her arm dropped to her side, still holding onto the gun.

"Come on, Agent Ryan, we need to get out of here."

*Agent Ryan?* So, he was pissed at her.

Her stomach tucked in as she trailed behind him, her heart betraying her body even though she needed to be strong right now.

A few minutes later, they found their way out to the street, guns tucked safely in concealed holsters. Guests were crowded outside the hotel beyond the perimeter the police had established.

"Let's go." Jake grabbed hold of her arm, and the touch of his fingers on her body created a sharp spike of adrenaline inside her. She allowed him to lead her through the throng of people and down the street.

She looked around for their team members, but she'd never

been introduced to the guys on Alpha or Beta team. She wouldn't even know whom to seek.

Alexa stole a glimpse back at the hotel as they began walking with quick steps down the street. The rest of the city twinkled around the hotel, which sat in a darkness of its own making.

"There's a restaurant up there."

She looked to where Jake was pointing with his free hand. His other hand tugged at her forearm as if she were a prisoner who might decide to run away.

"Hang on," she said, just as Jake pressed a hand to the door.

He dropped his arm and peered at her, and there was a blackness, an anger in his eyes that she'd never seen before. His past had hurtled into his mind all at once. He'd gotten twelve years of memories—good and bad (probably a lot of them bad)—and she couldn't imagine how it must feel to relive so much in such a short period. And he didn't even have the chance to make sense of it all.

"Did you get hurt?" She touched his shoulder where there was blood.

"No, but I clocked a guy a couple of good times before the son of a bitch got away."

"You have a T-shirt under there?" She lifted his shirt and was relieved to see a gray cotton tee.

"Take off the button-up. We don't want you to attract attention."

His eyes remained on hers as he worked at the buttons, and she tried to look away, but she couldn't. She was sucked into his pain. She could feel every drop of it.

Alexa only averted her gaze when Jake tossed his shirt in a waste bin off to the side of the little brownstone building. "Come on." He opened the door and motioned for her to go first.

Her body tensed as she crossed in front of him. Once inside, he came around in front of her and approached the hostess. He began sputtering Spanish, and Alexa was impressed. What else did he know? Of course, she was the same—spoke three languages. Such talents were to be expected in their line of work.

Jake faced Alexa again. "She's letting us use her phone. She's grabbing it from the back."

Alexa watched the long-haired brunette walk away before disappearing behind a door. "How'd you pull that off?" Her Spanish was piss-poor, so she hadn't understood but every fifth word Jake had said.

"Just offered her that pendant on your neck."

Her hand darted to the small diamond hanging there. "No." She rubbed the diamond between her fingers. "My dad gave it to me." She cleared her throat. "Before he died."

Jake threaded his disheveled hair with his fingers. "Shit, Alexa. Sorry. I thought it was just a piece of jewelry. You have any euros on you, then?"

"Not on me. Left my purse at the hotel." She released her necklace and bit her lip.

"Come on. There has to be a *locutorio* around here. No one will let us use their phone and rack up a bill without something in return." He grabbed her hand, and they rushed back out into the street.

"What's a *locutorio?*"

"A phone booth." He glanced around and then tugged at her elbow once again.

"Okay."

With hurried steps, they searched the street for a phone, medics blazing by.

Jake jerked to a stop a few minutes later, and Alexa careened into him, her hands landing on his back.

"Sorry." She stepped away.

"Here." He motioned to a building. The *locutorio* was more like a store. Inside, there were separate mini stalls with phones. Thank God the place was open until midnight, and it was empty.

Jake and Alexa entered the tight phone stall, and they pulled the door closed behind them. "Can you call MI6 collect?" Was that his idea of a joke?

Fortunately, there was a protocol for such events.

Jake leaned against the back wall as she dialed. She noticed his hand lingering at his hip, and he was biting back a grimace of pain. Had he been hurt earlier, or was he feeling the remnants of past wounds? She couldn't help but worry.

Alexa looked away from him when the low-pitched hum sang from the receiver, followed by a click. "Code: zero nine five three two eleven. I've been compromised."

She waited a few moments, and then there were two more clicks, followed by a ring.

"Alexa? Are you all right?"

Alexa had never been so happy to hear the sound of Laney's voice.

"I'm okay, but Jason Holms was taken. I'm not with my team anymore. We, eh, Agent Summers and I are looking for him, but—"

"We've lost the asset?" Laney snapped out. "Things are a bloody mess over here. We've had to shut down our servers to prevent further damage. We have people from GCHQ here. Hell, it's eleven at night and members of Parliament are crawling up my arse over this! They'll go ballistic when they hear we lost Holms."

"I don't know if Jason was somehow involved in all of this, or if Anarchy discovered his usefulness when they hacked us . . ." *God, this is unbelievable.* "I'm so sorry, Laney. I followed all protocol when I downloaded Gregov's files to our server, but I must have missed something. I can't believe it."

Then she remembered the reason they had called. "Agent Summers needs to talk to you. He has his memories back."

Alexa stepped out of the way and handed the phone to Jake, who studied her for a brief moment, his eyes flickering with confusion. "Ma'am, I'm not sure if these bastards have changed their target now that they know I'm alive, but when I was being held I overheard them speaking in Arabic. I only got fragments because they hadn't meant for me to hear—but from the neighboring room, I heard them mention the Palace of Westminster. Parliament. I don't know specifics, though. Sorry."

Alexa heard Laney swearing, but couldn't make out the rest.

"I don't know . . . I don't know. They didn't say anything else," Jake said. "I understand. Yes, ma'am." Jake handed Alexa the phone a moment later.

She swallowed and held it to her ear. "Yeah?"

"Alexa, this isn't your fault. These bastards tricked us. There was no way your team could have known you'd been lured to Munich so they could plant a virus in our server. It's damn genius on their part." She hissed. "And the virus moved so slow it was undetectable. If Sam hadn't had concerns about the servers running just a millisecond slower than normal . . ."

"What do you want me to do now? I'm meeting up with Xander soon. Have you heard from him?" Alexa's voice quavered, and she felt a punch of worry in her gut.

"No, I haven't. But Alexa, you need to hear me—everyone on your team has been compromised. The virus stole all the data related to Anarchy."

"They've been tracking our every move." She swallowed. "They knew we consulted with Jason before." She pressed a hand to her forehead and shut her eyes, trying to come to grips with the information.

"We've been playing into their hands like bloody puppets. It makes me so Goddamn sick. We led them to Agent Summers in Montana, and then they figured out we were coming to Barcelona . . ." Laney's voice was like the edge of a freshly sharpened knife.

"As much as I hate Jason, I don't think he had anything to do with this. He's known by hackers all over the world. Anarchy saw their chance to grab him and they took it." Nervousness spiked through Alexa so fast she thought she'd be sick. "What will you do about Parliament? If we close Westminster, Anarchy will either change the target, or . . . God, I don't even want to know what they'll do."

"I'll figure that out. We've alerted the Americans of the situation in case they've been breached as well. But as for you, right now I need you to locate Xander and the others and get everything cleared out of the hotel. Then get to the British Consulate and wait for further instructions. They'll be expecting you."

Once they were at the British Consulate, they'd no longer be on the case. They'd be trucked back home, and new faces sent in. Faces that @Anarchy hadn't already learned by heart.

"My family," she suddenly cried. Thoughts of her mum, sister, and baby nephew flickered to her mind.

"We have agents on their way to Manchester to protect them— same with everyone's family."

"Thank you." If anything happened to her family, she would never forgive herself. "But ma'am, I can't sit on the sidelines. I've been working this case forever. No one knows them the way I do—"

"We have this, Alexa. You have your instructions. I'll be in touch." The line went dead.

Alexa released the phone, her mind and body feeling almost numb.

"Alexa?"

She could barely hear him. She pushed open the door. She couldn't breathe in that tight space. Out in the open area of the building, she bent forward and pressed her hands to her knees, trying to gather air into her lungs.

Jake's hand was on her back. "You okay?"

She stood upright a moment later and faced him. They were alone. After all, who used pay phones anymore?

"We've got to find Xander, and then I'm supposed to go to the consulate." She blew out a breath. "They know everything, Jake. I'm done."

"Anarchy?" His brows pulled together, assessing her.

Alexa cupped the back of her neck with both hands and began kneading the flesh as she tried to find the right words. When her hands dropped heavy at her sides, she told him about the hack and how Anarchy had lured her team to Germany, just like they had roped Jake and his men to Italy.

He rubbed a hand down his cheek, his eyes widening when she finished.

"They brought us to Munich to infiltrate MI6, but do you really think they had you guys go to Italy just to . . . sorry, I don't mean 'just'—"

Jake held his hand between them, his eyes growing dark as pain fell over his face like a mask. Not only did he know that he'd lost his team—he remembered every moment of it.

When Jake didn't say anything, she pushed a little more. "Um. Now that you remember everything, is there anything else about the OP in Italy that could help explain why Anarchy brought you there?" She glanced at her wristwatch. "We should talk and walk. Maybe Xander found Jason." She could only hope, at this point.

Jake held the door open for her, and they went out to the street. "So?"

"I think the monument is this way." He pointed down the street, which was still bustling with life, despite the fact that a shooting had occurred just a few blocks away. Maybe the denizens of Barcelona were unaware that there had been a shooting, even though Alexa could still hear the faint sound of sirens in the distance.

"Well, like Trent told you back in Montana, our team was formed at the last minute to go to Sicily. We didn't have time to follow the proper matrix—to go through the appropriate channels of approval for the kill. The General at CENTCOM got clearance from the President, and so we were sent to Italy, where we broke protocol again by not alerting the Italian government that we were going to use Hellfire missiles against an enemy target. According to the intel, we only had a small window of opportunity to use our Reaper to take out the ISIS leader, Ansari."

And she thought Jake didn't break rules.

"You had a drone strike planned?" Her heart started racing in her chest, pounding fast as ideas pushed through her mind.

He looked over at her, the muscles in his face pulled together, and he nodded. "Our pilots are based in Las Vegas, but there are two pilots located at Sigonella in Sicily, as well. The MQ-9 Reaper has a slight delay, and that delay interferes with take-off and landing, which is why we need pilots locally. Drone pilots in Vegas pilot the rest of the mission."

Alexa knew this because if it weren't for that delay, Bekas's wife and daughters would still be alive.

"Anyway. About an hour into the flight, we lost connection with the drone."

"What?" She stopped, her face screwing tight.

"Drone pilots like to say, 'No comms, no bombs.' Something happened to the satellite—interference, maybe—which meant we lost control of the Reaper."

"So what happened to the drone?"

"There's a built-in default. If communication is lost, the drone automatically returns to the nearest landing facility. This keeps it from crashing or falling into enemy hands." His eyes grew darker as he spoke. "The ISIS leader was in civilian territory by the time we got another drone up, so we were called back to the States. I don't know what the diagnostics on the drone showed—my team was ambushed on our way out of Sicily, so I never saw the report."

The word ambushed was like a gunshot to her ears—splicing her open to her core as she recalled the loss of life of her own team members. Her emotions became mangled—twisted with anger and sadness as she drew up the images of the bodies lying on the cold concrete floor in Copenhagen.

Her voice was clipped when she next spoke as she tried to stifle her pain for the sake of the current issue at hand. "We need to call

Laney back. We need to let MI6 and the FBI know what Anarchy is planning to do." Alexa spotted the tall monument in the distance. "Let's meet the team first."

Jake reached for her wrist, stopping her. "You think it was Anarchy? That they hacked the Reaper? But they failed, right? They didn't overtake it, even if that was their goal."

Alexa was shaking her head. "Could have been a test run to see if they could hack it. Trent should have told us about this. I would have understood Anarchy's plan if he had."

"What happened in Sicily was highly classified." He released a ragged breath. "But what does it matter?"

"Because it tells us Anarchy's end game," she said in a rush. "To hijack a Reaper and use the Hellfire missiles." She stepped closer to Jake and looked at him, her lips parting as worry moved through her. "Bekas's family was killed by a drone strike, right? He's going to use our own weapon against us."

"Retribution," Jake said beneath his breath.

Alexa turned and hurried toward the monument, needing to see Xander. Maybe he'd be able to help. When she arrived, she checked her watch as she circled the statue. It had been forty minutes, but she didn't find any familiar faces. "He's not here. You don't think something happened to Xander, do you?" She was short of breath as panic crept inside her.

Jake pressed his hands over her arms and pulled her in with his gaze. "Give them time. Maybe he went back to the hotel, or he stopped to call MI6."

She looked beyond Jake's shoulders, searching the crowd lingering around the statue. Were any of them members of Alpha or Beta team?

No one screamed military, and most looked like couples in love or tourists. They were taking selfies with the monument behind them.

Alexa pulled away from Jake and sat on one of the steps at the base of the monument. A glow of light splattered the pavement around the statue, offering a romantic setting with the palm trees, water, and beautifully colored homes perched on the hills like layers of a cake. Why couldn't they be here for some romantic getaway? The work she did was meaningful, but at what point would she ever be able to find meaning in the simple things in life? Like admiring the color of the dark sky as the stars glittered above, with a man she cared about pressing his lips to hers. Or enjoying a steaming cup of tea, her feet kicked up over the side of a rocking chair as she watched sailboats drift by on the Mediterranean Sea.

She was distracting herself right now. She knew that.

In her heart, she knew something was wrong with Xander.

@Anarchy had him.

"It's Randall and Seth."

Alexa jumped to her feet at the sight of Randall and Seth maneuvering through the crowd. They appeared to be okay—no injuries that she could see.

"Where's Xander?" She blinked a few times as Jake came up alongside her.

Randall bent forward to catch his breath. "He's not here? We got split up at the casino. The power went out, and there was gunfire there. Several members of Alpha team were injured," Seth explained. "Same with Beta team." His words were like a deadly blow. She hadn't met the teams, but these were English and American servicemen. Good men had been hurt.

She gripped her stomach as her shoulders hunched forward.

"We need to get back to the hotel and grab our stuff once the police let us in. Then we need to get to the embassy," Randall said. "And you guys should head to the British Consulate."

"No," Jake insisted with a quickness that surprised Alexa. "You all should go. But I'm staying."

"What? Why?" Randall asked.

"I'm not going anywhere until we stop these pricks. I'm not going to sit back and hide." Jake was shaking his head, his voice laced with determination. "Both of our agencies have been breached. We don't know who to trust or what Anarchy already knows about us. If we're going to take these bastards out, we need to do things differently," Jake said.

"I have to report what happened," Randall said, his eyes narrowing on Jake.

"Please, do. You need to. And let them know we think Anarchy is planning on hijacking one of our drones at Sigonella. And we also think they'll be attacking the Palace of Westminster in London," Jake noted in a glib voice.

Randall stared at Jake in surprise.

Alexa barely heard as Jake updated the men on what they'd discovered. She was still looking around, panicked, hoping to see her best mate's face.

"What will you do? Where will you go?" Seth asked.

"I have a plan," Jake said, shrugging away the question.

This was news to Alexa.

"I don't like this," Randall said.

"You don't have to, but it won't change anything," Jake said in a firm voice. He swiveled on his heel, turning away.

"Jake—" Randall started, but Alexa held up her hand.

"You guys should go home. But be careful, Seth. Anarchy knows who you are."

Seth's brows quirked together and he stepped closer to Alexa. "You're not coming?"

*I can't.* There was no way she'd leave before finding Xander. And once he was safe, she wanted nothing more than to stop Bekas and the rest of the @Anarchy crew.

"I'm staying with Jake."

"Jesus, Alexa." Seth gripped his forehead with his thumb and middle finger.

"Can you get a message to Laney for me? Can you tell her about the drone—and tell her I'm sorry, and also," she cleared her throat, "tell her I quit."

"Alexa." Seth reached for her arm. He was older than she, so maybe it didn't matter to him if his identity was exposed. He could sit behind a desk for a few years and retire, or perhaps he already had enough socked away to keep him comfortable after they forced him out.

"I'm not going to push papers at the agency now that I won't be able to go on OPs," she hissed. Plus, after staying in Barcelona against Laney's instructions, she would probably get fired, anyways.

"You don't know that will be the case," Seth pleaded.

"How many agents do you know continue to work in the field after their covers have been blown?" She rubbed her hands down her face, her body burning as if coals were pressed to her flesh.

"If you want to quit, you'll have to tell Laney yourself, Alexa." He started to turn but stopped. "And Alexa?"

"Yeah?"

"Don't get yourself killed before you have the chance to tell her." Seth patted her on the shoulder, and she inhaled a slow breath.

Every part of her ached down to her chilled fingers as she watched the men leave then turned in search of Jake.

He was standing with his hands in his pockets, his head tipped toward the gleaming globe of the moon in the sky.

"They're gone," she said in a soft voice, wondering if they were making a mistake.

They were alone, with no resources or money.

How could they find Xander and stop @Anarchy like this?

"You should have gone with them, Alexa." He slowly turned to face her. She expected he'd insist she leave again, but instead, he said, "I have a call to make." He swallowed as the light from the street lamp spread across his face. "Are you coming?"

"But . . . what about Xander?"

Jake glanced down the street. "You and I both know he's not meeting us here."

# CHAPTER TWENTY-FOUR

JAKE WAS SUPPOSED TO BE A MESSENGER TO THE WORLD FOR Kemal Bekas. He'd managed to resist his attackers and snatch a suicide vest from their stash, using their tools of death as his way out the door . . .

And now, was Xander going to be in the same spot? Would Bekas try and force Xander to spread his messages of hate and death?

Jake clutched the small, folded piece of paper Emily had given him, trying to decide if he was making a mistake. Did he really want to drag his Marine buddies into this? To put even more lives at risk? They had fought side by side. He had dragged Michael's bleeding body through the desert after Michael had been shot three times. He had waited until dark when the chopper came to rescue them.

Aiden, Ben, and Connor had all saved his hide more than once.

They'd take a bullet for each other—some already had. They were brothers.

But that had been long ago, and now Aiden, Connor, and Michael were engaged or married. If things went bad, they would leave widows in their wake. And Jake couldn't be responsible for that.

But Ben Logan out in Vegas was single. Jake didn't value his friend's life less because of that, but he could feel less guilty about asking. There were lives at stake, after all.

Jake's hand trembled as he opened the paper that had the number to Ben's secure phone line. He wasn't about to call the man's personal phone, so thank God his sister had thought to write all those numbers down.

A rush of air escaped Jake's nose as the phone rang. He peeked through the glass pane in the door. Alexa was sitting on a bench in the other room, her head resting in her hands. Was she crying?

It only took two rings for Ben to pick up.

"It's me. It's Jake."

"Jesus Christ. Michael told me what happened to you," Ben blurted. "You okay?"

"Not really, man. But I'll be a hell of a lot better if you can help me."

"Of course."

Zero hesitation. *Thank God.* But Jake knew he could count on Ben; otherwise, he wouldn't have called.

He hung his head and pressed a hand to the door as the weight of the day began to bury itself inside him. It felt as if he were weighted down by quicksand, and he was slowly sinking to the depths of hell.

"I'm in Barcelona with no money and no place to go. And a crazy terrorist, hell-bent on revenging the death of his family, is trying to kill me." Jake almost laughed at the absurdity of his words. But it wasn't remotely funny.

"Well, shit. Sounds like a lot has happened since you last saw Michael." Ben paused for a moment. "I'm guessing you remember me. Since you called."

"I remember everything," Jake said grimly. He now remembered every death.

But also, every save.

Those saves were why he did what he did, after all. Why he put his neck on the line, and why he was about to put Ben at risk, too.

"I'll be on the first plane to Barcelona. Probably take me twenty-four hours or so to get to you, though."

"Actually, I need to get to Sicily. You, uh, know any rich people with private planes who can fly me to Italy?" Ben had high roller clients out in Vegas who paid him to keep them safe on their visits. Some of them were a bit shady, but Jake didn't care as long as they could help.

Ben was silent for a moment. "I do, actually."

"Good. And soon. I'm short on time."

"Can you call me back in twenty minutes?"

"Yeah. Thank you." Jake scrubbed a hand down his jaw, which was covered in stubble. "Don't tell the guys, okay? Not unless we have no choice. Don't take this the wrong way, but—"

"I know. You're right. Besides, I love nothing more than blasting a bunch of motherfucking terrorists." There was a hint of truth embedded in his humorous bravado. Ben had always been the wild card—the craziest of the bunch. But Jake knew he could trust Ben with his life.

"Why aren't you rolling with the Feds on this one?"

Jake toyed with the right words to say. "My cover has been compromised. Also, I need to color outside the lines on this one."

Ben snorted. "No more paint by numbers?"

Jake could picture his friend shaking his head, laughter in his eyes.

"I've missed working with you, man. Call me in twenty," Ben said.

When Jake hung up the phone, he stared out the window at Alexa, wondering how she'd react to his plan. Without her, it would crumble like sand.

He tucked the paper back into the wallet, wishing he'd thought to get some euros before coming to Spain. Then, at least, he wouldn't be relying on Ben's connections for transportation.

"So?" Alexa was on her feet as soon as he came into the room. Her hands were locked tight at her sides.

He shoved his wallet into his back pocket. "In twenty minutes, I'll know if my plan will work."

"Why twenty minutes?" She crossed the room to stand in front of him, and her hazel eyes landed on his.

To think he had once thought he'd never see her again. And now here she was, standing before him. A British spy.

"A friend of mine with a lot of contacts is going to help us. Well, hopefully." But Jake knew Ben would find a way. They always came through for each other.

Jake motioned for her to sit back down.

She hesitated, pulling her brows together, before going back over to the dark, wooden bench. She leaned the back of her head against the wall, and her hands fidgeted in her lap.

"We're going to Sicily." He sat next to her and pressed his palms to his jeaned thighs, staring down at his hands.

"Because of the drone?"

He could feel her eyes on him, so he dragged his gaze up to meet hers. "If Anarchy—well, Bekas and his men—are planning to hijack a drone, they'll need to be near it to pilot the takeoff."

"Won't the military ground all drone flights now?" Alexa asked. "There's no way Bekas will get a chance to overtake one."

Military recon drones had been hacked before, but none had Hellfire missiles on board.

Not yet, at least.

"Tell me, Alexa," Jake shifted to face her fully, "do you think it's even remotely possible for someone to hijack a drone that's still grounded at the base? Not just overtake it once it's taken off, but manipulate the power and control functions of the drone before it's up in the sky?"

"I barely know anything about the Reaper. But, considering we were able to manipulate the nuclear centrifuges in Iran to slow down their weapons program from thousands of miles away . . . and Anarchy was responsible for an explosion in Nevada all the way from Istanbul—yeah, I guess anything is possible. Well, especially now that they have Jason's help." She stood up and cupped the back of her neck before beginning to pace in front of him. "What's a Reaper's capable distance? Can it reach London from the Sigonella base in Sicily?"

"The Reaper has about a thirty-five-hundred-mile range, but combat range is usually a max of a thousand miles one way and a thousand back."

"And if they don't care about coming back?" she asked.

"I don't buy it. It's too far," Jake said. "It gives the military too much time to retake the drone or blow it out of the sky before it reaches its destination. Bekas wouldn't take that risk."

"Okay." She rubbed a hand over her face and then spun toward him. "Let's say Bekas and his men pull it off, and they actually jack a drone. Maybe we could manipulate the connection between the drone and its correlating satellite. Jam the transmission."

"If you could pull that off, and the drone loses contact with the satellite, then it would trip the default setting. The drone would autopilot right back to the base." Jake was on his feet, feeling hopeful. "Could you do that?"

Her lip pulled between her teeth as she stared down at the floor. "I don't know. May take more than just a computer. And it looks like Anarchy already got their feet wet hacking the drone, so they have more experience."

Jake reached forward and splayed his long fingers over her shoulders. "Let's hope we find them before it gets to that, but—"

"There are better hackers than me. Sam and—"

Jake was shaking his head. "You can do it, Alexa. I believe in you."

And he did. He knew she wouldn't let people die. She'd given up her life and her chance at love for the job. She wanted to help people, to do good in the world.

Alexa released a deep breath and nodded. "I'll need things, though."

"Give me a list." Jake leaned in a little closer, wanting to kiss her, to pull her into his arms. He wanted to tell her everything would be okay. He could see the response in her eyes, in the way her breath hitched, in the way her lips parted.

But instead, he backed away. She'd had her reasons for rejecting him in London last year, but it still stung. He had wanted her, regardless of his job and the ocean between them. But she hadn't wanted him—she wouldn't even take the chance.

And she had lied to him about it.

He couldn't think about that, though. He had no right to think of his personal life and feelings when @Anarchy was dealing the cards.

"Can you also ask your friend to try and access whatever files the NSA has on Anarchy, as well as the joint OP that took out Bekas's family in Afghanistan? There has to be something I missed. We need to figure out his target. I can hack the NSA myself, but that will take time—time we don't have."

"Yeah, I can ask." For a minute, Jake considered calling up Aiden. His fiancée, Ava, was a biochemist, but she was also a computer genius with great hacking skills. She'd get along great with Alexa. But what did that matter? The two of them would probably never meet.

Hell, he didn't even know if they'd survive the next twenty-four hours.

\* \* \*

ALEXA STARED UP AT THE MANSION AHEAD OF THEM. "YOU SURE about this?" she asked.

They'd been patted down and had to hand their weapons over

to some sketchy security guys—were they making the right decision?

The home looked like it belonged to a Spanish royal. It was massive in size and had an Old World feel to it, with white stucco cement walls, terracotta roof tiles, and multi-level roof lines. There were two, tower-like chimneys and even a turret.

Her gaze swept over the structure, admiring the arches and rustic windows, adorned with planters. The grounds before it were stunning, as well. Beds of red and gold flowers spread from the front of the house like the rays of the sun.

"Who'd Ben say this guy was again?" She wondered if they were at the doorstep of some Spanish crime lord.

"Someone who owes my friend a favor." Jake brought a fist to his mouth for a moment. "He's fine, I'm sure."

Alexa studied Jake's tight jaw as he looked up at the home. Maybe this was a bad idea.

Jake picked up their black duffel bag. "Come on." He reached for her wrist with his free hand and guided her down the path lined with palm trees. They skirted a circular, three-tier water fountain, and stopped in front of the massive double doors.

Before Jake could ring, one of the doors opened.

"We were expecting you sooner." The man was tall, well-built, and incredibly attractive. His dark hair was short on top and tapered at the sides. But it was his very light green eyes that pulled her in. "I'm Cristiano. Welcome to mi casa." He waved his arm and stepped back to allow them entrance.

Alexa had insisted that they scope out the city one more time before they went to see Ben's contact. They'd tried to get as close to the hotel and casino as they could, hoping to catch a glimpse of Xander. But no such luck.

They did have a chance to enter their hotel room and pack their belongings—since, unlike Xander's, it wasn't a crime scene. Alexa reminded herself to be grateful for the little things. At least now she had a change of clothes and a toothbrush.

Jake began speaking Spanish, the smooth words flowing from his mouth, so sexy it could cause flower petals to curl up.

Cristiano nodded and replied, and Alexa gave a curt nod and smile as if she knew what they were saying. She should have studied Spanish, or at least paid better attention to the basic Spanish lessons she'd had in primary school.

Beyond Jake and Cristiano rose the beautifully curved stairway, its every stair covered with hand-painted tiles. Bronze and orange, with hints of red, weaved through the flowered designs. The style was a bit over-the-top for her taste, but that was probably the point.

"What can I get you?" Cristiano rested a hand on the small of her back, which had her flinching.

She blinked a few times and pivoted to face the man. "I, um . . ." She didn't even know where to begin with the list of things she'd like to have at that moment. Like, for time to turn back a few hours so Xander would be safe. Or maybe rewind the clock to last year, when she'd first met Jake. This time, she wouldn't let him go.

"I think we're good. A place to rest, maybe, until we fly out." Jake stepped up next to her.

"Of course. We'll leave at eight in the morning and head to the airport. My pilot will have the jet fueled and ready," Cristiano said without taking his eyes off Alexa. She wondered how many women had been pulled into his orbit by the sound of his accent or the glimmer of those pale green eyes.

But then she stole a glance at Jake, and her heart truly fluttered. "Thank you so much. Eh, muchos gracias." She forced a smile and a nod toward Cristiano.

"De nada. Now, come this way." Cristiano stepped back and extended his arm in the direction of the stairs.

Jake's hand pressed to her back as she followed Cristiano up the steps. A group of men appeared below, exiting from a hallway under the stairs. They looked like bodyguards, with their dark clothes and well-muscled bodies.

Once on the second-floor landing, Cristiano pushed open the third door on the right and gestured for Alexa to enter. Jake followed close behind her.

The room was opulent, which was no surprise. A four-poster, king-sized bed took up the middle of the wall, with ivy and gold twining through the bedding.

Alexa sighed as she crossed the room to look out the large, expansive window. It was too dark to appreciate the horizon, but the pool down below was glowing with light. Even from above, the water appeared to drop right off the edge of the property, feeding down the cliff and into the sea where a few lit-up boats decorated the water.

Alexa's eyes caught Jake's in the glass, and she realized Cristiano had left them. She liked that the Spaniard was a man who didn't press. Then again, he was probably glad to avoid any questions about himself.

Jake touched the glass, and then lowered his forehead until it rested against the window. "When this is over—tomorrow, maybe —we'll need to talk. For now, we should get some rest."

*Oh.* The gravity in his voice was like a poke of hot iron against her flesh.

As he started to turn away, she caught him by the arm, and he looked down at her, his brown eyes steadying on her slowly as if it hurt to look at her. "And what if this doesn't end well?" she whispered.

Jake had been the only man who had come close to provoking her to think of the future, even though they'd spent only one week together up until now. She had thought she was crazy for feeling that way after such a short time—she had shrugged it off as intense lust. But now, with him standing right beside her, she knew without a doubt there had been a connection between them from day one. In all this time, it had only amplified.

"We'll get through this. Trust me," Jake said after a long minute.

She pressed a hand to her cheek and spun away from him, too much of a coward to confront him with what she wanted to say. "I need you to understand why I did it," she pleaded.

"I don't need to know. I get it." His voice was eerily calm but had an understated disappointment that she could feel in her bones.

Alexa sank on the bed, bracing her hands against her thighs as she looked up at him. He casually leaned his back against the window and angled his head to the side, studying the floor instead of her. "I'm sorry I lied to you, but I didn't want you to be angry at me."

"And I get it—just don't lie to me again. We need to be straight with each other if we want to take down Anarchy."

She chanced another look and saw his hand at his thigh, massaging ever so slightly. When his eyes caught hers, he dropped his hand. He didn't want her to know that he was in pain. She hated that. "Are you okay?" It was a stupid question.

"You should get some sleep. I'll take the floor."

"What? Are you bloody nuts?" She popped to her feet and came in front of him, and he took two steps back. "If you can't stomach the idea of sleeping next to me, I'm sure there's another bed you can sleep in," she said, spreading her arms wide, "somewhere in this massive home."

His brows pulled together, and his hand swooped up to cover her wrist, gently pushing her arm back down. His jaw ticked as he stared into her eyes, his chest heaving with a deep breath. "I'm not leaving you alone in this house. Who the hell knows who that man really is."

She almost laughed. "I thought you said he was fine."

"Sure. Look at this place," he grumbled, releasing his grip on her. He turned his back and faced the window.

The tension weakened a little, but Alexa still didn't think they were where they needed to be. They were going to have to depend on each other for survival. They would have to trust one another.

She closed her eyes for a moment and whispered, "Sleep with me."

"No," he quickly growled out the word.

"Why not?" Her eyes opened. "I don't want to shag." She perked a brow, trying to lighten the mood a little.

But he wasn't smiling when he looked at her in the window's reflection. His body remained stiff, radiating unease. "I need to accept the fact that there will never be a you-and-me," he said as he turned, running his fingers through his hair.

And yet, wasn't that exactly what she wanted right now? To throw out her rules, to ignore the thousands of kilometers separating them? "I was an idiot last year. I'm sorry." She swallowed and took a step closer.

Jake placed a fist over his heart and looked up at her with hooded eyes. "I looked for you, Alexa. Even after you turned me down before I went back to Dallas—insisting it could only be a fling . . . even after you said your goodbye—I didn't give up."

Alexa's heart landed in her throat. "You . . . what?"

His hand uncurled, dropping to his side. "I used my government pull to try and find you. But I only had a few photos on my phone to go on and no last name or address." He half-grunted his anger and scrubbed a hand over the growth on his jawline. "Now I know why we never went to your place in the city last year. Or why, with all my government contacts, I couldn't figure out who you were."

She was gutted at that moment.

"You see, Alexa, now that I remember everything, I know the truth. I know that I tried to find you. But you didn't fight for me at all." His face was close to hers, and her body trembled with anger at herself. She despised her fear so much that she could hardly breathe.

"I did want you." She paused. "I *still* do want—"

"But you're a spy, so . . ." He went over to the bed and sat down, shaking his head as he did. He raised his hands, palms clasped and pressed his fingertips to his forehead.

Maybe Jake had been right to put this conversation off until after the OP. She was so rattled that she felt like dropping to her knees and crying. How could she fight @Anarchy if she felt she could hardly stand?

"I never thought you would look for me," she said after a few moments of silence.

"Well, I'm not the kind of man to let a woman like you get away." His words had become thicker as he spoke them, the Southern drawl a little more noticeable as emotion cut through.

"Jake." She edged toward the bed, but was too afraid to sit next to him, worried he'd spring up and move away from her. If he did, she wouldn't blame him.

He lowered his hands to his lap, but defeat wasn't splayed over his face. Jake might be angry with her, but he still wasn't a quitter.

"God, Alexa, I want to be pissed at you. Despite everything we're dealing with, I still want to be stone cold pissed. Because I cared more about you than you did about me." As he slowly rose to his feet, her breath hitched. Her nerves tangled, ready to snap. "But in all honesty, I can only be upset that you lied to me in Montana. How could I hate you for the choice you made? We both put country first. That's who we are."

Her body was going to give out beneath the weight of his words. "It has to be country first," she said as her shoulders sagged. Although she may not be MI6 for much longer.

"You deserve a life, though. I hope you know that." He cupped the back of his neck and his gaze narrowed. "I hope it's not too late before you wake up remembering that you're a person in this world, too . . . and you'll end up having to save yourself." With that, he started for the door.

"Where are you going?" she asked, her body growing stiff at the thought of him leaving.

"To find another room." He peered over his shoulder at her.

She lowered her head at his words and tried to garner the strength she needed. "I thought you wanted to stick together."

"Looks like you're tough enough to take care of yourself, right?"

But she didn't want to be. She wanted to be safe and secure, with his arms encircling her. "I need you," she said as his hand rested on the brass knob.

His hand slid up the wooden door and pressed at the center as if he were trying to keep himself upright. "Don't do this, Alexa. I asked you to be straight with me."

"I am, Jake. I haven't thought I needed anyone, not since my dad died." They were words she'd never verbalized before, and she was worried she'd choke on her emotions as they wedged in her throat. "I was the strong one in my family. I held my mum's and sister's hands at Dad's funeral, and I kept us together after he passed. I had to stay strong, so they wouldn't fall apart." Alexa's eyes were like steamed glass—she could hardly see through them. "And even after everything I went through with Jason . . ."

She swiped at the fallen tears on her face and moved toward the door where he stood, his back to her. "I need someone tonight." She released an angry hiss. "Not just someone. I mean—I need you." She could feel the spider's web of cracks forming in her as she bared her weakness to him. "Please, Jake."

As her knees buckled beneath her and she gave in to the desire to fall, Jake's arms came around her, pulling her tight against him, lifting her up. He brought her to the bed and scooted up next to her, locking his arms around her, resting her face against his chest as she cried. His hands slipped through her tangled, dark hair as he kissed the top of her head.

"I'm sorry. This isn't like me." *I'm not supposed to be weak.*

"Tell me about him," Jake said after a few minutes, once her tears had turned to sniffles.

Alexa shifted back to look up at Jake, but he didn't loosen his grip on her. She was tucked away and safe in his arms as if the rest of the world and all of its craziness were backdrops for someone else's life.

She gulped, bringing her hand between their two bodies to wipe away the makeup beneath her eyes. "Well, I wouldn't be an agent right now if he was alive."

"Oh yeah?"

She smiled. "Yeah. He was overprotective, and I kind of adored being his princess." A slight chuckle tumbled from her lips. "I know. How'd I go from Daddy's Princess to a counterterrorist spy?"

"Princess. Terrorists." He squinted one eye. "Nope, not a stretch."

"Ha. Sure." She tipped up a shoulder before relaxing back into his embrace. "My dad would have lost his bloody mind if I had told him I was going to be a spy."

"What did he want you to do?"

"I was in school for computers, so he knew I'd be getting a tech job. My sister would have made him proud, though."

"She's an artist, right?"

"You remember?"

"Hell, I remember everything about everything right now. Some things I wish I didn't . . ."

She couldn't begin to imagine. "Lori had her first official gallery opening in Rome a few months back. She's brilliant. And she has a baby boy now." A squeeze of jealousy filled her heart. But would those things ever be possible for Alexa? A family? Kids?

He kissed her forehead, then brushed his thumb down her cheek as he held her gaze—and a fluttering in her chest that swept to her stomach had her feeling a glimmer of hope about the future.

# CHAPTER TWENTY-FIVE

ALEXA AND JAKE WERE AT THE CALTANISSETTA XIRBI RAILWAY station in Sicily. They'd taken a flight from Barcelona to Palermo before boarding the train to reach their final destination.

Cristiano had accompanied them to the private jet hangar before his guards, who carried themselves like military men, or all around bad asses, had flown with them to Italy. The guards had to have been packing, Alexa had decided when she saw the slight bulge beneath their blazers.

But the men were helping her, so she wouldn't complain. And Cristiano had supplied them with enough euros to last them a month in Vegas. Now that was a trip she could have used right about now.

Jake opened the locker and reached inside. His friend Ben would be in later that night. Getting from Vegas to Italy took time, after all. And, since time wasn't on their side, Ben had arranged for an old friend in the Air Force, who was stationed at the Sigonella base, to leave a computer at the hotel room they planned to stay in. She hoped Ben had been able to access the case files.

"Okay. We've got the hotel key and location. And the safe combination. Now let's hope a USB with those files we need is in the safe," Jake said while shutting the gray locker door. "Otherwise, you'll be breaking a couple of laws by hacking into the NSA—or the CIA." A brief smile skirted his lips as he pushed his glasses closer to his face. He had borrowed a razor from Cristiano to shave his beard, and his clean-shaven jaw was smooth, his firm lips beautifully prominent. His dimples seemed deeper than she remembered when he smiled. Not that he had smiled much today. Not until now, at least.

"I'm just relieved you have a friend who could pull all of this off for us in such a short period," she said as they began exiting the station.

"How are you holding up?" Jake asked as they waited at the curb for a taxi, stealing a glimpse of her over his shoulder.

"I'm as good as I can be, but I still think your friend could have stayed in Vegas," she said.

"I might need back up."

She scoffed. "You think I would let you go after these guys alone?"

Then again, where would they get a team? And Bekas had God knew how many armed men. Even with Ben at his side, it would be a suicide mission. The thought of Jake dying ripped at her heart.

"I faced these guys before and got away."

"And got yourself nearly blown up," she said as Jake opened the door for the taxi when it pulled up in front of them, and he waited for her to slide in before following suit. He read off the address to the driver.

"No English," the driver responded, so Jake handed over the paper with the hotel address on it, hoping it would make sense to him.

The man had looked back at them in the rearview mirror and nodded, before pulling out onto the street. She braced the seat in front of her with the jerking motion—and she thought drivers in London were bad. *Jeez.*

Jake's hand was suddenly resting on her thigh, and her lip

caught between her teeth, her heart fluttering like leaves blowing hard in the wind.

"I don't want anything happening to you," she whispered at last.

"What? You care about me or something?" he asked.

When she looked up at him, he was watching her, eyes hooded.

"Or something," she murmured.

* * *

ALEXA PUNCHED IN THE COMBINATION TO THE SAFE.

"Is it in there?" She glanced up at Jake as he came up behind her and withdrew her arm from the safe.

"Yeah." She clutched the drive to her breast and let out a sigh of relief. "Let's see what's on here."

She started for the living area, where Ben's friend had left a laptop for them. How much time would they have before Bekas followed through with his plan?

Then she felt the touch of Jake's hand on her wrist.

"What?" she asked softly, turning to face him.

His body was tense, his arms locked at his sides. "I want to say something before I forget. Before things get intense." His features softened. "I'm sorry I got upset last night. I was overwhelmed with what happened at the hotel. My memories all crashing back on me like that . . . I was feeling a whole lifetime of hurt."

She lowered her head, not able to look at this strong, sweet man. A man who could set her body on fire with a simple touch. "No, Jake." Her gaze traveled over his V-neck sweater now that he'd removed the blazer, admiring the tightness of his muscles beneath the fabric. "So much of what you said is true, and I hope that, after this . . ." *If we survive.* "I hope that we have a chance to figure out what this thing is between us."

Of course, she already knew what she felt.

Still holding her wrist, Jake gently tugged her toward him until her body pressed up against his chest. He tipped her chin up and sealed his lips over hers. Heat and desire threaded through every fabric of her being. It pulsed heavy and thick in her veins. With that kiss, she felt him inside of her, in her soul.

A moment later he stepped back. She didn't want to ever stop, but she was standing in Italy trying to thwart a terrorist attack— this wasn't some fairy tale. "What was that for?" she asked once she caught her breath. "For luck?" She smiled.

He wrapped a hand around her waist, keeping her close to him. Where else would she go? She was his. She had known it a year ago, even though she had pushed him away.

"Luck?" He squinted a little and his mouth curved up. "I don't need luck. I've got this."

"Oh, yeah?" His sexy confidence was nearly electric, and a little contagious.

She knew now, for sure, that Jake Summers was back.

"Yeah." He brushed the back of his hand down her cheek. "Because I have you."

Her heart almost leaped out of her chest at his words. In the faint lines around his dark brown eyes, forgiveness was etched. She realized that he accepted her for who she was—even for her mistakes. And that was rare.

His eyes smoldered as a look of passion—or maybe love?— spread across his face. Was it . . . love? *God, this is crazy.*

"Let's do this, Alexa." His fingers slipped to twine with hers. "You ready?"

*Am I?* She tightened her grip around the USB in her other hand. "After we take down these bastards, how about you and I have a drink?"

He shot her a full smile.

"On a beach. With a little umbrella in the drink." She pressed a quick kiss to his lips, and then backed away, trying her best to get back into the right mindset. It was time to take down @Anarchy.

She sat in front of the computer and plugged in the device. "It will take a few minutes for me to decrypt the files," she said. "Is there coffee in here?"

"Coffee?" Jake asked. "Not tea?"

"Guess you're rubbing off on me." She glanced back at him. "By all means, please sweeten it up." She still couldn't believe that it had only been a few days since she'd arrived at the cabin in Montana.

But maybe it would all be over soon. If Bekas was off the grid and his men had Xander, the countdown had already begun.

*Xander . . .* A stab of guilt spiraled through her. While she was joking around with Jake and kissing him, Xander was being held captive. Worse, he might be dead. Her body stilled, and she lifted her fingers from the keyboard. Her stomach grew nauseous, and she felt like she was on an out of control Ferris wheel, spinning round and round so fast she'd get chucked off.

*He's okay. He has to be.* She drew up the image of her best friend in her mind. Funny and caring Xander. She wanted him to walk her down the aisle if she ever got married.

*Marriage? Me?* She stole another quick look at Jake as he worked at the coffee machine in the room. His back was to her, and she remembered the scars beneath the shirt. And it reminded her of exactly how dangerous @Anarchy was, which meant Xander was close to death. And she and Jake might be the only ones standing between whether he lived or died.

Her fingers trembled as they touched the keys again, and she forced herself to take in a few deep breaths. She had to get back in the zone if she'd get to Xander in time.

After ten minutes and a couple of sips of coffee later, Jake was standing next to her, his glasses on, his arms crossed. He leaned forward to get a better look at the screen as she studied the files she decrypted that the NSA had collected on @Anarchy. Maybe they had information that MI6 didn't.

"What can I do?"

"Nothing right now. I've just got to look at this case from a different angle. There has to be something in here. Something I've missed." She switched over to the information on the drone strike that killed Bekas's wife and daughters. The evidence and documents were similar to those that MI6 had, but here she found that the key players involved on the American side were listed.

"Shit!" She frantically tapped at the keys. She pointed to a picture of a man in a naval uniform. He was tall and perhaps in his mid-thirties, with short blonde hair and a square jaw. "I know this guy. What was his name . . .?"

"What?"

Alexa switched back over to the @Anarchy files again. "It's got to be in here," she said as she scrolled through the folders. "Here." She clicked open the file labeled, "Vegas March 2016." "Remember when I told you that Anarchy had managed to kill people in Vegas all the way from Istanbul?"

"Yeah. How?"

She shook her head. "Don't worry about that for now. But look at who died in the explosion."

"Don Turner. Vanessa Shane. Brett Reeds. Sylvia Herald. Spike Anderson," Jake read down the list.

"Spike." She flipped back to the screen of the man in uniform. "He was one of the drone pilots that killed Bekas's family."

"And then he died six months ago in an explosion that was connected to Anarchy?"

"Looks that way. That can't be a coincidence, right?" Her body was thrumming to life as her brain worked faster than her fingers could move. "I didn't know the names of the Americans involved in the drone strike—not until now. But what if—"

"Anarchy has been systematically targeting those responsible," Jake finished. He cupped a hand over his mouth.

"It's possible. Maybe not every hit targeted someone on the drone strike because it would have been obvious, but if he buried his true agenda in the midst of other random strikes . . ."

It was all making sense to her now. For Kemal Bekas, this had always been about revenge. He wanted every person who had been involved in the death of his family to suffer. So, he had used his brilliant computer skills to orchestrate the movements of a cyber-terrorist group, using the group as an elaborate cover for his fiendish retribution.

"If this is right, we need to see how many of the people on that list are still alive." He raked a hand through his hair.

She would need to call MI6 after they confirmed their theory. They would need all the help they could get to stop the attack and rescue Xander.

"Where was the last attack?" Jake dragged a chair next to hers, offering another set of eyes on the case.

"India. A British bank." She pulled up the list of deaths and shook her head. "Nope."

"Before that?"

Alexa pulled up the next case, and they cross-referenced the deaths with the drone strike team members. "The pilot stationed in Afghanistan . . ." A lump formed in her throat as she processed Bekas's killing spree.

After an hour of scouring every file, they found five more people who had died from the drone strike team. And those were just the attacks that Intelligence had been able to connect to @Anarchy.

"This bastard killed over seventy people just to cover his tracks." Jake was on his feet, his face pulled together in anger. The vein in his neck was pulsing.

Once Alexa finished the records of known attacks, she started to search obituaries in both Britain and the U.S. for the remaining names on the list. She couldn't sign into MI6 for additional assistance. Fortunately, the men she searched for weren't undercover operatives. They were military and government employees. People who had Facebook pages and public lives.

Jake slammed a hand against the desk. "Jesus. Only one person is still alive. Goddamn."

"One person," she repeated in shock. A breath of air rushed from her lips. "And not just anyone. The General of CENTCOM." She curled her hands into fists in her lap and pushed back from the desk. "Bekas wants to destroy Parliament for revenge—that's an obvious target. But would killing an American general be enough for him?" The murder of anyone was horrific, but she'd expect Bekas to crave a bigger finale, to go out with a bang that would echo through the ages.

"I don't know, but this man is the *former* General of CENTCOM. He retired." Jake pointed at the image of the man in uniform on the screen. He had strong shoulders, a fit body, and silvery gray hair parted to the side, with a large nose and light green eyes. "He's a friend of my family's—I was at his retirement dinner two months ago."

"Shit. He's probably not part of the plan. I mean," she stood, "they'll try and kill him, so we need to alert your government. But that doesn't help us figure out Bekas's big target."

Jake shook his head and moved to the side table and lifted the phone from the receiver. "We need to let everyone know what's going on." He held the phone in the air in her direction. "Go ahead. I'll make the next call."

She came in front of him and took the phone, wrapping the cord around her finger as she punched in the number, her heart like a storm in her chest, furious, the blood pumping so hard she could hardly even see.

When the call was picked up, she sputtered out her code: "Zero nine five three two eleven."

"Access denied."

The call ended.

She scrunched her brow and quickly jabbed at the numbers to ring the agency again.

Jake was studying her, worry flickering across his face.

"Zero nine five three two eleven," she said in a rush.

"Access denied."

Her skin flushed as she slammed the phone down and gritted her teeth. "I've been cut out." She didn't know if MI6 was doing this to protect her, not to mention the intel. Or if it was because she had been fired for not following orders. Either way, it wasn't good.

"I guess I'll have to call someone else." Her mind spun as she tried to determine the best alternate course for communication. She had to alert them in one way or another, but she had wanted it to be secure. She had wanted to speak with Laney . . .

"It's going to be okay." He pressed his hands to her shoulders and slid them up her neck before cupping her face in his hands. "I promise, Alexa. Everything is going to work out."

# CHAPTER TWENTY-SIX

IT WAS JAKE'S TURN TO MAKE THE CALL.

He clutched the phone tight. He hadn't spoken to Trent since the team had left for Barcelona, and he wondered if there was any news on his side. Maybe something good, for once.

Alexa was back in front of the computer, doing her best to discover Bekas's target.

"Trent? It's Jake," he said once the line clicked over.

"Jesus Christ. What the hell happened? I've got guys in hospital beds in Barcelona, and no one knows what's going on."

"What do you mean? Didn't Randall tell you?" Jake asked.

Alexa swiveled in her chair, looking over at him, concern spreading across her beautiful face. Jake's chest tightened.

"Randall's not with you? I thought if you were calling that meant—"

*Don't tell me . . .* "Randall and I parted yesterday. He was supposed to go to the embassy and let you all know what was going on."

Alexa was on her feet, her arms folded over her chest. She'd called London PD and asked them to get a message to MI6. The officer she had spoken to had been skeptical, but she believed they'd do due diligence and follow through. But what if Seth never made it to the British Consulate? Perhaps everyone was still in the dark.

"Well, Randall didn't make it," Trent said slowly.

Jake hung his head until it rested against his hand. "Any word from MI6 about their agents in Barcelona?"

"No. MI6 alerted us to the hacking issue, and we've identified and shut down the problem within our servers—well, at the NSA, which is all that Anarchy targeted, so it seems. We also know what Alpha and Beta teams could tell us—you were ambushed, everyone split up, and the targets were lost," Trent answered.

"Well, it looks like Anarchy might be using Randall, Seth, and Xander as hostages." And he had to think that because the alternative was that they were dead.

Alexa turned her back and crossed the room to stand in front of the window, which offered a view of the city sprawled out below. "We also think we know their end game. Sort of." Jake's stomach rolled. "Shit. I just realized that since Randall didn't make it to you, you never got the message about the drones."

"What are you talking about?"

"You need to ground all drones. Monitor them at the Sigonella base," Jake said as fast he could.

"Hang on. What are you saying?" Trent's voice cut through the phone, the deepness seeming to vibrate against Jake's ear.

"The drone we used to try and take out Ansari in Libya from Sicily last month was hacked," Jake said. "And if you had mentioned the drone back in Montana we might be sitting in a Goddamn different situation right now." His heartbeat quickened as his anger ticked up a notch.

"Wait—you remember the mission?"

Jake should have lead with that. "I remember everything," he said slowly—almost as if he didn't believe it.

"That's great, but . . . well, shit, we don't know with all certainty the drone was ever hacked. It could have malfunctioned."

"Trust me, Trent. It was hacked. Anarchy is going to hack it again, and this time it won't be a trial run." Jake's gaze traveled back to Alexa. Her shoulders were hunched, her hand on the window pane.

"So, like I said, you need to get ahold of Sigonella and have them ground all drones. Lock them inside the damn hangars. I don't know if Anarchy can pull off a hijacking, but let's not wait and find out." He heaved out a deep breath. "Oh, and—more bad news—find Frank Warren, the retired General of CENTCOM. Anarchy is coming after him. They've already targeted and murdered everyone who was a part of the drone strike that led to the death of Bekas's family."

Jake couldn't believe he was saying this, that this was real and not some elaborate trial run like back in his Quantico days, when the government would throw every terrorist scenario at him, testing him on his ability to assess and handle the situation. He had graduated at the top of his class and even became one of the leading experts at counterterrorism in the U.S. He held seminars now at Quantico. But this . . . it was beyond anything he'd ever imagined, beyond even the farfetched trials at the FBI Academy.

Jake blinked a few times, squeezing his past from his mind.

Trent gasped. "Are you serious?"

*Do I sound like I'm kidding?* "Yes," he said through gritted teeth.

Trent took a long-winded breath, which crackled through the phone like feedback from a blender. Jake pulled the phone from his ear for a moment. "We'll locate Frank, but the drones . . . that might not be so easy." Trent's words were followed by a soft hiss.

"Why?" Jake's brows snapped together.

"Last month, the President finally agreed to order a massive strike against the ISIS compounds in Libya. We've been waiting for months to get this approval from the Italians and the President to finally go in and obliterate the ISIS military bases in Northern Libya."

"Well, post-fucking-pone it!"

"I'll see what I can do, but I think it's happening soon. Like, tonight."

"Do you not hear what I'm saying? This isn't some fucking coincidence that there is a strike scheduled for tonight!" Jake shouted, not giving a damn if he pissed off his boss. Rank didn't matter, not with lives on the line. To hell with the aftermath. "If those drones fly, you're playing right into their hands. They hacked our servers, which means they knew about this attack in Libya. They're counting on it. For once, we have the intel to stop them. For God's sake, let's use it!"

"I'll need to go to the President on this."

"Go to the Pope for all I care but call off the strike."

"Watch it, Jake. We're friends, but dammit—" Trent stopped himself. "Call me back in an hour. And . . . Jake? Don't do anything fucking stupid."

Jake slammed the phone down, anger billowing through him until he felt that he might erupt like one of the volcanoes nearby. Hell, maybe it should blow—and lava could pour right over Bekas and his damn men.

Jake pressed his palms to his temples, trying to lessen the intensity of his anger that flowed through him.

"We might be offering Anarchy a drone on a silver platter, so we need to find out where they're planning to hit. I hope your guys back in London are handling Parliament." His hands slipped down to his shoulders where he kneaded them, working at the tension.

He snapped his eyes shut as memories from the last twelve years ripped fresh wounds. So many men had given their lives for their country.

And Jake would be damned to hell if he refused to let anyone else die on his watch.

"You know this Bekas guy," he said, his eyes still closed. "We know he has been out for revenge all along. Aside from the general, what would he want?" He slowly opened his eyes to find Alexa standing right in front of him.

"Well." Alexa covered a hand to her mouth as her eyes darted to the ceiling in thought. Her eyes widened a little when her fingers slipped free from her lips. "Within a month after his family died, he began campaigning against the use of drone strikes. He even went to the media. He wanted his story shared. He hoped it would stop the strikes if the public knew more details about the deaths of his wife and children."

"What happened?"

"The story made the news for maybe a day or two, and then people forgot. I can imagine that he was upset. He wanted an apology, and he wanted the world to know—"

"Which is why he wanted to use me as a delivery boy," he interrupted, "to send some sort of message over live TV, maybe? He's most likely making this a suicide mission, too. That, or he has plans to escape to some tropical island and never look back."

Alexa tapped a short nail against her lip as she focused on Jake. "If he attacks the Palace of Westminster, it'll be empty. Not easy, either. Security has tightened after previous attempts in the past."

"If they can pull it off, destroying that iconic building would be symbolic, though," Jake said.

"Bloody hell. That's it, isn't it? He wants everyone to see the consequences of drone strikes. To put the fear of God into people, in the hope that the people will pressure our governments to stop using drones on enemy targets."

"It's a bit of an extreme way to get your point across, but we're still back to the question of where he plans to use the drone."

Alexa grumbled and grabbed a black hair tie from her wrist. She swept her hair up into a messy bun atop her head. "It has to be the American Embassy in Rome. It's close, and it would send a message."

"But we can prevent the loss of life by clearing it out. At this point, we have to assume he knows he probably won't kill anyone in London. And I'm pretty sure this SOB will want the world to see a loss of life among the chaos."

"Maybe a place where people feel safe. A target that people wouldn't expect, which makes it all the more frightening," she added. "Clubs, malls, markets . . ."

Jake wished he could forget all over again the drastic increase in terrorist attacks in the last several years. If the public knew how many had been stopped—all those that didn't make the news—people would be scared to do almost anything at all.

"It doesn't need to be a soft target since they'll have a damn drone. But it has to be close because Bekas must know he won't be able to override the drone for very long. The military will attempt to take down the drone's satellite or the drone itself . . ."

"So where?"

His gaze trailed from her hand, which was slightly trembling as it pressed to her core.

"The drone strikes in Libya are tonight," he said, reaching for her wrist to check the time on her watch, "which means we have about ten hours to figure it out."

\* \* \*

DARKNESS HAD FALLEN OVER THE CITY AND NEVER BEFORE HAD Jake been so worried about the setting of the sun.

He had touched base with Trent a couple of times, but the President had yet to lift his order for the strike that was supposed to start within one hour. There was a team back in the States debating possible outcomes and risks. They didn't want to lose their chance to hit ISIS, but they didn't want to be responsible for any loss of life at the hands of @Anarchy. Of course, no one truly believed it was possible to hijack the MQ-9 Reaper.

As for General Frank Warren, he'd been vacationing since his retirement, bouncing all over the globe. To Jake, this presented the possibility that the general was already dead.

"Reza and his men had to get to Sicily in the same way we did —by plane. And they couldn't exactly board a commercial airline with hostages." Alexa was sitting behind the desk, staring at her computer screen. "I'm going to check air traffic controls and see what private jets traveled last night and this morning."

"Okay. Good." He tapped her shoulder as he stepped back from her chair.

There was a knock on the door, and Alexa lifted her fingers from the keyboard. "Is it Ben?" she whispered, raising a brow and twisting to face the door.

"It should be." Jake grabbed his sidearm from the desk and removed the safety. He held the weapon down at his side as he approached the door. Once he checked the peephole, a grin spread across his face. "It's him."

When Jake opened the door, Ben was just as he remembered: tall, well-built, with dark hair and green eyes. He was also sporting a thick, black beard that Jake hadn't seen on his friend since Iraq. He immediately pulled Ben in for a quick, one-armed hug. "You're a sight for sore eyes."

"Glad to see you alive and with all of your faculties in order."

Jake stepped back to allow him entrance and then locked the door with the sliding chain. "Ben Logan, this is Alexa Ryan."

Ben dropped his black duffel bag at his feet and crossed the room to where Alexa was standing. "Good to meet you, ma'am."

Alexa smiled. *A real smile*, Jake thought.

"Ma'am?" She glanced at Jake for a moment as her lips curved deeper. "Not another guy who calls me ma'am." She shook Ben's hand.

"Oh? Not a fan?" Ben laughed.

"Makes me feel like an old maid." She retracted her arm, letting it fall heavy at her side.

Jake folded his arms over his chest, eyeing the way Ben took note of Alexa. His gaze traveled from her eyes and down so fast that it was almost unnoticeable. But Jake noticed. "You're far from that," Ben said with a quick wink. "So." He faced Jake and rubbed his palms together. "Who do I get to kill?"

"No one yet." Alexa scowled. "We're working on it, though." She sat back behind her computer. "And even if we do find these bastards in time, don't go thinking you're going in like two cowboys in a Western." She peered at them over her shoulder. "You realize those are only action flicks, right?"

"Oh, man." Ben pressed a hand to his chest and arched his shoulders back. "I'm offended. Jake and I, we're much more dangerous than a bunch of cowboys," he said in a low, smooth voice.

"Oh yeah?" She perked a brow and looked away from them.

"Trust me, sweetheart, these pricks don't want to mess with us."

"Damn man," Jake said while resting a hand on Ben's shoulder. "It's really good to have you here." He realized he'd made the right decision bringing Ben in.

"It beats being a bodyguard to some rich prick." He laughed a little and walked back over to the duffel bag and squatted down. "I got almost everything Alexa needed, plus a few things you might be interested in." He unzipped the bag and reached for a Glock.

"Where'd you get the artillery?" Jake asked, eying the contents of the bag.

"That officer friend of mine at the base hooked me up. This isn't all, though—we thought it'd be a little suspicious if I brought all the rifles up to the room."

Jake glowered. "We?"

With a mischievous grin, Ben said, "Well, I asked a few private security guys I know in Naples to come help. They have a van parked outside. So, this is just a little sample of what we have to blow these motherf—" he stopped himself, glancing over his shoulder at Alexa, "—these guys out of the water."

"You brought more men?" Alexa pushed back in the chair and faced them again, concern pulling at her face. "We didn't discuss that. And they're civilians?" She stood and approached the bag and kneeled down to study what Ben brought.

"Listen." Ben stood erect, his eyes catching Alexa's for a brief moment on his way up. He braced his hips with his palms. He didn't have to be in uniform to look like a Marine. His confidence and posture, and the glint of darkness behind his eyes said it all. Seeing Ben standing there like that was a harsh reminder of what they had gone through in the Middle East together, and the lives they lost. Jake's pulse quickened at the thought, and he wet his lips, turning away for a moment, trying to slow his heart.

"We need a little back-up, don't you think?" Ben finished.

"Oh, so you really aren't as bad as you said, yeah?" Alexa half-joked.

Jake faced the two and noticed the smirk on her face as she held what looked like a frequency jammer in her hand—a compact black box with eight six-inch antennas attached.

God, she was stunning. Smart, independent, caring, gorgeous, humorous—his perfect woman. Only, could he truly handle a woman who was always putting herself in danger? Then again, look at what he did. Why should he set a different standard of behavior for her?

"Jake?" Ben was snapping his fingers in his face. "Do we have a game plan, yet?"

"We're working on it," he answered.

"Let me go back to the van and update the guys then."

"How many men do we have?" Jake asked.

"Four more plus us," he answered as Alexa turned back to the computer.

"Six should be more than enough," Jake answered. Even if they were five to one—they would be facing about the same odds as they had in the Marines. Sometimes it was ten on one. Sure, they could do this.

Jake patted Ben on the back and nodded at him. "Thanks again for coming," he said as Ben started for the door.

"Oh, and I had to go through Michael to get those NSA and FBI files. I know you wanted him left out of this, but he's our best resource for that shit."

*Damn.* "What'd he say?"

Ben smirked. "He said to tell you, 'Welcome back.'"

*I am back, aren't I?* His mind had taken some crazy vacation—a road trip to Hell—but he was back, right?

"I'll be up in a few," Ben said.

After he left, there was just the sound of Alexa's fingertips clacking against the keyboard.

"There were three private jets that match our flight pattern, and one of them was ours," Alexa said a few moments later after Jake had once again secured the lock at the door.

"And the other two?" He came up behind her.

"Working on it."

"Okay, good. We have to assume they managed to bypass customs, which means they might have someone on the inside, as well." Just then, the hotel phone began to ring. "Should be Trent. Let's hope the President called off the strike."

Jake clutched the phone, released a deep breath, and raised it to his ear. "What's the news?"

"Good and bad. First, the good news is that General Frank Warren is alive. He's on a cruise right now. We're trying to get a message to his ship."

*A cruise?* Maybe the guy would be safe while at sea. "And the bad news?"

"The options have been weighed, and it's been decided to go ahead with the strike. They're moving the timetable in hopes of throwing off Anarchy's plans."

Trent's words hit him like a hard blow. Jake felt like he was losing his mind all over again.

"Don't say anything, Jake. I fought for you."

"Not hard enough for the people who might die!" Jake balled his free hand at his side, feeling his fingertips pressing hard against his palm as he tried to bite back the hot flash of anger inside him. "When do the drones fly out?" he asked in a low voice.

"Now," Trent said after a pause.

"Jesus."

"I'm sorry, Jake. Get to Sigonella and out of harm's way. Okay? They're expecting you. We have people on standby to try and stop the hijacking if it comes to it. And I've talked to MI6— they're tracking a good lead over there."

"Well, we're staying put." Jake shook his head and his eyes met with Alexa's as he slammed the phone down. He rubbed his palms down his face, releasing a breath. "The strike is on. Frank Warren is alive and safe."

"Where is he?"

"On a cruise." He approached her, his jaw clenched.

She angled her head, her eyes becoming thin slits. "What cruise? Where?"

"I don't know."

She immediately turned back to the computer.

"What is it?" he asked as her fingers moved with deftness over the keys.

"I want to know what cruise he's on."

"That's the least of our problems right now. We've got a drone hijacking to stop." Jake crossed his arms and looked over her shoulder as she worked, hacking into God knew what.

"I have a feeling this is important. It might take some time, though."

"Time is something you know we don't have." He followed his words with an exaggerated sigh.

"I know," she answered, but didn't pause.

She had worked for a good ten minutes before she stopped. Her shoulders sagged, and she seemed to wilt in front of him. "He's on a cruise in the Mediterranean, Jake." The screen cast a brilliant blue glow over her features. "It was a last-minute booking three weeks ago, and he boarded two nights ago with his wife, daughter, and two grandkids."

Jake shifted back in his stance, his body becoming stiff. "You're telling me the man who made the final call that killed Bekas's wife and twins is just a few hundred miles away from here —and with his family, no less?"

"That's got to be it, Jake. It fits. It's completely insane, but Bekas has killed everyone else over the years, and he's been waiting for the perfect moment to strike General Warren. He was patient. And he couldn't have planned it better with the strike in Libya tonight. Hell, he may have even orchestrated getting General Warren and his family on that cruise liner."

"Christ." Jake started back for the phone. "Can you pinpoint where the ship is right now?"

"Hang on."

Jake was amazed at her skill and speed, still stunned at her genius.

"It's one of those out-to-sea nights. I'd estimate it's about three hours from the nearest port off the coast of Italy."

"If I can get ahold of Trent in time, maybe he can get the drones called back to Sigonella. And bring that cruise back to port." He grabbed the phone and dialed Trent. "In the meantime, try to find out who flew Reza's plane."

"What about the drone?"

"There's nothing you can do until it's been jacked, right?" He held the phone tight, his fingers hovering over the buttons.

"Right . . ."

"Let's get the bastards before that becomes an issue, okay?"

"You think we can?" she asked as he dialed.

"You heard Ben, right? Well, now we have you—so, yeah. You'd better believe we can do it."

# CHAPTER TWENTY-SEVEN

BEN CHUCKED A PHONE AT JAKE THE SECOND HE OPENED THE DOOR to let him in. "Look at it."

Alexa rushed to Jake's side, pressing down on his forearm so she could have a look. On the screen was a Facebook live video of three men with their hands tied and their mouths taped. And they weren't strangers.

Xander.

Seth.

Randall.

There was no sound. And no one else.

All three agents appeared to have been roughed around, with bruises and small cuts showing on their faces. But there were no gaping wounds and nothing in their posture that would indicate they were in any great pain.

They were staring directly into the camera, an image that would haunt Jake for the rest of his life.

But they didn't look defeated. No—these men had known what they had signed up for when they made an oath to their countries. This possibility had always been forefront in their minds.

*Xander's alive . . .* "What the hell is going on?" Alexa's skin blanched, and her hand covered her heart, pressing against the thin material of her white blouse.

"Give it a second." Ben raked a hand through his dark, unruly hair.

Then the scrolling text appeared at the bottom of the screen.

**These men will die in less than one hour. And others will die, too. Will it be you? The death of innocents can only lead to more loss. #DEADLY CONSEQUENCES.**

"Jesus." Alexa turned away from the screen, her hands going into prayer position in front of her lips.

"Did this son of a bitch really hashtag his terrorist attack?" Ben reached into his pocket for another phone. "Shit. It's already trending."

"This is what he wanted—global attention." Alexa's head dropped forward.

"Yeah. It looks like Bekas is sharing the case file of the drone strike against his family." Jake handed Alexa the phone as images flashed across the screen. He watched over her shoulder as photos from the drone strike appeared briefly then drifted away.

They were classified documents.

There was a picture of his wife and daughters before the strike . . . and then after.

Alexa pressed the phone back into Jake's hand and hurried to the computer. "They're still alive, though," she said stubbornly.

"The Anarchy bastards are going to take out a cruise ship," Jake said to Ben.

"With our damn drone?" Ben's eyes widened.

"Yeah. The Air Force doesn't think the Reaper can be hacked, so they aren't pulling back. They said the air strike is too critical to halt," Jake answered, disbelief echoing in his words. "But the cruise liner has been notified and it's heading to the closest port. Of course, the closest port is three hours away."

"Anarchy is at least ten kilometers south of us," Alexa told Ben.

"Alexa identified the plane that the Anarchy members used to bring Xander and the others to Italy—then she accessed the video footage outside the airline hangar. Two black SUVs pulled away from the hangar shortly after the plane pulled in. She used traffic camera footage to track them until they reached the outskirts of town," Jake explained. "We don't know where they are from that point on, though."

"Damn, she's good," Ben said with a nod.

Jake came up behind Alexa and studied the screen as she switched over to the Facebook profile used to release the live video. "Can you trace it?"

"I'm sure he has it rerouted a half a dozen times, if not more. But I'm on it," she answered.

"Good. You can give us an updated location while we're en route." Ben tapped Jake on the shoulder. "Let's roll, brother."

Alexa looked up, her gaze soft and unfocused, and then she stood. "Wait. You're leaving?" Jake saw her swallow as her eyes flitted back and forth between the two.

"We'll head south, taking the last road you had them on, and then you can call us," Ben said in a calm voice as if he were explaining that he was about to go have a beer with the boys, and then he tossed her a phone.

Jake was getting the feeling this was the most intense OP she'd ever been on. And it wasn't even a regulated mission.

"Only you can tell us where they've gone," Jake reminded her.

Ben lifted his wrist and eyed his watch. "You'll let us know in ten minutes, okay?" He winked at her. "No pressure."

But Ben was not as nonchalant as he seemed. Four tours in the Middle East had hardened his heart and given him a live free or die mentality. A couple of Jake's other buddies had been like that until they had fallen in love. Maybe Ben needed someone to slow him down a little . . .

Jake glanced over at Alexa, wondering if she would be the one to change him. God, how he wanted to leave so much of himself behind. The loneliness. The nights assailed by memories of the desert. If it wasn't for his friends, Jake didn't know how he would have survived the punishment of those memories. But his friends understood—Marine to Marine, veteran to veteran.

But Alexa had her own painful past. She'd been the only survivor of a mission, just like Jake had. And she'd been betrayed by a man who was supposed to care for her. Alexa could relate to Jake. She could empathize. And maybe they could help pull out of the darkness together. Together, they could rise into the light.

"Jake?" Ben nudged him in the shoulder with his fist.

*Shit.* Of all the times to have his head in the clouds. "Yeah?" He blinked and looked at Alexa.

"I should go with you," she said softly. "I can create a Wi-Fi hotspot and work from inside the van."

"No." Jake shook his head and took a step back from her.

"Why? Because I'm a woman?" Her arms folded across her chest.

"Guys, we don't have time for this." Ben angled his head toward the door. "I have my number programmed in that phone."

"Give me a second, will you? I'll be right out," Jake said.

Ben sighed but nodded. "Okay."

Once the door closed behind Ben, Jake pressed his hands to Alexa's shoulders. He could feel the light trembling of her body. "I have no doubt you can handle yourself. But if we can't stop them, you should be here. If we can't contain Bekas, it's up to you and the Air Force to stop that Reaper."

Alexa's lip wedged between her teeth. "And what if there isn't enough time? They have Jason." Her shoulders started to arch forward, but he gently pressed them back, needing to see her confident.

She pulled away from him. "No, I need to be on-site. The best way to stop them is the most obvious, isn't it?"

His lips parted as he studied her, but he didn't know what to say.

"Once we find Bekas, I think I know how to end this. But I need to be close to him. Within sixty meters close . . ." She swallowed as her gaze lifted to meet his.

Was she crazy? Sixty meters? "I can't have anything happening to you," he said with a firm grit to his voice.

He moved back closer to her and her chest lifted with a deep breath. "Tell me what to do, and I can handle it."

She was shaking her head before he could even finish. "No. If something goes wrong, I might need to adapt. This is too important, Jake." She closed the gap between them, bringing her hands down over his chest. "We've got each other's backs, okay?"

He closed his eyes as his heart pumped harder.

"Kiss me one more time, Jake."

"Once more?" He shook his head as his eyes flashed open. "This won't be the last time, Alexa. That I can promise," he said roughly. He drew her in close, and his tongue roamed her mouth. Her breasts pressed against him, hard peaks against his taut flesh.

When he stepped away, he kept his hand cupped around the back of her head and the other on her cheek as his lips brushed a kiss along the top of her forehead. "Come on," he said almost inaudibly, even though everything inside him begged to keep her safe in the hotel room. But he couldn't—country first, right? That's what they had to do. They were built like that, dammit.

If Alexa could help protect innocent lives, he had to let her come, and it burned him deep to the core.

"You act like I've never done this before." She turned away and began to gather her equipment.

Jake caught her by the arm, and she bowed her head slightly. "Nothing is going to happen to you, Alexa. You'll be okay." He wasn't sure if he was asking or telling . . . but he needed to say it. To make it real.

"I promise I'll be okay," she said so softly that he wasn't sure he could believe her.

But against his better judgment, he replied, "Okay. Let's do this."

He helped her pack the laptop and other gadgets that she said she'd need, and they left the hotel without saying another word. What could they say, after all? They were about to go into enemy territory, and there was no guarantee that they would make it out alive.

Ben was standing in front of a black van when they came outside. His brows pulled together as his head cocked to the side when he saw Alexa.

"So . . ." Ben stepped back and opened the back doors of the van. He reached for her hand and helped her climb into the back.

"Plans changed," he muttered to Ben and slapped him on the chest, following Alexa inside.

"Hi," Alexa said.

Steel benches lined the interior walls of the van, each one with a guy sitting down at the end. In the center aisle, AK-47s, M-16s, and pistols were spread like presents beneath a Christmas tree, and Jake watched as Alexa navigated to a bench.

There were also grenades and canisters that were probably filled with tear gas. Thank God for Ben's friends.

Jake shook the hands of the two new members of their team and sat next to the door as Alexa reached inside her bag for her laptop.

"I'm Jake. This is Agent Ryan," he said, looking over as Ben closed the door and positioned himself across from Jake. They had Special Forces written all over them. Maybe former Seals, possibly Rangers. Of course, maybe it was just the bulletproof vests, black boots, and all black clothing—accompanied with black face paint —that gave him the impression.

"Tanner," the one guy said with a nod, his dark brown eyes meeting Jake's.

"Pat," the other guy announced.

"Thanks for coming." Jake looked through the rectangular glass that separated the driver from the ammo.

"This is Tom, and I'm Steve," the driver said, glancing at Jake in the rearview mirror. Tom turned around in the passenger seat and nodded as the van began to roll away from the curb.

"Appreciate your help," Jake said as Alexa looked up from her computer screen, her eyes already slightly fogged with the task at hand, and smiled at the crew.

Ben tossed a bulletproof vest to Jake, and another to Alexa.

Jake strapped it on, rolling his shoulders when the compression squeezed his scarred back. It was a painful reminder that they were heading directly to the men who had done this to him.

"You think you got this?" Ben tipped his head back until the base of his skull pressed against the metal interior of the van. His eyes slid to the side, glancing at Alexa.

Alexa's lower lip quivered as her eyes flicked up to Ben's. "Yeah."

"It's been a while since I was on a mission like this," Ben said as Alexa began to type again.

"Maybe you ought to change careers if the private security gig out in Vegas isn't exciting enough for you."

"It has its moments. Can't beat living in Sin City." He flashed him a grin. "Maybe you're the one ready to slow down, though?" He tipped his chin in Alexa's direction—and Jake got the message.

Jake scratched at the stubble that was starting to grow back on his jaw. "Since when have you ever known me to do anything at half speed?"

He heard the soft sound of Alexa clearing her throat— discreetly, but he wondered what she was thinking at that moment.

"Oh, come on now. You're a good ole Southern boy. I bet you're dying for a slower pace." Ben was trying to distract him. Maybe he was worried about him. Did he think Jake was getting too old for this? Christ, they were practically the same age.

"And what the hell are you? You grew up in Alabama," Jake said.

"But I've got Vegas blood now." He laughed as he looked at the weapons at his feet.

"You're such an ass." Jake smirked.

"Well, this ass is trying to save yours . . ."

Jake looked back up at his friend. How many times had they saved each other? He was beginning to lose count.

"We're going to be okay," Ben said, glancing around the van before his eyes once again found Jake. "All of us." He raised his hand and curled his fingers into a fist. Jake bumped knuckles like they used to do.

He and Ben had made it out of the desert alive.

Why not now?

* * *

IT WAS LIKE A FIST HAD FORMED INSIDE HER STOMACH AND WAS steadily punching its way out. There were too many lives on the line. She couldn't let anyone die.

"This is the best I can do. He's not exactly using internet dial up. He's either bouncing off someone else's connection or using a hot spot, like me. Either way, I can put him about here." She flipped the computer screen around to show Jake a spot on the map.

"That'll have to do," Jake said, and nodded at Ben.

"Hey Boss Man," Ben hollered up to the driver. He shouted the coordinates. "Keep your eyes peeled for two black SUVs, crazy looking fuckers standing guard outside a house, and whatnot."

*How are you so calm?* Alexa studied Ben. Her nerves were pinched so tight that she thought she might be losing oxygen.

"You did it," Jake said, and then nudged her with the vest, which she still hadn't put on.

She shook her head. "Just a minute." She handed her laptop to Ben and reached into her bag.

"Once we find these guys, I need you to call Trent and give him the location."

Jake's words had her snapping her head back up.

"And what if he orders Hellfire missiles to take out the place?" It would probably create a major international incident, but who knew what Trent thought was an appropriate countermove?

"He won't. There are three agents streaming live over the internet right now, and the video has millions of hits already. The world would witness their deaths," Jake answered.

"Isn't Bekas planning to kill them on camera anyway? Trent might weigh his options and choose to save the cruise ship." God, she still couldn't believe this was happening. Parliament in London, a whole cruise liner filled with people . . . all to kill the family of a general and send the world a message. *Oh yeah, and a fecking hashtag.* She wanted to pull the trigger and take out Bekas and his men herself.

"Don't call Trent until we're inside. That gives us enough time to do what we need to. But I'll feel better knowing we have back-up in case—"

Her stomach tightened. "In case what?"

"Either way, we'll need to escort them to the base, right?" Jake countered. "Even if it's just their bodies."

"Shit, you've got to see this," Ben said, and the growing swell of nausea that pooled in the pit of her stomach churned. "That's you, right?"

Alexa took the phone from Ben and stared at the image. It was her security clearance photo from the agency.

Her hand covered her mouth as her body tensed. Her life as an agent was now officially over.

It was the least of her concerns right now, but it was still a knife in the back. The decision to stay or quit had been taken from her. Her whole life's purpose had disappeared in a puff of smoke.

# CHAPTER TWENTY-EIGHT

"THAT HAS TO BE IT, MAN. I DON'T SEE THE SUVS, BUT THERE'S A garage," the driver—AKA Boss Man—said. "There's a guy out front, one on each side of the villa, and one in the back. And I'm pretty sure I saw someone on the rooftop patio. No rifles, but who knows what else they're packing."

"Okay. Park us a few houses up and out of sight," Ben instructed.

"No. I need to be closer." Alexa was holding the frequency jammer in her hand, along with some other contraption she had created on the drive over. She'd connected thin, blue and red wires to a microchip board, and these attached to a cell phone she'd deconstructed into . . . well, hell if he knew.

"I can't have them spotting us—or getting to you." Jake's fingers draped over her wrist, his eyes steadying on hers.

She raised her shoulders up, the bulky bulletproof vest shifting as she did. "If we're going to stop the drone strike, I told you that I need to be within sixty meters of Bekas. Closer would be better."

"She'll need to come with us on foot," the driver proposed. "There's nowhere I can park the van that close that won't get noticed. She can take cover behind the house."

"No." Jake removed his hand from her wrist and opened his palm. "Give me that thing and tell me what to do." His body was wrung so damn tight he was going to snap. There was no way he could focus on the mission with her life hanging in the balance.

"You need to deal with Bekas. Let me handle this." Her voice was stern, and he knew she wouldn't give in. She was as stubborn as him.

"What is your plan, exactly?" Ben asked as he screwed a silencer onto a Beretta M9 9mm and handed it over to Jake.

"Well, 'no comms, no bombs,' right? If they hijack the drone, I'll block their Wi-Fi. Once they lose communication with the drone, it will override their last directive and the drone switches to autopilot as a default and returns to base. It's much easier than trying to hack the satellite." Alexa raised the device in her hand and gave Jake a half-smile. "Taking a lesson from the moves Anarchy used against us in Barcelona."

"Shit, that's good. Simple, and yet brilliant," Ben said.

"But there's still a problem." She sighed and reached for the black box Wi-Fi jammer. "While this jammer can block up to eight different frequencies at a time, I'm sure Bekas, or even Jason, has an infinite amount of connections. Every time I kill the Wi-Fi, they will probably flip over to a new one. I'll do my best to keep up with them, but I may not be able to hold them off for more than five-or-ten minutes. We can't risk them retaking the drone," she explained.

"Which is where the guys and I come in. We'll take them out before that becomes an issue," Ben said with a wink.

"We'll cut the power, too . . . at the right time. They probably have a back-up for that, as well. We have to expect the worst case and be prepared for it." Jake looked over at Ben. "You got the earpieces?"

"Yeah." Ben rummaged around in a bag by his combat-booted feet.

"We'll need to split up. I don't know if they have security cameras or not, but let's assume that they'll know we're there by the time we are inside the building. I want them to think they have us." Jake shifted his attention in the van to the other men. "I want everyone except Ben and me to stay put here. We'll take out the guards. Once we're in position, you guys escort Alexa to a secure location near the house and immediately work on killing their Wi-Fi. Tanner, you'll stay with Alexa while Tom, Steve, and Pat follow Ben and me inside. When the power goes out, I'll need you to enter the house for the assist."

"How will the two of you take out five armed men?" Alexa's fingers slipped over to Jake's thigh, and he stared down at her hand. If only she knew he'd been in situations like this more damn times than he could count.

Then again, maybe it was better that she didn't know.

"Don't worry about that, we've got this," Ben said. "Here." He handed her and Jake an earpiece.

Jake tucked it inside his ear and pressed it on. "You got me?" he asked her.

"Yeah." Alexa nodded, her face growing tight. She had to be nervous. Her best friend was inside and there was an entire cruise ship full of people relying on her.

Jake patted her on the shoulder and reached for her hand, squeezing it tight. This might be the last time he ever saw her again. There was always the risk of death on a mission, but as long as she survived . . .

"Be safe." Her eyes became glossy, but Ben was pressing a hand over her shoulder.

"Come on, man," Ben urged.

Jake quickly touched his lips to hers, not giving a damn about the other men. When he pulled back, he looked away from her almost immediately, too afraid to see the look in her eyes. He grabbed his rifle and 9mm and followed Ben out the back door. "Call Trent," Jake said over his shoulder to her, and then he shut the door to the van and rested the back of his head against it for a moment, trying to compose himself.

Ben nodded at him and removed his earpiece, and Jake did the same and clicked it off for a moment. "You good, man?"

Jake pinched his throat and blinked a couple of times. "Yeah." As they began walking, Jake secured his rifle on his back and kept the 9mm with the attached silencer in hand.

"I like your plan—make sure they underestimate us."

"If Bekas thinks he has the upper hand, that will give us more time." Jake stopped walking. "After we take the guards out, I need you to hang back out of sight. That way you can kill the power. If I lose you on comms and can't give you a signal, then wait about five minutes and shut it down."

"Like old times, brother." Ben lightly tapped him on the shoulder and cocked his gun. "I'll get the guy on the roof, the one in the back, and the one on the left side of the house."

"Be safe, man." Jake placed the earpiece back in and inhaled deeply before nodding at Ben. He fell back, taking cover alongside the neighbor's garage as Ben stealthily crept forward. Once Ben took out the man on the roof, Jake could approach the other side of the house unseen.

A few minutes ticked by. "You're good to roll," Ben said into Jake's ear, and a rush of relief hit him.

Jake started for the villa with slow steps, his head bent to the side, his gun extended in front of him. When he reached the house, he stayed as close as possible to the shadows—noting the dead guard sprawled out on the ground. His eyes were open, his arm above his head, a gun in his hand.

Jake moved around the body and pressed his back to the siding, preparing himself to round the next side of the house. If there was any pain in his body, he didn't feel it. Adrenaline pumped through him, and his heart pounded in his chest.

He chanced a glimpse around the corner and spotted a man moving fast in his direction, gun in hand. The guards were already on alert. Of course they'd be in communication with each other.

Fortunately, Jake had expected this.

The slug from Jake's gun tore straight through the center of the man's forehead, and he fell back fast without a chance to fire or even open his mouth. Jake sprinted alongside the house, dodging the fallen body, and halted where the side met the front of the home, waiting for the next guard to come to him.

It was barely five seconds before the next man crossed in front of Jake. He was only inches away, and he locked his forearm beneath the large man's jawline and secured his other arm against the back of his neck. He squeezed tight, and the guard struggled against him. The man's gun fell to the ground, and he gripped Jake's forearm, trying to lift the pressure from his throat. The guard tried to yell, but Jake pressed against his vocal cords so that he could hardly squeak.

Jake shut his eyes, trying to separate himself from the killer he had to be. With one quick movement, he jerked both his arms and snapped the guy's neck.

He swallowed and opened his eyes as the man crumpled to his feet.

"Ben, are you good?" Jake whispered hoarsely, knowing Alexa could also hear him. He hoped she hadn't been too scared, listening to all the commotion.

"I'm in position, but I'm pretty sure they're waiting inside for you," Ben answered.

Helping and protecting people—the need to serve—became like water. A necessity. It was hard to turn off the man you became in war. Some, like Jake, Ben, and many of his Marine buddies, had never discovered how.

Once a soldier, always a soldier.

"I know." Jake tucked his 9mm into the holster at his hip and reached for the AK-47 that he had strapped to his back.

"Be careful, Jake." Alexa's words stopped him in his tracks. He wanted to respond, but what could he say? Being careful was not the mission objective. So he kept his mouth shut and tried to drown out the doubts that crept into his mind.

He approached the door and turned the knob. It was unlocked. After all, the house was guarded, and Bekas hadn't expected to be outsmarted. He'd been five steps ahead of them at every turn.

But not tonight. Not this one damn time.

Jake wondered if either man he'd just killed was responsible for his abduction in Italy and the massacre of his team. The slight tinge of guilt that had roiled in his stomach disappeared. He'd never believed in an eye for an eye, especially given how Kemal Bekas was going about it, but he'd be damned if he didn't want revenge for the men he'd lost.

Jake opened the door and slowly stepped into the villa. With the nozzle of the rifle pointed forward, he moved through the foyer, grateful for the darkness that masked his presence. At any moment, he'd be confronting the enemy.

There was a low rumbling down the hall where light glinted from beneath a doorway. Jake moved in that direction with slow and careful steps.

"Tell me you didn't really come with only one other guy."

The deep, throaty voice came from down the hall. Jake remembered that voice from London when he'd been hanging by his wrists, his back being whipped. But he'd never seen the face that matched it. He waited for the speaker to reveal himself, but instead, a door opened in the hall, allowing a splash of light to filter out into the dark.

"It's over, Bekas!" Jake shouted, securing his rifle tight against the top of his chest and right shoulder blade. "I'm coming in!" He closed in on the room.

"What? No!" Alexa cried into his ear.

He flashed his eyes shut, allowing images of his family, friends, Alexa, to grace his mind. When he opened his eyes, he offered himself as a target in the open doorway.

A gun met his temple the second he stepped into the room. No surprise there.

"Lower your weapon," the man ordered, but Jake held his rifle steady at the targets across the room. Jason was sitting behind a long, sleek desk, which housed three laptops and a joystick. So, they were planning for Jason to fly the drone, huh? Since his hands weren't on the joystick, Jake felt a surge of hope that they hadn't attempted to hijack it yet. Maybe there was still time.

Jake's gaze slowly moved across the room, accounting for every person.

Xander, Randall, and Seth were tied to chairs in front of a camera mounted on a tripod. Tape covered their mouths, and each of them looked his way. "A little light on security, yeah?" Jake poked.

"Drop your weapon or they die." It was the familiar voice again. The guy with his gun on him had been in the cabin in London. Jake looked forward to a little payback.

The man standing next to Jason was Bekas. The ring leader. His arms were crossed over his chest. And Jake recognized the other men beside him—Reza and Gregov.

Bekas still hadn't spoken, so Jake added, "Your desire to show off to the media is how I found you, you know. You only have yourself to blame. But come on, were you that confident no one would be able to find you? Maybe you shouldn't have relied on that asshole," Jake said while tipping his head Jason's way, "to cover your tracks." Jake tightened his hold on his rifle, despite the three other drawn weapons in the room. He knew they wouldn't fire without Bekas's order, and Bekas, who was on the receiving end of the barrel of Jake's rifle, couldn't take the chance that Jake would get a shot off first.

Bekas smoothed a hand over his black beard, and his gleaming dark eyes met Jake's gaze. "Tell me something, do you believe that the things you do for your country are justified? The murdering of innocent lives?" He released a deep breath and took a step forward.

"I've never killed anyone innocent so I wouldn't know. Why don't you tell me how it feels since you're so Goddamn familiar?"

Bekas's lips curved down. "I am sacrificing some lives now to save many lives later. The world will see the danger of your government's drone strikes. They will know the consequences."

"Perhaps drones aren't the best way to kill terrorists." Jake shrugged lightly. "Up, close, and personal is so much better."

Bekas narrowed one eye at him and slipped his hands into the pockets of his black slacks, seeming not to have a care in the world. "People will witness your death. And the death of many others. They will be scared, and they will attack what they fear."

Jake shook his head. "You're forgetting something," he said in a low voice as he glanced over the man's shoulder at Jason, who was working steadily at the computer. Jake realized he was running low on time.

"Oh yeah? What is that?" Bekas asked.

Jake slowly moved into the room and stepped in front of the camera, directly in front of the agents. The man kept his gun on him as he moved, but Jake kept his finger on the trigger and the nozzle pointing toward Bekas.

"We don't let people like you intimidate us," Jake said. "You knock us down, and we get right the fuck back up. You're going to fail because you didn't consider the strength of the American people. Or of the British. We won't surrender to you assholes. You want to fight? Bring it," Jake rasped.

"I think you're overestimating your people." Bekas's lips twitched. "But you and your friend won't be around long enough to find out."

Jake looked over at Jason, whose hand swept up to the joystick. His eyes focused on the screen in front of him as he shifted the joystick to the left.

"And your military will be too late. I assume they are on their way, yes?" Bekas raised an eyebrow as he cocked his head.

So, it had been a suicide mission all along. Bekas didn't care if he got caught, so long as he sent his message to the world.

"Fuck. I've already lost control of the drone." Jason's hand slipped free from the joystick as he began tapping at keys.

*Thank you, Alexa.*

"What the hell happened?" Bekas kept his eyes on Jake, glowering at him, as he came around behind the computer to see what Jason was doing.

"Someone is jamming the frequencies. It's going to take me a minute to get us online again," Jason answered, flicking his gaze up at Jake for one brief moment, a darkness in his eyes.

"We don't have a Goddamn minute," Bekas said while looking back at Jake, eyeing the nozzle of Jake's rifle.

"You did it, huh? You hijacked the drone. I'm impressed. I didn't think Jason was smart enough." A smile met Jake's lips. "Too bad you couldn't hang onto it for more than a second." Jake could no longer hear any sound coming from his earpiece so he assumed he'd lost the signal.

"Is it your pretty little spy doing this?" Bekas directed his attention to the man who was holding the gun to Jake's temple. "Why don't I send my men out to go get her?" He shrugged his shoulders, but the sweat on his brow beneath his dark hair, and the strain in his throat indicated the guy was rattled. "Git," the man commanded in what sounded like Turkish. "Şimdi."

*Hell, no.* Jake dropped to his knees in one fast movement, prepared to shoot—but darkness flashed through the room, stealing his chance. Only the glow from the computer screens at the desk— running on damn battery power—allowed for a little light.

"Get him," Bekas said, but Jake wasn't sure who he was ordering.

*She's protected,* Jake reminded himself as he tried not to lose focus.

Jake remained low on the ground and lifted his gun, angling it in the direction of the computers—then he quickly clipped off two powerful rounds, shredding the monitors.

"Motherfucker!" Jason shouted as flickers of light popped from the screens as the CPUs died. Too bad he hadn't hit Jason, too.

"Get the power back on," Bekas grumbled, and based on the sound of his voice, he was probably on the ground—hiding in fear. Good, it was where Jake wanted him to be.

Jake reached for the night vision goggles he had stowed in his cargo pants pocket by his shin. He slipped them on and grabbed the 9mm at his side.

Through the green tinted goggles, he could count the figures in the room. Bekas and Jason were crouched down near the desk. And the guy who'd first had his gun on Jake was now hunkered down with his gun clutched in both hands. At least he hadn't gone for Alexa. That was something.

But two men were missing—Reza and Gregov.

Jake army crawled across the floor, trying to get to Xander and the others. They were sitting ducks in what would soon become a shit storm.

He lifted his gun as the guy by the doorway started in Jake's direction, and he pegged the man in the head. His shoulders rolled before his body slumped forward.

"Hold your damn fire," Bekas urged with terror in his voice. Not so much a death wish now.

Ben and the others would be there any second. Jake just needed to keep everyone alive until then.

He secured a knife from the holder at his side and slipped it between the duct tape that was wrapped around Xander's hands. Xander couldn't see Jake, but he pressed a hand to Jake's shoulder as Jake sawed at the bindings that tied Xander's feet.

The room was dark, but Jake had to assume Bekas's vision had adjusted now—and at any moment Bekas could become a threat once again.

When Xander was free, Jake gave him his 9mm and the knife

and looked up to see Ben edging inside the room, a pair of night vision goggles strapped to his face.

Ben raised a hand into the air and clenched his fist, signaling for Jake to hold his position. He slowly moved toward the desk where Bekas was hiding.

"You're surrounded. Put your hands over your heads," Ben instructed.

"Not on your life," Bekas answered.

"Fine. Have it your way." With zero hesitation, Ben sprayed fire at the desk, adding additional damage to the software.

Jake moved off to the side, coming around to engage with Bekas and the others from another angle to cover Ben. As he approached, the lights in the room came back on, which prompted his goggles to automatically turn off, saving his eyes. As he yanked them free—Jake hissed, gritting his teeth as a bullet caught him in the vest, knocking the wind out of him. As he adjusted to the light and shook off the pain, not sure where the enemy fire was coming from—another bullet, like a breath of fire on his neck —grazed him.

More shots fired.

Reza and Gregov were back and engaging with Ben, but also with the rest of the team. *Thank God.*

"Fuck. Stop firing." Bekas threw his hands up in the air. He went to his knees and cupped a hand over his bleeding shoulder, wedged between two crumpled bodies. Reza and Jason's lifeless bodies were in front of him. Gregov was moaning on the floor, holding his hand against his abdomen.

"Screw your shoulder. Put your hands back over your head," Ben ordered.

Jake clutched his chest where it throbbed from the bullet, even though it'd hit the vest. He started to approach Bekas, but scanned the room for a head count, ensuring all of his men were safe.

When his eyes cast down onto Xander's body on the floor, a new pain crushed him. "Christ!" He rubbed a hand over his face as

271

he saw Xander gasping, making a loud sucking sound. He had a GSW to the chest, and based on the way he was breathing, the bullet probably pierced his lungs.

Jake quickly looked back at Ben who was securing Bekas's hands behind his back. Knowing that the situation was covered, he rushed around the fallen chairs and moved to Xander's side, coming up next to Seth who was covering the hole with both his hands. "Find me some plastic," Jake said to Randall who was over his shoulder, watching. "We need to cover his wound with it to keep air from getting inside."

"Got something," Randall said a moment later and thrusted something at Jake.

"Move your hands for a second, Seth," Jake said as Xander continued to gasp for air, a spurt of blood starting to come from the edge of his mouth. *Jesus, stay with me,* but he thought the words instead of saying them as he pressed the plastic over the wound. "You're going to be okay, man," Jake finally said to Xander just as his gray eyes slowly closed.

"Keep this pressed over the wound while I do CPR," Jake ordered to Seth as his hand slipped up to the groove of Xander's throat, checking for a pulse.

They were losing him.

"Won't that make it worse? He has a bullet in his chest." Seth raised his brows, his hands coming back over Xander's wound.

Jake's hands were slick with Xander's blood as he started compressions. "We don't have a choice. He's in cardiac arrest. We've got to keep blood flowing to the brain even if it causes more damage to his lungs." Jake was thankful for the medical training he'd had in Iraq—but he hoped to hell it would pay off right now.

"Hold your hands over that plastic—keep it tight," Jake said to Seth as he continued to push and pump—trying to keep Xander alive. *Please, God. For Alexa. She's been through too much.*

"I think he's gone," Randall said a minute later, his hand reaching across Xander's body to touch Jake's shoulder.

"No. Screw that. We can save—" Jake cut himself off when he heard what sounded like blades above. A Black Hawk?

Then Jake looked up for a brief moment, his jaw going slack as he caught sight of Alexa standing across the room. Her eyes landed on his and filled with a brief glow of relief to see Jake alive. Their light turned to horror at the sight of Xander lying bloody and motionless in front of him.

"No!" she screamed as she rushed their way.

Jake didn't remove his hands. He kept them there, but his eyes stayed on Alexa. His heart tearing apart at that moment. "Alexa . . ." he said in a hoarse voice.

Randall went for her, wrapping his arms around Alexa, pulling her back, trying to turn her around so she wouldn't have to see.

"No," she cried again, struggling against him, fighting for her friend.

"He's gone, Alexa," Randall said.

Jake continued CPR. He refused to accept Xander was gone.

Tears sprang to her eyes as she sank to the floor. Jake saw something in her eyes he had never seen—never wanted to. Her gaze drifted to a pistol on the floor just a few feet away from her. "You deserve to die, Bekas," she yelled as she extended her hand in the direction of the gun.

"Fuck." Jake stopped the compressions, grabbed his 9mm from beside Xander's body, and lifted it into the air in one smooth movement, shooting Bekas in the chest before Alexa had the chance.

Ben's brows pinched with surprise as Bekas fell back, his skull banging uselessly against the desk.

Alexa was still holding the gun tight in her hand, breathing hard. Then she pivoted on her knees to face Jake. He set the 9mm down and went back to trying to keep Xander alive as if the moment hadn't happened.

He hadn't just killed a man whose hands were tied . . . Jake wouldn't do such a thing.

"Why . . .?" Alexa crawled on her hands and knees over to Jake, coming up next to Xander. Emotion choked her words as her gun slipped and clanked to the ground. Her hands came over Xander's body, and she lowered her forehead to his stomach, tears breaking down her cheeks.

# CHAPTER TWENTY-NINE

A SLIGHT, SALTY BREEZE BLEW HER HAIR ACROSS HER FACE AS SHE stood in the parking lot at the Sigonella base.

Alexa studied the swelling on Jake's forehead and the dark ring beneath his eye. Her gaze skated down to his throat where gauze was taped. "Are you all right?" She swallowed, attempting to clear the emotion from her throat. "Did anyone else get hurt?" She'd been so overcome by sadness that she still hadn't taken a moment to thank God they'd stopped the terrorist attack. Or taken time to process that Jason had died, too.

But Jake was okay. She cared so deeply for him that she felt like he owned part of her heart.

Xander, on the other hand . . .

Jake's fingers played over the gauze for a brief moment. "No one else on our team got hurt," he said solemnly, his eyes darting to the black pavement.

"I talked to Matt at headquarters. They managed to stop the attack in London." She had spoken softly as if her words didn't really matter. She raised both hands to the back of her neck and gripped it, her body aching and her heart damn near breaking.

"That's good," he said.

BRITTNEY SAHIN

Was he feeling guilty? Although she didn't blame him for what happened to Xander, she didn't know what to say.

Chills blew across her skin and her stomach muscles clenched as she absorbed the reality of their situation. "I should get to the hospital."

Jake cleared his throat and finally tore his gaze from the ground to meet her eyes. He shoved his hands into his pockets and rocked back on his heels. "Yeah. I should, uh, fill everyone in about what happened."

"Will you get in trouble?" If he ended up in jail because of her . . .

"Don't worry, please."

"You didn't need to do that for me. I could have handled the repercussions. Killing Bekas would have been worth it." She'd been itching to kill the man for a long time. She hadn't suspected that she'd have an opportunity to do it with her own hands, but still. And Jake had done it for her, lifting the burden of murder from her shoulders. In that moment, he had sacrificed his morals, his values, and maybe even his career for her.

*What have I done?*

"Can I meet you at the hospital after?" Jake angled his head, finding her eyes.

She wanted to say yes as much as she needed to say no. "I'd rather be alone if you don't mind." And what if he wasn't even allowed to come?

"I don't think that's best." He took a step closer to her, lifting his hands from his pockets. There was still evidence of Xander's blood on his palms, and the sight of it made her stomach somersault. *How did this happen?*

"I think it's best if we take some time . . . wrap up the case officially, and then get in touch." She was pushing him away. She knew it. He knew it.

His eyes were coated with a pained sadness. "Okay." One word, full of meaning.

"I—I'll come to you this time," she found herself saying. "You looked for me last time, so I'll come to Dallas." She tried to tell herself she was speaking the truth, but doubt curved around the syllables of her words, wrapping them in fear.

*What am I doing? Stay with me, Jake. Don't leave.* She was crying on the inside—but she couldn't get herself to voice her words.

Her lips parted, trying to muster the courage to tell him how she really felt.

"Okay. Sure," he answered with hollow eyes, taking a step back. "Goodbye, Alexa." He turned from her, hiding his bloodstained shirt from her sight. When Jake stole one last glimpse of her over his shoulder as he walked away, Alexa's heart broke for the second time that night.

# CHAPTER THIRTY

JAKE WALKED ACROSS THE GRASS, WHICH WAS PARTLY COVERED BY slowly melting snow. The sun hung brightly in the sky as he made his way through the Arlington National Cemetery. Row after row of white headstones spread as far as the eye could see. A few trees were scattered in the midst of the nation's hallowed ground.

He hadn't been there in years. He hated himself for not coming more often.

Jake found his way to the first tomb he'd come to visit and crouched to one knee. He pulled a bouquet of flowers from the crook of his elbow and set it on top of the white arch.

When his memories had come back, with them had come a deep, throbbing loss.

It was like all his buddies had died all over again.

They had been sons, husbands, brothers. They'd served their country and died protecting it. They'd made the ultimate sacrifice.

Jake took a deep breath and closed his eyes. The bitter air brushed across his skin as emotions funneled through him.

It had been a week and a half since he'd left London.

Ben hadn't told the military that Jake had killed Bekas while his hands had been tied—but Jake had known Ben wouldn't rat on him.

So, Jake told on himself. He admitted that he killed Bekas out of anger, but he didn't mention Alexa's name. He would have rather gone to prison before allowing anything happen to her.

As much as he wanted to feel guilty for murdering Bekas—he didn't. He wouldn't hesitate to do the same thing again. He would kill for Alexa. Maybe that should have worried him, but it didn't.

But when his agency decided to act like they didn't hear Jake's admission of guilt—because Jake and his team had managed to thwart the terrorist attack . . . well, Jake couldn't help but take matters into his own hands.

He resigned. Besides, how could he be an undercover agent when the world had watched him stand up to terrorists on a live feed.

He'd even given interviews for three morning cable talk shows and had been a guest on all of the major news stations in the U.S. It hadn't been his idea, but after being hounded nonstop, he'd given in.

But he didn't want to stop helping people—that he knew. But he also wanted to plant roots and start a family. But with Alexa? He didn't know if he'd ever hear from her again. And he wasn't sure what to do about it. Would he chase after her once again?

Jake slowly rose to his feet and looked back out at the sea of tombstones.

More memories of men and women who'd donned the uniform flooded to his mind.

From the agents he'd lost in the FBI to the soldiers in Iraq and Afghanistan. Men and women who'd given their lives, who had made it possible for there to be a today and a tomorrow.

"Thank you," he said while bowing his head forward and shutting his eyes.

# CHAPTER THIRTY-ONE

ALEXA'S FISTS PUMPED AT HER SIDES AS HER FEET POUNDED THE pavement along the Thames. A roll of what looked like smoke steamed off the river, wafting over the sidewalk as she ran.

The muscles in her quads grew tight and pain radiated in her calves as she sprinted harder and faster than she had ever thought possible.

And then she jerked to an immediate stop, unable to push herself anymore. She leaned forward as her chest expanded, her ribs aching. She pressed her palms to her knees, catching her breath.

But as she sucked in the cool air, her eyes filled with tears. Alexa moved off to the edge of the path and raised a hand to cover her face, hiding the tears as emotion breached, pouring out of her with gut-wrenching intensity.

Her world had forever changed when the @Anarchy case closed.

She missed Jake, but she couldn't bring herself to call him. Let alone go to Dallas and find him as she'd promised. She'd seen him on TV, though. He had looked so uncomfortable being interviewed.

Still, she'd recorded the program and kept replaying it over and over.

Alexa swiped the tears from her wind-burned cheeks and sniffled as she tried to get ahold of herself. She brushed away her emotion, like she always did, and started back for her flat.

She climbed the two flights to get to her landing and unzipped her jacket pocket for her key. But when she opened the door, she stumbled back a step, surprise deepening the red in her already bright cheeks. "What are you doing here?" She closed the door behind her, tossed the key on the table in the foyer, and folded her arms.

"You're moving? I hope it's to Texas."

Alexa looked around her flat. Half-packed boxes cluttered the living area. Somehow or other, she had to find a new place to live. Now that the social media video Bekas had uploaded had over one-hundred million hits, everyone recognized her. Of course, moving wouldn't exactly solve that problem, but she felt like she needed a new home if she were going to start a new life.

So much for her life as a spy, though.

And she couldn't go back to work even if she wanted to, could she? She'd almost killed a man who had his hands tied, simply for revenge.

Guilt stabbed at her as she thought again about what Jake had done. She kept remembering the moment when Jake reached for the gun and shot Bekas without thinking twice. She'd heard Jake had quit the agency, and it seemed as though the Americans had covered up the kill.

"Alexa?" Xander rolled forward, gripping tight to the rims of his wheelchair.

She stared at her wounded—but, thank God, very alive friend, and cupped a hand to her mouth as emotions began to strangle her, yet again, today.

The soldiers in the helicopter had managed to keep Xander alive long enough to get him to the hospital. She thought they'd lost him, for sure. She'd gone to the hospital to say goodbye only to find out he'd made it through surgery and had a chance to survive. With physical therapy, the doctors thought he'd recover to live a normal life. He'd never be a hundred percent or be able to be an agent again, but he was alive. And the doctor said if it weren't for Jake—he wouldn't have ever had a chance.

Xander was okay . . . and the crisis had been averted, so why did she still feel so gutted?

Was it being apart from Jake? Something in her resisted going to him. Was it guilt at what she'd caused him to do? He had been a man who didn't want to kill a spider, but he'd killed for her in the blink of an eye. Surely he'd had to kill people before, but not unarmed, helpless, tied down people . . .

She knew what he had done for her, and she wasn't sure if she could forgive herself.

"You should be in bed," she said, coming in front of Xander and reaching for his hand.

"Maybe if I had a hotter nurse taking care of me! But, damn! The woman is old and annoying as hell."

Xander almost had her smiling. Even a near death experience didn't change his attitude. God bless him.

"I was hoping to find your place empty and you gone." He raised a brow and squeezed his hand tighter around hers.

There it was again—raw pain—a little jagged around the edges. Eviscerating.

"Go to him, Alexa." Xander's voice moved through her as her eyes closed. She lowered herself to the floor beside his wheelchair.

"I can't."

"Do you love him?"

She released a breath and opened her eyes to peer up at her friend. His dark, steely eyes caged her. There was a depth there now she hadn't noticed before. "I—" *Do I?*

"It's a simple yes or no, Alexa."

She gulped.

"Don't waste your time feeling guilty. Don't waste another Goddamn minute doing anything other than what makes you happy."

She cleared her throat and pushed back up to her feet. "Is that what you're going to do?"

"Of course."

"And what makes you happy?"

"Saving the world," he said, shooting her a playful wink to lighten the mood.

"No love life? Not going to settle down?"

He pressed a hand to his chest, and she saw there again the hole, the blood spilling through . . . "My heart is working beautifully, and I have so much love to give. No one person could handle my overflowing ardor."

"Jesus, Xander." She huffed. "You drive me bloody nuts." But she was feeling better. For now, at least.

"Good. Then all is right in the world." He pressed his hands to the outside of his chair and rolled toward the door.

"Where are you going?"

He glanced over his shoulder and smiled. "To find a better nurse."

She pressed a hand to her stomach, supporting the first bubble of laughter she'd felt in weeks.

"And, Alexa?"

"Yeah?"

"The next time I lug my arse back here, this place had better be empty."

She opened the door for him and said goodbye, then locked up and pressed her back to it, dragging her hands down her face.

Sore and slightly chilled from her run, she decided to have a bath.

Moments later, she was slipping below the bubbles, raising a cup of tea to her lips. She took a sip, savoring its flavor to the sultry sounds of Jazz, and then draped her arm over the side of the tub, the mug still in her hand.

Xander's words kept pushing to the forefront of her mind.

Jake . . .

*What if he doesn't ever want to see me again?* She'd let him slip free from her life a year ago, and now . . . what if he changed his mind and didn't want her back? What if there was too much damage between them?

Xander had almost died, and other people did die because of @Anarchy. And Alexa was adrift in the world with no job and, in two weeks, no home.

God, what she wouldn't give for a beach and a tropical cocktail. Instead of putting her nose in a book, she'd lounge at the side of the man she loved.

*Stop being a coward. Buy the ticket to Dallas.*

The water splashed over the edge of the tub as she shifted up, realizing she needed to get to a computer. Not tomorrow or the next day. She needed to book the damn ticket now. If Jake had changed his mind about her, well, she needed to be strong enough to face him and find out.

Alexa set the cup on the bathroom counter while she toweled off, and put on her red silk robe. She pulled her mostly dry hair free from its bun and shook her head until it cascaded down over her shoulders.

Her fingers went to her collarbone as she remembered her time with Jake in London when they had first met. What she wouldn't give to have his hands on her again.

She exhaled, blowing out her fear, and started for the sofa where her laptop was sitting.

Her shoulders flinched at the sound of the rap on the door.

Was that Xander again? Surely he hadn't expected her to move out in less than an hour.

Maybe Matt?

"Coming," she called, and then her heartbeat ticked up as she realized it could be an enemy at the door. Someone who'd discovered her location after Bekas had shared her picture with the world. She approached with cautious steps and pressed her palms against the wood. She wondered how fast she could get to her safe, which had a gun inside it.

Her heart thundered in her chest at the sight of the man standing on the other side of the peephole.

He was wearing a cream-colored sweater with jeans and beat-up, dark brown cowboy boots. The man had never looked sexier.

She unlocked the door and rested her hand on top of the handle. Her lip quivered as her body thrummed to life with an energy she had almost forgotten as she finally opened the door.

"Alexa," Jake murmured as if her name was meant only for his lips.

"You came for me," she whispered, and took a small step back, still holding onto the knob. He scratched at his throat before sliding his fingers through his hair. It was dirty blonde again. His natural color.

"I'll always come for you, Alexa."

She wilted at his words like a flower almost losing its petals, only to realize it was actually just now blooming. Her knees became wobbly, and she nearly collapsed, but he lunged forward and pulled her into his arms. He hitched her up, and her legs wrapped around his hips, gripping him tightly as his lips met hers. His tongue dove deep into her mouth, lighting her on fire with its sweetness.

God, she had craved his touch. To press against him and have him inside of her . . . where he belonged.

"I missed you so much," she cried against his lips and opened her eyes. "I was about to book my ticket to come to Dallas." He gently lowered her to the floor. "I was going to come sooner, but I —I was afraid you wouldn't want to see me after what happened."

When she saw the change in his eyes, the pure love glistening there—she knew she'd been an utter fool.

"Alexa," he swallowed, banding a hand around her hipbone, bringing her back against him, "you don't know me nearly well enough if that's what you thought."

She started to open her mouth to protest, but his finger slipped up to her chin, and he angled her face to capture her eyes.

"But we have the rest of our lives to fix that," he said. Then his mouth moved over hers, stealing her breath, her heart, her soul.

# CHAPTER THIRTY-TWO

"You got me tea?" A slow smile spread across Alexa's face as she looked down at the mug. Jake pulled back the covers, and slipped next to her in the bed, setting his cup of coffee down on the nightstand next to him.

They'd arrived in Dallas two days after Jake had surprised Alexa in London. It had been her idea to go to the States, and he happily obliged.

"Well, maybe I was a little confident I'd have you over some day." He trailed his fingers along her jaw, and her body spurred with the simple touch.

His hand fell on his lap and his eyes smoldered with more than desire. She still hadn't told him how she truly felt, but neither had he. But she knew.

"I can't believe we're sitting here like two people without a care in the world. So much has changed." But that was sort of a lie, right? They still hadn't broached the subject of the death of Bekas since the base in Italy. "Jake, there's something I need to ask." Her throat constricted and she forced out a deep breath.

"Yeah. Anything."

She placed her cup by the bed and faced him. "Do, you, um—" She looked down at her hands. "Do you hate me for what I made you do? Killing Bekas."

"First," Jake began while reaching for her hand, "I could never hate you. And second, I'm a big boy. I made the decision myself. You didn't make me do anything."

"Yeah, but you never would have—" Jake was shaking his head, his eyes narrowing on her, so she cut herself off.

"The guy was a psychopathic killer, Alexa. I didn't exactly kill someone innocent. I can handle what I did—I promise."

"But are you sure?" She forced herself to focus on his eyes, to read him—to make sure he truly was okay. "I mean, I thought he killed Xander, and so I reacted so quick."

"It sounds like you're the one that needs to forgive yourself and move on, Alexa."

He was right. She'd been beating herself up for weeks.

She finally nodded at him when she realized Jake had the kind of strength inside him that meant he could, in fact, navigate through his feelings about what happened and find the resolve to have acceptance.

And his strength was something she needed. Something she admired and loved.

"How's Xander and the others?"

She knew he was trying to distract her, and she decided to let him, because in all honestly, she really wanted a moment to be happy.

"Xander's still recovering, but he's doing well. Most of my former team members have accepted desk jobs with the government since they've lost clearance for undercover operations. But a few can't handle not being in the action." *Like Matt.*

And part of her knew that she should be upset that she was no longer an agent. It had been her life for the last eight years. Who was she without the agency?

But there was another piece of her that was relieved. She loved serving her country, and she knew she wanted to continue to help people in some way, but she also knew that being an agent had held her back in so many ways. Now, she was free to live her life out in the open.

"Well, about that." Jake scratched the back of his neck and closed an eye for a moment.

"Oh, God."

He flashed her his dazzling grin, and she lifted her fingers, pushing them through his hair.

His fingers lifted to cover her hand, and he raised it to his mouth and kissed her palm. "How about working together?"

"What do you mean?"

He rested their hands in his lap. "Well, remember how I told you back in London that my friend Connor and his brother sold their family business to start their own company, and—"

"I hardly call a rescue-slash-counterterrorist group a company, but, uh, yeah, I remember."

"Well, they have a lot of money to spend on the project, and they're thinking about opening a few locations. I mentioned maybe having one in the U.K." Jake swallowed. "I was thinking that maybe you and I could join. And if Xander wants in when he's better—"

"I love you." It wasn't how she had planned to say those words for the first time, but she couldn't hold them back. Her heart was thundering in her chest, and Jake's eyes glittered with the love he felt right back. He heaved out a breath—was that relief? Had he not known how she felt?

He tightened his grip on her hand. "It's about damn time," he said before his lips split into a grin. She relaxed at the sight of his smile. "I love you, too." He brushed his lips across hers, and she wanted to fall into his arms and stay there forever.

"Are you serious, though?" she asked a little breathlessly as their lips parted. She straightened, her body covered in goose bumps. "You want to live in London and continue to kick ass—with me? And with my mates?" Her heart was hammering in her chest so intensely she wasn't sure if she'd be able to hear his reply.

"They could use people like you and Xander. And since we can't exactly work for the government undercover anymore . . ."

Alexa leaned in and slanted her lips over his, cutting him off. He was giving her everything she could ever want. To continue to help, and to do it with her friends and this incredible man at her side. In London, her home. And this job could be on her own terms. No fake identities, no sleazy seductions. Although if Jake wanted to play dress-up, she supposed she'd give it a try.

She pulled away and rushed her fingers over her lips, trying to slow her thoughts for a moment. "But—do you really want to live in London? With me?"

"I thought maybe a few months a year we could come to Dallas, but yeah. I know this is soon, and all. I mean, I can get my own place over there, if you'd prefer."

"Are you daft? Of course, you're going to live with me! Well, we need to get a new flat in the city. Maybe outside London would be safer . . ." Her body was trembling, and it was as if she were floating—so light and free. "But."

"Oh no." He faked a groan. "There's a 'but'?" His eyes twinkled with amusement.

"Well, I would absolutely love to do this, but first I could really use a bloody holiday. Preferably to some place where my only concern is whether or not to wear clothes that day."

Jake's lips parted, and he laughed. He reached for her and gently dragged her naked body up and on top of him. She pressed her hands against his hard chest and stared down at him.

She wet her lips and wriggled against him a little, feeling him stiffen.

"If we're going on a vacation, I say we shouldn't have any

concerns." He held her wrists and lowered her until her breasts pressed flush against his chest. Her hands threaded through his hair as he cupped her face, her lips hovering before his. "No clothes, period."

* * *

ALEXA GLANCED AROUND THE ROOM, TRYING TO STIFLE HER laughter. "Did you really take me to a country bar? Or is this a dance club?"

At the center of the room was a wooden dance floor where couples were moving around—doing some sort of country dance, she assumed. Cowboy boots shuffled around the floor, and many of the men and women were wearing straw-colored hats.

The bar area circled the dance floor, separated by a thin black railing.

"I thought I'd teach you to two-step." Jake flicked his cowboy hat up to give her a better view of his deep brown eyes—eyes she could lose herself in forever. "Maybe someday I'll get you to wear some boots and a hat. You'd look damn sexy."

"Someday, but probably not today." She dragged her gaze down his button-up shirt, where his muscles were evident beneath his sleeves. His dark but well-worn jeans covered his brown boots.

*I'm in love with a cowboy. Who would have thought?* Her lips split open as her chest and shoulders lifted with a freeing laugh.

"Are you laughing at me?" Jake reached for her hips and lifted her into the air, spinning her around, and she stared down at him, her heart full of more joy than she ever could have dreamed it would be.

He slowly lowered her, and her breasts pressed against his firm chest as she slid down, her palms pressing between them when her heels touched the ground.

"We've been through a lot. I think we deserve to let loose a

little. Don't you?" He perked a brow and stepped back, holding his
hand out for her.

She stared at his hand, remembering how he made her sizzle
with his every touch. She swallowed, feeling a sudden tug in her
heart. There was no place she'd rather be right now. Even in a
country bar in Dallas where people held onto their belt buckles
while they danced.

Because she was here with Jake—with Mr. New Year's Eve.

She slowly placed her hand inside his, and he gently guided her
out to the center of the floor.

Alexa eyed the couples moving around her, nervous that she
wouldn't be able to keep up. Jake pressed a quick kiss to her lips
and then grabbed hold of her hands. "You've got this," he said with
a wink.

"I don't know." She shot him a nervous smile.

"Trust me." He pulled her into his arms, his hands smoothing
down over her bare back, where her shirt was split into a V. "Once
you're in my arms, the moves will come to you."

"Oh." She looked up at him. "You're that good?"

He gripped her hand, pulling their clasped palms up and
against his heart. He was quiet for a moment as he stared at her,
and then he suddenly stepped back and spun her around. She came
to a stop with her back to his chest before he dipped her, his eyes
catching hers.

"If I'm with you, I am," he said in a husky voice, and her body
shuddered with a chill that set her skin tingling. "If we're together,
Alexa, nothing can stop us."

He raised her upright and pulled her into his arms.

"*If* we're together?" she teased. But deep inside of her, she
knew that tomorrow was going to be so much better now that he
was in her life. And although her dad wouldn't be there to walk her
down the aisle when that time came, she knew her dad would've
been proud.

Jake squinted an eye as a smile tugged at his mouth. "You're certainly going to make my life a whole hell of a lot more interesting, aren't you?"

"Mm." She rolled her tongue over her teeth. "And you wouldn't want it any other way."

# BONUS SCENES

## WHEN JAKE AND ALEXA FIRST MET –
## NEW YEAR'S EVE

ALEXA

"If you don't find some hot guy to shag tonight, then I'll find one for you." Lori nudged me with her hip as she raised her champagne flute to her lips. She was pregnant, although you wouldn't be able to tell from her high-waisted, shimmering pink princess gown. So, unlike me, her champagne flute was filled with water.

"Babe, there's not a chance in hell I'm going home with any bloke from this party tonight." I took a sip of my drink, enjoying the sensation of the bubbles popping in my chest on the way down. I scanned the crowded room, which was filled mostly with rich and uppity men with whom I wouldn't want to spend one hour with, let alone a whole night.

No, I preferred a real man. A man who knew how to use his hands, and not just to tap at a keyboard and trade stock, or whatever the hell it was that most of the men at this party did. Of course, some of the guys in here were athletes, too, but they weren't my flavor, either.

Although my sister's fiancé, football player, Sean Houseman, seemed an all right sort.

It had been so long since I'd even seen a man naked, perhaps the time had passed when I could be so damn choosy. Maybe I wouldn't even recognize a man when I saw him.

But I was on holiday. What would be the harm in getting laid?

"What about him? I don't recognize him." Lori was pointing to a guy at the bar who was wearing a tux. His broad shoulders filled out the jacket well . . . hell, more than well. My gaze trailed up his tan throat to his hard jaw.

He was studying the drink in his hand instead of looking at the man who was chatting him up. He looked bored, or at least not in the least bit interested in what the man to his left was saying. He was standing probably twenty meters away from me, but when he looked up from his drink, his eyes found mine. It was as if the crowd parted before us, and he and I were alone. "Holy shit, he's looking at you." Lori's sharp elbow jabbed me in the ribs.

"Jesus, Lori." I winced. She'd caught me right in the scar. It didn't hurt anymore, but I still felt sensitive about the area. I frowned, no longer interested in sex.

"What's wrong?" Lori asked, coming around to look me in the eyes.

"Nothing. So, how're sales?" I asked instead. She'd had her debut art gallery show a few months ago. I went into a completely different field than her.

Shit, I didn't want to think about work right now. Otherwise, I might as well just skip the party and head back to HQ. Part of me wanted to say screw the holiday. I had to work straight through Christmas and up to New Year's Eve, though, but I still didn't think I needed a week off. What would I do with a whole bloody week?

"Your diversionary tactics won't work on me, sis. I think you should—"

Lori had fallen silent, and when I looked up, I realized why.

The not-so-stuffy guy in a tux was standing in front of me. He was holding a champagne flute, extending it toward me. It was good timing on his part—my glass appeared to be empty.

Lori didn't miss a beat. She snatched my glass and flitted off, probably in search of Sean.

"Would you like another, ma'am?"

If I had anything in my mouth, I would have choked. "Did you just call me 'ma'am'?" Dimples popped in his cheeks as he smiled, and I think my heart skipped about three beats.

"I could call you something else if you'd prefer." He was still holding the drink between us, and I stood stupidly staring at him instead of reaching for it.

The man was American. Most likely Southern, based on the soulful way he spoke. I'd played the part of an American Southern girl on an OP two years ago, and I had to watch a few movies and practice the accent. I probably spent only half of my job behind the computer screen where I belonged, and the other half working on my acting skills.

"My arm's getting tired," he prompted.

Sure, it was.

"Maybe you'd like something else?" He smiled again. No—his eyes smiled. Wow. And what eyes . . .

The idea of a shag was starting to seem more and more appealing.

"Thank you." I finally took the drink and brought the rim of the glass to my lips, but I couldn't help but notice his hands. They were strong and masculine—hands that could touch a woman . . . and protect one, too.

*Although I can protect myself perfectly fine, thank you.*

"I should get back to my friends. Thanks for the drink." Although it wasn't like he'd bought it—the drinks were complimentary. But it was still a nice gesture.

"No name?" he asked after I had turned.

I peeked over my shoulder at him. "Ma'am works," I said, chuckling.

Just then, I realized the room was buzzing to life. The countdown had begun. When had it gotten so close to midnight?

I faced the American again. "Ten. Nine. Eight . . ." He winked at me as he counted with the crowd. "Seven. Six. Five. Four. Three. Two. One . . ."

The room exploded with "Happy New Years," but my mystery guy was simply staring at me. Bursts of dandelion yellow and pinkish-red confetti fell over his head and shoulders. His lips parted, and he swiftly moved toward me and lowered my glass to the bar top table. He tipped my chin up, moving his lips to mine.

Oh, God, a New Year's kiss. How cliché . . .

Then I tightened my grip on the edge of the table as his lips slanted over mine because I thought I'd damn near collapse from the heat. He stepped closer, and his hand came around to my back, tugging me firm against his body. My mouth opened, giving him entrance. He could do whatever the hell he pleased at that moment.

"Mm." I had moaned against his lips before my tongue swept inside his mouth, and I became energized, filled with sudden need. He held me firmly as we kissed, my breasts feeling suddenly constrained in the bodice of the burgundy silk gown. I wanted his hands all over me. I wanted him to touch me everywhere.

When the kiss ended, I stood like a transfixed teen, totally stunned. I wasn't some primary school kid, though, I was a damn agent for Her Majesty's service. How had a simple kiss brought me to such a state? I felt almost . . . innocent.

"Can I have a name now?" He took another step back as he pushed his jacket back a little, shoving his hands into his pockets.

I stole a second by reaching for my half empty glass of champagne. And then an extra few seconds by finishing off the glass. I usually wasn't much of a drinker, but after that kiss, I could've used a bucket of ice water over my head to cool me off.

"You have to earn the name," I said before turning away from him. I couldn't resist a quick look over my shoulder at him as I walked, however. His lips curved into a beautiful smile that shone brightly in those insanely deep brown eyes.

Oh, God, was I in trouble.

* * *

JAKE

"Jesus," I muttered as Alexa wrapped her legs around my hips and we fell backward onto my hotel bed.

I had been wrong. So very, very wrong.

Misconception one: English women are straight-edge prudes.

Misconception two: An English woman at such an elitist party would never hook up with a stranger, let alone an American.

Misconception three: If you kiss a strange woman, you'll get slapped.

Okay, so I wasn't about to test the third one again anytime soon. But so far, the night was going far better than I had expected when my baby sister forced me to come with her to the party tonight.

I looked up at Alexa as she knelt over me, working at the buttons of my dress shirt. I propped a hand behind my head and studied the firecracker of a woman I'd met only two hours ago. I couldn't take my eyes off of her, but she was also making it pretty damn difficult to see anything else. She was wearing only her lace bra and panties. Her hazel eyes fused to mine like she owned me.

"You're beautiful." As she took a moment to unclip her bra, my eyes dipped down to admire her breasts. A scar on her hip bone caught my eye, and I couldn't help but smooth my finger over the faded line.

Alexa startled at the touch, and she started to scoot off me. I sensed her panic, and I raised my hands in the air between us. "Sorry."

"Kiss me," she commanded, her eyes narrowing.

I swooped a hand up and cupped the back of her neck, bringing her back down to me. "I'm going to kiss you all night," I whispered before nipping her pouty bottom lip with my teeth. I could taste her sweet champagne when our mouths met again, and I wondered if I should stop myself. Was she drunk? Hell, I knew I was.

*Damn.*

It took all my willpower to stop kissing her. "I don't want to take advantage of you. You've been drinking and—"

Alexa sat up a little, wiggling her firm butt against my cock. The woman was going to kill me.

"Don't worry, love, it's me that's probably taking advantage of you." And then she crushed her lips against mine once again.

\* \* \*

ALEXA

I scooped up my silk gown as quietly as possible before stepping down into it, trying not to wake Jake as I made my escape.

"I hope you're just planning on getting dressed for breakfast. Although I thought breakfast in bed would be more fun."

*Shit.* I turned at the sound of his deep, sexy voice as I slipped the straps of my gown over my shoulders. "I was leaving, actually." I took an extra step back from the bed, needing to put distance between us so I could hold fast to my resolve. He sat up in the bed and pulled the covers down, offering me the warm spot next to him.

At the sight of his golden, muscular chest, my fingernails bit into my palms. The man had a body that was meant to be enjoyed. He should have been posing nude for artists. Maybe my sister could paint him. The thought almost made me chuckle as I imagined this strong Southern gentleman sitting naked on a stool while my sister tut-tutted over him.

"What?" A smile teased his lips.

I could feel my cheeks warming, and I found myself moving back toward the bed—I couldn't resist the pull of him. "Nothing, I was just picturing . . . something."

"Oh yeah?" He shifted his hands up to his chest and clasped them together as his eyes bore down on me. Hah, as if anyone could read me. It was my job to make sure that they couldn't.

And that was reason number six hundred and fifty-seven why relationships with civilians never worked for me. I'd been there, done that, and almost got killed in the process.

My stomach flipped bloody somersaults as I remembered my ex. What a mood killer.

"You can't leave now. I mean, not after last night." He cleared his throat and grinned. "Although I guess it was this morning."

"Last night was a—"

He raised a hand, his palm facing me. "By far the best part of my trip here." Another smile skirted his lips, which had me wetting mine.

"I don't even remember what happened," I lied.

He leaned back against the tall, dark walnut headboard, his eyes drilling into me. "You don't remember kissing me? I mean, you started this whole thing, so I—"

"The bloody hell I did. You . . ." *Shit. Did he really just rope me so easily?* "Funny." I couldn't help but laugh. It wasn't every day a man could knock me off my game. In this case, it kind of felt good.

I was starting to enjoy my vacation.

"What do you English call making out, again? Snogging?" He mimicked my accent, and I laughed. A deep, belly laugh. Whoever managed to win this man's heart over would be one lucky woman.

"Snogging makes me think of two dogs rubbing their noses together. Not very romantic," he teased, probably hoping to bait me. And it was working.

"So, if I were to say I wanted to snog you right now, you'd say no?" I raised a brow and moved to the bed until my thighs met the mattress.

He tilted his head and closed an eye. "Okay, so when you say it, standing there in your dress that hugs every curve of your body like it was designed by God to fit you, well . . . damn woman, it sounds hot!" He gave me one of his incredible smiles again, and it was like sin had been handed to me on a silver platter. How could I say no?

I touched the straps of my gown and shrugged them down. Jake's eyes became darker, glinting with passion as the material fell to my feet. I was only in my knickers, and I had to bet he'd find that word amusing as well. "Should I take off my knickers?" I deepened my voice, faking a Southern accent.

He rubbed a hand down his jaw and swallowed. "Your accent is much better than mine." He laughed. "And the answer to your question is hell yes."

\* \* \*

JAKE

"How much did that cost?"

I waited for the doors to close before I moved up behind her, resting my hand on the small of her back as she looked out the window and down below at the water as we began to rise. We were inside a giant Ferris wheel known as the London Eye, which looked like a huge spoked bicycle wheel. "I wanted you alone in here. Couldn't stand to share you and this view with a bunch of tourists."

"And what are you?" She looked over at me, and her full lips parted, offering me her smile. God, the woman was gorgeous. I wrapped my arms around her back, and our fingers twined, our hands splayed over her stomach. "I'd like to think of myself as a visitor . . . although I'd like to come back again."

She stiffened against me, the very embodiment of her hesitation. Maybe she felt differently about me but damned if I couldn't picture letting this woman go. We'd spent six nights together, and I'd barely seen my little sister, even though she was the whole reason I'd come to London. But, as much as I wanted to extend my stay, I had an undercover OP coming up. I had to start hunting some scumbag who possibly had sworn allegiance to Ansari, an ISIS leader.

"I can't believe you leave today."

She had decided to avoid my hint and I took a step back, releasing my hold. I stepped around her and pressed a hand to the glass window. The city was spectacular, laid out before us.

"Jake." Her hand on my back had me straightening my spine, angry at myself for giving into the strange feelings that filled me whenever we were together. I'd never fallen for a woman in a week. Hell, I'd never really fallen for any woman. And Alexa . . . shit, there was an ocean between us. How would this work? We hadn't talked about it, and I was about to leave. Wasn't it worth mentioning?

Maybe she didn't feel the same way. There was something mysterious about this woman, and I wanted to discover her secrets —what lay beneath her gorgeous body, her beautiful face, her laugh, her fire, her quick intelligence. I wanted to know the real Alexa. But I needed more time to get through to her—time I didn't have.

And how could I explain to her that it was my job to hunt down terrorists?

"This week—well, it took me by surprise. This was the first time I've been unplugged from work, and you gave me the chance to see what life could be like if—"

I spun to face her, but when her lips pressed tightly together, I realized she would never finish that sentence. The woman shut herself off to people, even though she had opened up to me in small pieces, each time pulling me deeper under her spell. "If what,

Alexa?" My hand came down over her forearm as I met her hazel eyes.

"Mm. Jake. Let's just enjoy the last hour we have together."

One hour? The thought was unbearable.

"Just kiss me, okay?" Her chest rose and fell with slow breaths. "Kiss me one last time, Jake," she said softly.

"No." I shook my head. "But I'll kiss you for now, until next time . . ."

* * *

Jake's sister (Emily) guest stars in *Finding Justice*, book 2 in my new SEAL series. Emily's book releases June 6th, 2019- *Finding Her Chance.*

Jake & Alexa guest star in the Dublin Nights novella - *On the Line.*

# ALSO BY BRITTNEY SAHIN

A Stealth Ops World Guide is now available on my website, which features more information about the team, character muses, and SEAL lingo.

Also, check out this handy **reading guide**.

## Hidden Truths

*The Safe Bet* – Begin the series with the Man-of-Steel lookalike Michael Maddox.

*Beyond the Chase* - Fall for the sexy Irishman, Aiden O'Connor, in this romantic suspense.

*The Hard Truth* – Read Connor Matthews' story in this second-chance romantic suspense novel.

*The Final Goodbye* - Friends-to-lovers romantic mystery.

\* Alexa and Jake guest star in On the Line and Finding Her Chance.

\*Connor & Mason Matthews guest star in the mob romantic suspense - *My Every Breath*.

## Stealth Ops Series: Bravo Team

*Finding His Mark* - Book 1 - Luke & Eva

*Finding Justice* - Book 2 - Owen & Samantha

*Finding the Fight* - Book 3 - Asher & Jessica

*Finding Her Chance* - Book 4 - Liam & Emily

*Finding the Way Back* - Book 5 -Knox & Adriana

## Stealth Ops Series: Echo Team

*Chasing the Knight* - Book 6 -Wyatt & Natasha

*Chasing Daylight* - Book 7 - A.J. & Ana (7/30/20)

## Becoming Us

*Someone Like You* - A former Navy SEAL. A father. And off-limits.

*My Every Breath* - A sizzling and suspenseful romance. Businessman Cade King has fallen for the wrong woman. She's the daughter of a hitman - and he's the target.

## Dublin Nights

*On the Edge* - Travel to Dublin and get swept up in this romantic suspense starring an Irish businessman by day...and fighter by night.

*On the Line* - novella - the wedding.

*The Real Deal* - This mysterious billionaire businessman has finally met his match.

*The Inside Man* - 4/30/20

**Standalone** (with a connection to *On the Edge*):

*The Story of Us*– Sports columnist Maggie Lane has 1 rule: never fall for a player. One mistaken kiss with Italian soccer star Marco Valenti changes everything...

# CONNECT

Thank you for reading Jake and Alexa's story. If you don't mind taking a minute to leave a short review, I would greatly appreciate it. Reviews are incredibly helpful to us authors! Thank you!

*For more information:*
www.brittneysahin.com
brittneysahin@emkomedia.net

Join the Facebook group: Brittney's Book Babes

Made in the USA
Coppell, TX
28 September 2023

22144773R10180